Her Libyan husband imprisoned by the Gaddafi regime, Nita Nicholson taught at the university in Benghazi. Later, she studied Applied Linguistics at Birkbeck College London whilst campaigning for her husband's release. Reflecting on the long and dark years of state killings and disappearances, she turned to writing. When in 2011 the Libyan 'street' spoke out despite its fear of retribution, she was spurred on to conclude and share her first novel on the social impact of state terror.

To Fathia, my mother-in-law, always a peace-maker.
To the disappeared and their loving families who
deserve an answer.

Nita Nicholson

CHAMELEON IN
MY GARDEN

AUSTIN MACAULEY
PUBLISHERS LTD.

A CIP catalogue record for this title is available from the British Library.

ISBN 978 184963 675 9

www.austinmacauley.com

First Published (2014)
Austin Macauley Publishers Ltd.
25 Canada Square
Canary Wharf
London
E14 5LB

Printed and bound in Great Britain

Part One – Letting go

She had said goodbye to everything she had known that offered safety, just as Saad had done before her.

Chapter 1

No word of him

Neda was two, and a bit. That little extra mattered because, until very recently, she had not spoken a single word her mother understood – nothing even vaguely approaching a child's mutation of something recognisable – not 'mama' or 'papa'. Her life so far had been a predictable pattern of sleep, food and play, with her mother anticipating all her needs; she had no need of speech.

It had worried Sally that her second child never called for attention. Knowing she was content did nothing to reassure her. Perhaps her over-diligence had worked too much like clockwork. She knew Neda was capable of speech because she had heard her chatting away quite fluently with a little Gujerati-speaking playmate who lived next door. Together they had made up a whole new language of which not even the smallest fragment or morpheme was understood by either set of parents.

Since her birth in distant Libya, in Al Baitha in the hills of Cyrenaica, English and Arabic had swapped positions like dancers in a quadrille. On her mother's knee, English had been the most intimate, with Arabic the ambient background music. Then, as she mingled with the larger family in Benghazi, Arabic had come to the fore and her mother tongue receded. As her mother's running commentary, English was reserved for moments of intimacy, not for social mingling. Now in England, English was dominant again and Neda's passive Arabic was fading fast, though it figured on occasions when her father was at home.

Neither language had absorbed her attention like this wholly self-tailored toddler tongue, a multilingual hybrid which had encompassed all her desires and supported creative play. It had sufficed – until her nursery friend left one day for

Glasgow. Then, of course, unnourished, it fell away like pieces of a broken shell. There was only English for the most part to get along with.

Her brother, Nizar, being just that little older, could model the sort of language she would understand when they played together. He was not troubled by her silent company; he had a captive audience. His chatter in the English of their mother's stories, the wordplay of meal routines, was familiar. His guiding interjections as she rummaged through the toy basket were suddenly more meaningful. Then there was the more mysterious language her mother used for telling stories about the shiny items she kept in a wooden bowl – things like discarded buttons, Christmas cracker gifts, fossils, shells and shiny pebbles.

But now, there came the absence-of-language times, more frequent than before, times when her mother seemed to keep her own counsel as, between chores, she rested in the window seat. Sometimes Neda joined her there and watched the birds her mother must be watching. Silences were easy; but a little disconcerting. So when words did appear, they seemed like invitations to join in the wonder of things and Neda began to play with words, mimicking their stressed syllables, seizing on all that was salient about them and especially those little snippets that tripped easily off the tongue.

It was April 1973. Apart from the rain slashing at her bedroom window, it was quiet inside the apartment. Too quiet. Neda had been tucked in bed but was wide awake, listening. She called out for her mother who came to tuck her in for the second time. Her short dark curls framed her chubby face as she settled back on the pillow. Her eyes, large and inquiring, didn't look like they would close any time soon. With her chin up and eyes laughing, it was plain to see that she had inherited the lush features of her Libyan grandmother, now left behind in Benghazi.

Neda's apple-rosy cheeks just asked to be squeezed. Sally sang a nursery rhyme then kissed her 'sweet dreams'. She set the nursery chimes to calm her, knowing that Nizar slept soundly and would not easily be wakened.

Neda kept still in the position she had adopted when her mother had cuddled her with the blanket pressed gently round her shoulders. She was listening out for voices in conversation, one in particular – the one that had been missing now for far too long – her father's voice.

It had been days, perhaps even more than days, certainly longer than usual, since she had seen him, or heard him coming in, late as usual. A long time after she had gone to bed, the front door would close behind him with the softest of clicks. He would, it seemed, mostly be away and only ever dip into her life after a long time of not being there. Whenever she did hear him arriving home, sleep came right away. In the morning, she would be able to snatch a little of his time and attention. He would chuck her chin and give Nizar a high five; but only to dash away for another long not-being-there, leaving his green coffee mug steaming on the kitchen counter. The world outside the front door would always spirit him away.

But this time was not like the other times. His slippers were where he had left them in the hallway, still undisturbed, still neatly aligned. Letters meant for him were piling up on his desk, unopened. He had been away for that long. Her mother was restless, too preoccupied for chatting. Neda knew something was amiss, though Sally had said nothing to make her think so.

Then, as she lay listening, she heard someone clattering dishes in the kitchen, the noisy way he always did so that she was sure it must be him. She sat up to hear better, and decided she would burst in and surprise him. He would laugh, and lift her up, jog her up and down and swing her round like a carousel. He might even pinch her nose and squeeze her hands, plant kisses on her cheeks.

So she crept along the passage, pausing where she knew a floorboard creaked. It was her mother's voice that called out, "Now, who is that? Who is not asleep yet? Is that you, Neda?"

Finding herself discovered, Neda pushed the door and called out 'boo' all the same, rescuing as much surprise as she could from too-soon discovery. It wasn't her father in the kitchen after all.

Sally saw her disappointment and understood. She held her close, whispering "Not yet, my little one. He's not home yet. But he will come soon, I promise you. After all, what would we do without him?"

Neda dragged her mother round the apartment, finding all the things that belonged to Saad – "Daddy's towel, Daddy's slippers, Daddy's book, Daddy's coat, Daddy's mug, All Daddy's!" – until she felt disheartened by the absence of an answer to the question. As Sally tucked her back in bed, with the chimes playing by her pillow, she succumbed to sleep.

Neda would never ask again about her father. He was gone for good, for sure. People simply disappear like that, inexplicably. This is how things are, just as perplexing as other things that go missing in the world. It was a cruel caprice and a child must just accept. Things were just that way.

For Sally, it was the end of another day of longing for Saad, of waiting for any kind of news of him, listening to the radio, hoping for something to emerge in the news on the hour, at every hour. The many reasons that crowded in her head for what might have detained him were too dire to contemplate for more than a flashing second. But she returned again and again to all the possibilities. There were letters from the hospital asking for an explanation. She had no answers. There was no information to be gleaned from the international section of the news which seemed never to report on Libya. There were phone calls from friends enquiring, but none from him or his family.

"What would we do without him?" she had said. *What will we do?* was really the more pressing question slowly forming out of her distraught confusion. Managing without Saad was inconceivable. How much longer could she keep up the facade that everything would soon or ever return to normal? The tone of hurt in Neda's voice had shaken her pretended serenity. It was time to face up to the consequences of Saad's decision to make the visit, or go back home – which it was she could not say. Whether or not he intended to return, she might have to carry on without him. She would have to carry on alone.

She had not agreed with Saad's decision to return to Libya, if only for a short visit. But an invitation to advise on the founding of a heart hospital in Tripoli had been too important, too enticing, to resist. She had argued passionately against it. *It isn't safe and you know that, Saad. Why would you take the risk and leave us here?*

He had dismissed her pleading as emotional, irrational even. Libya was a place he knew well, better than she did. He would be safe amongst his own people, with relatives he could trust. Furthermore, it was an invitation from a distant uncle, in the Ministry of Health; that fact alone would guarantee his safety. *An uncle would never put a nephew's life in jeopardy. People are basically good, despite what you may say,* he had said. *In any case, I'm needed there. You don't need to worry – it will only be a few days, not a week even.* He had been so sure.

Now it had been long enough with no word from him to suspect things might not have been as Saad had imagined. Either he was detained there, held against his will, or he had deserted them, intentionally. Had he not considered the consequences for their children? The apartment was not theirs. The hospital was waiting for the rent. The letters were sounding impatient and taking on a detached administrative tone.

Chapter 2

Missing

The following morning, Neda was unusually quiet and still, content just to watch her brother play as she sat cross-legged in a deep armchair. Nizar had tipped a jigsaw from its box and they had fallen like a landslide onto the fireside rug. He was methodically turning the pieces face up. Neda was not moved to join him as she usually did, but instead reminded him that a piece was missing. She remembered searching with him for it. Didn't he? But Nizar was undeterred. He loved this particular set with beetles of every hue from petrol blue to toxic greens, all aligned in rows like collectors' items. He knew the picture well and returned the scattered beetle bits to their whole selves with practiced ease.

With predictable contrariness that seemed to be a part of jigsaw mystery, the lost piece was not lost after all. He whooped with joy. Neda sprung to life and joined in. They turned to their mother for her approval of this surprising outcome.

Sally was still sitting at the breakfast table, though breakfast was done with long ago. She had her back to them but sensed their anticipation of her reply. "You've found it then, Nizar?" she said, not turning round, not really sharing in the find. "That's a nice surprise, isn't it? How clever of you. Nothing missing after all." It was that *Nothing missing after all* that punctured her reverie with such finality.

Her voice was strangely flat – no lilting tones in it. *Nothing – missing – after all.* She was staring though the window, seeing nothing in particular, other than the hedge that marked the boundary of the garden. That was where Saad used to leave nuts for the squirrels, so that he and Sally could watch them turn them so adeptly in their little fists. Nizar stretched up to see if anything in particular was going on in the garden, but there was nothing he could make out. His mother was clearly somewhere else in her head, a place where things bigger than jigsaws demanded her attention, the kinds of things that often filled the minds of adults, he supposed. Nizar saw that she held a letter in her hand, not reading it, the same letter he had brought in from the post earlier that morning. She had been far away ever since, he realised now, ever since opening it – that is until *You've found it ... nothing missing after all.*

The little Big Ben clock ticked more loudly on the mantelpiece in the silence. Still she sat there turned away from him, with her hair hiding her face. He studied her hair, the way she had let it fall without pushing it away. Silver hairs, he thought, just a few; they come when you get older. She had told him that when he had asked about them once before. He felt he knew a little about growing old and how it led to dying; it worried him. His father, Saad, had explained the link once when together they had found a dead bird in the gutter. Saad had moved it to a garden bed. "It was probably old for a bird," he had said, intending to reassure him. "It's time has come."

"And in the garden, it won't get hurt any more," Nizar had added, not sure if this was really a truth or just a question. There was nothing reassuring about the chain of thought that led from silver hair to being old, and not getting hurt any more.

When Nizar moved closer to his mother, he saw that she had been crying. This was not the first time since his father had left at least a week or more ago. Only the other day, on a morning at home just like this one, she had been doodling with his crayons. Little boxes had taken shape, completely filled with crouching figures, as though their cages held them tight, row on row of them. It had been a scary kind of crying then, a slow straining deep inside her, more like a sighing than a crying.

"Don't worry, Mama," he had said. "I can do it for you, if you want. I'm good at colouring in."

The letter must be the reason this time. She would explain when she was ready. She would lift her head and with a flick of her hand make the silver go away. While he waited for her to do just this, he continued to admire the finished jigsaw, all pieces present, every beetle in its place.

"You're pleased I've found the piece, Mama, aren't you?" he asked, not necessarily expecting an answer.

"Yes, of course I am," she said. "And you did it all by yourself, didn't you?" This time she spoke with genuine enthusiasm, pleasure sounding strong in her voice as she turned to look him straight in the eye.

"All by yourself," Neda mimicked, jumping from her chair. "You find missing, don't you? All by yourself!"

The words *You find missing* spoken with the innocence and trust of a child were disquieting, stroking her like a fingered shiver down the back.

"It wasn't really missing, Neda, love. Just mislaid." Sally stood up to clear the table, determined to shake off the feeling of so much helplessness.

"Is everything okay now?" Nizar asked.

"Sure it is, my sweetheart. Don't you worry. I must get a move on, mustn't I? My goodness, it's getting late."

Chapter 3

Torn

Clearing the table, Sally filed the letter beneath the miniature Big Ben clock on the mantelpiece. Weighted there, it was comfortingly reduced to the red and blue edge of its envelope: dealt with, tamed. Surely silenced. Catching herself in the mirror, she stopped to finger through her hair. She must return things to the way they were before the letter. She paused to pose with a coping smile, the way her mother always did, as if the tidiness of things could banish all disquiet, as if a carefully arranged smile could make things better.

Tracing her forefinger over the mirror's surface, she left a track in the static dust. She wiped it, and then the clock's face, lifting, wiping and restoring the items alongside one by one to their assigned places on the mantel shelf. She fussed around the letter – not done with after all.

With the writer's words still fresh in her mind, she imagined the writer's voice modulating them with different intentions. Throughout, the language was matter-of-fact and dry. She imagined the writer's voice, stern in timbre, speaking them. She had signed off as "Eva, a well-wisher," but sympathy had not been much in evidence. "You desert him," the voice challenged, ambiguous with the inaccurate choice of tense or aspect. Sally set the words free to echo in her head. Lifted off their written shapes, they could more easily be tested for how they might have been spoken. But whichever way she modified the intonation, the words still offended her. They hurt, for the opposite was true.

"I've deserted him?" She couldn't help the bitter tone tumbling within earshot of the children.

"Deserted who, Mummy?" Nizar asked.

"Oh, take no notice of me, love. Something very silly on my mind."

"But what's 'deserted'?" he persisted.

"Nothing, darling. Daddy's coming soon, I told you, didn't I?"

"Has Daddy deserted?"

"Oh, never. He would never desert us. Don't you worry, my little one, Daddy's coming soon, I'm sure of that. What would we do without him, anyway?" There it was again, that cry of need for him. And yet she could not rid herself of the niggling doubt that he had perhaps deserted them and if so she should not be feeling the need of him. There had been signs. He had been restless, keen to get away. There was anger in her thoughts.

"Coming soon," Neda mimicked. "Daddy coming soo-oon." She slid down from the armchair scattering the jigsaw across the hearthrug.

"Hey, you. I wanted to keep that. You've messed it up and you don't care, do you?" Nizar complained.

"Coming soon. Coming soon. Daddy coming soo-oon." Neda sang the words over and over to herself as she skipped around the room, oblivious to the damage she had done.

Sally read on silently: "I cannot imagine what possess you to be away." She cannot imagine? What has possessed me? The words were deeply wounding. She would not hear them any more. She put the letter back under the clock and then bent down to help Nizar collect the jigsaw pieces. She set the box at the table for him to assemble them where they would be safe. Neda was still singing, making up a flow of lyrics from a confusion of partially assimilated words, and dancing to their rhythm.

This, everything we have here, is all unreal, Sally thought. *We won't be able to stay, without Saad, if he doesn't come back. We will lose all of this.* Nothing was theirs, not the Parker Knoll furniture, the porcelain plates, not the furnishings – it was an apartment furnished more lavishly than they could ever have afforded. Even Saad's car, a Volkswagen Beetle, would have to go. She could not drive it anyway.

Now at last, she had hit the brick wall that was the truth about her dilemma. She had no idea where to go from here.

Perhaps she had after all been possessed, in denial of the crisis they really were in. Certainly she had been unable to begin the search for solutions. Finding a job seemed a mountain of a task, and that was only the first of many things she would have to do, on her own.

It was Saad who was possessed – by dreams, by impossible desires, by goals beyond his reach. They had left Libya because it had not been safe to stay another day, and nothing had happened since to change that naked fact. It was, she remembered, almost a year to the day when a stranger had accosted Saad in the street in Benghazi, to wish him well and warn him that he was at imminent risk of arrest or worse. That night they had travelled back to Al Baitha in the mountains for a few items, said goodbye to friends under cover of darkness and left Libya the next evening from Benghazi airport. It had been the safe thing to do. But whereas leaving meant returning home for Sally, it was tantamount to exile for Saad – that terrifying choice of an ending, a cutting-off never wished for. What had made for prudence at the time soon came to seem to him like cowardice.

Sally thought, too late now, that she might have tried harder to understand what exile had meant to Saad, leaving behind so much that defined who he was. On reflection, it was easier now to make allowances for what had seemed at the time like a rash decision. He had been forced, panicked even, into exile. Libya was where he wanted to be. After all, with the first flush of altruism, he was one of the few who had answered the Colonel's call for trained professionals to leave the coastal towns and work in the countryside, reversing the trend of migration from rural to urban areas. Saad had volunteered right away, seeing this as his honourable and patriotic duty – repayment for the scholarship he had been awarded years before.

Sally had been proud of his decision. She had supported him. She still had the photos of Saad standing on the steps of the hospital in Al Baitha with his staff, including the ambulance driver and the carpenter. He had directed a successful campaign against the cholera epidemic that had swept across the Middle East from Pakistan, leaving a trail of devastation in its wake. Despite having no kinship links to the area, he had been able to win the trust of the Bedouin against all odds, persuading them to accept vaccine injections administered by volunteer nurses often from feuding enemy tribes. He had travelled to their desert camps and spent time with them, winning their trust. He had explained the campaign on television. He had done more than most.

Unexpectedly, his endeavours had stirred up some resentment, made enemies, and given him a higher profile than was prudent. He was drawn irrevocably into controversial matters of public health, a politically charged question. Sally saw quite clearly that this had brought him up against vested interests much more powerful than he was. She had sensed the growing hostility. She felt the danger.

Even so, the decision to flee had been a difficult one, for them both. With hindsight, it was easy to see that abandoning all he had achieved was a bitter pill. But it seemed he had come to terms with this disappointment; he was happy with his internship at the General Infirmary in Leeds. He was diligent and dedicated, ultimately obtaining the privilege of presenting a paper at a global heart conference in Madrid, under the guidance of a famous heart surgeon. The future looked promising and he could still make headway in his career, albeit in a different direction, in a different place.

Then out of the blue had come an invitation to help with the founding of a new hospital in Tripoli. It had seemed plausible, given Saad's recent success and profile. She could not blame him for hoping that it might be a preamble to rehabilitation, easing the way for a permanent return. Exile was not perhaps to be forever.

This was why he had overridden her appeals so vehemently, why he had dismissed the anonymous calls she had received, the calls that warned it was not safe for him to return to Libya. He did not want to be restrained by caution, for, after all, no one could be trusted one way or another, and he could not let his life be shaped by such uncertainty. She realised his decision had not been a sudden impulse. Her pleading would have seemed misjudged, poorly reasoned, selfish even. The limits she had placed on his choice had only given further cause to take the risk.

"You always like to think the worst and put obstacles in the way," he had said; unfairly she had thought. He had been adamant; and, within the week, was gone.

Sally returned the breakfast dishes to the cupboard. She was reminded of the other side of Saad's nature as she did so – his caring side, his love of children that had attracted her to him in the first place. And there was his favourite mug with its green Celtic pattern, hidden now in a corner at the back of the shelf, its green self out of place she had said when he had chosen it, out of place for not blending in with the white porcelain. Feeling regret for this pettiness, she brought it forward now right to the front, even though it meant reaching past it for other items she preferred.

Had she been unreasonable in other ways? Had she driven him away? How she wished they could still share a coffee break together, she with her white mug, he with his green one.

Other doubts hung about in the background, hesitant as unbidden guests always are. The blue and red line of the airmail envelope forced its way into her ruminating thoughts. *You're always ruminating*, he would say. She was ruminating now. She lifted the clock to read again that irksome phrase – something about 'a wife's place' – something she could not commit to memory. Yes, there it was – Eva had written that a wife's first duty was to follow her husband, to give up everything and accompany him wherever that might take her. Doing otherwise suggested infidelity on her part.

Oh, there were things this woman Eva needed to know, this anonymous Eva she could not put a face to, this stranger out of nowhere who had no knowledge of her side of the story. Should she enter into a dialogue with her? She decided she would not. She felt there was nothing she could do to turn the writer's bias to her favour.

Chapter 4

Bearings

Sally, like Saad, had not wanted to leave Al Baitha. But with no time to waste, the imperative to flee was paramount. She trusted Saad to judge the situation better than she could. They grabbed a few essential items that could be squashed into the children's baggage along with infant toiletries. They left many precious things behind. Saad had driven in stony silence. Benghazi was two hours away.

The children slept in the back seats, leaving their mother free to think her own thoughts, with time enough to commit to memory the place they were leaving behind; the lie of the land, the way it dropped from the hills to the limestone plateau, a plain that spread like an apron to the coast in the west and north, banked up by more hills to the east. Hills she had walked in. Coastal towns she had visited. She remembered it all passing by like a grainy film, so swiftly, so vague and dream-like. She had stared out through bleary eyes, wondering if they would ever return, fearing that they never would.

The old wooden bridge that spanned the largest wadi as part of the old twisting track around the hillsides had once been the only route. It was made redundant now by a new highway that cut right through the hills and spanned the valleys in a straight line. A series of wadis lay below the highway, mostly hidden by thick canopies of lush vegetation, lemon and juniper, olive and *pistacia* and other species she could not name. There was even almond, and always the hardy shrubs that survived the summer droughts like acacia. She was keen to see again and maybe for the last time the familiar pockmarks that had been blasted into the sandstone rock with bullets from the gun of a World War Two soldier. Most likely his epitaph. But she did not find it this time.

Then came to mind the scene she and Saad had come across journeying back to Al Baitha from Benghazi, a trip they made frequently. Passing by where the road dipped down to the plain, they saw again the burnt-out chassis they had passed only weeks before. They had known what it must be, whose accident. They had stopped to examine it. The body of the young dentist had been removed for burial, the door removed; but his charred brain remained, spilled on the steering wheel and dashboard. She remembered how all of Al Baitha had awaited his return from Egypt, his family ready to celebrate his graduation and his forthcoming marriage.

It had been the middle of the night, or early morning. Sally was wakened by the barks of wild dogs more clamorous than usual, the crowing cocks that never seemed to wait for dawn. She had opened the windows wide to make sense of the commotion, hearing the crickets and the frogs croaking nearby. But it seemed the whole town was awake. And then she heard the wailing, the unmistakable high-pitched plaintive sound. She knew at once a disaster had hit this close-knit community.

There was no obvious obstacle the car might have hit, no second car involved. The road on either side was edged by barren soil as flat as the tarmac road. But the chassis was skewed across the edge, inexplicably. Saad had said nothing, perhaps he knew, perhaps he guessed what must have happened. For Sally it remained a mystery, a memory charged with startling inclusion in the overall sadness. She had felt the loss as though it was a loss of someone close, though she had not known him. It had bound her up with the community – and now they were leaving that behind. On one level, it made no sense at all to be leaving. On another there was no choice.

She often asked herself how it was that this different place had become so special to them both. How it was that life there seemed lived at a higher pitch. Their stay had not been planned as permanent, but it had ended up as something more than a casual sojourn, not easy to detach themselves from. Despite her limited freedom, she had grown to love it for its difference, its character born of its unique location. There was more to discover than there had been time for. It was an unfinished project, a dream in her head.

Al Baitha was a small town in the highlands east of Benghazi. It had once been a key meeting place for commerce, perhaps still was. It was a niche where old and ancient trade routes met and crossed. It was part of a wider network of connections all around, across and through the Sahara. More recently it was the capital city under the late and dethroned Senoussi King Idris. At the time of its elevation to administrative capital, there were quaint stories of camels poking their heads through the windows of the council chambers where parliament met. The habits of a desert life had lingered on to mingle with the new ways of a semi-settled urban lifestyle. The Bedouins hedged their bets and lived a life between two mutually exclusive options. Different eras had met there, ancient and modern, and people were trying to forge a link between the past and the present. It was a place where the past abided, and the present century could easily be dismissed as a giddy latecomer, yet to prove its worth.

Nearby was the village of Shahhat, nestled in the hills alongside the ancient Greek antiquities of Cyrene, once devastated by an earthquake. The ruins that spread over the flank of a long hill faced the Mediterranean Sea. In Sally's memory, its sparkling sheen was mirrored in the bright expanse of air and land that lay before it. So much space the lungs could breathe more generously. Further to the east the coastal road reached Susa and beyond to Tobruk. Further still was Derna. Susa's Italianate municipal buildings stood back from the ruins of Apollonia and the inland sea, a bathing pool guarded by the pinnacle rocks, known as Cleopatra's Needle. Cyrenaica was a green and fertile stretch from the coast to the desert, its lush terrain lured the ancient Greeks and Romans, and in recent times Italian colonizers.

What fixed Cyrenaica as an enigma in Sally's recollections was a walk in Cyrene. It was a day of free roaming, so rare at the time, of warm sun and a strange kind of very pleasant weariness that came with being heavily pregnant with Neda, her second child. She had stopped for respite, while Saad had taken Nizar on the more demanding climb up the incline to the arched caverns that housed the ancient water system. She had sat on the steps of a temple, before her the view of the baths lined with a mosaic of what she imagined to be lapis lazuli perhaps, at least a stunning blue that held her attention so that she would never forget it.

Refreshed a little, she had carried on to explore further afield, on her own; another sense of freedom. She had picked her way through the grid of rock-strewn streets that mapped the urban centre. She was drawn on to explore even further, attracted by the sound of an animal, obviously in pain. It seemed to come from below the amphitheatre.

The ground there had slipped away from the theatre's boundary, no doubt in a flash flood. But stone steps had been lodged into the soft earth descending into the lower land at the foot of the landslip. It was something like a little glen made of young saplings. There, in the shade of an olive tree, lay the suffering creature – a camel, lying prone on its side in a foetal pose. Someone had built a protective pen around it, a low wall made of antique stones.

Saad had said the creature was comatose. He thought the camel had most likely eaten the silver leaf of *sylphium*, or *drias*, its Greek name. He had heard about it from Bedouin camel herders. It was a highly toxic plant, to be avoided at all costs. He could not be sure that this was the case since the Bedouin had told him the plant was rare, probably extinct – they had tried to eradicate it from their pastures to protect their herds. Coma could lead to death, as, if the animal failed to rouse in time, it would starve to death, or die of thirst. There was no known antidote, except for the camel to have eaten the yellow flowers in the previous spring before the plant turned silver. "A prophylactic," Saad had said, musing on the fact that the Bedouin must have discovered for themselves this scientific principle, a wisdom which was part of their own inherited tradition, long before modern medicine had invented vaccines. There was admiration in his voice as he spoke about it. He said he would like to search for the plant and rediscover it, since perhaps after all it was perhaps not extinct. But nothing could be done for a camel once intoxicated. The camel's owner must only wait and hope. "*Bi yithan Allah*, the camel is in God's hands," Saad had said as he led Sally up to the amphitheatre. "*Bi yithan Allah*."

And so her memory of that short-lived happiness was sullied with misgivings, misgivings that she knew she must extend to the brutal purpose of the amphitheatre itself, the sadistic fights and cruel deaths enacted there so long ago, against a backdrop of bloodthirsty roars of human approval and jubilation. The moans of the camel still reached her and came to symbolise the pathos of the place. From that time on, it was impossible to think of Cyrene without remembering the camel's moan.

Sally's memories of their home in Al Baitha were tenacious too, for different reasons. They had left so much behind. Her portfolio of drawings was irreplaceable; Saad's library of books, including some she knew were banned – they worried her; her own books, especially Paul Klee's *Thinking Eye* in two heavy volumes. And there were the more sentimental things, gifts they had been given, like the two purple velvet fish embroidered with sequins and Bedouin glass beads. She had hung them on the children's beds for protection from the evil eye, not out of any real belief in superstition – more because they symbolised a kindness. The ordinary task of straightening the children's pillows, or sharpening their pencils were constant triggers of a lingering nostalgia. If she reached for a book no longer there to refer to, she could see it in her mind's eye just where she had left it, jutting forwards for easy discovery.

But more often than she could account for, nostalgia took her back to that acute sense of outsider helplessness, when Saad had declared the camel's fate was in the hands of God. There was nothing to be done, that was what he had meant. Libya had come to mean for her a bewildering fusion of beauty and suffering that could not be helped.

It was impossible to convey this sense to anyone around her, not friends or family. It was an understanding that isolated her. She discovered that to most people Libya was a closed book, little known or understood and thought to be of no great consequence. Her stories made little impact or sense in the telling. Libya was obscure, located somewhere in North Africa along the coast, or maybe in the Levant, for it was often confused with Lebanon. She had always to explain its worthiness of attention. But it was impossible to garner much interest beyond a few simple facts. Its geography was a contradictory mix of presumed barren desert and a rarely-mentioned narrow but fertile coastal strip. Interest in this largely unknown state was limited to two periods: a current fascination with its military leader and the desert conflicts of the war years. The Colonel's bloodless coup was much romanticised in the Western media, so easily distracted by his eccentric and entertaining behaviour, and increasingly celebrated by an international following that knew little of his domestic policies.

Once a monarchy, now republic, Libya was, in Western eyes, exotic – not a term Sally liked to use. Those who travelled there for commercial reasons were mainly charmed by the notion of a Bedouin commander briefing from his tent, with his camel tethered to a tent peg. They were enthralled by the chance of a little of his aura transferring to themselves, perhaps. The rest of what might constitute Libya, apart from its oil reserves, was nothing of much interest, except to the rare intrepid traveller.

Reeling the camera backwards twenty years or more, following the end of the Second World War, the pages of history, it seemed, had indeed closed themselves shut. The project that was Libya was in stasis, or so it seemed. For War veterans, it was still remembered as the arena for a gruelling campaign, a place of extreme endurance they were glad to have survived. Even for this tested generation it was difficult, almost impossible, to convey to the next the rigours of a desert skirmish – the interminable forays to and fro, the horror of being becalmed in a sand sea by desert storm or lack of fuel. They at least knew how the desert was not a place of romance, that it would more willingly bury you than offer refuge.

Sally herself knew nothing of the desert. There was time enough on the long road to Benghazi to contemplate this disappointing fact. As the road took them further away and dropped down from the hills to the plain, and along the plain to the shanty town suburbs, Sally committed to memory her sense of what was being lost, made up of all the things she might never see, or never see again.

She knew of, but had never seen, the snowy mountain peaks further south, now left far behind them. Such distant places were to become ghosts in her imagination, detailed only by Saad's recounting of his outreach work in Bedouin encampments. There was much to cherish about his stories, like the new understandings he had reached bridge-building with the Bedouin tribes, the gazelle hunts he had been unable to avoid. There were the times when he had stayed over and kept company with tribal leaders sipping hot mint tea, wrapped in a camelhair blanket, talking through the cold night. The blanket was another gift they had left behind. It was there in her mental store of everything that had once been theirs.

Although Sally had not made it to the desert, she had at least discovered other places in the limestone hills that were scored through here and there with caves. She remembered how Nizar had once run through them and out to the other side laughing at the idea of a sky momentarily lost and then found, a sort of grand scale hide and seek. Saad had shown them the cave reputed to be the one Rommel had hidden in during the last war. Other times in spring they had made picnics with Saad's parents on flower-covered hillsides, and wandered through fertile wadi farms with almond trees in blossom and fields of fawn rabbits basking in the sun. They had collected wild artichokes and eaten pomegranate and walnut desserts with friends, and *tanour* bread dipped in butter ghee. Libya was full of good memories. It was not at all an empty place.

Nor could it be an empty place, she mused, when engineers prospected for precious resources. The idea of a desert being an empty place was, she thought, a screen fabricated for reasons she could not fathom. Reasons that were best not to ponder. For now, there was only one kind of information Sally longed for, hungered for. She needed news of Saad.

News from Libya was beginning to trickle out. There had been vague reports for some time of political unrest. More of its detail had come to the fore in recent newsflashes. There were reports of exploration for oil resources hidden beneath the Sahara in places that would inevitably revive old tensions with neighbouring countries. There were frequent clashes at the border between Libya and Chad, a frontier riddled with all the dangers associated with a frontier. European powers were keen to defend Chad in the long-standing dispute over sovereignty of the Aouzou Strip and the map of the Sahara was coming under close scrutiny. Gaddafi, the Colonel now at the helm of his country, was seeking expansion into the Sahel and had sent his forces to defend an old claim to this territory. His attempts at annexation were making headline news.

And there were other conflicts in the region, with some aspects brewing inside Libya itself. A civilian plane bound for Egypt had left Tripoli, stopping over at Benghazi briefly before it lost its way and flew into Israeli airspace. Israeli forces shot it down, after warnings were not heeded. Troubled negotiations between nations added fuel to the internal unrest occasioned by grieving families and their unmet demands for compensation from the Libyan government. The news came in fragments, obscure enough to hide the looming dangers.

Sally had risen early as she did most mornings, some time before the children did, partly to prepare for the day but also for the necessary quiet for listening to the radio. It had to be the earliest broadcast for information on Libya since Libya was likely to drop out of later newscasts. She was making coffee, listening to the weather forecast – "outlook warm and dry with above average temperature" for the time of year. May was often a time of indecision about appropriate clothing, she remembered. She would stick with winter clothing. She was not ready in any case for the summer. How easily she let her mind wander to the smaller preoccupations of her life. In fact, she didn't want to make herself ready. There was no money for new clothes for growing children. It was easier to hang on to the prevaricating present, harking back to winter when Saad had still been with them.

While the coffee percolated, Eva's letter came to mind. Something she had missed now worried her. Eva had mentioned arrests, her own husband's but not Saad's specifically. Hopefully Saad's was not implied. But she had hinted at it in a guarded way: *I am here on my own. It is same as you. Out of our apartment they locked me when they took Abdul. I will stay and wait for him. He needs me, like Saad needs you.* There was nothing certain, nothing clear enough to know for sure.

The news gave no confirmation of the internal situation apart from a report on peaceful demonstrations in Benghazi from a correspondent based in Tripoli. There was no viable opposition to the regime of the "idealistic young officer who had staged a bloodless coup only four years earlier". Not a military dictatorship, she noted, not a police state. An "idealistic young officer". Yes, she nodded, and remembered her own excitement when she had stood just yards away from the podium on the plaza below the monument to Omar Mukhtar, the famed Bedouin leader who had led the rebellion against Italian colonialism and was executed after a long and heroic campaign. Now a young and handsome officer had taken the reins. The crowds, all men, apart from a coterie of women around the young officer, had been ecstatic.

Idealistic and idealised, she added, for her own silent commentary, as the foreign correspondent continued: "... the Colonel, Leader or Guide as he is known to his people, has cracked down severely on what was a peaceful demonstration. There are reports of casualties, numbers not yet known."

So Benghazi was in turmoil. Sally felt her skin go cold. The risk had been real, and the political situation graver than she had imagined. Now she understood that a complete stranger, herself quite vulnerable, had been brave enough to take a risk writing a letter – something very serious had compelled her.

Sally sat in the bay window, where the sun was streaming in without her feeling its warmth; she felt the fine hairs on the back of her neck rise with a sudden chill. She examined the letter with a new understanding.

Eva's hand was European, though not English in style. But she had already guessed she was European from the name and her small grammatical errors. The handwriting itself was fluent and looked confident. It seemed honest or frank, if it was possible to assign such human qualities to a style of handwriting. Perhaps it was a little harsh in its vertical strokes but this was being overcritical, a trick of bias. Who could say for sure what kind of motive had moved Eva to write? Saad's family must have provided the address. Possibly it was a message from them asking her to bring the children home, as they would see it; and Eva had written to console a grieving mother out of duty, under social pressure.

The address was not written by Eva. It looked like a hesitant attempt at an unfamiliar script. The scribe had laboured over it. But why the change? To deflect attention from Eva, perhaps? The awkward scrawl on the envelope starting with Sally's name was so near the top of the envelope that it was partly concealed by the date stamp. It would have been the perfect decoy, this child's uncertain hand.

Sally found some comfort in the thought that Eva might be someone she could turn to after all. But there was something other than friendship implied in her letter. She had provided crucial information on arrests, not reported before today as far as Sally knew. Now, the newsflash confirmed it. Prisoners had been taken from the crowd of peaceful demonstrators. And Sally had a name. The story wanted passing on, and, the telling of it had fallen to her. The letter had not required an answer – it had demanded action.

Chapter 5

We have your number now

There were many questions in Sally's head, none with answers. No matter how much she might wish it otherwise, the answers would not present themselves voluntarily, not without some effort on her part. Nothing more came by post or phone, not in newscasts certainly, not in articles as far as she was aware. As for effort on her part, she had no idea where to start. Her attention was distracted by the need for survival, in the here and now, with two children to take care of. They had to move from the apartment. She had to find a place to stay. She needed a job.

She found a teaching post, covering a maternity leave in a school on the other side of Leeds; it would begin in June in a few weeks, giving time she hoped to find a place to live. Maternity leave meant possibly another term or two, giving scope for sorting out their housing needs. She was beginning to gain some control and a sense of independence. She found herself strong enough to abandon her self-imposed isolation and helplessness. No need to hide away.

It was strange to return to a life where everything around her was as normal as it had always been, and had been so all through the time of her losing Saad. Her story was not an easy one to tell. It didn't fit socially. It made no sense in this other normal existence. She met other doctors' wives, who knew and offered their sympathy, politely she thought, distantly, not wanting to become involved. Life flowed in this other world largely on the general assumption that the events of the next day were more or less predictable. The parameters for variation were well known, and so naturally taken for granted. There were few surprises.

Clearly, her upheavals had taken place in a world apart. Her panic had been managed by the pretence of coping. It was hard to explain now what the crisis had been. Even now, as the crisis deepened, she would have to continue looking normal. On her visit to the school, in the staffroom, she could see that she was just another unfamiliar face fulfilling a prescribed role, most likely to be short-lived and so passing through without much significance to anyone in their social terms. She was just another anonymous individual albeit remarkable for her inexplicably foreign surname. No one could remember or pronounce it. No special effort was made to master it. Strange, how a name pushed her further into the background. People were not curious. No matter, she did not want their curiosity. She was happy to retreat.

Sally realised that had it not been for the need of an income, she might have found her re-entry into a setting she had become estranged from impossibly daunting. But she knew the ropes well and she could muster courage. She could begin again, even though this was all an act, a show of being in the moment, of fitting in, when in fact she was somewhere else in her head, somewhere else in her feelings. In the event, it had taken a disembodied voice on the phone, someone from social services, speaking in such a matter-of-fact way, telling her that her children would be taken from her if she could not earn enough to pay the rent, that had been the spur. She knew now she could manage on her own.

Since marrying Saad and living in a different culture she had exchanged her previous self-sufficiency for reliance on him. How foolish to have done so, she thought, to have relied on someone who had so easily walked away. And how to explain what Saad had done? She felt she would cut a pathetic figure in the public perception of her, if she told her story. It was after all humiliating to be abandoned, to be dependent. No doubt to others she did not look so helpless. Nor was she.

Sally decided to make one more effort to make contact with Saad's family in Benghazi. This time she might be lucky – someone might be there, ready to take her call. She imagined Fathia, her mother-in-law, sitting in the family room, making tea. She imagined her in her everyday Libyan dress, the broad sleeves of her blouse with a floral pattern caught up with a gold chain, sleek and flexibly fashioned like the body of a long narrow snake, the silver and pale green stripes of her robes, pleated round the hips and held with a sash. This time she might get to speak to her. She would let her know she was all right. The children were fine but missing their father very much. Fathia would want to know that. She would tell her the children were in school and growing strong. She would tell it with a certain pride in herself that she had managed on her own. Fathia would tell him. Perhaps he would regret leaving them. Perhaps he would even speak to her. If he was there. If he was not arrested, not lying in a cell. She would know.

She found the old number which had drawn a silence on previous attempts, and also a different one, an earlier entry in Saad's diary, now faintly crossed out in pencil but still decipherable. But her own telephone was cut off; she had not paid the bill. She could ask Jan upstairs if she could use hers.

It was late. The children were asleep. She could leave the front door ajar and listen out for them. Jan was just one floor up, another hospital apartment a short flight of steps away. She wondered why she had not called on her weeks ago. Jan was sympathetic, a doctor's wife like herself. Not someone who kept her distance. Her husband had worked with Saad. She found that Jan was relieved to see her. Her eyes betrayed a bemused and inquiring concern. She made her welcome, and gave her privacy for the call. She must know something, Sally thought. She must be wondering.

Sally dialled the same number and again the line was dead. She tried the new one. Surprisingly, there was a dialling tone. She hung on for some time, until at last a man's voice answered.

"You called?"

She hesitated.

"Speak, will you!"

"Who is that?" she asked, timidly in Arabic. "Is it Buya?" – the term she used to address Saad's father. She knew it wasn't – Hassan's voice was smoother and warm.

"Go ahead, will you, and speak. Say what you want to say, and hurry up." The tone was aggressive now. "This number is being [unclear, blurred by static]. What do you want?"

She paused again and another voice butted in with, "We know where you are, you know. We have been waiting for your call. Don't you worry, we can find you. We have your number now."

She slammed the receiver down on its cradle. Her first thought was that she had disturbed a family. Her foreign accent and hesitation must have irritated. Perhaps the speaker had taken her intrusion as a threat. But the more convincing explanation was that this number had been commandeered by an intelligence cell. Saad must have discovered this and crossed it out, but never told her, the way he never told her anything. He liked to keep her in the dark, not to worry her. *It's best you don't know anything*, he had said many times. And he was right perhaps. So was it really true that they knew where to find her? Did Libyan intelligence have the means for tracking people down even here in England? Was she somehow considered a threat?

Jan brought in a tray of tea and cakes.

"You look shocked," she said. "Are you all right?"

"Yes. Well, no, I'm not really. I'm probably imagining things. You know, paranoid. Making mountains out of molehills. I don't know. I need someone to talk to, to sort it out in my own head. It's been absolutely awful." She forced back her desire to cry; she must hold it all together.

But now her proud independence deserted her. It seemed so useless. Jan put her arms around her and made her feel a little safer. "I know. Something but not much. But I can guess, or perhaps I can't even begin to imagine what you've been going through. I didn't want to pry. I thought it all very private and hoped that you would come to me, to tell me yourself, if you wanted to."

Jan told her what she knew. First when Saad had been gone for a day or two and not answered calls from his secretary, the department had decided he was irresponsible and it had been a mistake to employ him. They were surprised he had thrown away such an opportunity. Jan's husband had thought it out of character. But his was a lone voice. Then Sally's letters in response to the department's enquiries altered things. They guessed he had been unable to contact them, that perhaps Saad had gone missing in Libya. Still, then they wondered if he would return at all. Which put them in a quandary. Whatever the explanation, Saad's uncertain status was untenable.

This was not all Sally gleaned from Jan. She sensed that Jan was holding something back. She had not wanted to pry, she had said. She was Sally's nearest neighbour and yet had never called in, despite knowing she must be struggling on her own. There was more and Sally felt she only needed to push a little harder on the envelope not fully opened and Jan would tell her. But there was no real need to ask. She preferred simply to leave her doubts undisturbed. But she would test the waters, just a little.

"The secretary has offered to help me sell Saad's car. I thought that very kind of her." She delivered the last statement in a questioning tone.

"You don't need her. We can help. We would be horrified – if you didn't let us help, that is."

It was enough. It was confirmation. Sally knew. She thought she knew. She did not want to know more than what she might tolerably bear. She acknowledged the warning in Jan's voice and accepted her help.

"Now," said Jan very purposefully. "What about housing? Surely if the Council has given you a job, it can find you some accommodation." Jan managed to be capable without taking anything away from Sally's new-found independence. "We're leaving England soon," she added. "Back to New Zealand. But before we go, we'll see you settled and safe. I promise you."

So this was how the world went, a friend at last and soon to leave – nothing and no one was ever permanent. Sally felt she had been drawn into Jan's safe world only to have it spun away from her. But if Jan was a guardian angel, Sally would trust her while she could. But how easily she lost people, she thought. How easily people could be lost. How easily she might herself disappear. *We have your number now.*

Sally knew about surveillance, the very obvious kind that declared itself publicly. The Mukhabarat, or secret police, had operated openly in Libya, not always under cover. Intimidation was an effective tool. She remembered being surprised at how openly they had operated, all along the central reservation of the main road in Al Baitha. Men with clipboards had sat on dining chairs recording registration numbers and directions, noting times and dates, and the identity and number of passengers. She had been followed on one of her rare shopping trips, Neda in the buggy, Nizar running alongside. Just as Nizar had run some way ahead of her, a man in the street had asked if she loved her son, because she should know, he added darkly, that he could be taken at any time of *their* own choosing. She had hurried on to get the honey and the eggs from the single grocery store and the same man had followed her inside, gone behind the counter without needing to excuse himself and picked up the grocer's phone. "The doctor's wife has just bought a jar of honey and six eggs."

This petty reporting of the minor details of her shopping list was a powerful signal. Sally made sure Nizar held tightly to the buggy all the bumpy unpaved way home. It was her last outing.

It was widely known that children were kidnapped for ransom, sometimes for political reasons, often for money. Even the son of the chief of police had been taken, with no word of him until now, as far as she knew. She did not need to be told that phones were tapped and shared walls bugged. Back then, the technology had been crude and you could hear it whirring. You were meant to hear it. You were meant to know.

But then surveillance had not relied entirely on uncertain clicks and whirrs of bugs or taps on phones that often failed to pacify as intended. If the people could not be pacified, they must be alarmed. Dissident renegades needed to know for sure that they were being watched and could be hurt. The machinery of state had resorted to shouting out its threats. Its anger was not the temper tantrum of a child, she reminded herself, but the scorn and spite of brazen power. Unbridled power would silent dissent at any cost.

Silencing dissent at any cost – this was the intention that only now Sally fully grasped. It seemed unreal, but inevitably she too must be silenced – for she was the untidy detail, the voice still left out in the world outside, a voice free to blurt out whatever she wanted, or so 'they' might imagine. But with Saad possibly at 'their' disposal, she was not free to speak out. And they had her number now.

They had even been waiting for her call. And she had made it.

Chapter 6

Reaching Out

The next steps were difficult. Sally was shaken by her new understanding of the way things really were; but she was not rendered silent by the threat but convinced she needed to tell someone what she knew, perhaps what only she knew. She was unsure of all the facts but she knew enough to feel pressured to convey what little she did know. She could not involve or speak for Saad when she knew nothing definite about him but she did have information on someone, albeit a stranger about whom she knew virtually nothing. The source of her information was difficult to evaluate. She could guarantee the safety of no one. Action or inaction, it made no difference. She had no choice but to take Eva's message at face value. Who was she to decide on its accuracy? Besides, the inference that Saad too had been taken was not at all far-fetched.

Sally knew of only one organisation that might help. For that, she would have to travel to London. It was arranged speedily. She left the children with their grandparents in Liverpool and travelled from there by train. It was late May and the weather was unusually wet. With her head down against the driving rain, she felt she was battling her way not just along the streets asking for directions, but battling through a storm of mental chaos, seeking reassurance from every nuanced meaning of the words of someone she could hardly trust, did not know.

She took in nothing of the crowd around her, the grey streets, the unremarkable brick buildings. It was all noise. She was in a bubble, surprised by the unexpected stress of branching out this far on her own. She imagined someone was following her, lagging just yards behind on the other side of the road. In the blustering weather, it was impossible to be sure. In the emotional storm, impossible to dismiss as mere paranoia.

Once there, she was unsure of the wisdom of her coming. She sat stiffly on a straight-backed chair in a very small office, with a researcher behind the desk clutching a file. The desk almost filled the room. The researcher seemed too young. Sally told her her story, haltingly, not even sure at this stage of its narrative. It seemed so incomplete and implausible. But it told itself. And as it did so, sounded like someone else's life. Impossible to have happened to her.

"So you have the name of just one person besides maybe your husband. And your husband is missing, you say." The young woman's voice was steady and businesslike. "I can tell you that we know about the arrests from another source. We have more details, other names I cannot reveal to you. They are imprisoned. Without trial so far. We are considering their adoption as prisoners of conscience. Your husband is not one of them, I'm afraid. We can do nothing. Not until we are sure."

Her tone was so neutral, so calmly objective. So unconnected to the anguish Sally felt. Her details had been few, they had added nothing remarkable, it seemed. And yet, they were precious to her, and rapidly gaining preciousness as she shared them. She noted how sanguinely, with so little expression of sympathy, they were received. The details of her story, cluttered with emotion, were scrutinised by a professional objectivity.

"However, even though we have no idea what has happened to your husband, his name has been reported to us. I can confirm that at least. For the present, he is regarded as missing. We do not know where he is. We know his family has been looking for him. Our source is very reliable. As for the other name you mention, you are another source which crucially confirms his case. It gives us the substantiation we need to progress it. Your husband's case is possibly confirmed. But first it will have to go before a committee and then decisions will be made."

"You will keep in touch with me?" Sally's voice was shaking. She sat with her hands tightly folded round the letter to stop the trembling.

"Of course we will. But we will need to have the letter you mentioned for our files before we can do anything much."

"The problem is, I will be moving soon. I don't know where I'll be living."

"A contact address will do. And we do need the letter."

"My parents' address. I can give you that."

"Very good. But Sally, we do need the letter."

Sally was unwilling to give it. The writer could be traced. Perhaps she had already betrayed a confidence by coming here. She folded it away and placed it in her bag. "I'm sorry, but I can't do that. It isn't safe."

"It will be very safe, I promise you, it will be safe with us. Without it I just can't present the case, and nothing more will happen. Your words will just be hearsay. If your husband is located and he is being held and if we do adopt him, we can get our volunteers to write to him, to write letters of appeal for his release. Without your evidence, we can't do that. We don't proceed on the basis of one source only."

Sally felt compelled to hand the letter over, but withheld the envelope. She reasoned that Eva's husband's name was already known and the wife would be easily identified even without the letter. In no way had Eva exposed either of their husbands to any danger. It was a letter meant to call Sally in, appealing to her as a wife. There was nothing political in that. It was the writer of the address, as willing go-between, who was vulnerable perhaps. So Sally satisfied herself that keeping the envelope was a fair compromise, and her conscience was appeased by the thought that Eva had been careful in her wording. She had written nothing incriminating.

"Is there anything else we can do for you?" the young woman asked. The calm expression on her young face certainly belied her years, or sentiments. She seemed well trained, courteous if restrained, and certainly methodical.

Chapter 7

Coming to terms

A few days passed with no further news from any quarter. It gave her time enough to adjust to the changed circumstances of her life. She was pleased she was able to make a living and keep her little family together. She could pay the rent. Now they needed to find a place to live. The General Infirmary would not wait another month. The whole affair of Saad's unexplained absence had become an embarrassment. She could no longer trespass on polite goodwill.

Sally's mother came to help her sort things out and search for somewhere. She had offered her accommodation but Sally wanted to be independent. They met at the station. Sally's mother was in the habit of reining her emotions in, and she did so now, wringing her hands. Sally flung her arms around her, and held her tight, saying she was all right, not to worry, she was coping fine.

"A job? You've found a job? What kind of job?" Her mother's face brightened.

"Yes. They rang this morning. Temporary. But it suits. Covering a maternity leave. A class of twelve year olds in a middle school. Nizar can join reception on the same site, and Neda the nursery."

"That's amazing. A job. I didn't think you'd find one so soon. To begin when?"

"Next month. And so I'll be paid for the summer too."

"That's amazing, Sally. I've been so worried about you, about you all."

They found a cafe in the station, and ordered coffee. Juice for Neda and Nizar.

"Don't worry, Nana," Nizar sounded so mature. "Something will turn up. It always does. Doesn't it, Mummy?"

"Yes, the sky doesn't fall in, after all, does it, love? We will manage."

"We'll manage without Daddy, Nana. When he comes home, he'll be surprised."

"He be surprise," Neda echoed.

The children left the table to choose a cake from the counter display case. Sally's mother took her chance to express her still unappeased concern. "But you need a place to live, Sally. I can't believe Saad has left you in this mess."

"It's isn't fair to blame him, Mum."

"I'm not blaming him, my love. But he should have thought about the consequences."

"About what, Mum? Who could have known this would happen? The whole country seems to be in crisis. He could not have known. No one's safe. Perhaps not even here. The regime behaves unpredictably. It's almost mad. If you can describe a state in that way – mad?"

"But he knew it wasn't safe."

"Sticky buns, Mummy – please." The children's faces were beaming with the promise of a treat.

Sally's mother bought the buns. It was her treat she declared. Sally was glad the children had managed to close down the topic of Saad and whatever mistakes her mother thought he had made. In restrained silence, mother and grandmother watched the children chomp through their buns. Sticky faces, shiny eyes. It was a pleasure doubled by the undivided attention they had won. It was true – the sky had not fallen in.

It was Neda who broke the silence. "Henny Penny say sky fallin'."

"But it didn't, Neda," corrected Nizar. "It didn't fall in. Anyway, that's just a story for babies."

They had sat long enough in the café. Later, on the bus, Sally's mother whispered in her ear, "As I see it, he left you, Sally – you and the children – left you with nothing. I can't get over that. Never will. But then I'm sure I can't know the truth of it."

"Oh, but I have the car. And it will all come right in the end, I am sure of that."

"Only the car, and that is all? And you don't even drive."

"I've sold it. The money will help."

"What about all the rent you haven't paid?"

"I'll pay it back, Mum. I've got a job, remember."

"And you aren't even a little bit angry with him?"

"Anger seems a bit pointless, doesn't it? I've got things to do."

"What about his family? Can't they help?"

"I've heard nothing from them. I'm fine I told you. I'll manage."

"And do you love him still? You wouldn't go to Libya, would you? Not now?"

"Of course I do. I think I understand what he did. I can forgive him."

"You wouldn't go to Libya, would you, though?"

"Oh, Mum. Where would I begin? I have no idea where he is."

They did not speak of the unspeakable – for Sally it was the fear that she might never see Saad again; for her mother it was the certain knowledge that Sally would never let go of the idea of him.

Chapter 8

Decision

That was spring turning into summer. Now it was July. The Council found Sally and the children a place to live, not near the school, on the other side of town. It was a back-to-back terraced house, a condemned property bequeathed to the Council, but with a suspended sentence, while the Council's housing stock needed replenishing. Sally had taken up her temporary post, and by the end of the summer term it seemed to those around her that she was living a normal everyday existence, much like their own. But the journey to school and back was a gruelling routine of buggy-pushing and hand-holding through a busy thoroughfare, her shoulders laden with exercise books. Yet they had adapted to some extent. Libya seemed so far away, Saad's disappearance a myth and unfathomable. It was a background story, not quite possible to slot into everyday existence; and yet its weight bore down.

Sally was unable to settle in her mind. She had tamed whatever residue of anger had lingered on even beyond her conversations with her mother. She found it easier to reflect more kindly on Saad. She did not want to harbour bitterness. Sometimes she blamed herself for their separation: she should have sensed his dilemma, his ambiguity, the allegiance he felt to his own people, and his scorn for a too-easy existence in refuge. Perhaps Saad had found escape dishonourable, especially when his homeland was in foment. Now it seemed to her that even her own almost normal existence had begun to weigh on her conscience, while Saad was still a disappeared person. It was impossible to live without an explanation.

So it was that Sally reached the point when she was ready to meet Libyan authorities at the London embassy and make her own enquiries. Once her focus was galvanised, taking the decisive step of making an appointment with the Ambassador was easy. The support of her father made it easier. He accompanied her to London.

London was not his favourite place. He thought it was too busy. After several wrong turns, they found themselves at last in a grand part of Kensington. The elegant terraces adorned with marble pillars were a homage to expensive elegance and empire, and all of it belonged to a class and culture he felt reduced by, but not without a touch of his own kind of Northern pride. The elegant avenues were wide and empty of people. The noise of traffic was soaked up by the foliage of plane trees. It all gave the impression of stately stability and historical continuity, reiterated in the width of roads, the breadth of doorways.

They found the embassy. A surly youth at the entrance demanded their purpose and sent a chain of commands to other youths down the dark corridor behind him to check the authenticity of the visitors. They were allowed in after a sufficiently impressive amount of time had passed.

A measure of defiance might have just registered on her father's face as they passed through a long hallway. Sally sensed it. They were being made aware of the threatening presence of a surprising number of ill-defined characters leaning on the walls on either side. Ruffians, her father had said later. Their dress was more than casual; they flaunted a creased and unwashed look, the better to affect a rebellious disregard for the usual mores of diplomats. She was reminded of a children's game of passing under a gamut of arches of up-stretched arms. But this was not a game – they were the suspicious foreigners whose intrusion was regarded an affront.

Her father was required to remain in the visitors' lobby. Sally was escorted to a side room to meet 'The Minister.' His assistant stressed the title in a manner that suggested a lofty and superior status: "The Minister is ready for you now."

The Minister had the kind of enigmatic aura about him that explained his capacity for survival through all shifts of power. He affected casual disinterest. The Minister had always been here, in this place, at this desk. He would always be there, come what may. He maintained his anonymity behind sunglasses, improbably worn in a darkened room. There was no window into his soul. He further obscured his corporeal presence by sitting silhouetted his back to the window. Heavy velvet curtains only partially drawn afforded a narrow glint of light that ran along his cheekbone and jaw, cut along the firmly padded shoulder of his military-style jacket, touched the Rolex watch loose above his closed fist that resting on the pristine blotter before him. Though the hand seemed to reach a little way towards her, it did not invite communication, let alone a handshake.

In contrast to him, Sally's face was wholly lit by the light from the window. Her chair was lower than his on the other side of a huge mahogany block of desk. He remained seated. He indicated her subservience. He did not open up the discussion, but sat unmoved, affecting disinterest, flicking at times for his own distraction at an invisible speck of something on the blotter.

There was no hint of movement in his darkened face to suggest he would begin the discussion at any time soon. She must speak first, to an intimidating emptiness. His hand opened in a gesture that seemed to ask "What?" Undaunted by his show of power, his lack of courtesy, she presented her case firmly, opening up with the bare and simple facts. Her husband had travelled to Libya, Tripoli, at the request of the Minister of Health. It was important business. But he had not returned. She requested reasons, information.

His inscrutable self remained unmoved. His sullenness bore down on her tenacity. But she surprised herself. He had met his match in determination. She wanted information. She insisted. Did he think he could break her in this way, make her weep, make her plead? He had touched a raw nerve and she was offended by his uncivil stony resistance. She was ready with a feisty challenge, almost verging on a threat.

"If you know nothing, I hope you will make it your business to kindly find out something at least. There is one thing I must warn you" – and here she felt her cheeks burn – "if you so much as touch one hair of my husband's head, I will expose you and what you people do. I will go to the press. I will tell everyone what I know. I have my contacts."

There was a visible ripple in the tight muscles of his neck. He leaned back and pulled at the joints of his fingers so that they cracked, loudly. Then surprisingly he let slip just one sliver of humanity, "I will do as you ask. I will find where he is. If we find him. If we find him anywhere, I will let you know." Then he turned his face away from her towards the darker side of the room so that his profile was lost to the velvet drape of curtain. A dismissive wave of his hand shook the Rolex watch hanging loosely on his wrist.

Uniformed officers led Sally quickly to an antechamber where an elegantly dressed man guided her to a chair beside a long coffee table. He sat opposite and ordered coffee for two. His manner was quite different. He spoke on the level with her and with an obvious concern, even sympathy. He introduced himself as the Minister of Agriculture, and an acquaintance of her husband. He said he would do his best to help, but warned that his influence was limited. The conversation was easy and wandered over other matters, the lingering drought in Benghazi, the humidity in Tripoli, the problem with locusts, the need for more education, better hospitals, and surprisingly his belief that wealth from oil was not yet trickling down to the masses as they hoped it would soon.

"Has oil been a blessing or a curse, do you think?" she had dared to ask.

"Ah, you strike the nail on the head," he answered. "The question is a good one. I think a curse. Why do you ask?"

"Well, I never understood why the money never reached far. The hospital in Al Baitha had only one ambulance and Saad had to fetch the medical supplies himself – all the way from Tripoli, on the long coastal road. We didn't seem to get the benefit there. Like it was a poor country with no resources."

The agricultural minister looked pained. The conversation had stumbled into a wall. Sally's directness had alarmed him; she had drawn him into matters he was not free to comment on.

Even so, despite her lack of diplomatic prudence, he was gracious in his manner and wished her well.

Chapter 9

The tipping point

Two weeks later, another letter tracked Sally down. Someone had discovered her new address, not airmail this time, but inland. The large buff envelope had been posted second class and bore a London postmark. It contained a small and unassuming swatch of folded sheets, of waxed paper, the kind that backs the foil lining of cigarettes packets. They were written on in a minuscule hand that was unmistakably Saad's:

I am writing from a hospital. They have just moved me here. I'm surrounded by guards round the clock. They work in shifts. I write when they are distracted. I have been in solitary confinement in an underground cell. It was very damp and my joints are now inflamed. Here it's clean. No cockroaches. No rats. The male nurses are kind. There are soldiers in uniform and carry guns. They seem shocked with it all. I am thinking of you. I miss you. Hard to remember you. Your bird-like face, your staring eyes. You would stare now if you saw me. My bones stick out, my ribs are a cage, only no bird inside. Time plods on. Can you forgive me? I've had time to think. I'm thinking about love. No tales of love here. I never explored love as a way of giving. I only found an existential loneliness. Now I know better. Do I deserve a second chance with you? If you can forgive me, please come. Please be near me. You could stay in Tripoli and you and the children could visit me every week. Please come.

The words hardly registered their meaning at first. They only served to tell her Saad was alive. Alive. He had been through hell; the details needed time to be absorbed. But at the end of the ordeal, and the end of it all, thank God, he was safe, in a hospital bed, recovering, from what she could not tell, but being taken care of. The letter offered her a path into a future, hazy and uncertain it may be, but a future where Saad would continue to figure as the focus of her life, her life and the children's. He asked for forgiveness. She could forgive. She would have to.

From then on, the future just happened of its own accord, drawing its own sequence. Sally merely followed its prescribed path, subjugating all other options to it, ignoring all possible consequences, good or bad.

Good or bad – there was no certainty. Outwardly, she may have seemed untroubled; perhaps she sleepwalked, but doubt was always there. She wrote something in her notebook. It illuminated the disquiet beneath the surface, behind her public face, her not-so-sure hope that things would be resolved if she threw her lot in with Saad's, no hesitation, no dithering:

He called me / mine is a choice half-made/ half retracted / Either I live like a tortoise / hiding in its shell / fearing the hawk / that hovers over me / or I leap / a bright spark to be consumed / enveloped in a shroud of medieval fabric.

Chapter 10

Leaving

In the terraced back-to-back house that had been their home for almost a year, the mismatched jumble of furniture was waiting to be collected by a council van. Most of it was second hand but there was also a newish Mary Quant sofa bought on a whim with money she could hardly afford. It would go to her mother. She had paid all outstanding bills by cashing in her teacher's superannuation. The family cat had sorted out its own future, wandering off during the packing of boxes and suitcases. But she had returned to sit on the gatepost every morning, purring loudly, waiting for an affectionate ruffling of her fur.

Sally had been offered another post teaching Art. It was attractive and tempting but she turned it down after much unease about the rightness of her choice. This was only the first of the many little deaths of herself that followed, the first in a series of denials of who she was, obscure in the reason for their casting off. Who she was, who she had been, all that was retreating into a past, all hardly relevant or known about in the place she was moving towards. The lure of an alternative faded, its attraction less painful once her mind was made up. She was going to the place where Saad belonged, had always belonged, a land tagged in her mind with the label 'Caprice', for she knew it to be a wilful and unpredictable territory.

The one aspect of her own identity she could hold on to was that of 'mother'; it was a role that transcended cultures, through time and space. It was a role that gave her a dominion of a kind, an undisputed function and purpose: mother, and also wife, as 'mother' seemed automatically to infer. And yet, in this new culture, which was not her own, she had yet to understand that as a foreigner, she could not legally claim her children as her own.

That was for the future. For now, she had come to terms with the inevitability of her choice. The way her life would be lived through a series of prison visits, in a city a desert away from family in Benghazi, was a vague proposition; vague enough to dismiss all consideration of its latent dangers and promises as pointless. Whichever way she looked at it, she was leaving behind certainty, and the options would never present themselves again.

The flight to Tripoli was uneventful. The children were a welcome distraction, playing games, having stories read to them, being entertained by the friendly air hostesses. Sally took in little of the detail. She let it pass over her. Her resignation deepened with the increasing distance between herself and a place where she could no longer be. She trusted in a basic fund of benign will to protect her children and herself, yet kept the children close to herself all the way. The act was done and could not be undone. She had said goodbye to everything she had known that offered safety, just as Saad had done before her.

Part Two – Separate worlds

But few words passed between them as they sat together, cloaked in their separate worlds of different meanings and different means of survival.

Chapter 1

The gift

On arrival at Tripoli airport Sally and the children were met by Hassan, Saad's father, and his uncle, Sidi Ahmed to Sally. As brothers they were quite unlike each other – Hassan unshaven and dishevelled in an ill-fitting suit, Ahmed clean-shaven, taller and too large for the jacket that did not reach over his front. Ahmed loomed large in personality too. He was more than generous in the largesse of his smile and hearty handshake. Hassan was quiet, not assuming much authority, hesitant even, though he was the elder of the two. Perhaps it was the strangeness of Sally, this pale foreigner that was by some accident his daughter-in-law, that made him stand back, away from her. Perhaps it was more difficult for a father to accept his son's aberrant choice. Ahmed seemed at sufficient ease for two in his role as go-between, bridging the gulf between cultures with charm. His welcome bubbly chatter smoothed over any awkwardness. Sally warmed to him right away.

The motley group left the cool of the airport lounge for the taxi rank. The humidity of a Tripolitanian summer oppressed them like a damp blanket. It took her breath away. Still adjusting to the moist air, they were whisked away in the first taxi available. Whispering as though in conspiracy, Hassan explained they were going to see Saad, now, no time to waste. The taxi driver was given a vague destination, and he dropped them off in the commercial high street; any convenient stopping place would do. No doubt he was bemused by this unlikely collection of solemn adults, the female clearly a foreigner, and two excited children speaking English.

They found their way walking to Porto Benito Prison. The building was imposing from the outside; it was once an Italian military base during the years of colonisation, so Hassan told them. They stood a while staring at its forbidding gates. The children were silenced by its bleak aspect. They had not imagined their father in such a place. If they had imagined him anywhere, it would have been in an open doorway somewhere ill-defined. He would have been waving from a distance, walking towards them but never arriving near enough, always fading. They drew closer to their mother, unsure of entering the compound.

Hassan tried to reassure them. He and Ahmed had seen Saad the day before and everything was fine. He was fine. Now this was their day, and they could have their father all to themselves. Hassan, a little diffident, presented the children and Sally to the guard who was sitting behind the open window of the gatehouse. It was Ahmed who ushered them in with confidence, bending down to speak to the children, encouraging them with messages to give to Saad when they saw him. This focussed them. When Ahmed righted himself to a standing position with some stretching effort, Sally saw his eyes were shining in a reddened face. Sweat was pouring down his temples, down his cheeks, or were they tears – she could not be sure. The dark hallway with its high arched ceiling echoed to their whispers and their footsteps. It opened onto an expansive yard, once a parade ground, now its function seeming obsolete. It was flooded with sunlight. They paused to blink and shade their eyes before stepping into the blinding light.

"Go on," Hassan urged, raising his hand with a seemingly impatient gesture more out of anxiety than irritation. "You'll find a place to sit when you get inside." Ahmed nodded his approval.

As far as sally could make out scanning the perimeter in all directions, the open yard was empty, except for a dark equestrian statue to one end. A colonnade around the court offered shade in little porticos. Constructed of stone, they were cool as well as shady. She chose the nearest one and settled the children on the simple wooden bench fixed to the wall with a chain, while she kept a look-out for movement at a spot where the colonnade gave way to a large opening of some kind.

Before long, the prisoners could be seen filing out of there in an orderly fashion, collecting into a standing area. A long metal chain like a low fence prevented their further progress and they stood still behind it. When, at a signal, the guards released the chain, the men rushed towards their visitors.

"Here they come," Sally called and Nizar ran out searching for his father in amongst the prisoners. He found him in the crowd. He was waving. Nizar ran ahead to meet him. Neda followed hesitating as she came close; for this was not the father she had remembered from his wedding photo, so formal in a suit, now wearing a long shirt down to his ankles. Saad approached her gently, understanding her shyness. He crouched low to put his arm around her. Only then did she remember the smell and touch of him.

Sally stood back, giving this special moment to the children. She longed to be held close, but a public show of affection man to wife was unthinkable here. She felt tears pricking her eyelids. But Saad had prepared for just this difficult interface where two cultures clashed. Firstly he was the only one with a wife. Who knew if the others would ever find partners now? There were more than cultural reasons for damping down his own expression of his love for her. But he had found a way – a gift, something he had made for her. He passed it over by sleight of hand, a slim box fashioned from a cigarette packet. She opened it a chink to find a butterfly, a *painted lady*, pinned down in crucifix repose.

He touched her hand and whispered, "Hide it. Underneath the butterfly. There's something underneath. Don't look now."

The shock of it! She looked around to diffuse any slight commotion the exchange might have caused, but there was none. The gift and its surprise had been private. "I'll be back," Saad was saying, as he led the children to the other family groups, childless families. It moved her to see how much her own children meant to them. She watched from a distance and saw how the older women fondled them and passed them on like precious prayer beads, mothers who may never have grandchildren of their own. Nizar and Neda were painful reminders of their childless present, the futures denied their sons.

Sally felt herself set apart, not by anyone's intention, just for the absence of a point of reference in the culture. In her paisley-patterned dress, coloured like the underwings of a butterfly, she was the *franji*, the outsider, the foreign one. Appropriately sombre she had thought the colours, but now strikingly bright in contrast to the pale garb of the other women. She stood out, in a way she had not expected, as if she was ignorant of local norms of female dress. The other women merged in a sisterly oneness, their individuality hidden under outer robes that covered them over their heads and down to their ankles. They held the draped covering tightly between their teeth to reveal only one seeing eye.

Sally stepped away to find her distance of ease, and turned aside to look again at the bright thing in the box. *Trapped*, she thought, *clearly in its* coffin.

The heat from the sky reflected back from the ground was overpowering; best not to resist the pressing down, Sally thought, and let herself feel cosseted in, swaddled by the light. Sweat was pouring off her. She felt her dress was inappropriate – the skin of her forearms was exposed and burning. Long loose sleeves would have kept her cool. She looked for shade, but there was only the thin retreating shadow of the equine statue disappearing in the midday. Above her the towering statue offered no shelter.

The horse reared up, balanced on muscled flanks, and frozen in bronze. It would have thrown a rider easily; but it was riderless. Appearing to emerge from a pond, it symbolised triumph. Bold and beautifully fashioned, dramatically dark despite patches where the patina was a bronze green, it was, Sally thought, overly grand as a centrepiece for such a drab pool. The rough cement walls did not match up to the refinement of the superbly moulded sculpture. The crumbling render exposed the brickwork underneath and was crudely repaired with daubs of cement.

Sally trailed her fingers in the water. It was turgid. A scummy film of reddish dust hid its murky depths. There was no fountain to relieve the sombre stillness. Though the unsaddled horse struck a rampant pose, it gave no illusion of freedom. Was it straining to rise above the dirty, brown liquid, Sally wondered.

Then a familiar cry made her turn. It was Neda. The guards were herding the prisoners out of the prison yard and away to their cells. Sally collected her children, Neda clinging to her and Nizar resisting and defiant, demanding his father back. A guard stayed him with gentle firmness; there was a flicker of disquiet in his eyes as Sally retrieved Nizar. She caught the look of regret in the guard's eyes and understood that underneath the facade of harshness there was perhaps compassion, and embarrassment.

Sally and the children joined the other visitors being shepherded towards the exit. The iron gates slammed behind them with a force that made them shudder in their frames.

Chapter 2

Home

They found Hassan and Ahmed waiting for them on the street outside, surprised by the briefness of the visit. They disguised any concern they may have had and reassured Sally that the prisoners could not be in any danger. It was just another example of the petty administration they had grown accustomed to, Hassan had said, knowing in his heart that it was more a display of power, an expression of its capricious nature. You could never know when it might show itself and that was how it worked. The whole point of being unpredictable was to engender a seemingly irrational fear. But Hassan would not worry Sally now with such misgivings, his growing dismay and cynicism. Instead he reiterated how relaxed and friendly things had been the day before.

The taxi shunted its way through the traffic chaos of the commercial centre. Then it sped along the airport road making up for the lost time. Transfer to the plane was straightforward. Soon *terra firma* was left behind and receding at a steady pace. The smallholdings of semi-settled Bedouin farmers were patchworks of green giving way to the deceptive emptiness of the desert, its vastness interrupted at intervals by the ridges of dunes and a few oases with their shining water stretches glinting in the sun. Then the distances between places of settlement lengthened until the only sign of human habitation was the thin thread of a tarmac road, intermittently erased by the encroaching desert.

When the dunes below were wholly obliterated by cloud the children slept, leaving Sally to her private thoughts. She tried to come to terms with this very different and unpredictable territory that was to be their new home. The children seemed more vulnerable than before and she would strive to keep them close. She was not able to tell them when next they would see their father. It could be a month or more. It was clear she could not live in Tripoli, on her own, and would not be near Saad as she had hoped, as he had promised. She would be staying instead with his family in Benghazi, a whole desert away.

They arrived in Benghazi, at night, too late for the welcome Saad's family had planned for them. They were taken up the external marble staircase to the apartment above the family villa, the children too sleepy to walk and needing to be carried. The largest room had been prepared for them; it was furnished with one large bed, a bedside table and reading lamp, and in the far corner a dark red velvet armchair, worn thin at the edges. The children found the bed inviting with its heavy blankets and snuggled in.

While they settled, Sally explored an adjacent room. It was dusty and stale-smelling, so she opened the French windows onto an adjoining balcony to refresh it. She smelt the salt of the Mediterranean in the air and heard its rhythmic booming tones as it washed on the near shore. She was physically tired but her mind was still racing, anxiety rising and falling with the distant waves. She returned to the children and found her own narrow slot between them, where she lay quite still, listening to their steady breathing, waiting for her own sleep.

Neda and Nizar were still in a twilight sleep and stirred to turn themselves towards her.

"Will we see Daddy again soon?" whispered Neda.

"Of course we will." Nizar was as sure of this as he was about things in general returning to their rightful places.

"You know when?"

"Yes, soon, Neda. If you go to sleep." Neda believed him, because he was two years older. It was a promise to himself as much as to his sister; it allowed them both to sleep.

Sally could not sleep. She wanted to examine Saad's gift, to find again that 'something hidden' underneath the butterfly. It was almost three in the morning, that time in the night when the temperature drops suddenly. The children's sleep was deep. She eased herself from the warmth and felt in the dark for the lamp. Carrying it over to the chair in the dark, she found a socket and rummaged in her bag for the box. She lifted the butterfly on its mount and underneath was the familiar waxed paper Saad had used for his first smuggled letter. His second letter to her was written in that same minuscule hand, not easy to decipher in the dim light.

We struggle to stay hopeful here. I am with some good men. They are decent, missing their families very much. One of us is upset because his fiancée has broken off their engagement. She is to marry another man. She is not prepared to wait. He is not bitter. He has forgiven her. There has been no trial, no charge against us. They keep us separate much of the time and try to divide us, but they cannot. We only have each other. You will see a pond in the prison yard. It has a black statue – a horse. It's where we are tortured. They choose us at random, who and when. They push us under until we think we must drown. I'm okay so far. I miss you. You are my freedom. The butterfly is my soul flying to you, free. Be strong, I must come home one day. Give our children twice your love and then some more from me. Let them know I love them. My dearest darling, keep this letter safe. Tell no one what I have told you.

Chapter 3

Painted Lady

The images conjured by Saad's words could not be put aside. They would hover in Sally's liminal inner sight, always ineradicable, impossible to forget. In her mind, the words could not be tamed to oblivion. Minuscule in size, they were a whispered haunting, too shocking to consider in their full meaning. Like wild spirits, his words repeated and repeated, filling the night with their discomforting message of violence and death: "where we are tortured... until we think we will drown." The dirty pond where they were tortured! The towering horse fixed in dismal concrete, the shadow of its mass bearing down on them as they struggled for another breath. She read his words again and again. Somewhere out of all the pain and misery came the butterfly, the symbol of his longed-for freedom. And she was his butterfly, his impossible freedom.

This was not how Sally had imagined her return. Libya was still the place they had once escaped from. But how could it have been otherwise? Now it was no longer a place she could escape from, not a second time. She had become attached to it like a bird is restrained on a string. She was the awkward uninvited guest in a strange and whimsical tyranny, her sole charge and function to double her capacity for love. *Give our children twice your love*, he had written. Could that be done in such a loveless place? The freedom that had been hers she had thrown away. It was impossible to embrace even the smallest measure of freedom when a prison wall cast such a long shadow.

There was no choice but to carry the burden of what she knew without complaining. Knowing the pain of others was a burden; saying nothing, since nothing could be said, was a burden increased.

Sally was not new to the sensation of fear. Two years living in Al Baitha, in the eastern Green Mountain region of Libya, known as Cyrenaica or Barce, had taught her something of the capricious nature of surveillance, its terrors in a place of great beauty. It always seemed surreal.

It had been a cold day in winter. The children had needed an outing and Saad had chosen the crescent beach just beyond Shahhat, below Cyrene. They were followed by a police car. Scowling faces had peered through misted windows as it overtook them. At the beach, the same posse of police sat a short distance away, hurling insults.

The outing was made unbearable. Their little family was an odd phenomenon, deviant and mostly not approved of, just as her walking out alone with the children had been unacceptable. Sally remembered the child kidnappings. *You love your son? Take care. We could take him from you.*

Then there was the other time – a call in the night, to resuscitate a soldier rescued from the sea, a full hour's drive away. A fabricated emergency if ever there was one; but Saad could not resist the call. He was not the doctor on call that night; it was someone else's duty. Even so, he answered the call and left in a hurry, as if haste from this distance made some kind of sense to him. In her panic, she had struggled to draw breath at an open window and finally found the wit to call a colleague who had dutifully followed after Saad. There had been no incident. The drama had dissipated as soon as the colleague arrived only minutes after Saad. Saad said nothing to Sally to explain his rash behaviour – if rash it was.

While Sally knew she could be sure of nothing, she had sensed that fear would silence everyone on the matter., this and others. Saad was no longer there to advise her. In surmising what or who might be normal or dependable, she had only her 'ruminations.' It was safest to join the silence.

She stayed in the chair through the long hours until dawn relieved the gloom. Two slats in the wooden blinds hung askew so that light came in as a narrow beam, crookedly, spotlighting the red of the armchair around her. The velvet glowed crimson, like the blood of a sacrificed lamb in the first gush from its cut throat. She remembered her first experience of a slaughtered lamb, its blood spreading. Up against the window a moth's wings trembled, caught between glass and wood. She caught sight briefly of its dun-coloured form as it dropped into the gap. Or perhaps she only caught sight of the dust it left behind, a barely visible puff of its own bruising.

She shook away the thought. She must have dozed off, because she had not seen the children leave room. Saad's voice came louder to her. *Give our children twice your love and then some more from me. Let them know I love them.* She could hear their voices in the villa downstairs. She wanted to tidy the room. She wanted the blind to be straight. She tugged at it to no avail. She straightened the bedsheets and folded the blanket on the chair. Removing Saad's letter, she placed the butterfly box inside her travel bag which from now on would serve as a hiding place. Tidying things made everything seem better.

Tidiness and order helped Sally to cope. Collections added to the impression of order. Already there was the beginnings of a collection of Saad's smuggled letters. She had kept an old Clan tobacco tin of Saad's for keeping foreign currency in. It still exuded the smell of Clan and reminded her of him. Now it held both his letters, and she was ready to present herself to the family downstairs.

She closed the door behind her very softly. Not quite ready yet. For her children's sake, she wanted to appear serene and in control and so paused to collect herself. From the almost-top of the marble staircase looking down, she saw how the usual film of sand had been disturbed by their footsteps. How easily they adapted! And what did they make of her in these changed circumstances?

She had to be the person she had always been, even though she could no longer be the same mother who had kept them safe before; even though the family had accepted her only by dint of Saad's love for her, his choice of wife. She would love their children extra, if that was possible, as Saad had asked, for they carried her identity with them. This was her purpose: they needed her protection. Then the doubt crept in – could she really be that intrepid protector in this place where she was the stranger, an outsider. She felt again the greasy slip of pond water on her skimming finger tips. She imagined the butterfly alive in her open hand, readying itself to fly away, free from all of this. She imagined the light touch of its take-off. But it could not fly and its deathly stillness held all the pain of drowning. The butterfly had become a conceit; it was not, could not be, freedom. It was instead everything that could not be told. And yet: *You are my freedom. The butterfly is my soul flying to you.*

How we claim to know only as much as we can handle, she thought. We suppress what we fear, especially when it has the power to stop us in our tracks and turn our little worlds upside-down. Nothing is what it seems. And who am I in this place but the actual painted lady butterfly safeguarding the future for Saad, keeping alive his stolen freedom?

Chapter 4

A second disappearance

The children had settled in with apparent ease. The container holding their possessions from England had arrived and boxes filled the rooms. The once empty apartment was ringing with their chatter and squeals of delight as they rediscovered old toys and assigned them to makeshift cardboard furniture. They liked the new routines of morning school with afternoons for play.

Afternoons were meant for siestas but were often opportunities for both of them to explore the garden, even for forbidden trespass outside the garden gate onto the wasteland of wild olive trees. When the villa came to life again at four, then they separated into male and female roles. Nizar would go with his grandfather, *Jeddi* Hassan to the shop, in the middle of the busy commercial centre of the city. Neda would lean on the balcony wall, peering through the balustrade, enviously watching them leave, wondering what kind of streets they passed through on their way. But soon enough she would be drawn into the female conversation around the tea tray, treated to sweets and nuts and fruity syrups. By the time Nizar and Hassan returned in the evening, she would be asleep.

Weeks passed with no more news of Saad. At first Nizar had pressed for information but there was never anything to tell. Neda never asked about him. It was as though the visit in Tripoli was all a dream, a reminder that a father is not for always, that a father would fade from memory unless you worked hard at remembering. After months of waiting, of spring turning into summer and approaching autumn, his name was rarely mentioned. But it was there, lodged in a place where many crucial things were lodged and not spoken of, yet longed for. It was avoided. Skirted around, especially by adults.

Sally noticed how Saad had gone missing from their conversations. Neither Fathia nor Hassan mentioned him. Perhaps they did but in a private, coded way without her noticing, though she listened acutely for his name. She waited for mention of another visit but there was nothing and the dark days at the end of November installed their own kind of gloom at the villa. Sally feared the worst and dared not ask the question.

Fathia prayed in the garden most times of prayer, near the spot where Saad had planted beans some years before. She prayed in earnest, adding special supplications. Prayer like other routines sustained her so that every afternoon, she would be sitting on the veranda making tea, whispering her pleas at each step in the process. She melted the resin of frankincense on her charcoal burner and wafted the *bukhour* over the grandchildren for a blessing. At other times, she kept busy pruning and cutting, sweeping and baking, always brooding on the fate of her eldest child.

As for Hassan, he stayed in his room most of the time. He revealed nothing of what was on his mind in conversation with his wife; he did not need to. Fathia had learned to read his moods over the years and she explained his behaviour as that old malaise of spirit which showed itself whenever he was thwarted. Sally supposed it was the inevitable male condition, when the authority of men is usurped by an all-invasive state. Hassan must bear his troubles in isolation, and try to sublimate his sense of powerlessness in his own private way. Hence his habit of retreating from family discourse. It seemed to her that Saad in some way must bear some of the blame, leaving the care of his family to his ageing father. Even so, Hassan never complained apart from the occasional comment such as: "He could have been here looking after his mother." She saw him as a good man, if disagreeable at times.

Neda often sat near her grandfather, wishing him to be closer to her. Sharing an early morning reflection at the kitchen table was the closest she could get to him. She imagined Nizar was closer, because at least he took him with him for company; but at home there was little sign of much between them, other than the way Nizar imitated his grandfather's expressions and posture. So as he supped his espresso coffee from a little cup in one long sip without much sign of enjoying it, she wondered what it was that could give him any sort of pleasure, make him smile just a little. If there was anything, it was well hidden. Sometimes, she caught a glimpse of him in his bedroom, listening intently to the wireless, usually with a frown that creased his forehead.

Only Fathia could join him in his room; but even she only did so for minutes at a time, mainly to tidy it, to tidy him and clear away the clutter he created. She bustled round him, sometimes overstaying her welcome, for there was a limit to the tidying up around him that he could tolerate. No more could she tolerate his crumpled clothes which were as crushed and dishevelled as his unshaven face. The most he could achieve in grooming was the monthly close crop to his grey hair, cut like an army recruit, so close it narrowed his head and puffed out his full cheeks. But this was the man she had married, whose face she had not seen before marriage and which had never pleased her after marriage. Yet she had always given him wifely and charitable attention, never questioning his expectations of her. She knew he was basically a good man.

As the days went by, it seemed Hassan sat ever more heavily in his chair. Once seated, he was as immovable as a rock. He was a defeated man, a man who had given up the fight, a man who now let his shoulders slope, his back collapse, when he sat at the table waiting for his food. The sight of a despairing man was wearing, and impossible to ignore. With his head cast down, he seemed to pass judgement on the idleness of his hands as they rested in his lap.

Fathia chivvied him on to drink some water, she straightened his collar, fixed his tie for him. She put the keys to his shop in his pocket and made sure he had his watch. She tended to his basic needs for the day, some change, a biscuit to put him on, so that it would seem that he was turned out like a man still in charge. But there were always limits to how far she could go in her exhortations. Hassan had his own well entrenched habit of dismissing her when she had gone too far. It was that flutter of his hand, that exaggerated expression of disgust that accompanied a disdainful expression on his face that was the most unappealing thing about him. Fathia had the impression that he had no desire to curb his disdain; it was his weapon for guaranteeing he would not be disturbed.

And so it was that, one late afternoon in late September, when the time of waiting for news of his son had dragged on for far too long, Hassan's acerbic disdain got the better of him. He had left Nizar in the shop, knowing Mohamed the driver was nearby to watch over him, and had gone to his usual cafe, a short distance away, He entered the cafe in a fractious mood, barely acknowledging the armed youths leaning in the doorway, pushing past them. Perhaps he grunted something. No doubt his uncouth manner had seemed disrespectful, or was taken as an insult. It was always best to give respectful distance to a man with a gun in his belt.

Then he was sitting at his usual table, alone as he always chose to be, and gazing at the proprietor's newspaper, the official broadsheet approved by the regime. It was open at the centre page spread, displaying a large image of the Brother-Leader whose face was staring out at him, staring down. Hassan wanted to turn the page but could not take his eyes off this life-size portrait of the man who had whisked away his son. He placed his elbows on the table and rested his chin in his hands, hiding his pursed lips. He scowled. He looked around for his coffee. He had been waiting longer than usual. It seemed it was delayed for no good-enough reason.

So he hitched his chair forwards as much to draw attention to his waiting as to make himself more comfortable. Then he read the caption beneath the photo. It hailed the Brother-Leader as a hero for extending national boundaries into disputed territory. This adventure was being hailed as a victory when Hassan knew for a fact from his radio and other sources that the Libyan forces had been routed. And worse, they had been forced to flee back into the desert with no retreat plan in place to rescue them. The defeated men, mainly young inexperienced recruits had starved or died of thirst in their hundreds, maybe thousands. No one had wanted to fight the Chadian army who were fighting for the land where they lived. And now a generation of bright young men had been sacrificed for an ill-considered project to gratify the Leader's own personal territorial hubris.

Hassan whacked the page with the back of his hand, that same disdainful wave of dismissal that he used to finalise matters, and muttered something under his breath. It sounded angry. It sounded subversive. It could have been seditious. It probably was inflammatory. Certainly his meaning would have been obvious in the crack of the torn sheet as it ripped across the Leader-Brother's face.

What followed was a lightning sequence of action as the armed youths at the doorway moved in to surround Hassan. They kicked the chair from underneath him. They yanked him to an upright stance. His body recoiled against the onslaught. Chairs folded, the table tipped. Hassan was dragged across the floor, pushed through the doorway into the cold night air. They wrestled with him on the pavement where a Mercedes waited to steal him away.

At Hassan's shop there was another commotion. Soldiers arrived to board it up. Mohamed, the family driver, rescued Nizar and rushed him home. Angry youths closed the shop with its metal shutters padlocked down. There was no news of Hassan. Nizar was in shock. Fathia sat him on her knee and said it would soon all be fine, but she kept to herself the thought that Hassan might not be coming home that evening or the next.

For the next few days Fathia prayed in the orchard incessantly, whispering, and pleading with a power she knew to be in the sky. Nizar would not talk to anyone but the driver. Nothing made any sense to Neda, only the certainty of routines. So she helped her mother sweeping steps, sweeping paths, sweeping steps again.

Several nights passed before Hassan came home. The family had heard a heavy vehicle pulling up at the gate, then pull away. They found Hassan leaning on the gatepost. He was confused. His face was badly bruised and swollen, bloody cuts were not yet healed. He could barely hold himself upright. Together Sally and Fathia, feint with shock, tried to help him up the steps without stumbling. No one said a word, except for Fathia in her whispered phrases of thanks for his return, mixed with cries of *Ya Rub*: Oh God.

Nizar wanted to stay near his grandfather and so a bed was set up in his room, small enough to fit into a little alcove. Hassan did not object.

Chapter 5

A child watches

As time passed, Hassan seemed to have recovered from his arrest, finding new resolve to take control of his life. He had always enjoyed fishing along the coast and decided to take it up again. He set about repairing his tackle and his boat. Fathia tried to discourage him, something about it being too demanding, not worth the effort or the risk. There had been raised voices and it was clear to everyone that Fathia was aggrieved, and Hassan stubbornly resolved. His mind was firmly made up.

So when Neda followed *Jeddi* Hassan down to the jetty one early morning, she knew he was defying her grandmother. He turned around to caution her with his finger pressed to his lips, meaning that she must not tell.

"Not even Jdaidi?" she asked. He shook his head and raised his eyebrows meaning: No, not even Jdaidi, who would be very angry. Neda felt her loyalties severely tested but that was Jeddi all over, always setting one against the other. The frown on her grandmother's face would make her feel bad. She hoped he would come home soon enough to save her from the shame of complicit silence.

Neda spent the day watching her grandmother. She glanced at the clock so many times, the intervals between each glance shortening as the day wore on. If she wasn't checking on the time, she was looking out to sea, or putting her head round the kitchen door for no obvious reason. Sometimes she disguised her purpose by placing a rug on the veranda wall and giving it a good shake. Several shakes she would give the rug, just to take another searching look into the orchard. Sometimes she went into the orchard with an empty bowl in case some figs were ripe for eating. Neda knew she was only making a show of looking busy just like when she fed the garden cat for the chance to whisper another *Bismillah*.

As the big hand on the clock slipped ever closer to the nine, her grandmother checked on the veranda again. She sensed that Neda was watching and turned to smile. But only her grandmother's eyes smiled back – her mouth was tightly pursed. She cupped Neda's face in her broad hands, and with eyes staring back at each other, each confirmed the other's fear that it was getting very late.

The television was blaring in the family living area. As her grandmother started serving supper, Neda helped lining up the plates. It was her job to set Hassan's place at the table in the formal dining room. Her father's was permanently laid opposite, awaiting his return. The television in the lounge blared its cartoon cacophony and Neda recognised the crash of Tom chasing Jerry through a wall just as she fetched the biggest plate for Jeddi's pasta. She placed the plate on the kitchen cabinet. There was the big glass water jug waiting by the kitchen tap. Next a napkin from the linen drawer. She imagined Tom's eyes spinning round like a Catharine wheel and Jerry's stretched whiskers being let go with a stinging smack.

The clock sounds louder in the dark. The tea tray's ready. I love it when we're all together and Jdaidi pours from high up, Neda thought. *She makes it frothy and the glass gets sticky, splashing all the tray things. Let me have a sip. The sugar round, with nuts bobbing at the top. Bobbing on my lips. But we wait 'til Jeddi comes. Throws his bags on the sofa. Goes to his room. Jeddi always bangs his door shut. Don't like it when he does that. Wouldn't mind one little bit tonight though if he did. He can bang it all he likes. Jdaidi's lit a lantern on the veranda. Rug's still there, fringes lifting. Just a little wind. Dark red it is, they call it gazelle blood, and zig-zag patterns all around the edges. I like it in the window here. I like it when he fills the view when he comes, fills the place of Daddy. Don't know where to go to look for Daddy.*

"Come on down, sweetheart. It's too cold there. What are you doing to my window?" her grandmother called, pretending to be stern.

"Drawing, Jdaidi. See, a smiley face. And a cat."

"Well here's a fish to go with your cat." Jdaidi Fathia drew fish on biscuits too, when there was something to celebrate. Neda thought of Jdaidi's biscuits filled with dates and figs, shaped like fish.

"You're good at doing fish, Jdaidi. Show me how."

Fathia drew another fish slowly, two symmetrical curves that crossed to make the tail and a dot for its one eye, saying, "Come down and have some sweetened milk, sweetheart."

Neda shook her head. Jdaidi draped her woollen cardigan over her and left her watching in the window nook, shuffling away on her aching feet. Neda knew her feet must ache, on her feet all day. Jdaidi Fathia opened the kitchen door to peer outside again, letting in a draught and the chirping of crickets.

Jdaidi's cardy keeps me warm. Smells of sandalwood and frankincense. It's nicer here, nicer at the back, nicer than the balcony at the front. There, I have to sit on marble. Marble's cold. Music plays of soldiers singing, when the guns stop in the barracks. At night there are the lights, the shop down the road between the trees. I can smell the honeysuckle. Hear Jdaidi with the water hose. The lemon tree and water sizzling down the leaves. Splashing. Washing feet and hands for prayer. All the time I'm listening for Jeddi's shoes crunching on the gravel, keys jangling, shoes sliding on the path, in his worn-out shoes.

"You still here?" It's her mother's voice. Neda hummed her answer.

"I brought you hazelnuts, little one. Here hold out your hand." Sally funnelled roasted nuts into her palms, and kissed her curly head. Neda hummed her thanks.

"He'll be all right, you know. Jeddi that is. He'll be all right. You know that don't you?"

"Do you really know for sure?" was Neda's excited reply. When her mother didn't answer, Neda hummed again. Sally left her at her vigil, saying, "Time for bed soon, little one." And Neda carried on with humming.

Can't sleep now. Mustn't fall asleep. Eyes wide open, nose pressed on the glass. Please God, let him come soon. Let Jeddi come home safe.

Chapter 6

Remorse

Once on shore, Hassan tied his boat to what remained of the old jetty, a skeleton of weathered planks precariously balanced on a rickety frame of stilts. It was something he would have to attend to if fishing proved worthwhile, which he doubted, given the obvious depletion of the fish stocks near the coastal waters. The tie-rope was frayed in places, which meant he had to knot it many times to secure the mooring. Bending over the hull of the boat, he worked slowly, exhausted now, his clothes flapping in the breeze lifting up from an agitated sea. He sensed the landscape around him more acutely from the wind, its touch and noise, than with his eyes. The sun that in the day had burned his face while out at sea was setting fast.

I'm later than I meant to be, he thought, scanning the scene a full circle around himself in one slow turn. He was just in time before the weather changed for the worst. There was still a streak of light atop the distant hills, but it was thinning fast and as for moonlight, there was none at all. He made to gather up his tackle but let it fall back into itself, thinking better of it. The drag up the sloping beach was more than he felt ready for.

"Nets'll wait 'til morning," words spoken out aloud to convince himself; but he was still unsure, not quite ready to leave his thoughts behind on the beach that was his haven.

A little movement in the shadows of the boat's hollow caught his attention. "Ah, you little nipper, found you, didn't I? Nice hole there you made. Have to set you free or you'll never make it on your own, will you?" He was whispering now, though he was far from any eavesdropper.

"Pinch me now, is it? Wouldn't eat you anyhow. Can't sell you in the market, can I? Always throw you shelled stuff back anyway." And he placed the crab on the wet sand within reach of creeping waves and watched it scuttle off into the foam.

It was a relief to have made it back, and without being seen, at least as far as he could tell. Only now did he realise how stressful the fear of discovery had been, even to the extent of feeling exposed each time he threw the line. Had his courage been sheer bravado? Only now did it cross his mind that his defiance had probably been foolhardy. But what choice had he, circumscribed as he was by regulations and the expectations others had of him as provider? Necessity had driven him. But luckily, in the event, he had seen no naval vessels passing along the shipping lanes. No lights had flashed a warning from the coast, and no police speedboats had come searching for him. He could afford to feel at least a little pleased with himself.

But, as he placed stones under the barrel of the boat to lodge it there against the brewing storm, another memory disturbed him. He turned to face the hills. It was instinctive this searching for their outline. He had always done it since that fateful day in his boyhood, as if he needed to touch base with a time in his youth, despite the cruel reminder.

He scanned the horizon where the separate undulations were just about discernible. He could trace their shape in the sand if he wanted to, and even locate precisely the wadi he had wandered through, searching for his father who had gone missing that fateful day on his way to market. He knew every little dip and fold. He knew the many caves and wild goat tracks. He knew the place where he had found him at last.

Looking now at their silhouette against the backlit night sky, the memory of his wounded body that must have lain there for hours came flooding back to him. This evening, his sense of guilt was amplified. The sky darkened altogether.

The hills slipped into the sky. It was impossible to know for sure, after all this time, just which one his father lost his way on, the place the mine was hidden. Hassan never wanted to go there. It was not surprising he avoided it. It was water under the bridge, so long ago. Other matters distracted him. Always other worries stood in the way.

Hassan needed a rest for a little while longer, so he turned away from the hills with the chilling wind on his back. He watched the place where the crab had sidled into the sea. He crouched at the water's edge and let the lapping waves break over his feet, rising up and falling down the steep incline without ever gaining the upper shore. He could lose himself in the ceaseless ebb and flow. But memory of the recent past would not let him go.

Can't think about it any more. Perhaps I've overdone it for the first attempt. To be expected, I suppose. Not getting any younger. I'll be stiff for days, no doubt about that. Surprised me though – not a single mullet. Even one red mullet would have been respectable. Fried fish for supper at least. And strange no baby hake either. Not even silversides. What an effort and all for nothing. And hurting in every muscle, aching like I'd taken another beating.

The beating. That was it. The feel of recent barely-healed wounds resurrected in his ageing body, the reason why his body ached the way it did now. They had beaten him senseless. They had beaten him about the head until he had collapsed unconscious. He had had dizzy spells ever since but had never once spoken about it.

All for what? Just for calling him an upstart. Well that is what he is – an upstart. Came from out of nowhere. We never expected that. Should have kept my mouth shut though. I knew the kind of freedom he meant. Freedom to own a gun. Freedom to settle a score outside a court of law. Freedom for revenge – any old excuse will do. Not the kind of freedom I was thinking of. Should have known that. Should have kept my mouth shut. Silly fool. Ah, here it comes again, coming at me like a storm every time.

Hassan fell again on the wet beach. He tried to get up but failed each time to stand quite upright before his legs collapsed beneath him. He surrendered to each fall like a helpless baby. Then he lay quite still, aware and conscious of the damp on his back, the little runner waves rippling at his trouser turn-ups then his shirt sleeves, the wetness seeping all along his legs.

Swirling round me like a pack of hounds, they were. They aimed their blows where it hurts the most. Thrashing me at every drag of breath they took. I heard their heaving sighs mingling with my groans, my suffocated gurgles blowing bubbles through the blood. Blood bubbles at my nostrils. Struggling for air. Didn't think I'd survive it. Squirming like a harpooned weever, wriggling in my own blood. But I did survive. I made it through. They didn't think I would. They didn't want me to. Wanted my death. Me too, I wanted it like you can't imagine. Couldn't let them have it though. Couldn't let them have me that way. Had to get myself together. Had to pull myself together somehow. Couldn't see for blood.

Eventually, he managed to lift himself to his knees, and then push deep into the sand with his fists to bring himself fully upright. He steadied himself and made to move homewards with a swinging gait. He could make it, if stumbling, from boat to rising beach. Then, with his shoulders lunging into a swerve, he lost his balance altogether and was tipped into a dive. He hit his head on the broken pier.

"Get up! Get up, you dog!" That's what they said. Made me stand, propped me up against the wall. "Stand up," they bawled. "Salute our leader!" and they showed me the middle page spread where his face looked up at me, looking down on me. The bastards. There, I've said it. That feels better. Sliding down in my own blood, they found my efforts funny. Ha! Hit my head falling, heard the crack like wood snapping. Waited for the blood to seep. Heard them laughing. The bastards! Again, say it again. The bastards!

Hassan lay where he had fallen. He made no effort to get up.

Out of it. Out cold. Couldn't tell how long for. I'm there again, here again, pressed against the tiles, cold and hard, cockroaches searching every part of me. I see them in the dark even, feel the ugly touch of them. The slightest thing sets me off. Just let it happen. Best to let it have its way with me, until it goes away. Fall like an infant, no sense of space nor my place in it, not like an infant though, the heavy bulk of me crashing like a mighty cod, thrashing in the wet. Can't talk about it, not to anyone. Wouldn't want to. Can't let them know what they did to me. What they do to anyone. What they do.

He felt the push and pull of waves rocking him, making his body roll. He heard the wheeling of seagulls, their cries drowning his. The world was spinning, flying round him like a loosened sail in an all-out gale. The seagulls pulling in their wake dark clouds, bunching up together in the gathering storm. Screeching.

Pull by pull, he hauled himself up the slope to where the waves could not reach. "Pull yourself together, old man. You're made of stronger stuff than this!"

Is that my voice? How loud it sounds, how raw, how it carries on the breeze and seems to float higher with the seagulls. But it stops the squirming, doesn't it? The sliding to the waves, the rolling. I'll shout some more: I didn't die like you wanted me to! I survived, didn't I? Can't get rid of me that easily! Can't take that away from me. Not soaring any more. The birds have gone. Quieter now, calmer. Calmer's better. Could stand up now and brush the sand off. Make myself presentable. Not hurt after all, you see. Best forget it. Can't let them see me in this state. You bastards!

He was damp and feeling chilled. Despite the heat of the day, the night air retained none of its warmth. He listened to the sea hollering as it rose up around him, slapping at the boat, lifting it so that it floated and tugged at the ropes. Dogs were barking in the distant hills. He turned to face them one last time, staring. For a minute, the curved contour of one held his attention as he made out the gentle incline to the summit where it flattened like a plateau.

A light wind rippled down his spine where his shirt stuck to his skin. He shuddered. No glimmer on the horizon now. No moonlight. He could see neither the hills nor the fishing nets he had been folding. He was resigned to the fact of his empty basket and the need to dispose of it without it being seen. It was a little humiliation. Turning to face the house, looking for the track home, he made a mental note of the direction and cast his eyes down to find his way.

The scene was familiar, except for one piece of shadow cast over small hollows in the sand, scooped out by hand. He knew his grandchildren must have been playing there earlier in the day, tossing pebbles. Now sand, blown by a land-hugging breeze, was covering up the evidence. He shivered again and felt the wistful tug of time-to-go. He felt the stretch of muscles and the weight of his old bones as he stepped out.

Jeddi Hassan did not see the sand lizards that darted across the track before him into the long esparto grass, nor the chameleon holding onto the swaying branch of an almond tree with its feet and tail. He was aware of a silhouette at the window. Approaching the lamplit veranda, he saw a small hand waving excitedly. His youngest grandchild ran out to greet him as he snuffed out the light. An exchange of glances made him touch his head to ruffle the sand from his unkempt wind-tousled hair.

Chapter 7

Tough love

Fathia met Hassan at the kitchen door. "Where have you been?" she demanded. She almost cried and then regained composure since she knew he could not abide a woman crying. "What kind of time is this? Do you have any idea of the time? It's gone nine! It's almost ten! Even little Neda has waited for you all this while! Do you have any idea how we worry about you? There's the police out there, trawling for smugglers or foolish men like you! Isn't one arrest enough? Isn't losing a son enough for you? What can you be thinking of!"

She paused for breath while Hassan attempted to straighten his shirt, wet and sticking to his arms, all twisted. His hand strayed to his head meaning to shake it free of sand but he thought better of it and, hand part-raised, he thought better of answering her too.

"And look at you! All soaking wet. You'll catch your death of cold. What has happened to you, you foolish man? I can't believe you stayed out there so late, scaring us. What happened to you? Did you have a fall? It's all too much for you, you know, a man of your age! It's not expected of you. You don't have to do these things, Hassan. We'll manage. Don't you know that? We'll manage like we always do. It's not expected of you. Do you hear me? Taking risks like that. We'd rather have you here in one piece, do you know that? Have you thought of that?"

Fathia's voice had gradually softened in tone. She fussed around him trying to help him take his shirt off, brushing sand from his hair and finding the little wound on his head. Hassan stood up stiffly. His wife's kind attention threatened to weaken him and being rigid was his only self-defence. Something told him he should be grateful for her touch, even though she was tugging at his sleeves, and rubbing sand from the wound gently but still hurting him.

"Oh, don't mind that. It's nothing. The sunburn hurts much more. Hit my head on the jetty, tying the boat. Oh, you wouldn't understand. Stop fussing, woman. I'll see to it myself." Despite the roughness of the words, he spoke quietly with some embarrassment, pushing her arms away and placing them back to her sides where they took up their natural position, akimbo. Then he touched her again with a reassuring but apologetic pat on the shoulder.

"I'm back now, anyway," he turned to say, and went directly to his room to change while she heated up his supper. Nothing more was said between them. He ate alone. He had told her nothing. He shared nothing of his anguish. He just left her in the dark. It was best that way, he thought. Knowing nothing was a kind of protection for her, just as saying nothing was a protection for himself.

Shut away in his room, he was unobtainable and inviolate. It was where he did his thinking, slept and smoked, smoking being unseemly in the company of women and children. Here he slept the afternoon siesta and the long isolating sleep of night which he did not share with his wife any more. Here he could let go of the pretence of coping and of being in control.

He removed his clothes and let them drop to the floor. Then he wrapped himself in a dressing gown. He leaned from his bed to switch on the old wireless balanced precariously on a dining chair that served as a bedside table. At a touch, it surged into life with light and noisy static.

The radio was the centre of all things, linking him to the networks of the world. While night reigned, he indulged in surfing through the radio waves. First he part-raised the lower slats of the wooden blind to check for signs of activity outside. The lights in the lanterns at the front gate had gone out weeks ago and he had no intention of replacing them. The headlights of passing cars would not trace their beams across his bedroom walls once the blind was fully down. There was no car waiting under the single street lamp way down the road, alongside the army barracks. Satisfied that all was clear, he let the slats drop slowly, not to wake his grandson sleeping in the alcove as he did now, for a father's company.

Chapter 8

Taking risks

Someone had disturbed the settings on the wireless and it could only be his wife. He was too tired to fine-tune it now and in protest let it blast away, while he lit a cigarette. He drew deeply on the unfiltered tip and then exhaled. The ash accumulated in suspension before it fell, succumbing to the force of gravity like his face did. He had generous cheeks that had lost their plumpness long ago. Now they were covered in a white stubble which he would shave off in the morning. He shook his head from side to side bemused, until a whirl of pattern on the blanket caught his gaze and drew him into something vague and comforting.

The door burst open and his wife's voice dragged him noisily into the moment. The whining pitch of the wireless could be heard even from behind the closed door. Now the door was open, the din was oppressive. Her mouth fell open and she covered her ears in protest. This was all that was needed to make the point but on seeing the ash that had fallen onto the bed sheets, her next words rose above the din:

"Is that ash on the blanket, Hassan Ali? You'll burn the house down next. You'll not be satisfied 'til you harm us one way or another!"

"Go away, woman. Bring me my ashtray if it bothers you so much. Meddling all the time. That's what the trouble is." Hassan, never known for social graces at the best of times, was more irritable than usual; she mused on this as she turned to leave.

"And turn that thing off, will you," in the end she was feeling unreasonably chastised. It helped if she could have the last word.

She waited until he turned the wireless off, nodded her approval and left to fetch an ashtray. He fell back on his pillow, irritated. Silence was all he wanted now. Not agreement. He tried again for the station she always feared he listened to. He was still trying to locate it when she returned with the ashtray. Seeing he was completely absorbed and his back turned, Fathia seized her chance:

"Not that station again! You'll bring more trouble than we're in already. They'll find you out one day, that's for sure. Out there in their radio cars, they're most likely at it this very minute. You know that, don't you? Or am I wasting my breath?"

He heard the resignation in her voice. He noticed too that she was short of breath; her breathing was difficult these days with any kind of exertion. Seeing her bend down to gather up his clothes from the floor, he regretted he had left them there. Even so, as she left the room, he flapped her away with his hand, as if to brush away a worrisome fly. She caught the gesture as she turned to close the door. More regrets, the habit of a lifetime. She would not have been surprised by it, he supposed. It was his signature gesture that smothered the more felicitous feelings he had for her, deep down.

Fathia was a patient woman, a perfect choice of wife. She had tolerated his ungracious manners throughout their married life. It had occurred to him that she deserved more gentility in return for her selfless attention to his needs. But he knew that a long time ago, at the very beginning, when she was fourteen and he was twenty.

He smiled as he remembered the They met as photographs, she the village beauty, her face freshly tattooed but discreetly so as not to spoil her looks entirely; he a stocky build even in his youth, an honest face with blunt features and dark eyes burning with the passion of ambition.

They had found a way of sharing love through the synergy of parenthood. But there was neither intimacy nor communication between them now; perhaps a vestige of compassion lingered, a sympathy that struggled to survive in the ordinary routines of life.

Fathia let the door close behind her. It moved by its own weight, clicking quietly into place. A subdued, emotional closure it seemed to Hassan, who knew his defiant ways did not dovetail with his wife's gentler demeanour. Even so, his defiance remained.

Feeling provoked but a little contrite, he switched to the official station, that was allowed. He had expected the same manic voice to threaten retribution to all dissenters and apostates, but the degree of venom in the message never failed to surprise him. The rant, for that is what is was to him, followed a predictable pattern, creating first the spectre of the enemy at the gate or border, then a gloss on the failed attempt to confront and reform him, whoever he was, and finally the call for the avenging angel. It was all part of the daily fare that upbraided the nation; but it always seemed to speak directly to himself, adding to and feeding into the fears that had gripped him ever since that morning when soldiers had taken his son from his bed, and hidden him away.

The news after all, on this occasion, was unremarkable; there had been no further skirmishes at the border. There was still that same absence of narrative on the retreat. According to rumour, their troops had fled to fallback positions that were not defended, retreat not being envisioned as part of the campaign. He could not imagine the horror of being lost in the desert and abandoned there. There was no news of victory. Their enlisted soldier-sons had not returned in the months that followed. He like so many others awaited a nephew and other more distant relatives. But the obvious disaster had passed without public declaration or media comment. It had not surprised him, this callous disregard for human life. But it shocked him. Of course there would be a news famine. It would be left to rumour and grieving families to flesh out the details. This was nothing new.

Before the broadcast had ended, he had fallen asleep where he sat, on top of the bedcovers. The radio was humming on and he slept on, until a drop in temperature in the early hours of the morning woke him with a shiver. Feeling the chill, he pulled the sheets around him up to his chin and stared into the cavernous dark of the room. He was suddenly aware of serious matters still not attended to. A son was gone missing, hopefully was still alive, but heard no more of for more time than he dared account for.

Could it be that even at this very minute Saad's life was hanging on a thread? Hassan had that awful sentient feeling of something prescient. Could it be that all it took to rescue his son was a certain daring, and a dogged determination to break through his own disabling fear? Was there something he had overlooked, something that he, and only he, could strive for? The questions were insistent.

But before he found the will to face the striving, his old recalcitrant self gave way to despair. It was unlikely, he argued with himself, that he would ever find sufficient courage for the quest. The risks were high. The task unfairly imposed. He knew it was a noble quest, but it was a mantle that had fallen on his less than sturdy shoulders. His greatest anxiety was that either way he would be found wanting, just as he had been found wanting as that young boy who had not dutifully heeded his father's call.

In the morning, Hassan finished his prayers as usual with an intercession for his son. He shuffled down the corridor to the kitchen in his soft leather mules, flattened at the heels like slip-on slippers. After shooing away the nervous cat that waited at the kitchen door for scraps, he sat down heavily at the kitchen table. He turned his face towards the sea as he waited for his breakfast, a glass of milk with bread and olives, for he was dependent always on his wife for sustenance.

The cat returned following Fathia who had been hanging a rug on the washing line for a beating later in the day. In the night, a mild sandstorm had deposited a film of fine red sand everywhere. Hassan sat on the wicker chair, his slippered feet shuffling sand, pondering on the thought that, although different reasoning separated them, they both had wisdom enough not to challenge the other too far. Fathia joined him in the breaking morning light, bringing with her two glasses of hot sweet tea. But few words passed between them as they sat together, cloaked in their separate worlds of different meanings and different means of survival.

Part Three – Schism

Fathia's words signalled a crisis of trust never reached before
in their married life.

Chapter 1

Rain

December was a cold month. The garden was barren. The trees were stripped of foliage. Leaves had been pulled from the vine and gathered in long ago, and were now stored in brine, ready for wrapping a stuffing of chopped lamb and herbs in savoury parcels. Fathia had preserved strips of meat in butter ghee, meat that had first been dried in the sun at the height of summer and hot-peppered to keep away the flies. Now, as the longer nights drew in, she would use the meat to add substance to her home-made pasta. If they needed couscous, there was a year's supply. Sally had helped her mix the flour and water and press the dough through a series of mesh sieves from the widest gauge to the finest, a long and laborious process. She had been her constant helper, with Neda looking on, absorbing the scenes of domesticity and especially of communal friendship. It was Neda who had collected the black olives and, though they were very small that year, she had taken pride in helping to preserve them.

Now that the days were cold and short, Neda would be layered in woollen clothing, since she liked to spent her time sitting on a rug laid out on the veranda. From there she watched the feral cat, the cat that had no name but *Gutoose*, Benghazi vernacular for 'cat'. It criss-crossed the pathways in and out of the orchard, always on the lookout for the off-chance of scraps from the kitchen as it passed by. The resident chameleon was nowhere to be seen, at least not from this spot. She had searched for him all day. There was no foliage to hide under. Any leaves that were left hanging now shuddered in a brisk wind, rattling like dried parchment.

Then the cold changed to wet. It rained for days. Neda heard someone mention 'forty days and forty nights.' She wondered if that made eighty somethings. In any case it was never going to end. The land around could not take it all. The drain were full. The brittle earth absorbed the first few lashings and then was full to saturation. Water swirled around wherever it could, looking for a sluice, an escape into ditches. The wasteland at the front of the villa was a lake, ankle deep. Some workmen had started a month before to dig a trench for a purpose no one had any idea of. They were Egyptian workmen who toiled without question or protest. But the trench was filled to the brim with rainwater and all work had stopped. No one had thought to build a defence wall around it. Neda had strict instructions not to wander near it. It was a drowning hazard.

The eucalyptus trees along the avenue had shed their seeds some weeks ago and now the empty seed cases floated around in the swill, hard as stones and clogged up the grids and gutters. The problem of flooding was exacerbated by the absence of a proper drainage system. Everyone stayed indoors, avoiding unnecessary journeys out.

Then one night, one of the many indistinguishable nights of the rainy period, Sidi Ahmed, her grandfather's brother, visited. He spent a little time with Neda and made her laugh a lot. He was unusual that way, she thought, with his cheery smile and kindly compliments; he was never serious and forlorn like her grandfather. But Sidi Ahmed had really only come to see her grandfather. She could not imagine why except perhaps if it was to cheer him up.

Neda crept up to the door of the lounge where Jeddi and Sidi Ahmed were discussing something – it sounded like a problem. Mostly they were agreed but now and then her grandfather raised his voice and Sidi Ahmed laughed a little, nervously, as though to break the tension.

There was a new word she had not heard before, it sounded like 'merchdise', or 'merchndise.' It was her grandfather's anyway, this 'merchndise.' How many times did they say that word? And Sidi Ahmed kept it for him in his shop, near the Dark Market. It seemed far from the flood, she thought, and yet they were worried about it, whatever it was, for whatever reason. It might get spoiled. "Ruined," her grandfather had said. "And it's all I have." And this is where he raised his voice, which worried her. Sidi Ahmed spoke quietly. She could not exactly make his words out, but his voice was kind if firm. Jeddi said no more. She felt sure it would be all right in the end.

For the next few days, school was closed. Some children had tried to paddle there on planks of wood, but this would never do. Neda spent her time helping round the house. Outside the cat did not show up. Neither did the chameleon.

Chapter 2

Finding her way

Hassan was surprised one day when the chief librarian of Benghazi, also a patron of the Association for the Blind, visited him at home. He had come to ask if his daughter-in-law Sally would do some voluntary work for the Association. Hassan was at first alarmed, fearing that it might bring too much social exposure to the family, and Sally so untested in this new environment. But he had too healthy a regard for the chief librarian's good standing to refuse him, the cause also seeming so worthy. It took him a day or so to bring himself to the point of certainty that convinced him it was right to pass the message on to Sally. When he finally did so, he gave it his genuine support, and she had his blessing for her so-called 'outing' into the wider society, outside the safe confines of family.

There were three students she hoped to help with their studies at the university. It would be challenging, since they had no textbooks in braille, none provided by their respective university departments. There was little wider institutional support for her role. But the principal had diligently and courteously prepared a letter of introduction to the faculty that she would take to explain her role before her first support visit.

In the event, Sally's explanation was met with raised eyebrows. An urgent phone call was made to another authority in a different department. Within minutes, the offer of support for the blind students had been turned down and Sally was transferred instead to the faculty of Science, where she would teach English. She had been catapulted into a milieu that was more 'out there' than Hassan had anticipated or would have given his assent to. In this new post, she would be in plain sight of the regime's intelligence, for its spies were everywhere where minds were engaged in ideas.

There was nothing Hassan could do about this turn of events. It was a shift which felt like more an intrusion than an advantage. Ostensibly, Sally had gained something favourable. He was not resentful of the opportunity. But, nevertheless, he felt that somehow the network that he so mistrusted could now reach deeper into his private domain than was desirable. He could only trust that Sally would be discreet and circumspect in her work.

Sally had no choice but to accept the offer; but she did not forget the blind students. A way was found to offer language support to one of them. Twice weekly, at night, a car arrived at the villa to take her to the Blind School and there she would spend two hours teaching, mainly working on Shakespeare's *Hamlet*. A female social worker, whom Sally knew as Selma, supported her in her clandestine teacher role. It felt clandestine because they listened to Sally's tapes in the dark, lighting being superfluous; and Sally spoke in a low voice though only Fatma her student was there to hear. Fatma absorbed every word of interpretation. Adding to the conspiratorial atmosphere, Selma hovered in the background like a chaperone, informer and guard all rolled into one, waiting to escort her home in her own private car.

Selma was a robust sort of woman with a ruddy weather-beaten complexion. She cared not for her appearance but dedicated herself to her charitable work. She moved silently and swiftly despite her full and rounded figure, always alert to unexpected sounds and movements in the vicinity. She kept and lit a candle for Sally and often made her tea. There was something strangely energising about the whole set-up.

The Science College did not provide Sally with the chance to meet people and make close friends as she had hoped. She was under constant surveillance, with tall and burly guards, mainly Cuban, sitting on chairs outside her office, always civil and relaxed but imposing in their presence. She learned to find her own way round, never asking for help since to do so attracted unwanted attention.

The college was separate from the main campus in Gar Younis, being an old school building close to the commercial centre of Benghazi. The drivers of the minibus who took her to and from home and college and sometimes to the main campus were the kindest of acquaintances, always courteous and mindful of her safety. She trusted them. Somehow, despite the outward signs of her separation from everyone, she felt accepted, like a quaint mascot, tolerated as the authentic voice of English, publicly condemned and secretly aspired to. The college seemed to be a sheltered ground for her gradual assimilation into her new environment.

The professors and senior lecturers offered help with the scientific concepts she had to master before conveying it in English. They were generous with their time. She had no idea if they knew the facts of her situation. She did not dare to tell her story. They never probed and perhaps were not aware of anything remarkable about her presence amongst them. Being remarkable or questionable was perhaps only a self-conscious gloss she had assumed, an invisible cloak she felt placed around her shoulders. She was a secret mystery in their midst. A person out of place. Wanted and not wanted.

Having completed one week, she felt the first six days had gone without a hitch. She had constructed a language curriculum and syllabus for the various departments. She had given a few lectures and found the students warm and welcoming. She felt at ease at her desk, with all her books and stationery filling the drawers as though they and she had always been there.

On the sixth day she had been late for the bus home, and had sat with a later shift driver in his little gatehouse, waiting for the next. Together they had commented on a lonely figure standing shoulders above the wall of a balcony of a building opposite. Sally had seen him there every day and asked about him. At first the driver had hesitated but he did reveal that he knew the man, had been his chauffeur once. Then with his hand over his mouth, though no one was there to see or hear him, he told her that he had been the Dean, the one who was arrested a few years back, early into the new regime. He had been kept in solitary confinement all that time. he had disappeared and was thought to have died even. Since his release, he had never once walked outside his home. The nearest he came to the outside world was this balcony, where now he stood, only ever for a few minutes every day.

"I don't think he knows that I can see him standing there, wishing him well, wishing he felt safe enough to come down into the street."

Chapter 3

A rift

Fathia prepared a packed lunch for Hassan. She knew he had planned this fishing trip deliberately to avoid having to spend time with her brother, Salem, who was visiting later that same morning. He packed his bag with a sense of guilt, she knew that, as well as with some worthy contriteness, which she also knew. His was a thinly disguised humility that went a good way to appeasing her, despite his rough manner.

Hassan did not feel good about the way he treated his wife so churlishly, especially since he depended on her for her constancy. He took advantage of that. It was her constancy that allowed him to wander off the way he did, following his own selfish whims and ideas of enterprise. He trusted that their relationship had not completely lost its reciprocal bearing of goodwill. But it was unfair that she who had to do all the bending, she who had to make all the compromises. He knew it and could not deny it.

Even so, he could not stop himself from saying, "I'll have nothing more to do with that snake of a brother of yours, you know that, don't you?"

At this his final pronouncement on the matter, Fathia had merely raised her eyebrows. They are the words of an embittered man, she thought, for he was a bitter man, almost a stranger to her in his bitterness. Did he ever understand how much his words could hurt her? She could not fathom what he understood or knew of her anxieties. Her brother, the snake in question, was now the only person they could turn to, a fact he was too proud to admit, at least not publicly, certainly not to her, if ever to himself.

And so he left without a word of comfort spoken on either side. From the veranda steps, out of earshot, she whispered a blessing for his safe return. She watched him disappear into the orchard and listened for his steps on the shingle path, and imagined his stooped shadow disappearing into the tall esparto grass.

Turning round to face the villa, she noticed a face at the window; someone else had seen him leave in the direction of the sea.

"Don't you tell anyone," she warned. "You'll get us into trouble if you do, stubborn man that your grandfather is."

Chapter 4

Charm

Salem was Fathia's successful younger brother. He delivered his wife, Salha, that same morning at the villa, along with half a lamb and a round of Edam cheese. Salha stood there anticipating Fathia's effusive welcome. She held herself upright, corseted by a tightly fitting dress, her face radiating charity and benevolence.

Salem's manner indicated he had pressing business elsewhere. Fathia understood. There was no need to ask. He belonged to an elevated strata, and she never doubted his importance to the regime. Though her faith in him was unshakeable, it was not without its nagging doubts. Not once had he intervened for Saad. On that score, he had always placed himself just beyond her daring to ask the question. Now he hovered somewhere between the front door and the garden gate; it was clear he had no time to talk.

Salha charmed Fathia with her contagious smile. Her effusive manner never ceased to transfix her audience. She treble-kissed her husband's sister, bending her head to either cheek, and showered her with greetings. But she doled out her charm with premeditated measure. For Sally there was only the briefest show of perfect teeth, that abortive kind of smile that fades even before the other has reciprocated. Sally was the emblem of strangeness that for Salha stigmatised the whole family. A single kiss on either cheek met the minimum standard of politeness. At the same time it signified a limited acceptance, setting Sally apart so that as Sally leaned forwards to offer a second kiss Salha stepped aside, leaving the proffered kiss frozen in mid-air.

As the child born of a union between 'a stranger' and a father falsely accused of treachery, an uncertain identity within the family had attached itself to Neda, or so Salha thought.

Little innocent Neda could not have guessed at the web of lies that had destroyed her father's reputation. She stood behind her mother, shy in the presence of this clearly very dominant female, an aunt perhaps or a distant kind of grandmother, she could not be sure. She managed an uncertain smile.

"You gorgeous little beauty!" Salha exclaimed planting imprints of her manicured nails into the soft flesh of Neda's cheeks as she squeezed them. Neda's smile withered in the strike of pain.

Salha turned and made her way to the lounge, where cushions were arranged round the edges of the room. The others followed her. Shaking off her sling-back heels, she flopped down onto the plumpest cushion and invited Fathia to join her, absurdly usurping Fathia's role as hostess. As an afterthought, she beckoned Sally to join them but Fathia stepped neatly in and gave her a small task in the kitchen.

Neda hesitated at the edge of the carpet. The two women seemed to fill the room. Her grandmother towered above her, with her voluminous skirts pleated deeply round her hips and tied with a broad and shiny sash. Neda was struck with how sturdy she seemed towering above her, standing barefoot and steadily placed full square on the velvety deep-pile carpet. Neda loved her for the way she made her feel so safe.

But Salha was different. She saw how her grandmother was in awe of her brother's wife. She had stopped in her tracks to take a second look at Salha's hands, in particular the elaborate gold rings that decorated her fingers. Salha was serene. She rested her wrists on her thighs as she sat with her legs disconcertingly spread out in a 'V' before her, painted toes curled and pointing up. Her skirt had ridden up to reveal her shapely calves and rounded fleshy knees; her legs were freshly stripped of hair.

Salha knew she had impressed, and yawned inelegantly making no attempt to stifle the yawn. Fathia turned away to ease herself down onto a floor cushion, conveniently erasing the impression of Salha's lack of grace and etiquette. Then the two women fell into the usual routines of formal enquiry each into the family of the other. In that way, they were able to construct a proper sense of decorum which Salha's behaviour had threatened to dispel.

However, in the careful exchange of predictable question and answer, they managed to skirt round the one question that never could be framed in words. The matter of Saad was not approached and remained pregnant and unresolved, when the tray arrived as a welcome diversion.

Sally placed the tray on the carpet, handed first Salha and then Fathia a glass of fruit juice and then passed around a bowl of chocolates and sweets. This new routine of delicate politeness restrained Salha further for it was impossible to eat with obvious pleasure when the matter of Saad still lingered on in their minds. She took a polite sip of the juice and set her glass aside. She refused the sweets and assumed a posture of sobriety. The significance of the shift in Salha's manner was lost on Sally as she sat down to join them; but Fathia understood it very well.

Fathia offered the sweets again, this insistence being customary and expected, knowing Salha would not hesitate a second time; and, as expected, Salha scooped up a generous fistful and dropped the sweets into her large bag.

"For the children," she explained. "They expect them after I've been visiting. They let me go without making a fuss when they know they'll get some sweets later. It helps to get away."

"You should have brought them with you," Fathia reminded her. "They would have been company for Neda. She is left on her own too often. Nizar's at his cousin's. They have a beach hut, you know."

"So why isn't Neda with them, enjoying the sea?"

"She keeps us company," Fathia replied, the tone of her voice implying closure.

But the question of why Neda never was allowed to enjoy the sea like her brother went on reverberating, at least for Neda if for no one else. The uncertainty of her mother's social standing was not a complete explanation, since her brother was not similarly neglected. She shook off the disquieting doubt and inched up closer to her mother preparing to absorb the thrill of conversation with its twists and turns beyond her comprehension. She felt her mother's little shivers of discomfort; and like her mother did not interrupt or ask a question.

For Sally the way the conversation – mainly a monologue by Salha – unfolded was a revelation. Its course was unpredictable. She could not tell if others felt the same confusion with the rambling flow of topics or whether she was right to be incredulous. One thing she had learned – it was wrong to imagine that women lived their lives in the shadow of their men, that ideas and wisdom came down to women from above, imposed by the world outside the home. Women did not live their lives cut off from the bigger political events. Maybe they worked in the garden, orchard and the home, as living models of the virtue of domestication. But they visited one another in their homes, their knowledge was augmented by their shared experiences. They were not left ignorant or helpless. If their roles were those of duty and caring, their destiny that of waiting for male decision and permission, that was only partly how it was. Women like Salha could be very powerful.

Women, Sally realised, had everything essential for their social advancement within some obvious limitations, limitations not too much different from those that shackled men. Women cannily safeguarded the sanctuary of their separate lives in the ceaseless rounds of afternoon visits whilst only seeming to serve the aspirations of their menfolk. The world of women, impressively represented here in front of her by Salha, had its own feisty dynamic; it was more active than its male counterpart supposed.

On another level, it did seem to Sally that women's lives were too separate from those of men. It caused misunderstandings, left little gaps or lacunae in the conversations and fabric of social life. That was patently clear from the way it was Nizar and not Neda who was taken out on car jaunts to the beach or for picnics in the foothills. It was Nizar who prayed with his grandfather at the mosque while Neda was left to amuse herself around the house.

As for Neda herself, she had felt the division like a punishment. She was excluded from everything and the world outside the walls of the villa remained a mystery to her. Of course she was fascinated by the way Salha brought the outside world in. Of course she was charmed.

But what Neda did not yet see was her own particular otherness, that being the fatherless child of a foreign and socially isolated mother excluded her even further from the action. For now, it did not trouble her. She thrived in the care of two mothers, in the freedom of the orchard and the shelter of a sandy bay with its great expanse out to the sky, where she and Nizar still spent time together. This was enough: an stretch of land inhabited by lizards, chameleons and geckos, butterflies and bee-chasing birds, and a feral cat.

But Salha had planted a seed in her mind. She had suggested new horizons even in the way she had announced herself with a rustling of her skirts, the tapping of her high-heeled shoes on the marble tiles, and the waft of expensive perfume that followed in her wake. She had disturbed the daily humdrum of their lives with a certain frisson.

Chapter 5

The grapevine

Neda and Sally nestled together next to Fathia. Salha sat before them. They sat before her, a ready audience. This was Salha, who had endless stories to tell, Salha who visited women every afternoon, spilling the stories of one lounge into the next, and who was about to spill more stories in Fathia's lounge.

Salha knew very well the power she had over her listeners. She lowered her head and cleared her throat as they leaned in towards her. Light caught the strands of henna glowing in her hair. Her long earrings swung like pendulums as she moved her head and they shone as brightly as the many rings on her fingers. She looked up to assess her audience and saw how Neda had imitated her pose. She avoided Fathia's gaze, noting that her eyes were shiny and welled up with tears. And then she looked directly at her, speaking with unexpected directness, with words that were too harsh in the way they homed in so swiftly to the heart of the matter.

"You know I saw the Leader, our dear Brother-Leader, don't you?" Salha began, setting her voice into the conspiratorial tone of insider gossip.

Fathia felt her heart beat harder.

"Oh, you don't? Well then, I must tell you all about it. It was, well, he's a soldier, you know, Abdul Wahab, an officer based in a barracks somewhere in the mountain region. Well, he was an officer but he's something bigger now. A colonel or whatever the title is. The wedding was amazing! You weren't invited but you came to the engagement, you remember. They slaughtered thirty sheep and thirty goats. So you weren't invited to the actual wedding, then?"

"Yes, I was invited. But I haven't been to weddings since... I sent a gift anyway. But you met the Leader there? If I'd known that I would have come. A pity you didn't tell me he'd be there."

"Well, it wasn't like that at all. We didn't know. He always comes unexpected, you know. Besides, you being there would not have made any difference."

The briefest of pauses underlined the implausibility of her claim. Fathia did not seem convinced. Salha hurried on with the tale, embellished here and there, Fathia suspected, but possibly holding a nugget of truth, a seam of crucial detail that would be revealing of something useful.

"The bride's sister was married at the same time, you know. It was a bit confusing as to which families, who belonged to who. The bridegroom was poor. So poor, you must know, that they have to live with his father in a one-storey house, where they let their few goats roam between the buildings. They say he's a night-watchman, the father that is, at the old café in the bay there, just along from here."

Fathia had to fathom for herself just which bridegroom Salha was referring to, but it was not important enough to delay the story telling.

"No one even goes to the café nowadays. It's very isolated. People don't go out at night do they? Not any more. He minds it for someone else who's taken his family abroad. He watches all the comings and goings along the coastal road that way, and I suspect that's how he managed to make the right kind of connections despite having little money. The kind of connections he needed for making a good match for his son, I mean."

Salha's account of the wedding rambled on, in and out of rumour and gossip, details of the wedding preparations, the bridal dress and the wedding feast. Fathia's thoughts fled to her husband sailing now along the coast. What if this man watches the coast and out to sea as well as the coastal road? I must warn Hassan.

"Far and away above him socially, she is. They say she'll never get used to his Bedouin ways but he gets everywhere, now. Very popular with the Leader. How people's fortunes change, don't they? Just a few years ago he was a nobody. Just hung around with gangs of youths until one day he joined the army. Anyway, he must have done well and it must have been a posting with opportunity to better himself because now he can pick up the phone at any time and just ask for you know who. Very close he is."

"Is this Abdul Wahab you're talking about? Is he your contact, then?" Fathia interrupted.

"Well, yes. He's quite a find, he can get hold of just about anything anyone could ever want. You should see the gold she wears now, even in public, his wife, and you know this is forbidden now, to wear gold. Abdul Wahab brings trays of gold from the market for her own private viewing. He's at her beck and call. She gets us all together to advise her which is best, always the biggest of course. That way we all get something too. Look!"

Salha thrust her gold-laden hand forward for Fathia to admire the largest ring Fathia had ever seen on a woman's finger. It was studded with blood red precious stones and diamonds, a ring within a ring that came apart to form two only marginally more modest rings. The gold setting was baroque, almost grotesque on a woman's finger, and it gripped Salha's finger like a vice leaving an impression in the flesh. Fathia was secretly impressed but remained outwardly indifferent. Sally observed it all from a reserved distance unable to simulate the smallest amount of enthusiasm. Neda crept an inch or so from her safe niche beside her mother and peered a little closer.

"So the Leader was at the wedding, you say?" A note of urgency sounded in Fathia's voice.

"Well, let's get back to the wedding first. You need to make it your business to find out about these people for yourself, Fathia dear." There was a tinge of criticism intended in the remark. "What you won't believe is this. The Leader invited himself to the celebration and came into the room where the woman were. Took us quite by surprise. Naturally, we were fumbling to cover our faces. We had no warning. But what noble bearing he has to walk wherever he wishes, mingling with his people from the highest to the very lowest without indicating a difference. But you only understand his charm when you meet him in person. He was as close as this" – she leaned towards Neda who was by now sitting in the centre of the carpet. "He is so serene, moves slowly and with power. Then he springs up from the floor like a lion and leaves as suddenly as he arrived."

Salha made note of the shine in Fathia's eyes. She had not meant to raise her hopes so much and hastily resumed her story, talking faster to reach its essentially disappointing end, rushing over the impression she had given of an opportunity, an opportunity missed.

"Well, it was Iman who touched his arm. She was the one near him, not me. He seemed to know her. 'Iman.' he said how are you?' Called her by her name. 'How is the Hajj. Haven't seen him for a long time.' Well, we were amazed, as you can imagine. It seems Hamid, Iman's father, has known him since his school days. Went to the same school. It is a strange world indeed. Such a coincidence that now the Leader returns to pay tribute to his teacher by promoting his son-in-law. It seems like perfect justice and all quite by chance, you understand."

Fathia waited. Surely there were words spoken, a communication about Saad, a request was made, or why the effort of this elaborate account?

"I have to tell you, Fathia – we did not expect to see him there. We were truly taken by surprise, you must believe me. I had no time to prepare myself. The Leader is a very illusive man, as you know. Ah, I know what you want, Fathia. You want me to ask about Saad, get an interview. I wish I could arrange it for you. I'd pay with this ring if that would help, I promise you. I nudged Iman, tried to catch her eye but she was gazing into the Leader's face, totally unaware of what was going on around her. I tried, believe me. And told her off afterwards. I said, 'What a pity you didn't say anything, didn't speak up for Fathia,' I said. 'Just one small word would have done it, that's all.' But it would have helped if you had been there and spoken for yourself."

The silence lasted minutes. The failure was Iman's, of course, Iman who was a more distantly related kinswoman, and then the blame was shifted on to Fathia herself. She left that preposterous thought with them, and let it settle in their minds, while she played with the rings on her fingers.

Sally turned away. It was too much to bear. It was callous to have made light of Fathia's hopes and expectations in that way, cruel to have turned the tables so unjustly. She could not disguise her disapproval – she knew it must be written on her face.

Neda too felt the sudden jolt. It came like a shock though she did not the know the reason for it. She cast about, looking to her mother for an explanation. Something had shifted; the story had foundered at its end. It had disappointed. She tried to catch the storyteller's eye. She could not read her grandmother's expression. The spell of charm was all gone. All those images that had entertained her now fell away, dissolving into the patterns and colours of the carpet before her, like mist evaporates in the sun. She felt cheated.

"Maybe there will be other chances, Salha," Fathia broke the silence. "Maybe Salem could help." She spoke firmly so that her wishes would not be mistaken for criticism. She sounded angry.

As Salha busied herself searching in her bag for something. Fathia noticed how her jowls sagged when she was sullen. She saw how the fine creases in her previously smooth brow deepened. Salha's beauty was transient, lost to the darkening shadows under her eyes as she pouted her lips in pretended concentration; she found her lipstick, and smoothed the red gloss in a double swipe on her waiting lips. Then, with a sudden flutter of her long black eyelashes the flaws were dismissed in an instant, like magic.

Salha looked up with her eyes large and doleful, even springing tears. The two women faced each other in silent defence of their different positions. The air was so charged with the unspeakable question that it took some time for Salha to extricate herself from Fathia's discomforting gaze.

"God willing," she answered. "But the chances are slim, Fathia. You expect too much of Salem."

"Maybe you could talk to Iman, then, to her father even." Fathia was undeterred. "He's a good man, I know. He knew my father once. They came to these parts together from the same village. They were together when their land was taken and they were forced into camps by the Italians. As children we all worked together, piling all our belongings onto a shared cart. His cart, my father's donkey. There must be many connections like that between us. For Saad's sake. On this his daughter's head, let it be so. For the sake of Neda, his fatherless child. Young, innocent Neda here."

At the mention of her name, Neda stopped playing with the tassels on her mother's scarf and looked up. Suddenly the talk was about herself. Her grandmother was speaking from the heart. Direct and true with so much feeling that nothing more could be said on the matter of finding her father. Salha, the mesmerising story-teller had fallen silent. She was short of what to say.

It didn't seem right to Neda that Salha chose just this moment to loosen her hair from its bun and let it cascade over her shoulders, before reshaping it back into a coil. She was making a drama, or so it seemed, out of a petty detail, inexplicably needing to make the bun tighter than before, so tight, in fact, that it pulled the skin at the sides of her face. With the final hairpin secured, Salha still managed to secure even more time for finding her stride, tidying imaginary strands of hair and sweeping them away with her hands. She found her earrings where they dangled and pinched the warm gold; she fingered her golden rings twisting them round and round. But all attempts to diffuse the tension failed. Neda was surprised that her grandmother had sat tight throughout this display, bristling with impatience and irritation.

"Trust me, Fathia, my dear," Salha finally said. "I will handle things, but in my own way. Just point me in the right direction, that is all." And with that, Salha reached for the sweets and biscuits and pulled the tray towards her, to offer it her in perverse way to her host.

"Sweets, anyone?"

It shifted the topic. She had brought a convenient close to the vexed question of Neda's father.

Chapter 6

The uninvited guest

An hour later, the three women and Neda were still seated cross-legged on the carpet, around a tray, this time filled with nuts, mint and tea-making paraphernalia. The doorbell on the garden wall at the gate rang – once briefly, then again, ferociously and persistently.

"Now who would come at such an hour!" exclaimed Salha.

"It's maybe Salem, home early," said Fathia.

"I wouldn't think so, not at this time. He wouldn't ring like that, not even if he's in a hurry. It's probably a beggar woman – you know what they're like. They get about a lot these days, don't they?" Fathia didn't know. "One came to my sister's only yesterday, and my neighbours get them frequently."

"I hope it's not bad news," said Fathia. "I am not sure we should answer it. Hassan wouldn't like me to. Not a stranger."

"Oh, best to. You don't know who it might be. Could be good news, could be important too. Besides we can't pretend there's no one at home with the windows flung wide open as they are. They'll have heard our voices. Whoever it is, and possibly a beggar woman, I wouldn't invite their mischief, if I were you."

"But anyone with manners would phone first. No one drops in just like that – not these days, anyway."

"All the more reason to think it's a beggar," said Salha, laughing. "What do beggars know of phones? They wouldn't know how to use one, would they? Answer the door and see who it is," she urged.

"May God protect us," Fathia intoned.

"Just give her something to make her happy and she'll go away. Besides it's a good deed to help a beggar. Allah will reward you."

"How can you be so sure it is a beggar?" Fathia feared she had challenged Salha unfairly, but no matter – Salha was leaning through the open window, pleased to find her surmise conveniently confirmed.

A tall female figure stood at the gate. Her head was turned away from her. She was covered from head to toe in a robe of modest quality, worn and frayed in places. Quite obviously she was poor and surely a beggar. As if she were the mistress of the house, Salha herself called out she was coming and the figure turned, slowly so that Salha had time to withdraw and was no longer there to be seen.

Fathia was thrown into confusion by the haste that had been forced on her. She began searching a cupboard for something suitable. In her hurry, she pulled out a precious shawl. It was shot through with silver thread and embroidered with a holy scene from Mecca – a souvenir from her last pilgrimage.

"Oh, that's far too good, *ya Hajja*. Best give it to me if you don't want it," said Salha. "Anything will do for a beggar. What does she know of quality? Here, this roll of cotton cloth. It's nothing special but a beggar would appreciate it. I'll give it to her if you like, and send her away."

"No, I'll give it myself. You are right – the cloth will do. But it is my gift – my opportunity," said Fathia assertively. "My blessing. So I will give it. It could even be a good omen."

They rushed to the door, the bell still ringing but now in short sharp bursts, evidence of a very impatient and uncouth caller indeed.

On the step, silhouetted against the light reflecting from the gravel of the wasteland behind her, stood the erect figure of a tall woman. Her face was masculine in its bony structure and sharp straight nose. Her deeply wrinkled skin was evidence of an outdoor existence. But her physical vigour and youthful energy belied her apparent old age. She did not wait to be invited in, not even for a preliminary greeting. If Fathia had thought she could so easily dismiss her with a present and a blessing and be done with her, she soon knew otherwise. The woman, certainly with the appearance of a beggar, glided over the threshold, sweeping the women aside before stopping to turn towards her presumed benefactor, clearly indicated by the roll of cloth tucked under her arm. She addressed her as if she had known her well.

"So kind of you to invite me in, *ya Hajja*. May Allah bless you and bring all good things to you and your family, *ya* Fathia." She knew her name. "And to this beautiful child and... Oh but who is this foreign woman? Allah save us from foreigners, they bring nothing but disaster. Stealing our land and our most cherished menfolk. Allah save us and bless this wonderful child and you, oh *Hajja*! May God reward you for your patience in the midst of all the tribulations and trials of life. Is this woman foreign? Is she the child's mother? Oh pestilence! What a burden this must be! But maybe she brings her own blessings – for it is blessed to be burdened, to suffer with patience. And you are a patient woman, I know!"

Chapter 7

The Comb

The beggar woman continued speaking in her turbulent way, the pace of her speech sometimes halting, sometimes swift. Her utterances were a mix of blessing and threat. Her rambling style identified her either as harmless harpy or suspicious intruder who knew very well the effect her malicious babble would have on her ambushed audience. She spoke in a dialect Sally had not heard before and so most of what she said was unintelligible to her; but the manner of her speaking and the furious emphasis of her gestures, amplified by the darting glances of her small sharp eyes, were sufficient to convey malign intent.

Having ushered the woman in against her better judgement, Fathia felt uncomfortable about entertaining her. Her height, her bony face and skinny frame marked her out as ugly, making it hard to imagine her in her youthful past. It was possible she had been a lady of the night, one of those who had served foreign armies in the war and whose only source of income in her old age would have to be a lucrative trade in information. Deprived of honour, family and progeny, she would have no other place to run to. Such women, Fathia thought, naturally lacked all social charm. *May Allah curse the Devil in all his guises,* she thought.

The beggar woman turned purposefully to Fathia to introduce herself as Hajja Jazia. The title of *Hajja* seemed to be spoken with emphasis as if to chide her for uncharitable thoughts. Ignoring the tone and accepting the woman's worthiness of charity, Fathia led her graciously into the lounge where the food still awaited them. She enjoined the intruder to eat with them.

Hajja Jazia shook her dusty plastic sandals off her wrinkled and hennaed feet and washed her hands in the bowl provided.

She let fall the wrap from her head to reveal strong wavy hennaed hair, with wide borders of grey on either side of the parting. The wiry hair bounced up from her skull. As her outer wrap slipped to the floor, her overly thin body was startling with its boney frame apparent under her brightly coloured dress. It was as if a moth had spread its dull wings to reveal its gaudy underwing. She wore a blouse of huge dimensions, too voluminous for her skeletal frame, its mix of floral patterns clashing with a swirling mass of green and orange sleeves set in a strident yellow and bright vermillion bodice, all printed on soft brushed cotton. The sweep of her gaze gleaned more detail than most gazes would, her head swivelling like an owl's, perfectly maintaining its horizontal level as it turned. She gazed down at Neda even as the child moved away in fear; she still gazed at her as she eased herself down from her remarkable height to join her host at the spread of food laid out on the large round tray. Neda backed away.

Sally was bemused, unsure how to respond. She brought Neda closer to herself. Fathia offered reassuring blessings on their company and appeased the stranger with formal salutations, then bid them all to eat. Hajja Jazia required no second invitation. It was a wholesome collection of delicacies – stuffed vine leaves and *kofta* left over from the night before, eggs freshly fried in minced spiced lamb, Edam cheese and home-made flat bread baked in an earth-oven, all accompanied by soured butter milk. Both visitors had the heartiest of appetites and the dishes were soon emptied. Sally brought out the tea tray and the charcoal burner, prepared for making sweet mint tea.

The beggar, however, asked for coffee instead. Salha offered to make it and Fathia joined her in the kitchen. Neda left to fetch water. Sally sat in silence in the room alone with Hajja Jazia who fiddled with her robes within which a small pouch was revealed, briefly but long enough to make its impression on Sally. She returned it to its hiding place hanging from a leather belt just as Neda returned with a tumbler of water tightly gripped in her hands.

Coffee was served but Sally showed no inclination to drink hers. Salha was visibly agitated and reassured her it was very sweet and wonderfully flavoured with cardamom. Sally obliged and complemented her on its taste, then no sooner had she finished with her cup than the old woman seized it from her. She placed it to one side and left it there, uncommented on. Several minutes later she turned the cup in a circular motion and deftly placed it upside-down in its saucer. Now the drying residue would settle and dry to reveal its mysteries.

A complicit silence descended on the little group. The beggar checked on the progress of the drying coffee grains and finding them ready she turned the cup upright in its saucer with aplomb. They were almost ready. She straightened her back, placed the cup between her crossed legs and rested her hands in her lap. Now she was ready.

"Let me read your fortune, my girl," she said to Sally. "It will cost you nothing. No, please wait!" Sally had made to leave the room.

"Now, do be patient and let the grains dry. A little more." Salha nodded, indicating she must stay.

"The secrets of your fate are traced here and only I can know. You will be better armed to face the future once you've heard my reading. What is written? Your face tells me. Tells me all..." But the beggar woman is studying the grains, not her face.

"...tells me all I need to know. Tells me that and so much. So much more I can see. In your eyes you can hide nothing from me." Still she gazes at the cup.

"I hold your secrets in my heart and so. You need to heed my words. I can tell you what will be. In the grains what will be will be revealed. To me only. It will be clear to me which dreams are foolish to hold on to. Which hopes are to be dashed like precious vessels thrown against a wall. Your heeding of my wisdom will repay you a thousandfold."

"*Ya Hajja*, wait." Fathia interjected. She was alarmed by the beggar woman's cruel words and suspected Sally had not understood them. "I would love you to read my cup for me. Read my cup instead. Sally's destiny will be written in mine in any case. Our destinies are twined together after all. Perhaps you can see my son's future in my grains. His fate. Perhaps your wisdom could guide us to him. We both have lost him, you see. He has disappeared. Perhaps you didn't know. No one can tell us where he is. There is only prayer to guide us in our patience."

All the while through Fathia's pleading, the beggar woman's demeanour remained stern and infelicitous. "Some things I do not touch upon, my sister. It would be unwise. You must see a sheikh for that. I have not come to disappoint you. Only to show you a way to help yourself. I know a Sheikh who'll do it. I'll tell you later. But please let me continue."

Hajja Jazia then resumed her task. She stared unblinking at the coffee grains in Sally's cup, making a show of seeming to be troubled by what she saw and yet feigning a little reluctance to reveal anything of it. In the pause, Sally's heart leapt at the small and foolish hope that something enlightening might be about to happen. The beggar woman heaved up her sunken bosom and drew in a deep breath. She narrowed her eyes as she spoke, her stare directed straight at Sally for the first time.

"Your face tells me you are far from home. You are rootless. You wonder why you are here among a strange people. Why did you leave your homeland? Who would leave the green hills of Europe to live like a lost goat in a desert? "

There was another pause as she turned the cup in the palm of her hand. "You are living where your heart has led you. It is a hostile land for sure. And a mistaken heart. You are lost. Abandoned. You fear the truth of the grains. The truth that I know. I will speak it simply so that you shall understand their unmistakeable meaning. You shall know what I know."

The beggar seized the coffee cup in both hands with unexpected relish. She wriggled in her seat, like an animal shaping its nest around itself, and after a brief hesitation, she began.

"Ah! The grains are ready. So clear they are to me. So perfectly reduced to simple truths. Now. Three heads I see. And they whisper, all three, to each other. Whisper so that you shall not hear them. Here there are the eyes of an owl, and tears, many tears, wailing and tears, a loud wailing. The owl lives in the dark and is part-hidden. It covers its face. The women cover their faces so that you shall not know them. There is a strange mark like a scratch, a broken line that runs across the grains, around the cup. Something is lost. A child may be. A child as yet unborn, stillborn or dropped too early as in miscarriage. It means you will have no more children. This is what the three heads are saying. This is the curse they place on you. The curse you place on your husband by staying. I can't say who they are, these three heads. But they are powerful in deciding your fate."

The old woman finished her reading, her shoulders shuddering for a few seconds, feigning the end of an ordeal, as if she had been possessed. Then she remained subdued for minutes afterwards as if in a trance. No one dared to disturb her. It was all so artfully contrived.

Sally was troubled. Fathia saw the concern on her face. She was shocked by Hajja Jazia's curse-like reading. She wanted to be rid of her. She must somehow eject this wicked woman from her home, be rid of her and all her evil influence. She was surprised that Salha, for her part, seemed content to let the woman be.

Fathia went to the kitchen to search for items she could use to eke the woman out of her comfortable seat, out into the street. She found a tin of little cakes she had made some months ago for Saad, hoping to hear of his whereabouts, hoping for a visit. But no, they were too precious, even though a little stale, and she put them back.

In her absence, the beggar had awoken from her trance and was addressing Sally: "You seem upset, my dear, shocked even, by my readings. I speak honestly from the heart, you know, believing you would prefer to know the truth. It is best that you should know there are enemies about. Foolish not to be aware. And so beware. You will thank me one day. But I can do no more than this. I cannot protect you unless you trust me. I can protect you if you trust me, and you do need protection, believe me. Just give me some small item belonging to yourself and I will perform a blessing for you with it. Something small that I can carry with me, a useful item you use every day. Perhaps a comb. Yes, a comb. I need only a comb and then I can protect you. Go now, go and fetch it."

"What does she want with a comb?" Sally asked Salha.

"She wants to comb her hair, that's all. She'll give it back to you. Go on and fetch it quickly before she changes her mind. It will be a blessing to lend a comb to a beggar. Then she will feel blessed and content to go. It's good to please her and Allah will bless you."

Sally felt compelled to please the beggar and Salha too. She left the room to find her comb. Hairs caught in its teeth shone in the light as it passed into the beggar's clutch. The hairs were the crucial thing. To Sally's dismay the beggar did not comb her hair at all, but carefully retrieved the hairs and placed them in the small pouch that hung from the belt before placing the comb in the drape of her voluminous blouse. Sally felt a sinking feeling. She had been violated.

"We'll seek protection from Allah," whispered Fathia under her breath. And she seized the opportunity to overwhelm the beggar with a bag of provisions she had collected from her kitchen store. This was a clear sign for the beggar to take her leave, it being unseemly to stay beyond this generosity. Hajja Jazia was content to go and uttered blessings on them all as she quickly wrapped herself in the drab colours of a night moth. She assumed again the harmless air of a poor old woman in need of charity.

Salha saw her to the door. Hajja Jazia leapt outside with an energetic stride over the threshold, into the bright blinding light of the wasteland in front of the villa, still muddy from the receding inundation. From the balcony, Neda watched her pick her way around the puddles, her flimsy shoes were surely soaked. Gradually she faded into the dreary distance. Neda was glad the old woman was gone and ran to her mother who was gathering the debris of biscuit crumbs and sweet wrapping papers from the carpet.

Chapter 8

Crisis

Salem was going to be late for lunch. His share was keeping warm in the oven. When he finally arrived, Fathia hovered over him as he ate, and chatted. With mild interest, he asked about her day and she touched on their unexpected visitor, careful not to burden him with too much detail. His eyes glazed over and she said no more.

Fathia knew that Salem shunned beggars and what he deemed to be their murky unproductive lives. To him, they were members of an underclass for which he had no pity, no proper charity. He had always found Hassan's indulgence of them reprehensible. She switched topic and rambled on, raising matters of no real consequence until Salem rounded their conversation off with routine compliments about the food and impressed on her how tired he felt.

While Salem had been eating, Salha had slept in the guest room. Now it was time for Salem's afternoon siesta. Leaving Sally to clear the dishes, Fathia joined Salha in the guest room, offering her a glass of sweet tea.

"Salem seems very tired, like you said. He's sleeping in the lounge," Fathia said, waiting for Salha to join her in reflection on the morning's events. Salha took her time tidying her hair. She let it fall in cascades around her shoulders, something Fathia, whose own hair was much more sparse, admired. Her profile was strikingly handsome, though not pretty. Then Salha turned to face her frowning. It was the same alternation of opposites that had bewildered Fathia earlier.

"You didn't mention the beggar, or the fortune-telling, did you?" Salha seemed alarmed at the thought. "You know how Salem hates fortune-telling and any sort of superstition."

"Of course not. He wasn't interested in any case."

"You mean you did but he wasn't interested?"

"No, my dear. I only said we had a strange visitor, a beggar woman. I was glad to see the back of her."

"You didn't mention her name?"

"Why would I do that? I'm sure he wouldn't know her. Would he?" Fathia thought for a second or two about the significance of mentioning the name, but then dismissed all possible conclusions.

"Men don't understand what women do and it's best left that way. Don't you think?" Fathia agreed. She knew very well that if men wished to make mischief they had no need of fortune-telling. But she wondered if men kept their exploits well hidden like women did.

The conversation trailed off with no further mention of the morning's visit, as if both women had agreed not to let it trouble their consciences any further, each for their different reasons. At least they didn't worry themselves until, after a long lull of no more to be said, Fathia raised the question that Salha had failed to answer – did Salem know Hajja Jazia?

"So, does Salem know Hajja Jazia? Has he met her any time?" Fathia preferred not to look her in the eye as she spoke for fear of what she found there, a pretence, perhaps a lie. Glancing away, she missed the merest, slightest shudder that flickered across Salha's face before she answered, still avoiding the questions, with, "Did you actually tell him you were glad to see her go, then? That would be very foolish, if you did."

"No, Salha. That's only what I thought. A wicked woman she seemed to me. You could tell that by the look in her eyes."

"But you didn't say that to Salem, did you?"

Fathia shook her head, bemused now, feeling that something had been carefully avoided and just as skilfully supplanted by the insinuation that she herself was a foolish, undiscerning woman. Best to draw a curtain over the whole affair, and so she turned her energies to preparing the tray for afternoon tea. She transferred the action to the lounge where Salem was now awake and ending a conversation on the phone to someone. Salem and Salha sat stiffly on the settee, while she sat cross-legged on the carpet. Sally had absented herself knowing Fathia would be relieved – Salem could relax with just his sister and his wife.

First Salem moved to sit beside his sister cross-legged on the carpet and then he stretched out with his elbow crooked as a support. He was quiet, grateful that the sound of tea pouring into glasses from a height filled the silence for him. Once the tea was ready with a little froth piled up high in the glass, he sat up to drink. But Fathia saw he was not happy. He was more serious than she could remember.

"That's good. I needed that." He spoke quietly but without gentleness. Something firm in his voice warned her of something disagreeable he was about to raise.

"There's been trouble this morning, my dear sister. A disturbing incident," he said. "I'm sorry I have to bring it up but you should know about it. Some youths trying to avoid the draft. We've been combing the streets for weeks looking for such lay-abouts, the ne'er-do-wells, traitors some would call them. But what is serious, and here I'm afraid you will be shocked..."

He ignored the look of apprehension on Fathia's face and continued, "... what is really serious is their apparent connection with Hassan." Again he ignored the look of incredulity on Fathia's face. She was too surprised to interrupt or challenge the ridiculous suggestion. He continued. "They were spotted in a flat above a certain shop, an empty flat or supposedly empty. So I was told. It turns out it was Hassan's shop. The soldiers had to scale the walls to reach one of the windows they were seen at. They smashed the glass to break in and all three were caught. One was injured. They were packed into trucks and you can be sure that they are not destined for the usual cadet training. I have always said it's better to volunteer, because the army will have its way in the end no matter what. The same goes for Hassan. But he never listens, does he?"

Fathia felt the reprimand was meant for her. He had not elaborated on the suggested connection between Hassan and the youths. She felt he must have made an error, was referring to another situation, a different set of circumstances that could not possibly involve Hassan. As for volunteering, it was true Hassan was courting trouble by avoiding the military training arranged for his age group. She herself had urged him to join the others, believing it would bring some badly needed advantage. She felt the need to make excuses for her husband's omissions, saying he was getting old and no longer in good health. She did not like to add that since his arrest he had withdrawn even further into himself, and there was little she could do about that. In any case, she felt Salem was too harsh in his judgment and was prepared to say so.

"You don't understand him, Salem. Things have been hard."

"My dear sister, Hassan is so blatantly uncooperative that it has become an embarrassment even to me. Do you realise just how damaging his last little tantrum was? Any more of this and it will jeopardise my visiting you. He damages me too, you know. I don't think you can have any idea."

"I wouldn't call it a tantrum, Salem. Foolish, yes. I've told him so, many times. But it wasn't just a tantrum. It comes from losing too much. First he lost half his land and that was bad enough. His land given over to that grass, esparto they call it, and the living it could have given us went as well. Now he's lost his shop, the fruits of thirty years of hard work. Allah will help us to bear that sort of loss. But to lose your son! That is just too much to bear. Too much altogether."

"Yes, and that's just the point, isn't it? Having lost his son, he should have kept quiet. One thing just leads to another, doesn't it?"

"It's not Hassan I'm breaking my heart over. It's not him that I pray for every day, is it? Could that be my greatest worry, by any stretch of the imagination, d'you think? Hassan will settle given time. Just give him time. He'd settle now if it wasn't for this one thing."

"You expect me to sort Saad out as well? Well, that's not how things work, I'm afraid. Hassan has to understand that the regime does not have to bow to him – he has to bow to it. But he's too arrogant. They have all the power. How could it be any other way? That's what we all have to do. Forgive me, sister, but this is the truth of the matter. And it's better to hear it from a caring brother than from..." Salem preferred not to finish the sentence.

Fathia's eyes were burning. "Why are you so hard on him, all the time?"

"Why, you ask. And I am here especially to have it out with him. To explain the 'whys and wherefore.' So where is he? I expected him to be here. After all, I was late enough. I gave him time."

Fathia could not answer. Her silence told him all he needed to know; and now that he understood Hassan was unlikely to return any time soon, he knew he could not expect Fathia to wait for a proper explanation of the incident he had only partially reported to her. And so he gave her the briefest of outlines of the day's events which had so troubled him.

He was very clear on one point. More sinister than the fact that the said shop was Hassan's shop was the fact the youths had had a key for the flat above it. Worse still, the soldiers had found subversive literature in the flat and leaflets written in the same vein, all tucked away at the back of Hassan's shop. He, Salem, just happened to be passing by, he said, when the raid had taken place and he been regaled with all these inconvenient facts.

"Perhaps I can give him some advice, Fathia. But, as for being able to help him, well, forget about that at this stage."

"Are you saying that Hassan gave them the key?" Fathia was indignant. "That's nonsense! He'd never do anything like that, never. He's far too cautious, nowadays. He keeps himself to himself, as you well know. Everyone knows. Even you know that."

Salem did know that the allegations he had just insinuated were without substance. It was the police after all who had taken the keys away from Hassan some months before. Hassan could not reasonably be held responsible for anything that had taken place there after that. Salem knew this well enough, but it suited him not to say so. Furthermore, it was entirely feasible that the apprehended youths had entered the premises with permission from the police. Possibly, Salem knew this also was most likely the case, but such an admission here and now would have thrown unwanted light on his connections. In turn, it might suggest a deeper involvement with the regime than Fathia imagined, perhaps even one that extended into the conspiracy of silence surrounding Saad's disappearance; even his current whereabouts if he was still alive. If so, perhaps Salem was involved more deeply than he imagined since he himself could not be sure of the truth or otherwise of what he thought he knew. It was prudent to hide his insecurities and collusion, unwitting or otherwise, from his sister.

"Besides," Fathia continued, "He didn't even have a key any more."

Salem replied, "Who knows what's the truth of the matter, these days? (And so he absolved himself) Hassan just needs to understand the danger he is in, the danger he is putting us all in."

After this ill-tempered exchange, they had no appetite for further talk. Each fell silent, reflecting on the issues from their own perspectives. Fathia poured the second brewing of the tea from the pot, holding it high above the glass the better to create a froth, then meticulously dividing it between the smaller gold-rimmed tea glasses, and emptying them back in the pot to pour again until the froth itself was equally divided. It was a routine that usually comforted her with its familiar sounds and aromas, and its repetition; but it failed to do so now.

Salem remained and waited for Hassan. The afternoon had dragged on into early evening and the night was drawing in. The house was very quiet. Fathia was troubled by the way her brother kept apart, sitting on his own in the guest room. He was the only person she could turn to for help. She could not afford to lose his sympathy. The day had been so full of evil boding and perhaps there was more yet to come.

She took the second round of tea to Salem and then for the third glass, refreshed with mint and roasted hazelnuts, he joined her in the kitchen. They sat around the kitchen table where Fathia had spread the remains of their lunch, supplemented with cheese and olives, and a plain pasta dish to make a simple evening meal. There was no real conversation, only awkward comments on the weather, the winter closing in, the wind in the orchard, and the voices of the children sitting on the veranda steps, waiting.

Salha was restless, clearly indicating her impatience to return home. The stress of it all played on Fathia's usual calmness of mind and the morning's mischief had lost all its urgency.

Chapter 9

Good Intentions

Hassan had not meant to take his boat out far. He had steered as close to the shoreline as possible. The crystal clear water was almost still as he veered up a gully carefully avoiding sandbanks. He killed the engine and hauled the boat all the beach into his favourite cove. There, a crescent of white sand edged the flow of sea that was never quite a full tide. Crouching low as if that was sufficient to make himself unseen, he unwrapped his lunch and quickly polished off the bread, the cheese and olives, and sweet red grapes.

His sights were set on the hill slopes, their inclines gentle enough for a younger man but now a fair challenge for someone past his middle age. The bulky haversack slung across his chest, was another handicap.

He knew exactly where to find the caves, and one in particular, or so he thought. As a child in the war years, he had come with his father to this same bay in search of Rommel's hideout. On that occasion, they had reached it from inland on a dirt track that wound through the valleys, taking it in turns to ride the family donkey. But today it was easier and wiser to approach from the sea.

Rommel, 'that wily fox' as he was known, filled his father's stories with all the panache of a pirate's tale. Wartime outlaws, deserters from the German army, nuns, monks and smugglers peopled the cast. Perhaps they were never real. His father had pointed out the cave but Hassan never knew for sure if they had really found it. But now he believed he could see one that fitted the description. It was a good size with plenty of cover in the sprawl of yellow-flowered gorse.

In places he lost his footing and slipped quite some way. It began to bother him that the suddenness of each fall would reveal him. He imagined an all-seeing surveillance even in this deserted place. And what would be his reason for attempting such a climb. No man walked the hills alone.

How would he explain the documents in the haversack, topped with fishing tackle for disguise. And if that worked, he would still have to explain the presence of a fisherman in the hills. He could tell the story of his father's quest. But doing so would shatter any chance of using a cave as a hiding place. His papers, his manuscripts rolled up tight and tied, wrapped in newsprint and sealed in plastic bags with string, they were all a burden to him. He had to take the risk whichever way. After all, he was here to free himself of the unbearable load of opposition, the loneliness of his isolated rebellion.

The caves from here were highly visible, like a line of pockmarks, recognisable as a colonnade of dark holes in the limestone outcrop. Perhaps they were once use as food cellars, or stores of other items, for he knew that many of his troubled countrymen had been forced to leave their homes and inhabit caves during the war. When confronted with the choice, he opted for the cave that seemed the most improbable, being narrow at the entrance, a tight-fit and uninviting. He did what he had to do as quickly as he could. He pressed the secret bundles into recesses he found gouged in the walls, perhaps by human hand, he thought. Then he left feeling more panicked than he had expected. He progressed down to the foot of the hill with surprising agility relying on a pebbled goat track he had discovered.

The sky out to sea was mainly blue but an angry-looking rabble of dark clouds had accumulated on the horizon, though far enough away not to worry him, far enough away not to sabotage his plan for an alibi to satisfy his wife's inevitable curiosity – if nothing else, a modest catch at least would do the trick. There was time to catch a fish or two, before turning round for home.

The little boat sped away from the shore to a vantage point from where he could scan whole the line of caves before they disappeared into the mottled green of the hill. He stalled the engine and was surprised to find shoals of herring swarming nearby. He took a net and scooped them up. Then he saw larger fish and threw his net to trawl a while, making an arc out to sea and curving back again. He felt the tug of something large, several tugs and hoped for red mullet at least. When the net felt sufficiently heavy, he hauled it in and in the bottom of his boat there wriggled twelve good-sized fish of various species, some viciously spiked with razor-sharp fins. He was satisfied for many reasons. The sea still had promise.

Sailing home, Hassan thought about his reception when got there. It would be awkward, considering his deliberate avoidance of Salem. He reflected on how he might make up for his churlishness, explicable only if the reason for his absence could be told, which it couldn't. Some kind of peace-making with Salem would be in order, something he could do without losing face. It would have to be impressive, not too much of a gesture but something that put himself in a reasonable and honourable light.

The lift and dip of the prow ploughing through the heavy water made a pleasant numbness trickle though his body like warm honey. It was a sign that he had overstretched himself. But the direction home was straight and the boat was on automatic pilot. He found the remains of his lunch, fish-shaped biscuits filled with dates, and devoured them with gratitude for his wife's thoughtfulness. This unfamiliar felicitous mood sustained him for the homeward trek.

Besides, if for no other reason than she deserves a bit of peace, he thought, gathering the sweet crumbs in his fingers, *I could do something to make it easier for her at least.*

He puzzled on the form his peace-offering might take. He had the fish, enough to share. He tried several tacks speaking his offering out aloud, to see how the words sounded – regretful, apologetic or lacking in dignity. With the noise of water drowning out his voice, he could hardly hear himself: "By my son's life, you must share these fish with us" or "I stayed an extra hour, so that I had enough to share," and then anticipating the customary polite refusal he added, "It must be quite some time since you tasted fish this good."

But none of these would do. It was a wonder he had not remembered. Private fishing of any kind was banned along the coast. It was not the convenient alibi he needed. Salem would disapprove and could make trouble for him. He could hardly credit his forgetfulness. He must, then, leave the fish outside and offer Salem something else. The beans in the kitchen patch, they had come up early and were sweet and plump with the recent rain. His words rang boldly in his head. He would invoke the name of Saad.. That would do it.

As he approached the villa, it occurred to him that Salem and Salha may have left already and he would be cheated of the chance to make amends. The poignancy of his dismay surprised him and he quickened his pace, labouring up the incline through the orchard, barely stopping to muster breath. He would place the fish at the kitchen door and turn back to pick the beans and collect them in the front of his shirt.

He steadied his laboured breathing and composed himself at the kitchen door. His hair was unkempt, his face glowing and he smelt of fish. No matter, he could say he had been checking on his nets, the pomegranate trees, and then the trees in the long alfalfa grass. The fish he could have bought at market. There was nothing for it but to break in upon the scene with the assurance of a man who was answerable to no one in his own home.

But pausing for second thoughts, he noticed there was silence on the other side of the door. They must have left already. He would leave the beans and if he found his guests still there in the lounge or somewhere else, he could dispose of the fish in the kitchen before announcing his arrival. So, feeling like a thief in his own house, he pushed the door inwards and wiped his boots on the mat.

"Ah, at last. You're here!"

Surprised faces all around. Startled not only to find them sitting there at the kitchen table but also a bowl of beans already at its centre, Hassan stood aghast, vacillating between shock and disappointment. Greetings were truncated by the arrival of the fish centre-stage. But while Fathia's gaze rested on the fish, it was the beans that registered with Hassan – his dismay perfectly mirroring hers for different reasons. Hassan placed the fish on the table beside the beans, explaining somewhat incoherently that they were a gift.

"A gift for you, that's what they are. Just come back. My brother's, you know."

Fathia ushered everyone out of the kitchen and, from the door, she looked back to glare at him.

"A gift from your brother, you say?" The tone of Salem's voice re-arranged Hassan's words into some kind of alternative meaning, converting his intended vagueness into an unexpected certainty, bringing the guilt into full focus.

"How kind of him! Likes his fishing does he? Must be feeling better then. That is a blessing. Thanks be to Allah."

Chapter 10

Distrust

Did Salem know for certain that Hassan was being less than honest with him? It was hard to know but Hassan thought he did; he looked so decidedly composed, so intolerably in control.

Of course he was composed, he always was. And here he sat so smartly dressed, cuffs unbuttoned and hanging loose Italian fashion, shirt collar open casually authoritative without a tie. Ties were considered decadent, Hassan knew that, and in his position of course, Salem must conform. He could not fault him there. He did not seem unfriendly at all. He leaned back on his chair tilting it backwards, not like a man ready for a challenge. But it was irritating that he wore his sleeves unbuttoned, his wrists resting limply like a dandy. Even so, the extra elegance of draped cloth gave the impression of a man too relaxed to be ready for argument.

"So how are things with you, Ya Haj?" Salem was being very formal. "It can't be easy. Can't be many visitors, in the circumstances. No customers these days either, I shouldn't wonder."

'In the circumstances' grated. Of course there were no customers. And with no shop, that was obvious. This was an intrusion into personal matters that Hassan did not appreciate. He dipped his bread in the stew Fathia had heated up for him, appearing too preoccupied to answer, his mouth so conveniently full of bread.

"So your brother fishes still, does he? Recovered from his heart condition? Fishing not too arduous then, the fish being so far out? He goes the distance, does he? They say the stock is almost depleted by the coast. Have you noticed that yourself?" Hassan felt trapped, the questioning touching so closely on the details of his fishing route. After all, it was common knowledge that there was a ban.

"Well you've got me there, brother. I'm really out of touch, you see. Spend my time on the jetty, wishing I had the energy of my youth. Still no point is there, with the ban. Like I said, my brother's fish. Not mine. No idea how he got them. Market, I should think. Forgot the time, you see. Sorry if I kept you waiting. And you so busy these days." Only afterwards did it strike Hassan that he had uttered 'and you so busy these days' in a sarcastic tone.

"Didn't say you had been fishing, not today at least," Salem watched him like a hawk. "Merely enquiring. Mentioned it because I wondered if you noticed anything along the coast. From the jetty, of course. Only from the jetty. Something unusual, smuggling and stuff like that. Little boats hiding in sheltered bays."

Hassan's eyes widened inwardly but outwardly he conveyed neither shock nor recognition of the danger so casually implied.

"It's said they use the caves," Salem continued. "You can reach them from a number of places along this stretch of coastline. You've seen nothing then?"

'Using the caves' and 'smugglers' struck him sharply. He stopped for a moment and looked up. Alarming details best forgotten. There was still no sign of 'yes' or 'no' as Hassan gulped water down his stricken throat and wiped his mouth with the back of his hand, forgetting the napkin Fathia had set there for him.

"That's fine. Just let me know if you do. It would be very helpful."

Hassan had been mulling over Salem's turn of phrase 'in the circumstances', detecting in it a poorly disguised sarcasm, perhaps an implied criticism. He dipped the last of his bread in the gravy, pushing it around the dish. This last 'would be very helpful' was a puzzle too. Did Salem mean to offer him a bribe? Was he inviting him into his circle of intelligence or simply trying to tap into his own private fund of secrecy? Either way, he was in no mood to cooperate and muttered something quite pathetic by way of hoping to end the matter: "Wouldn't know anything about it, would I? No. I'm telling you. Don't know a thing so don't be asking me."

Somewhere in the back of his mind, it registered that the risk he had taken was very real indeed. His secret place might even be discovered. Reaching for a knife to peel an apple, he reflected on what had passed between them. Clearly Salem was in control, so effortlessly establishing his politically dominant position. Hassan re-arranged the dishes on the table for no particular purpose and made an elaborate ceremony out of peeling the apple and slicing it into segments like an orange. He offered Salem a slice, then took a noisy bite himself.

"Your health, *ya Hajj*. You must be hungry after all that fresh air. I see you eat well, considering."

Hassan swallowed the remains in his mouth too hastily. What did he mean to insinuate by "fresh air" and there it was again, that 'considering'. Something sinister lurked in Salem's 'considering.' Would it be best to cooperate after all, 'considering'?

"We do well enough. Smuggling, you say. Have I seen boats, from the shore you mean? Well, no, I can't say I have. Never that far out at sea, as you imply, you see."

"Who's talking about boats?" Salem pounced. "Doesn't have to be boats."

"Must be boats. No other way to reach those caves. You said yourself."

"No. I said the coast. You said 'boats'. Not me. And by the way, I'm implying nothing."

"Oh yes you are. You're implying plenty. There's nothing passes your lips but it's insinuation. Think I don't know what you're up to?"

There it was, done. A remark too blunt to be ignored. And here their conversation deadlocked over things implied but not quite said; Hassan denying the mention of the coast and Salem denying he had implied anything at all.

"You get me wrong, old man. You twist my meaning with your own ill-considered thoughts. How is it that you take offence so easily?"

"I understand your meaning well enough, young man," came the sharp attempt at a put-down, an impossible reversal.

But it was Salem who played sage to the older man, saying:

"If you end up a lonely pauper, unable to provide for your family, it doesn't matter to me. It's only Fathia I care about. It's your own arrogance that will get you in the end. Mark my words, it is, old boy." Saying this Salem stressed his words by poking the air several times with a sharp forefinger, and then made to leave the table. His bluntness had surprised them both.

"I'll take care of my own wife, thank you, and I won't be needing your interference, that's for sure!" Hassan nearly choked on his words spoken with such unexpected vehemence that Salem felt himself under physical attack and rose up, scraping the legs of the chair on the floor as he did so.

"I've had enough of this. It's getting very late," he said heatedly. "Let Fathia tell you what happened at your shop today. And after that, come and see me if you're feeling reasonable and I'll see what I can do, in the circumstances."

This was the signal. Both men were standing now. Hassan had pushed his chair away so forcefully it clattered to the floor and alerted Fathia who had been listening at the door. She found both men were stunned to silence in a stalemate which she mistook for a reluctant truce. She pressed the bowl of beans into her brother's hands. No one thought to parcel up the fish, tainted as they were with their uncertain provenance.

Chapter 11

Impasse

A little later that same evening, when the kitchen had been tidied, dishes washed and put away, Hassan and Fathia sat opposite each other at the cane table on the veranda. Their weary faces were animated by the flickering light of a paraffin lamp which swayed above them in a gentle breeze. Mosquitoes were biting at their ankles and moths hovered in the air charging at the lamp. Beyond the sounds of crickets in the orchard, they could hear the wash of waves on the shore. They felt the sea's vapours touch their skin. A house gecko clung to the wall behind them, a pale transparent yellow-green. According to superstition, it was a dangerous toxic little creature and was burdened with the local title of 'father of yellow fever' for its colour.

Children might flick pebbles at geckos, but two weary people sitting on the veranda were oblivious to mosquito, moth and gecko alike.

The cane chair creaked as Fathia leaned forwards to pour tea and pass a glass to Hassan. She sensed that he was tense and so preferred not to open up the discussion. She assumed he would be musing on the difficult situation at the shop. She hoped that Salem had offered him a solution and that he had graciously agreed.

"I suppose there's no more beans." Hassan's sullen voice suggested beans had been the pressing issue of the day. The pettiness of his complaint disguised his real thoughts which were too complicated to marshal into a coherent sentence. It was trivial to turn the issue of the beans into a complaint but it helped him to skirt around what was really troubling him about the beans, the march Fathia had stolen on him offering them before he had a chance; an unreasonable grievance, he knew. But it would have both pleased and dismayed her to know that it had been his intention to give the beans himself, that her own generosity had thwarted his. So he let his inadequate words fall into oblivion, unaware that he spoke too economically.

For her part, Fathia was not surprised by his enquiry about the beans. She expected him to be irritated by anything she did for her brother, but his complaining now confirmed him in her mind as uncharitable. She did not make this charge against him but told herself it was a bitter disappointment that he was not the man she had hoped she'd married, many years ago.

"I didn't think you'd mind so much. There were only a few left, although I did give most to Salem."

"No. I don't mind. I'm not angry about the beans," but he sounded defensive.

"After all, he's been so generous to us," she continued, forgetting that Hassan was unaware of the joint of lamb and tins of cheese and butter Salem had given them that very day.

"I'm not angry. Not with you anyway. I'm angry with myself. With myself, do you see that, Fathia? Are you listening to me? I'm angry with myself. I wanted to patch things up but somehow it all went wrong."

"I don't understand what you have against him in the first place." She wasn't listening to him. "You mean to put things right and instead you lose your temper. Well, isn't that just fine. Just when he wants to help us, you push him away. He's doing his best to be tactful and you attack him."

Hassan knew she had been listening to their argument at the closed kitchen door, but he did not expect her to comment on a conversation she had not been part of.

"Tactful? Is that how you see him? Tactful. That's it, and of course I'm not. You don't see it, do you? You are never there when it happens. He's careful in front of you, of course. But with me it's different. I can't stand a man who always puts a twisted interpretation on things. Who manipulates everything to fit his own agenda. It's quite clear to me that he's one of those sort. I'll tell you what he gets up to when he's away in important places, why you can't find him when you need him. He keeps an eye on things, that's what he does. He's one of those who watches all the comings and goings. Puts his nose in where it's not wanted. Oh, yes he's interested all right, likes to know what we all get up to. He's interested that way. That's why, that's why he's busy all the time. And that's why he's so tactful as you like to call it. Has to be, to hide his tracks, doesn't he?"

"Well, that's very contrary of you now. One minute you say you want him to help us. And you expect him to go searching for our son while you sit at home and do nothing about it yourself and then you complain about him knowing other people's business. That's rich, I have to say. And I wouldn't mind if you weren't such a liability yourself, so careless you are about the shop and everything else you do. Always offering to help any lame dog without bothering to find out who they are and what they're up to. If you weren't so foolish, *ya Haj* Hassan, Salem would be able to do more for us, an awful lot more."

Striking at the truth so remorselessly in this way, Fathia's words stung him. He felt foolish and vulnerable. He felt severely scolded like a child with no plausible defence. She rarely spoke with anger, so when she did, it hit its target. There was a long silence while Hassan reflected on her words 'careless about the shop' and 'helping any lame dog' she had said. They seemed unfair, unworthy of his wife. He had taken risks to retrieve as much of his stock as possible without drawing attention to himself. Even his brother had taken risks storing it in his own shop and selling it himself without a license to. Together they had worked hard to find a market for his fine cashmere woollens. Against great odds, they had been successful, though in a modest way since he had been denied access to the majority of it, it being in his locked up shop, no longer his. Had she forgotten this?

"What's this about the shop? About me being careless? What have I done now? How can I help it if the police have closed it down? Boarded up the premises and confiscated the keys? You know I'm doing my best to sell what I can so that we can eat. That's a risky business, you know. The black market. You don't give me credit where credit's due."

It struck Fathia that her husband knew nothing of Salem's news. There was no sense of panic in him as there should have been, only unreasonable indignation. Simultaneously, a second thought alarmed her, that, contrary to his claims, he did have access to the shop after all. But how, without a key? Was he doing something illegal after all? If so, that would explain his evasive behaviour.

"So you didn't talk about the shop with Salem? Salem didn't tell you about the shop? So, tell me, what was all that shouting for if it wasn't about the shop?"

"Shouting? We didn't shout. We argued. About irrelevant things to do with smuggling, along the coast somewhere. Nothing I know anything about. Just Salem's usual innuendoes about things going on that I'm supposed to know about and he tries to implicate me. And you think he's tactful. I wouldn't trust him for one minute. He speaks dangerously, without thinking of the implications of a loose tongue. That's why I lost my temper."

At this, Fathia's face registered disgust and horror in quick succession. "So he didn't tell you that your shop has been raided? This very morning? That they found books, leaflets or something? Subversive stuff anyway, against the regime? That they found youths with your keys hiding in the flat above? Trying to avoid the draft they were. Traitors they called them. Associated with you, Hassan. Traitors. Associated with you. They had your keys. How come? What nice company you keep!"

"No, he told me nothing." Hassan was stopped in his stride, his anger suppressed temporarily by shock and then revived by yet more rage. "So that's why he waited to see me. Wanted to cast more suspicions in my direction, didn't he? And now he's turned even you against me. And he knows I don't have the keys any more. Even you know that!"

"Have you ever thought that I know nothing? What do I know? I have no idea what you get up to, do I, Hassan? You tell me nothing. You never let me into your secret world. Perhaps you know about the smuggling too. How would I know if you did or you didn't?"

"I can expect little support from you, then. You'd be the first to condemn me. You'd support your brother sooner than understand your husband."

She heard the hurt in his voice. He saw the hurt on her face. He saw that it was beautiful still, despite the passing years, spoilt at this moment only by his own cruel words and her understandable distress. The lamplight found the furrows across her forehead, the wrinkles round her eyes and now about her pursed lips.

"You tell me nothing, Hassan. You are far, far away," was all she said.

Fathia's words signalled a crisis of trust never reached before in their married life.

Part Four – Alignments

But it was a heavy duty, not unlike a mythical trial of torment, knowingly unreasonable and beyond his physical and mental means.

Chapter 1

Wild dogs

Over recent nights, packs of wild dogs had been roaming the wasteland outside the villa. A sharp volley of barking broke the silence some minutes before sunrise. Nizar stirred in his sleep and lay still, waiting for an idea of what had wakened him so early. It seemed close as if it had come from somewhere within his little chamber, a bed-sized adjunct to his grandfather's bedroom. He was used to being woken by the wireless at his grandfather's bedside blaring unattended to; but this was something different.

It came again, the interruption, from somewhere beyond the villa walls and Nizar pictured the scene with the olive tree that never bore olives, its gnarled trunk spiralling upwards from the hard earth like an exclamation mark. He had climbed it once to impress his sister. What he could never have imagined was the lone mule leaning against it this very moment, in the semi-dark, rigidly motionless, and fixed to its place by a trap of snarling teeth belonging to a troop of wild dogs.

When their barking woke him, he could not have known that it signalled the moment they had pounced to savage the mule's neck and hindquarters. Nizar had never known nature in the raw; he had never seen the merciless hunt of the helpless victim known as prey. With teeth gripping its bony shoulders, and legs gnawed at, the mule shuddered. Its moan was barely audible as an intermittent undercurrent to the barks of dogs on the scent of blood. Birds whirled around in a pre-dawn sky, adding their screeches to the canine clamour.

Nizar jumped up to raise the blinds at the window above his bed. He tugged at the thick cord that lifted the heavy wooden slats, but could only see the trellis against the garden wall. In the shadows, a cat was disturbed by the clatter of wood and dashed across his view, swift as an arrow.

A muffled voice of complaint came from the adjoining room. Nizar let the blinds fall and the dead weight of the slats dragged the cord through his palms scorching them. He nursed them under the still warm sheets. He was wide awake now, while the rest of the family slept on. He hated quiet times when there was nothing to distract him from thoughts of his father. He tightened every muscle in his body to dam the welling tears.

Then shock shook him bolt upright. He had not done his homework; he had not memorised the *sura*. He would have to recite it in front of Abla Fawzia. He would falter and she would show no mercy. Abla Fawzia had never once shown kindness to the children entrusted to her care. The class had learnt not to expect compassion; she was said to be in a cadre in the Leader's party, a position that emboldened her to break all rules. And Nizar had seen that boldness play out on a daily basis. She meted out punishment as if satisfying a deeply personal need to be brutal.

Nizar threw off the bedsheets and, careful not to disturb his grandfather, closed the bedroom door behind him. He found his school bag and dragged it to the kitchen, surprised to find the door ajar and his grandmother already busy in the orchard. He could hear the drop of apples into her basket. Otherwise only crickets. No dogs barking, no mule braying. Sitting on the cane chair, he pored over the sacred text, and, hugging his knees, rocked back and forth. His recital began with deceptive ease:

"'In the name of Allah, the most merciful the most compassionate…'," and there he stopped to scan the words that followed. They were familiar and the metre was compelling, and he had one whole hour to go. He could do it.

The sacred text urged believers not to choose enemies as friends, an idea that struck him as unlikely at first until it occurred to him that enemies could play tricks on you and pretend to be friends. Then it was possible to make such a mistake. Thoughts of war came to him, reminders of the television broadcasts calling for volunteers, ranks of soldiers training, recruits lined up and bawled at in a wide parade ground, crawling on their bellies in dust and mud, the film repeating many times, endlessly it seemed, the sound of pounding feet and deeply breathing lungs drowned out by the dolorous, the tuneless bellowing of the parade officer. He searched again for the words, wanting their music to fill his mind.

Again the sacred text exhorted him to vigilance lest the enemy try to deceive him. He had visions of his grandfather listening in the night hours to broadcasts from banned stations. Were they the voice of the enemy? His grandmother always warned of dire consequences. Perhaps she knew. He gripped his knees tighter totally absorbed by the task of committing the sacred words to memory.

But the words sent shivers down his spine. He was sure his grandfather did hide things. There was a hoard of papers, nothing official-looking, but reams of handwritten pages which his grandfather had stashed away in a little safe hidden behind a clothes rail, alongside his own small bed. Once he had found his grandfather placing a bundle in it and he had looked distinctly guilty. He had been sworn to secrecy and was proud of the fact he had kept the promise. But now the sacred text warned him that nothing could be hidden from Allah.

For some precious minutes, this revelation opened up the glaring fact that his grandfather lived a secret life. There was no denying he took risks for which his grandmother constantly upbraided him; risks that were all the more worrying to Nizar for being nameless. Every morning in the intimacy of the shared bedroom, he woke to his grandfather's wireless blaring news of a different kind from the news on the official station, spoken in an accent he did not know. The promise not to tell another soul of this act of defiance seemed to include him in the treachery. Was he defiant too? If listening to foreign channels was forbidden, was he a traitor too?

The pulse of blood beating in his temples carried a rhythmic certainty. He could hear the sea. The waves came lapping to him, with washing sounds so persistent they could maybe wash away his unease. For after all, it was surely fear that engendered secrecy and the crime could not therefore be so terrible that even Allah's compassion would slip away, as transient as the banks of sand that rolled down under the weight of falling waves. He stood on tiptoe on the veranda, then on the wall to see above and beyond the canopies of the fruit trees. The energy of the sea came to him, leaping at his anxiety, infusing itself deeper and deeper with each thunderous roller.

Still the text swooped down on him like a bird with its beautiful and terrifying language: '... in secret strayed...' He could remember it. He knew it all and it all made sense. His grandfather had strayed but ultimately nothing was ever hidden. He had been forced to secrecy. In the end that too would be known and he would be forgiven. He would not then lose Allah's mercy.

Nizar ran down the path to the sea, stopping at the jetty where the fishing boat was tied. He was almost free of doubt but one last sliver of fear came slicing through his new found calm. Where did his grandfather go when he went fishing? Were his fishing trips forbidden like his listening? Could it be that the fact of secrecy alone was sufficient to condemn him?

Once again, the sacred text warned him that the enemy can take control and with false words put him in a dangerous place, a place of crisis where the soul is disturbed in its serenity. The message was not clear to him, but there was no time left to wrestle with it. What he had learned was still too fresh and in a fragile state. It could easily be lost between now and the moment of recital, his performance for Abla Fawzia. He ran like crazy to the water and let his toes sink into the sand at the foaming edge of the sea. He felt the sand sink away underneath his tread. A seagull flew high in the sky calling out and wheeling round in unbounded circles.

Coming into the kitchen from the veranda, Nizar surprised his mother who was preparing his sandwiches and breakfast. She was quiet, as she always was, and difficult to make easy conversation with. For weeks she had been grieving inconsolably so that he did not know how to approach her. If he could not console her, she was strange to him. Usually he avoided her but meeting there in the kitchen, there was no running away. She brushed the sand off his pyjamas and they sat sharing breakfast, nothing said between them. She wondered at his silence, thinking it a rejection of her. As she stood to clear the table, she meant to touch his shoulder but he ran away.

He listened at his grandfather's door. He had to get his school clothes. He could hear the wireless buzzing and so he knocked loudly. When he put his head inside, he saw his grandfather sitting on this bed with head bent down listening intently. He ignored the usual impatient wave of the hand signalling him to go away and waited by the wireless. Eventually, Hassan looked up. His face was gentle now and enquiring.

"Jeddi? listen to me recite a *surah*. I only have a few minutes."

The old man sat in a large low chair, rubbed his bristly chin and nodded. He listened. The vague glazed look of anticipation hardened when he recognised the passage and remembered who had been entrusted with his grandson's religious instruction. He interrupted.

"So Abla Fawzia has asked you to learn this one. I wonder if she's really capable of explaining it to you? Properly, I mean. Do you know what it's all about?"

"Oh, Jeddi. Don't ask me that. I don't understand it much but I can recite it. And that will have to do." At this Nizar grabbed his kit and left in a hurry. How unhelpful to say that about his teacher, he thought.

He ran past the room where his little sister slept recovering from a lingering fever. He would be travelling to school alone this morning and could rehearse the passage more on his way. His grandmother was settled into her second sleep on the settee, after early morning prayers. She lay straight and perfectly horizontal under her blanket, like a statue. His mother stood at the doorway holding out his morning snack. He snatched it and ran out of the dark hall into the bright sunlight and went on running until he had reached the old dry eucalyptus tree whose leaves and hard seed cases choked the gutters in the rainy season. He slowed down to rehearse again from the beginning the words that warned of Allah's all-knowing presence.

The recital halted at the sight of the carcass of a dead mule lying in his path. Flies swarming from a pool of blood beneath the olive tree smothered the animal's open wounds. As they rushed up in front of him, Nizar dropped his sandwiches and flayed his arms about, thrashing through a cloud of shiny insect bodies. He ran on, his little satchel bumping on his back, hindering his stride with its unrhythmic thuds. In the distance he could see the green Volkswagen always stationed on the road for surveillance.

Just ahead of him was a fellow classmate, Omar, a *child* referred to by his teachers as 'the wretched one.' Sight of him compelled Nizar to rehearse the *surah* one last desperate time, recalling the part that dealt with hands stretched out and tongues that spoke with evil. For Omar, the wretched one, knew a lot about hands and tongues; he was beaten almost every day at school. Nizar had found him embarrassing and wondered at the stubborn way in which he never could recite a *surah*. If he must be rebellious, he thought, then he should at least be brave. But Omar always cried when he was punished. His humiliation was a depressing feature of their shared schooling, a humiliation for them all.

Nizar caught up with Omar who continued in silence despite having company. There was something curious about his personality, an inexplicable something which disturbed Nizar and made him want to run ahead. But he didn't.

"We're late," was all he said and this spurred them both to run the last stretch together. They passed through the school gates without being seen, joined the rear of their class standing to attention and in file, and joined in the national anthem with as much zeal as the rest, their backs as keenly straight. With the rest they marched into the school and down the wide corridor to their classroom. Forty desks in formal rows occupied half the space. There were no cupboards for books, and no pictures on the walls. The children kept their own books in neat piles bound together by elastic straps underneath their seats. At Abla Fawzia's bidding, the class was seated and each child sat bolt upright on the edges of the wooden benches which were fixed at the base to the desks, creating an impossible distance between seat and desktop. The sun blazed into the room through large windows high above their heads.

Abla Fawzia sat large and dominant at her desk. Her voice was a monotone and echoed through the airy room. Apart from desks, the only other item of classroom furniture was a large wooden slat that was propped up in the corner by the open door. Everyone avoided looking at it but its presence was a potent thing, tempering everything that happened in the room. It waited.

Administrative routines cleared away, the class began the dread procedure of each child's recital. It took an hour at least and the order always seemed vicarious. The pupils could never work out whether Abla Fawzia was aware or not of the advantage that the last had over the first. But no matter what the order, only one child's attempt was guaranteed doomed first or last.

There was nothing comforting for Omar in the appeal to Allah's mercy and compassion; he always stumbled at these opening words. Was it possible that he did not understand them, never having experienced such charity? It seemed that no one ever intervened for him, no one checked if his teacher was worthy. He must submit to Abla Fawzia's mockery and abuse, and wait for it to pass. He took up his relegated position, a ritual now, next to the wooden slat. The others dreaded joining him. But when it was over, usually only Omar waited there.

Abla Fawzia rose up from her desk. She asked generally around the class for the explanation of the sura they should have learned by heart. Several eager hands went up but she ignored them. She stalked the room up and down the empty aisles between their desks, prowling like a hunting animal. More hands, less eager now, no longer saved by the company of those who really knew. Nizar wavered, unsure if pretending to know was a protection against discovery. Seconds too late and she had seen his hesitation. Like a bird of prey she pounced.

"I'm pleased you can explain, boy. This sura has special meaning for you, you and your family indeed. It has a special message." But turning sharply on her heel, instead she confronted Mahmoud who was feeling safe in the desk behind.

"Mahmoud, you don't seem sure. Is your hand up or down?" Mahmoud's faltering hand went up and he began to mutter something only to be abandoned as she swung round again to face Nizar, the look of relief at her passing over him seconds before still registering on his face.

"Just who are the foes we've been hearing about, Nizar? You can tell us."

Everyone looked at Nizar, willing him to please her. Desperately hoping that he would not, like Omar, turn them into unwilling voyeurs of his disgrace. He felt himself transported to the beach before a violent sea under whose monstrous waves he was about to fall. He struggled to suppress the feeling in his stomach which he suspected were the pangs of treachery of which he and his family stood accused. It all seemed so unfair. Not daring to look Abla Fawzia directly in the eyes, he sized up his position and knew he was defeated.

When he spoke he did so calmly and with dignity. It made him seem mature beyond his years. "Foes are those who are against us," he stated boldly.

Abla Fawzia's voice was quietly threatening. She stood over him, large and heaving under her uniform. Her eyes were wildly vibrant with unbounded energy. She took hold of one of his ears and pinched it firmly between the large robust forefinger and thumb of her left hand. Then she twisted it. Her rasping whisper raked over him like a flame drawing blood to his face.

"Don't try to be clever with me, you donkey. You'll have to do better than that. Now try again."

"They're people who try to make you think they are friends but they are not," he offered boldly without hesitation.

Abla Fawzia smiled triumphantly. She knew as all his classmates guessed that he had not learnt the authoritative interpretation of the sacred text.

"Stubborn like the rest of your family, aren't you? It's a fact that's been well noted." A final tug at his ear directed him to the corner where Omar waited by the wooden slat.

The class was silent. Each child bent their gaze downwards, eyes staring into vacant lapses. Abla Fawzia laced a pencil in and out of Omar's fingers on the right hand, his writing hand. She raised the plank using both her arms and let its falling weight strike the back of his fingers with a cracking sound. She did this several times. Omar cried out and went crying to his desk.

She exercised herself more ferociously on Nizar since his greater mistake was not to mimic Omar's meekness. He stood with his head erect, ready to watch her face, her eyes especially, as she meted out his punishment. His impudence had excited her. The class noted her heightened appetite for punishment. Nizar yelled once then staunched his cries until the bitter final stroke, which seemed to satisfy her.

Chapter 2

A place of torture

A strange affinity now attracted Nizar to Omar. Like him he was avoided by the others for the rest of the day and so at home-time at midday he gravitated towards him. He followed him down the corridor and out of the school gates, catching up with him when the others had passed them by. Nizar tried to engage his attention by describing the dead mule he had seen that morning, but his new friend was not impressed by the gory details. He knew of things more terrible. He wanted Nizar to know about them too and his eyes were enlivened by a certain furtiveness. Nizar was intrigued and, forgetting time and family, he agreed to take a different route home. Omar led the way.

They crossed a main road into an estate of public housing, tile and plaster clad tenements several storeys high. Despite their newness, the walls were riven with cracks and visibly crumbling. Some tiles were missing. The road was untreated hard earth that disintegrated into dust at the hard worn trodden and fissured surface. In the rainy season, it was awash with mud, and mud was trailed up the steps and into the communal hallways. Each flat had its own balcony, small recesses flush with the outer walls, dark and unloved by the sun. Their balustrades were hung with either washing or carpets left out for an airing. Lines were stretched across the openings, and used for curing strips of meat.

The two boys passed by but at a distance. From the opposite side of the street, Omar waved to his younger siblings and cousins who played on the steps. Other children sat in the road, seemingly at home with hens that moved amongst them scratching the earth. With an eager curiosity they observed Omar's neatly dressed friend, his smart leather satchel and his shiny shoes.

They left this friendly compound behind them and turned a corner into a road that led straight up to the main highway. Here there were no gates, only long high walls around an ancient camel market which was empty. The intrepid pair crossed the very busy highway which Nizar had only ever seen from the window of his grandfather's car. There were little shops with their merchandise spilling out onto the pavement, covered with dust and grime from the traffic, shops with windows glazed over with the deposits of alternating seasons of sandstorm and muddy rains, so that you could neither see in nor see out through them. The warm inviting smell of freshly baked bread blended with the pungent smells of paint and kerosene. Old tyres and second-hand fridges jostled on the forecourts of larger premises, and plastic bowls of every shape and size towered up the cracked white plaster of the walls, colonising every available space with their bright and gaudy colours.

The two friends, looking quaintly odd in their new association, negotiated their way through boxes of coriander and flat-leaf parsley wilting in the midday sun, aubergines shining darkly, defying the dust, and great orange pumpkins that seemed to go on swelling in the heat until they burst, as some had done already.

At the end of the row of shops they turned another corner into a grander residential avenue off the main street where huge villas were set back from the road, concealed from public view by high walls. Trees lined the pavement and provided shade. Halfway down the avenue, Omar stopped at a large iron nondescript sort of gate, its paint peeling off. Beyond it was another great villa, which he claimed to have seen once through open gates. An oleander tree grew higher than a bush just above the wall and honeysuckle trailed in and out of the balusters, with only a meagre show of flowers that gave off no perfume. Nizar stared at the padlocked iron gate and was puzzled.

"Hush," said Omar. "Just make a note of it and I'll tell you all about it on our way back." Not until they were around the corner did Omar explain: "That's where they torture people."

They found a little alcove in a wall where they could lean unseen and, against the din of traffic, Omar explained that he had listened in to adult conversations and found out some things which he had then investigated to be certain of their truth. His daring impressed Nizar. He believed him and began to see him in a different light. He spoke with strength and earnestness. He was no longer the pathetic schoolboy Nizar had thought he knew so well; he was a slightly weird preposterous kind of child who found out more than books could tell just by his own initiative. If he was unschooled, he was impressive just the same.

The terrible details poured out of Omar like water in a river that has broken through its dam. He had never told anyone before but he trusted Nizar since the threats of Abla Fawzia and her insults to his family had sealed a kind of bond between them. This trust was compelling for Nizar, but, for what he was about to hear, he must swear yet another secrecy.

Omar's testimony was not to be repeated on pain of his father's life, for Omar's father had disappeared too. just like Nizar's The secret oath was sworn. They moved on, retracing the steps they had taken past the vegetables, the kitchen stuff and all the chaos of used and unused goods so untidily strewn across the path.

Omar explained that he believed his own father was held prisoner in that very villa. He had often waited outside at night hiding in the shadows of other gateways, hoping to see him. He had watched the comings and goings of dark-windowed Mercedes that pulled up at the gate and disgorged the bodies of victims and he had watched the perpetrators of whatever crime they committed there glide quietly in and out, nodded to by a security guard. He had heard the slithering of passive bodies on the ground and the suppressed struggle of limbs when the victim resisted the captors. He was always unable in the darkness to determine just how many human torsos were engaged in the desperate struggle. He claimed to have heard screams, muffled by hoods or scarves, maybe sacks, but they no longer filled him with the same dread he had felt creep over his flesh the very first time. Fear had scoured his mind so many times by now that it had diminished his initial horror. His father's rebellion had gone to ground. He must rebel for him.

Omar had felt compelled to return to this villa again and again. Perhaps it was a morbid curiosity. Perhaps it was a longing to find his father. Every cry of an unknown prisoner could be his father's and each degrading reduced his own humanity. Humiliation had so far become his life stance, his only way of engaging with people outside family. In this respect alone, he had the greater maturity of all his peers for he was set apart by the simple fact of knowing what he should not know.

Perhaps this was why Omar could not read and never did his homework, Nizar thought. He had chosen to be punished because he did not care. He cared about other things. Things like school must seem quite trivial. But did that mean he scorned his school work, even sacred text? Omar anticipated the question:

"Is that why you never do your homework?" Nizar asked. "Homework must seem so unimportant to you."

"No, Nizar, of course not. Don't tell anyone, please, but I simply can't read. I've tried but I just can't. Besides, there's no one now to help me. And there's nowhere to study. We live in a very cramped space with my uncle's family. My mother is ill and stays with her mother. I live with my cousins. In the afternoons, I have to help out by selling things in my uncle's stall. That's where I get to hear about things I'm not supposed to know. You should come and see me sometime. I sit on the pavement at the front of the Dark Market, the old covered market down town."

By now they had reached the dilapidated flats where Omar's uncle lived. Some children were waiting outside for Omar and rushed up to him as he approached. To them he was a hero. Nizar watched as they clamoured round him while he stood waving.

Nizar ran the rest of the way home. He arrived to find his grandfather at the gate looking out for him, his anger mixed with great relief. He was not rebuked too much. The family drew together in a circle of protection. The different perspectives that separated them in their daily lives, the burning issues they might wrangle over, the different cultures and identities that they comprised, these did not matter now. They had thought that he was kidnapped, since child-snatching was commonplace, part of the accelerating political mayhem. It was yet another way to silence opposition, the ultimate tool of control.

His mother had searched for him in the wasteland around the villa in near distraction but the family had prevailed upon her to come indoors. Hassan had kept watch at the gate, his thoughts running over the words of the *sura* Nizar had recited in part to him that morning, wishing he had listened more, regretting the lost opportunity for reinforcing its real and actual message.

For Nizar, his detour after school that day and his late return home was a milestone in his growing up. He explained his lateness with a few dismissive details that gave little away. There was a secret he must keep. He held back his innermost thoughts which he had not yet had time to make sense of. He watched his grandmother serenely brew the tea as if the panic of disorder could be reassembled into order by the simple ritual of tea-making. He watched his grandfather wait patiently until the brew was ready. Grandfather and grandmother made each a different contribution; each filled their position in the family with an unquestioning acceptance of their separate gender roles.

Even tea, Nizar noted, described the hierarchy of male over female, of bitter taste over sweet. His grandfather drank the bitter first pouring, while the women waited for the second sweeter brew. The chubby face of his sister peered at him from behind his grandmother. Neda smiled an exaggerated smile wondering at the solemnity of the family group, trying hard to melt them all into something more light-hearted. Nizar felt himself far removed from her world of innocence and could not return her smile. She won instead a loving rub of her curly head from her grandmother and settled back between her and her mother. From this place of safety, she struck a more thoughtful, imitative pose, taking her cue from Nizar who took his from his grandfather.

Hassan suddenly spoke with great decision: "I will take Nizar fishing with me tomorrow. Don't worry. I'll avoid the banned area, too far out for me. I go the safe way."

Nizar became more acutely aware that it was his grandfather who had authority, that it was the women who must demure to his intent, even if they disapproved. He also saw that it was his mother as the foreigner who was the most distanced of all from his grandfather's authority. He loved his mother, but his love for her must now be circumscribed by a manly assumption of distance from things female, as well as things foreign. It was his grandfather who would nurture him from now on. Hassan took him aside and kept him apart in the formal lounge where male guests were entertained. Nizar looked back as he left the family room and observed his mother's face stained with dried tears and strained for not being able to hug him as she wished she could.

Chapter 3

The saint's shrine

"The bird has gone." Hassan muttered, more to himself than to Nizar who was too eager for the motor to be started to notice the strangeness of the remark. The engine burst into life with a shudder and the boat was off. They were cruising and the motor too noisy for conversation. Nizar was exhilarated by the feel of speed beneath his feet and in the air around him. But the sensation was curdled by fear; he was forging yet another secret with his grandfather. This was the first sea trip he had made with him, and some of the sea was forbidden.

Any first experience is impressive but this one was marked with an additional frisson for Nizar because it had given him a status that took him away from the women. This giving of greater scope to the boy-man seemed to take something away from the girl-woman, his sister. There was a spike in the cocktail of being both separated and favoured all in the one moment. It drew a definite line between the two conditions of male and female. But the excitement he felt was accompanied by a new unease. This was a preview of manhood, a perspective which his grandmother, his mother and his sister could never have. He knew they were unhappy with his grandfather's plan but imagined it was simply their regret at his growing apart from them.

Nizar leaned over the side of the boat, trailing his bruised hand in the salt water. He watched the spray rise up against the prow. It mesmerised him. He did not notice the coastline change so when he did look up at his grandfather's cry of pleasure, a cove had already opened up before them. It was a sandy beach spread out apron-like below gently sloping hills. The cove was a crescent curve guarded at its wide mouth by narrow sandbanks. They needed to take care because the banks were hidden, submerged just below a gently undulating surface that rolled incessantly to the beach, never gaining a higher reach. Hassan turned the motor off. The engine spluttered to a stop and the silence in its wake drew attention to just how noisy their approach must have been. He navigated the boat carefully along the gullies gaining traction with an oar until they reached a shallow stretch and the boat was carried by the momentum of the waves to the shore.

Looking upwards under shading hands, they saw how the dazzling white beach give way to earthy slopes, patchy with grass that had faded in the sun. A rough stone track led up to a small white domed shrine. Nizar led the way to it, full of energy, invigorated by the midday heat of an autumnal day. Their presence was ignored by the long-haired goats browsing on low bushes or standing on their hind legs to reach the lowest branches of trees. Boy and man moved through the landscape like ghosts, the only sound being the crunch of pebbles underfoot. Their skins were moist and shiny in the humid air.

The walls surrounding the shrine were draped with tattered cloths stained pale terracotta from recent sandstorms. They were the prayers and appeals of pilgrims to the local saint, Sidi Bu Fakhra, who rested in his tomb under the dome. The cloths did not move but their torn shreds gave evidence of the violent energy of the gales that blew in winter over this exposed terrain. Thistles grew round the walls and there was the heady smell of wild oregano.

They stood outside awhile catching their breath. Nizar turned round to take in the view, the shrine and all the hillside that it nestled in. He asked, in breathless bursts of whispering, still breathing heavily from the rapid climb, what this place could be. His grandfather explained it was a special place where a holy man was buried, a man who had been much revered by all the tribes for his wisdom and learning. A man so revered that many generations after his death people still came to tell him about their worries and asked for his intercession in their prayers. The little cloths signified the different worries people had brought to him. But Hassan admitted he had not yet hung his own prayer flag. He was unsure of his own connection to the saint, he explained.

"Come," he said, "let's go inside."

Hassan led Nizar through the low entrance and into the dark cavern. He lowered his head to accommodate his height to the low ceiling. Inside the air was cool. With Nizar following he slowly paced the sanctified narrow space around the tomb. There was barely room enough for his bulky frame to manoeuvre the corridor around the monumental rectangular block that held the saint's body. Nizar heard his grandfather pray and whisper his son's name many times over. His breathing and whispers echoed over each other around the tomb. Nizar could imagine that they emanated from the tomb itself. He lingered at the threshold of this enclosed and filled space that reverberated with his father's name – Saad, Saad, Saad. He stayed at the entrance waiting for his grandfather to emerge. Warm air touched him softly on the one cheek and chill air from the tomb touched him on the other. Hassan emerged at last with moisture standing in beads on his forehead. Nizar could not be sure if there were also tears in his eyes.

Nizar could clearly see the blue raised veins that lined Hassan's temples and rippled down his hollow cheeks. His eyes were deep-set in their sockets and made him look weary even as he urged his grandson to go inside and make his own prayers there.

Nizar did not dare to pray or whisper. He touched the cold stone of the tomb. Its solid mass towered above him and its shape seemed so abstract in form that he struggled to imagine that it held a man who once had been alive. Could his father be in such a place? The thought made him feel cold.

He joined his grandfather outside the shrine. He was sitting on some bare hard earth some little distance away. He looked dependable and unperturbed as he delved deep into his pocket and fetched out a handful of unshelled nuts. Nizar waited for him to crack them open with his teeth. He would have to wait until a fair number were assembled before he would be given some. There would be no talking until all the shells were despatched; most were stubborn and had to be smashed open with a stone. There were many questions he was burning to ask, some that he had stored away for a long time and others that were new and all the more urgent for their newness. They were questions with answers likely to be too fearful to be asked in ordinary circumstances; but now was not ordinary and so they tumbled out, uncensored.

"Where is my father, Jeddi? Where have they taken him? I saw a villa yesterday. Omar took me there. It's where they torture people. Is that where my father is? With Omar's father? He's there, isn't he? He's being tortured there, I know. Is my father in that villa too?"

Hassan was not prepared for such questions. He was shocked that a child had learnt about such matters. This was not what he had intended for their precious time together. Nizar saw the bewilderment in his grandfather's eyes before he averted his gaze. He noticed then how his shoulders drooped, his chest caved in, as if all life had been taken from him. He saw how he let his hands drop the smashed shells he had scooped up with the intention of tipping them into his pockets – it being essential to leave no trace of their visit to this place, or so he said. Nizar had not imagined that thoughts expressed aloud could be so shocking. Neither did he guess that adults only fleetingly acknowledged such painful matters before banishing them altogether from their thinking.

Hassan reached forwards to place his hands heavily on Nizar's shoulders. "Who put these ideas in your head, Nizar? We don't know about such things. Ridiculous even to imagine. You mustn't listen to your friend. No one would want to harm your father. Allah will take care of him, my child. Trust in Allah. Believe me, your father is safe. Or we would know. How would Omar know all this crazy stuff?"

Nizar was not so easily rebuffed. He had all of yesterday's punishment still freshly imprinted on his hands, the grazed palms and the bruised knuckles. Yesterday had been a brutal day. And so he told the full story of Abla Fawzia's reign of terror, of Omar the wretched one who could not read, of his exclusion by his peers and of the poor neighbourhood he lived in. He described the villa with the honeysuckle where terrible deeds were done. And then he ended with his greatest fear:

"Is my father the enemy..? If he is, would Allah still look after him..? What is the enemy..? Abla Fawzia said we are the enemy, so will we be punished..? Is it wrong to keep secrets? Is that why they took him away?"

This and much more the child asked of the old man. It was a confused collection of misunderstandings and innocence. Out of consideration for his grandson's troubled mind, Hassan answered with a measured gentleness. He saw that he had neglected him; wallowing in his own self-pity as father, he had not considered the pining of the son. He thought it best not to answer Nizar's enquiry challenge by challenge, for fear his words would be repeated in an unsafe place, perhaps at school where Abla Fawzia would come to hear of them. He abandoned his usual dogmatic posturing and spoke simply, seeking to protect his grandson where he had not been able to protect his son.

"I don't know who has put these worrying thoughts into your friend's mind. It seems very unwise to have done this and so I think I must explain things better to you. I know I haven't talked much about it. I haven't spent much time with you at all. I could have told you more about the *sura* but there wasn't time, you see. But you have got it all wrong. Perhaps you didn't understand your teacher. Oh yes, I see you shake your head. But listen to me first and then have your say and after that I will tell you a story.

"Abla Fawzia understands it seems only one kind of enemy. Those who don't agree with her. Those who don't support her friends, those who stand aloof and criticise. She thinks she and all her friends are right and so Allah must be on their side. And they are powerful because they have the army and everything on their side. And so they must be right, she thinks. She thinks power is good because then the strong can do what they want with the weak. When they have power, they can make everyone on their side. It seems simple to her.

"Now Omar your friend is weak, she thinks, because he can't read. That's true isn't it? She believes this gives her even more right to do what she wants with him. She is a foolish woman who disregards even the law since she is not supposed to use the stick. But she is powerful, so she can break the law. She is not the only one. No one stops them, you see. Perhaps she picks on you because she knows you have no father to defend you, no one who will dare to complain. Could that be right?"

"She picks on Omar too, but not because he's weak. It's because he can't read and she can make him look weak. Omar is not weak. He's only weak at school, in her class."

Hassan was impressed with Nizar's insight, more akin to an adult's than a child's. He paused a minute to reconfigure his own position, while he watched Nizar's eyes searching his for reassurance.

"You see, Nizar. There you have it. You don't agree with what she says about your friend, even though she is your teacher and can tell you what to do and what to think. So why should you believe what she says about your father? You see, truth does not necessarily belong to the strongest. That is the problem with truth. Sometimes it needs protecting too, because like people truth can be hurt. So what is there to say about the enemies? Are they the ones who fear the truth? How can we know who they could be? Who then can we trust and who should we be fearful of? Or more important, who should we be loyal to? That is what the *sura* makes us think about. It is a message for us all, not just for the powerful ones like Abla Fawzia. But sometime, we'll read the *sura* together and analyse it piece by piece to find its hidden message.

"But remember. I did not tell you this. You never heard it. You must never repeat my words to anyone. You understand? Good. Now I will tell you a story. It will help you understand more of what I mean."

Nizar settled himself cross-legged, eager to listen.

Chapter 4

The banished poet

"Once, in this beautiful bay, there lived a poet. He was a young man. But that was in the days when fishing boats came to these shores every day and fish were plentiful. Fishing was a real occupation, then. This shore was a sheltered place for trawling with large fishing nets, catches full of jumping fish. The noise of all the fisherman could be heard along the coast and up the hillside where the poet lived in a little wooden shack. I mentioned the poet already, didn't?

"He had not always been a poet of course. He had trained once as a lawyer, dealing in land registration. He used to know every little plot of land, the names of its previous owners, the history of its sale and new ownership, all of which had to be safeguarded against false claimants and usurpers – people who wanted to steal the land.

"That was, as I said, a long time ago. Sadly, the work of a land lawyer was not needed any more because the land was taken by a tyrant all for himself. No one ever asked to see land registry documents any more, and even the lawyer himself, we shall call him Bu Shi'r, was forbidden to practice law ever again. There was in any case nothing left for him to do. The papers in his filing cabinets were just papers after all; they had lost their power to defend the various ownerships they had once established as fact. That old system was swept away by a new regime which disregarded everything that had gone before it.

"One of its very first acts was about land. It gathered every designated piece of land to itself, and then over time divided it amongst its most loyal supporters, as rewards for their service, so that no one had need of Bu Shi'r and he was mainly forgotten. People thought of him as a vagabond, a disinherited son who lived in a hovel with no particular address.

"He did, in fact, live as a recluse and rarely spent time mixing with his fellow men. It was only his closest friend who knew where he lived as a hermit. He knew he was a poet. No one else knew.

"Problem was, he had no paper to write on. So he wrote his poems on the backs of the old land certificates. His poems were hidden or coded by the names of the land printed on the certificates. So, on one side of each paper was a record of land which was not to be remembered, and on the other was a poem which could not be read. The papers were full of secrets, dangerously full of a forgotten history.

"The poet was always meticulous in his shack-house. Everything was ordered and in its place, although he himself looked shockingly scruffy. His appearance was a trick, meant to fool you, you see. It kept people away and that was what he wanted, to be ignored, so that he could go on writing about truth, you see, without anyone ever knowing. His aim was to live without drawing attention to himself, lest the tiny spark of truth be snuffed out. And this worked well for a long time.

"If his name was ever mentioned, it was always with disgust about some aspect of his person, such as his dirty clothes, his crazy mind, or his old bent body. Some remembered him from his better days and spoke with a patronising pity, but either way, he did not care. He was the guardian of truth, and no role could be more noble. It was his lonely destiny to guard it.

"So, he was an old outlaw, witless and demented everybody thought, or else why would he store away as if it was gold this old collection of dusty documents relating to absolutely nothing that was real? He was a misfit, deviant and erring in his lonely vigil, outside family and even community, some might say.

"And so he was left alone.

"But even so, he felt anxious still about the truth. He felt his duty like a heavy stone on his back. He worried about the order of his collection and at frequent intervals re-arranged it, shifting files into new sequences, reclassifying them perhaps by alphabetical order, perhaps by geographical position, or historical precedence, and even – and this was his last most recent system – labelling them according to a hierarchy ranging from most dangerous to most innocuous of his poems.

"This last was the safest method since it defied any obvious logic; time, geography and alphabet all succumbed to the over-riding importance of his poetry. So the filing system seemed chaotic, convenient proof of a failing mind. That pleased him. He worried, you see, because truth is dangerous and must be hidden or men will attack it with great ferocity. As I told you.

"In his vigil for truth, the poet-lawyer was pure and untainted by other men, unworried by beggars, unsought after by sages, not counselled by the new thinkers. He was ignored by every living thing except for the wild creatures of the beach."

Hassan shuffled in his place. Nizar leaned against him, watching his grandfather's hands as they helped with the story, waving this way and that, coming together and opening up in declamation like the wings of a bird.

"Strangely, there was one exception to this," he resumed, "a very learned man, who visited him without warning from time to time. His visits kept Bu Shi'r busy hiding his poems. The learned man was Faiz, a public benefactor who spent all his time helping the blind and the poor, the unloved and the outcast.

"Faiz sat on all sorts of public boards, the board for the local libraries, the board for the Institute for the Blind, the board for the re-integration of beggars, the board for the rehabilitation of prisoners, the board for… oh, so many boards. He judged the appeals of the accused before their sentences were carried out; he found menial jobs for the unemployed and funded the kitchens of hostels for vagrants."

At this point, Nizar was growing restless on the hard, ungiving ground. Hassan realised he had tested his patience and decided to cut to the chase. He didn't bother to add that Faiz was revered by all who gained from his attention, that he was called pilgrim even though he had never made the holy journey. And did so much more in the way of public acts of generosity.

"Any way, Faiz was the only person who treated the poet like a human being," he hurried on. "But still Bu Shi'r didn't quite trust him. He couldn't think why. But when he heard his Mercedes roar to a halt at the foot of the hill, and raise a cloud of dust, he would hurry to hide his poems under a pile of boxes under layers of folded robes and cushions. He would stuff his pen and scraps of paper in the nearest file. Then at the end of each day, he returned every item to its proper place, like lambs to the fold.

"But one day, Bu Shi'r was caught out by unforeseen events following the arrival on his beach of a turtle. A turtle with a soft leathery shell on its back, quite unlike any other turtle he had ever seen had caught his attention. The creature seemed stranded and unable to return to the ocean from which she had come after laying her eggs in the sand. Instead of making for the waves, which female turtles usually do, she turned her head towards the sky, where a bird circled high above her. The bird mesmerised the turtle who stood stock still in the sand, neck craning upwards.

"The poet returned to his shack to write about this uncommon event in his diary. He had barely completed the entry when the bird itself flew into his room and settled on his desk disturbing the papers. It seemed upset. He touched the bird and calmed it down so that it appeared to fall asleep. Now the poet felt the urge to write a poem about the bird feeling out of place, just like himself.

"The poem was still incomplete when the bird swooped out through the door and flew in a straight line over the hill and down its incline towards the beach. That very same hill it was, over there." Nizar followed his grandfather's pointing, surprised that the story was suddenly so real.

"The poet followed the bird to the beach and realised the bird was following the turtle who was swimming in the water below. Both bird and turtle were heading in the direction of the war zone, just down there further down the coast. A place banned to all fishing boats. The poet worried about the turtle getting hurt, especially because of its soft leathery back. But there was nothing he could do. More worried about the poem left on his writing desk, he left them both and hurried up the hill to his shack.

He knew all was not well. An army truck was waiting at the bottom of the hill. A soldier was standing at the entrance to his shack and brandishing a piece of paper which was his unfinished poem. They had ransacked his room, and found many more poems hidden there.

"'You are an enemy of the state!' they screamed at him and denounced him as a traitor, fastening him roughly into handcuffs. They dragged him down the hill and threw him on the floor of the truck just like a sheep.

"They questioned him about the meanings of his poems written in a style they could not fathom.

"'Why do you write nonsense?' they asked. 'You seem to go to a lot of trouble to make it impossible for anyone to understand what you write. What messages do you hide in your riddles? We can only suppose that you are an enemy of the people.'

"The poet refused to translate his poems. He knew they would not understand them in any case, even when interpreted. So they took him away and put him a cell, and left him there all alone for two months. He was visited by Faiz, his noble friend who had, it seemed, urged his tormentors to be more gentle with him.

"Then, when the poet's health was dangerously failing, Faiz at last arranged to pay the fine that released him. Faiz reasoned that this little interlude would be a lesson for the poet but suspected that his isolation had further impaired his sanity. If that is the case, he thought, justifying his own actions to himself, he will certainly be safe in future because everyone will finally be convinced that he has indeed taken leave of his senses. No- one will ever be interested in his poems again.

"They were after all, you remember, the poems that must never be read."

Hassan paused a while. This last point seemed quite sad and needed a respectful silence.

"But that is not the end," he added, rubbing Nizar's curly head to be sure he was listening still.

"The poet still writes, now even more obscurely than before. No one understands him and his mind wanders from one thing to another, a jumble of testimonies about injustices long since forgotten and new ones not yet known.

"But he made a lot of sense once when he sat by the sea, sharing thoughts with a passing fisherman. He had been looking about in vain for the turtle, hoping she would return to lay her eggs like she had done before. The fisherman said he had seen a turtle answering to her description further up the beach. It had been accompanied by a bird wheeling in the sky above. But sadly it was dead and lay among the debris of discarded shells and shrapnel, its leathery back slashed by cruel cuts, from a ship's rudder, he supposed."

Nizar was startled. "That is very bad," he said angrily.

"Well, the fisherman did go on to explain that the turtle had strayed into unknown territory. Such turtles were never found in these parts. It had wandered off from its own kind. 'Like me,' the poet said to the sailor. 'It must have found its own way. That's a very lonely journey. And a dangerous one. But don't say I said so.'

"The fisherman kept the poet's confidence. He felt honoured the poet had trusted him, you see."

There the story ended. There was no more to say. The tale was cruel in the starkness of the turtle's fate. Too cruel for a child. But Nizar's new understanding of the world around them would not have been satisfied with a trite and happy ending, Hassan had understood that.

He continued with a kind of summing up: "You see, it isn't easy to know who is friend and who is enemy. Or to know the truth. The poet, was he really mad? Was Faiz a friend or had he grassed to the police on the poet? The fisherman was a stranger; but was he not also a friend, honoured as he was by the trust the old poet placed in him? Who seems like a friend might be an enemy and who seems like a stranger or an enemy might be a friend. In the same way, your father is not the enemy as Abla Fawzia says. He is someone to be proud of, because like the poet he loves the truth. And that is dangerous, as we now know."

"'Is the poet still alive?" asked Nizar.

"There are always poets when truth is in danger. The poet lives on. Only poets are not called poets, they are called The Enemy or Traitors. I think of them as poets. But, Nizar, I have trusted you. Remember, this afternoon is a secret," he said. "The shrine, the story, this place. We did not come here. I did not tell you this story. And because you are a man just like the fisherman, you will keep this secret because it is a test of your manhood."

Nizar pondered on this obscurity, this riddle and his grandfather's contradictions. He was not sure that his question had been answered. This new secret was yet another burden which he decided must be paid for by his grandfather with a promise.

"I will keep the secret but only if you make me a promise in return. Which is, you must find my father. You will search for him and never give up, no matter how hard."

Hassan was taken aback as much with the assertiveness of his grandchild as by his shrewd bargaining. By way of making a pact with him, he squeezed his grandson's hands tightly in his own, feeling the greatness of his mission in the smallness of a child's hand.

"That is a promise," he said.

"But is the poet alive? You didn't say."

"I think he may have died, sad to say. I have heard nothing of him for some time."

Chapter 5

Promises

In the brief time Hassan and Nizar had been away, the world had turned again. Salem and Salha had arrived and were standing with the family in the orchard as Hassan and Nizar came through the orchard.

"What's all this?" Hassan mumbled, irritation clearly registering in his voice, his discomfort erupting in his shortness of breath. "That's all we need," he muttered.

But Nizar noticed two goats tethered to a pomegranate tree and wondered at their meaning. "Might be something good, Jeddi. Might be something good." Hassan shook his head, meaning he doubted it. Nizar read the scene more favourably. His sister skipped a figure of eight around her mother and the goats with a playfulness he had not seen before. Salha was dressed radiantly, her clothes gleaming even in the shade of the fig tree. The way she stood there so confidently arms akimbo and face awash with smiles gave an impression of regal graciousness. It only irritated Hassan all the more.

From closer up, it was evident that Salem was about to be the proud deliverer of some good news, hopeful beyond their wildest dreams. He had discovered where Saad was held.

"Hassan, they've found him! They've found him and he's okay. They've found him and Salem can arrange a visit. Just imagine! Look what he has done! Thank Allah, they have found him safe and sound." It was Fathia's delighted voice calling him.

Hassan was stunned by the news, bowled over by his wife's jubilation and then confused by competing emotions: an irrepressible joy mingled with a cloying sense of unmet obligation, his own. His suspicious turn of mind made him wonder at the contacts Salem must have made, but it seemed ridiculously churlish at this juncture to question his authority.

Besides, indebtedness together with a sense of shame were effective pacifiers. And so he lingered at an unfriendly distance, standing back, not rushing forward to greet his brother-in-law as Fathia had expected.

Salem seemed offended by his reticence and walked away to dissipate his anger. He may have meant to indicate a wish to leave, but Salha was so obviously enjoying her role that he relented. Hassan too thought better of his coldness and summoned up the strength to express his gratitude and ask where Saad was being held. Salem for his part was not prepared to divulge the location just yet. How it rankled Hassan that Salem should be privy to this crucial detail and then withhold it from the anxious more deserving father.

Nizar had begun take note of how adults postured and jostled for position. He knew that they never quite said everything they were thinking, but held back those thoughts that were secret, difficult or not ready for an airing. His grandfather's promise seemed to have been overtaken by events which he could not control. Someone else, a younger man, had more influence, was better at making things happen. He felt his grandfather's loss of authority as a loss of dignity, which made no sense since he should be pleased, doubly so for in a small way he was released from the pact they had made only hours ago. Instead he looked perplexed and it was obvious that he was reluctant to greet Salem with much gusto.

There was another layer of perplexity for Nizar – a worry about the responsibility of keeping a secret. He felt he was still bound to keep his side of the bargain – he must tell no one that they had sailed along the coast to visit a saint's shrine and pray for his father. He would try to forget the rambling story. That would be easy – it was so long his mind had wandered anyway. It was in any case way above his head for the most part. Something about a poet, that much he could remember, who wrote dangerous words, so dangerous he was imprisoned for writing them, and kept them hidden. He wondered what kinds of words could be so dangerous, or so compelling that they must be written down despite the risk.

In contrast, his mother's mood was upbeat. An unfamiliar loveliness burnished her thin wan face. He guessed it was a loveliness born of loving denied for so long but now promised yet again. She held Neda close and looked across at him, communicating with her eyes. He regretted the inexplicable chasm that had opened up between them and passed close by to brush against her skirt. Then she hugged him, and he did not mind the show of affection from this foreign woman who was, after all, his mother.

Chapter 6

Strange seeds

There was no certain date for the visit. Salem could not even say where Saad was. But they trusted him. He would have good intelligence and surely would not mislead them. Even so, Fathia was cautious. Hassan detected a certain quietness in her bearing. Her initial excitement did not register in her eyes for long. Seeing her subdued, Hassan was predictably more voluble in his criticism.

"It's like I said," he insisted, keen to drive the point home. "Salem likes to sound important. Makes a lot of noise. And delivers nothing."

A fit of pique, Fathia thought and chided him for his scorn. "Well, at least someone is trying to do something. Which is more than I can say for you. And it was bound to be Salem who made the first move. He has the contacts which you don't, now be fair."

Hassan did not argue. He merely nodded. After a length of silence had passed, sufficient to let the truce between them take root, he said, "I just don't want to be disappointed. We haven't even got a date. We are still waiting for one, and how many days is it now? And does he really know anything? Like where he is, how he is? Not even the smallest piece of information. So how close is he really to finding him?'

"It has been almost a week. You are right. But I'm going ahead with my plans. A few guests for an afternoon, just one, that's all."

Hassan frowned but before he could chip in, she added, "Hajja Sana has asked to visit. She wants to wish me well, especially since her son has just been released. He was with Saad and some others, so she says. She may have information. Her son's wife will come with her, a foreign woman, like

Sally. We have lots in common. It would be rude to turn her away, now wouldn't it?"

Somehow this last piece of information satisfied Hassan and he gave his approval.

And so a few chosen guests, including Hajja Sana, arrived one afternoon. The guests' lounge had been furnished with the best cushions all plumped up, tables dusted and polished. The best silver tea tray was prepared, draped over with a silk crocheted cloth. Fathia prepared the charcoal burner with an aromatic resin of frankincense heating on a tin plate, pleasantly giving off its protective vapours.

When the women had settled and reintroduced themselves to Sally, and then the foreign woman, Hajja'Sana's daughter-in-law, there was a slight chilly pause, caused by Sally's obvious surprise. The foreign woman was Eva. It was Eva's husband who had now been released, before any of the others or so it seemed, on which fact was not wise to dwell. Eva's knowing smile was itself a kind of closure on the question of her letter written long ago.

Eva spoke English well and so they chatted together, though with some awkwardness, first about the letter being Eva's intention to bring Sally over, and then about the other men who were still imprisoned. Eva had no idea where they were. She could tell Sally nothing of their prison conditions, only that they were all alive. Quite how she knew even that was not at all made clear. Her husband had been in a separate block, she said, and not been allowed to make contact with the others, including Saad. And yet he had been certain they were well. With no news to the contrary, it was best to think it so.

Eva made a fuss of the children. Her own child, left with a sister-in-law, was younger as Sally knew. She said they must come and visit, and once Saad was free their two families could spend a day together on a picnic. Eva was keen to turn the topic to something neutral and asked if Sally was interested in growing indoor plants, since most of the foreign wives shared seeds or plants. She had some she could give away, like a sweet potato plant, just sprouted, and some castor oil seeds. She would drop them round when she was passing by one day soon. Sally warmed to the idea. Eva could be a friend after all. She had been wrong to doubt her.

When the guests had gone, it was clear that Fathia was pleased to have met another woman with a foreign daughter-in-law and whose son had despite that been returned to his family. She was pleased Sally had a friend. It seemed less foolish now to be hopeful for Saad, and she had fully justified the expense of the occasion. Through Eva, Sally would make contact with more women in the expatriate community. They would be mostly wives of Libyan men, and quite safe.

Eva dropped by a few days later, with the sweet potato plant and some castor oil seeds, as promised. Sally held the dark shiny seeds in the palm of her hand, then placed them carefully on the top of a tall cupboard, away from the children's sight and reach. She would have to ask some colleagues at the college how to germinate them. She knew nothing about castor oil plants.

Hassan, however, was not impressed with the lack of information from the afternoon visit. Nothing meaningful had transpired from his point of view. Precious money had been spent, for no obvious gain.

Chapter 7

Prison visit

Another week passed before Salem called in with news of a date. But on the day, at the agreed time, his chauffeur came alone, which surprised Hassan. He would not be taking them to visit Saad after all but came only to explain that the visit had been cancelled, hopefully just postponed, Allah willing, to another day.

Hassan would have preferred Salem to have had the courage to deliver the disappointment himself. The chauffeur's manners were impeccable but his words hurt deeply. Not pausing for a minute, he drove away at speed, the wheels of his saloon car churning a spit of stones and a cloud of dust in its wake. The family gathered round Fathia who did not move from where she had stood at the open gate to receive him, facing onto the barren space beyond.

Nizar ran out through the gate and watched until the car disappeared down the avenue of trees and into its deep foliage. And then he waited a little longer, not wanting to find joy gone from his mother's face or to see his grandmother's shock. Her sobs were strange, strangulated, more a moan than a cry, so deeply stored that they pained her visibly. He tried to support her as she leaned heavily on his shoulder, holding one hand to her heart. Neda held onto her pleated skirts.

Hassan was too choked for words. He held back his chafing "I told you so," and tried to find some words of comfort. Just now, words could not do sympathy. "Bastards," was all he mustered; but, if words could only curse, better to be silent. So all words seeped away like rain on parched earth. He touched Fathia gently on her shoulders. He did not try to catch her gaze. As he turned away, Neda, still holding close to her grandmother, caught his blank expression, his empty eyes, sunken in their darkened sockets. His jaw was set against the impulse of adding to his last remark. *Bastards* hung on the air, as he made his shuffling way to his bedroom retreat.

Nizar was secretly angry. Why did everyone depend so much on Salem? His promises were always hollow and empty. Cruel, he thought. In the following weeks, new dates came and went without success, each one delivered by Salem's driver. He noticed how his grandfather's face became gloomy as the baskets were being filled, provisions tightly arranged in the baskets . He saw his lacklustre when he tried to encourage the women in their preparations with a damning "Bravo, Bravo." It was the kind of faint praise he usually reserved for children.

Nizar understood his grandfather – he was beginning to feel the same himself. But still, his mother baked cakes and stored them in tins, clearly meant for his father. And always on the day before the hoped-for visit, the baking was more frenetic than ever, so that he knew this was the day. Then the hour came and went, each time as before.

However, one afternoon, there came another date, this one more believable than the others, if the new enthusiasm it caused was anything to go by. Salem had come himself, insisting that nothing would go wrong this time. This time he could tell them where Saad was. His own chauffeur would take them to an old Italian-era prison, on the outskirts of Benghazi. It was not as far away as they had feared and knowing the place gave them reason to believe Saad was going to be alright.

As before, they filled the baskets, enough for forty men, including Saad: honey cake and roasted nuts, spicy fillets of fish and slices of potatoes filled with minced lamb and herbs, apples stored through winter, green tea from China, soap and biscuits from Holland, rosewater for perfuming blankets, incense sticks and gum arabic from Mecca. They were all packed lovingly, eased and patted into place, and covered with checkered kitchen towels, then placed at the side gate waiting for the appointed hour.

Neda sat on the steps near the baskets, and waited. The side gate opened onto a road that passed under the eucalyptus trees and met the bigger road that ran alongside the army base. The sun was reaching higher up the sky, hidden now and then by fast-moving clouds. The garden cat came to sit beside her, smelling food no doubt. She loitered round the baskets. Neda felt she had company.

Then the chauffeured car drew up and seemed about to stop but didn't. The engine roared as it backed closer to the gate. In the same instant, the cat leapt up and ran under the chassis where it was caught by a nearside wheel and carried round the tyre in the traction. The car stopped. The cat was lying still in the gutter. The chauffeur had felt the hump of something unexpected, a small shudder. He stepped out as Neda screamed, "The cat! You hit the cat!" The chauffeur was dumbfounded. "It isn't yours, is it?" he asked.

"No, just a wild cat," Hassan said, emerging from the house, trying to defuse the situation. "But the children feed him." There was no consoling Neda.

They set off as quickly as they could to move things on. Sally held Neda close in her lap. With three adults, two children and many baskets, the car was very full. They travelled in silence, partly feeling shocked, the cat's death seeming ominous, an omen, and partly because they were reserved in front of a stranger – Salem's chauffeur was so very stern, not friendly like Mohamed Al Sudani, their own.

At the prison they found other visitors already arrived and gathered in family groups. Many were from Al Baitha, some with trucks being farmers. Their shaky hopes were confirmed by such a congregation. They gathered to one side of the main entrance, in small family groups, dwarfed by the sprawling backdrop of the prison building. The land around it was a wilderness, untended, full of weeds, and rampant prickly pear bushes. A cement wall marked the boundary, tall enough to obscure the prison from the road. It was a single-storey construction with no adornment whatsoever, no windows looking out. Standing apart like an afterthought there was a mosque, a concrete block. Its minaret so low it could not be seen. Its windows were darkened glass and barred with iron grills. These forlorn structures, hardly architecture, stood alone in the great expanse of a flat plain, squat against the earth. It was featureless and so without design or imagination that the human spirit dropped.

The main door was the focus of attention. It was made of metal mostly and large enough to allow military trucks to pass through when open. It was shut. Set within it was a small wooden door of more human proportions, and within its frame there was a chink that moved inside a metal casement. The crowd waited for one or other of these devices to open. They waited for the tiniest of movements or quietest of footsteps emerging from behind the door. Feet could be seen bobbing at ground level, in the gap between the gate and the ground. They could hear voices shouting, the volume set to military function, and the rattling of keys not set in locks but dangling or shaken.

They waited and exercised a little, shuffling places. The men passed time making solemn greetings, their initial enthusiasm gradually reducing with increasing premonition of a cancellation. The women were more reserved, but made polite exchanges with other women they had met at weddings, funerals and births. The men meandered round their families forming a protective circle. Some were surprised to discover who was in their company, who else like them had a son detained, perhaps only now daring to declare their involvement. They were comforted by the knowledge they were not alone. They felt less defiled and ventured out to speak with each other, giving comradely hugs and hearty handshakes.

Then they turned as one at the sound of metal bolts sliding in their shafts and the grinding noise of heavy doors turning on their hinges. They moved forwards not having seen three trucks that had slowly trundled down the tarmac path. An officer jumped out of one of them and showed his papers to a guard who appeared at the gap between the opening doors. The trucks were waved in and they rolled slowly into the great dark chasm inside the prison. The doors were closed behind the trucks and locked with a prolonged sequence of moving parts, of bolts jamming shut.

Chapter 8

The prisoner

The prisoner lay on a thin foam mattress. Confined by the dimensions of the cell, he could not accommodate his body extended fully, nor was he at rest. The mattress was a little longer than the cell, so that it must bend up the wall at one end, subtracting from the length of the cell. The prisoner could only lie on his side with legs bent at the knees – a rigid pose he kept for long hours, inducing pain in the joints. He could vary his position pulling his knees right up to his chest or placing the soles of his feet on the filthy ceiling where spiders hung their webs. These were some of the few positions the prisoner might adopt – there were others he could use to flex his muscles, searching for relief from cramp and easing aching bones.

Along the length of the cell at ground level was a metal grill just high enough for him to identify the feet of those who passed by. High enough to see the grill of an opposite cell of similar proportions. Unoccupied, they deepened his sense of isolation.

Footwear was a guide to the personality of the passing being. It might be the bare or sandalled feet of a fellow prisoner, or the sturdy shoes of gaolers. Less often seen were the combat boots of soldiers and at other times the buffed leather of those who came to torment him.

The grill was a source of air, stale air, but air nonetheless; and drafts, cold drafts that indicated an opened door, drafts that chilled the prisoner to the marrow. Grills were the two-way conduit for perfunctory orders and insults, and the prisoner's unheeded pleas. Mainly the communication was one-way, the prisoner having given up on seeking pity. Alongside the grill, a drainage grid provided a route for rats that wandered through the maze of similar cell blocks in this 'could-not-be a building' sort of holding place. Cockroaches hid in cracks in the walls and flew through the grills. Sometimes they were brushed in by the careless cleaner along with the filthy prison swill.

Only the prisoner knows the fears that haunt the solitary isolation cell, living ghosts that demean and humiliate, the nightmares that make him cower in its inhuman space. Only the prisoner keeps a memory of the threats. Fears like conspiracies flutter in his mind, like birds with clipped wings.

Outside the family groups still waited, weary and apprehensive. A chink appeared in the metal aperture with a clatter of its moving parts. Two expressionless eyes, divested of their human face, moved in the metal sockets, observing the gathering of visitors, registering how they moved forwards triggered by the smallest of movements, each with their loaded baskets lifted from the ground in anticipation. They inched forwards, straining their ears.

The officer on his way to the prisoner, and who had handed in the papers at the gate, did not speak to the guard on duty at the next door, nor to the guard at the third. He unlocked and locked again the doors with his own set of keys. He stopped to light a cigarette partway down a passage and as he did so dropped his keyring with its elegant silver fob. He stooped to lift it from the dirt floor, wiping it and his hands on his trouser legs. The next door was already unlocked. The guard behind it clicked his heels and stood to attention, pressing himself flat against the wall to let the officer pass by. The officer stopped briefly at an office to register his visit. Then he pushed through two more doors turning left and then right, this way and that, pleased that he could recall so easily the twists and turns of the maze. He paused to stub his cigarette out on the wall and then to flatten a running cockroach with the heel of his boot. He hated cockroaches.

An old woman, frail and emaciated, stepped out of her family group, not minding that her head covering had slipped to her shoulders. She approached the great door and stretched her arms in a gesture so wide in its reach that it swept both the earth and the sky. An arc of yearning. The chink in the great door closed with a reverberating ring. An old man moved to shield her, uttering a blessing as consolation.

Nizar broke away from his mother's side and hurled abuse at the iron door. He shook his fist at the empty air. No one had the will to restrain him.

At the next door, the officer felt for a handle which was not there. It had not been there last time either. Irritated by the disrepair of his surroundings, he kicked the door open. The door swung easily on its hinges but he had exerted such force that the handle on the other side hit the wall behind and chipped away at its crumbling brick and mortar, falling then to the ground with a heavy clink. He lit another cigarette and in the flare of his lighter saw the rubble on the ground, and the festering pool that collected under a dripping pipe. It protruded through the decaying wall unfinished and unexplained. Fecal droppings indicated the pool was a watering hole for rats. His cigarette failed to light. He walked on to the next door that hyphenated this infested corridor. It struck him that for a prison, this was a shambolic sort of construction, a series of underground tunnels extended at random, with no particular design. It was worthy of its inhabitants, he thought.

Once on the other side of the metal door, he paused. A flare lit up his face as he made another attempt at his cigarette. It flickered over his unhealthy complexion, and he squinted in the light. Here he met the prison guard working the daytime shift. Together they walked in step, left down another turning, this one lit by a well of light in the roof. The guard opened yet another door and his hand offered the officer entry. The place was dimly lit but when his eyes adjusted he could see the battery of cells on either side, each with a metal grating for ventilation at ground level. Some of them were empty. One was not. He would not bend down to observe the condition of the prisoner. He would merely interrogate the hole.

"Where is my father? What have you done with him?" It was a child's voice so justly pertinent and full of righteous indignation that its pitch was almost adult and yet more compelling for not being adult.

The chink moved again. Two eyes searched for the owner of the insolent challenge. Hassan stepped forwards as volunteer spokesman for all the families. He held Nizar close to protect him. The voice behind the chink asked him to wait while instructions were sought from the governor. The chink was closed. Maybe the eyes felt embarrassed by a child's reprimand. Perhaps he was a father himself. Or maybe he was manoeuvring to play for time, to give the impression that he could not act alone without orders, or to extricate himself from his duty. A small amount of time passed, perhaps sufficient for an internal phone call. The eyes reappeared at the chink and the voice attached to them explained that the governor knew of no instruction to allow the prisoners visits of any kind that day.

"We have your son with us, prisoner. Waiting just two rooms away. Waiting to see you, call you Daddy, waiting to embrace you. It can all be yours. For just one small favour. Easily paid in kind, one turn for another. How could you refuse him? He thinks you have deserted him. He thinks maybe you don't exist anymore. But I told him. I said. You're here. Here with me. I'm looking after you, being nice and kind to his daddy.

"So just confess. You are a traitor. You married a slut, a dirty foreigner. You just wanted to subvert the state and against the rules, married a foreigner. Say you will divorce her to prove you are a patriot, for your kid's sake, disown her. She has deserted you in any case. You didn't think she'd stay here did you? Didn't think she would be faithful, dirty foreigner? She's done like they all do, and gone away. We made sure of that. Just say the magic words and you can see your son. If not I'll have to send him away myself. Might worry him a bit, might rough him up. Slap him. Abuse him if I wish. In any case, I'll send him away unless you tell me otherwise. Up to you now."

The metal aperture had spoken. It took a few seconds to take in its denial, its lie, its blatant lie. Hassan turned around to face the gathering. They had understood. The men uncomplaining, not daring to complain, ushered the women and children into their various vehicles; farmers' trucks, lorries, well-used family estates.

Fathia stood at the roadside and appealed with a mystical fervour to the young saplings that had found a niche in the stony earth around the prison walls. Trees were nearer to humanity than concrete walls and iron doors. They could be appealed to. Perhaps they were a conduit to a source of influence that a frustrated mother could not otherwise reach. Perhaps their spirits mingled with the spirits of the air and would chance upon a meeting with the Divine, and intercede for her. Never mind that this kind of faith was frowned upon.

Those around her smiled at her superstition. It was an indulgence allowed an elderly woman in the circumstances. Neda watched her grandmother as she stretched out her arms, restrained as they were by the folds of the shawl wrapped around her body and held tightly with teeth to conceal her face from strangers. She opened her palms skywards to show that though she had received nothing, like a good pilgrim, she waited still for Allah's blessing. And as her arms reached upwards, Neda saw a stream of birds pass overhead. Low in flight at first, they circled round and round the prison perimeter in ever increasing arcs, gaining height until they were lost in grey cloud.

"The birds have gone, Jdeidi. Where have they gone to?"

"Don't worry, Neda. Birds come back. They always do. They'll come back next year. They always do, my sweetheart. It's stolen men that don't."

Once in the car, they travelled home under a darkening sky that threatened rain. The quiet engine purred soothingly making the journey seemed unreal. The new dual carriageway passed a power station, a silver-columned confusion rising upwards like the pipes of a giant church organ. It shone briefly as it caught a sunburst through the clouds. Along the way, children and women were gathering dry wood. Some were carrying it in bundles on their heads while others wrapped the branches in bright cloths and balanced them on the backs of their donkeys. They were returning to their tents, which could be seen some distance off, seeming flimsy as they flapped in the wind. Nizar wondered how they endured winter, existing on the edge of the town with very little. Their goats were nibbling at papers wind-blown from urban rubbish heaps. Hens were scratching at a wintry barren earth for seeds; some were crouching in basket cages at intervals along the road, scrawny and unproductive and so for sale. Cows were rummaging in rotting refuse tips, eating newspaper and melon skins, their hides drawn tightly over their skeletal bodies. At one place, a cow floated in a shallow stretch of water, upside down and bloated, its limbs stiff and pointing skywards.

The chauffeur stopped to buy some chickens being sold at the roadside. A young boy sat cross-legged beside some cages. He pulled the live chickens out, grabbing roughly at their flapping wings, and passed them over to the chauffeur who carried them away swinging them by their legs. They did not squawk or move suspended in this way. They were thrown unceremoniously into the boot of the car. The door was slammed shut.

Chapter 9

Hassan's burden

No one spoke about the cancelled visit. Fathia, ever stoic,
unpacked the baskets with a heavy heart and returned the
different items to kitchen store or fridge. When it was done,
she sat at the kitchen table where a handful of flat-leafed
parsley stalks lay on the chopping board. She stifled a long
deep sigh and covered her face with her hands. She rested there
a while and drew her scarf from round her neck to cover her
head, tucking in the few escaped curling wisps of hair. To
Hassan, who had retired to his room, she had said nothing.
Sally and the children sat in silence in the family room, with
the television playing quietly, a romantic serial set in Ancient
Persia, that did not attract her. Nizar had asked her for a photo
of his father and while he watched held it tight, his father
staring out to sea on the coast somewhere in the south of
England.

Hassan stirred from his den for lunch in the kitchen and
spent the afternoon on the jetty looking out to sea. He couldn't
look Nizar in the eye, he couldn't face that questioning that
demanded so much of him. In the villa, he was in Fathia's way.
There was nothing he could do there, and almost nothing in the
world outside the home. He felt diminished. But there was
always the fishing, a risky business, true, but rewarding in a
modest way if he dared; and there was the orchard though not
yet in season. He had checked the trees for pests, and pruned a
few bushes but mostly he left the orchard and kitchen garden to
Fathia. So with nothing to distract him, he moped around on
the beach letting the sea swirl about his idle feet.

He was weighing up the situation. There was still the pact
he had made with Nizar to keep. It haunted him. He needed his
trust for there were no more consoling conversations with his
wife on the veranda, sipping tea together. Her silent criticism

stung him. It was not enough to have his son taken, not enough to be without a livelihood, but now he felt the humiliation of his failure more keenly than ever. He felt interrogated by the questions his family could never bring themselves to ask, and the reasonable expectations of an innocent child were a constant chiding. There was so much he had failed to do.

He knew that it was pride that ruled him. And this was the crux of the matter. He could not find a happy accommodation with the regime, not until his son was returned to him. He had paid a price for his own rebellion and knew that somewhere along the way he could be forced to surrender even more of his independence than he had already. His voice had been silenced, but not his thoughts. There he remained defiant still.

Could his wife, he asked himself, not guess at the terrifying void he was cast into, let alone the unforgiving chiding of his own conscience? Did she understand what havoc six days of incarceration had wrought upon his ageing body? Did she even see how he was down and humiliated by the confiscation of his shop and merchandise? Could she imagine what risks he would be running operating in the black market with dubious anonymous dealers, every deal a necessary loss of value to avoid the risk of betrayal? It hardly mattered that fishing was banned when all up and down the coast west to Ajdabya and east to Derna, Sousa and Tobruk, the fish had migrated for better feeding grounds. Where was he to turn for help?

Left only with despair, and with so little to occupy him, Hassan fell into thinking of the past, not the recent past but the deeper history of his childhood. It too was littered with tragedy and failure, again his own failure, so harsh that the test of his manhood should come when he was barely eight years old when there was occupation and war. The Italians had settled, taking all the best land, some of it his father's.

With his back to the sea, he turned to scan the profile of the plateau, looking for that particular hill. He remembered what had transpired there in all its painful, recriminating detail.

Land mines lie in those very hills. Too distant to make out even on a good day, but a grey gloom ranges over it always in my mind, rises up as gentle as a dove and drops into a dry wadi somewhere out of sight. Now, looking down the coastline, I can see the headland jutting out to sea. And beyond that, more hills I can't see but know are there. Hills my father farmed. Hills that seep into the blue horizon there. And into my memory. Hiding the truth of it. Half-forgotten. Yet not in any way forgotten. How could I forget? Ya, Rub! What rotten memories.

But it must still be there, that little hollow. The place where he fell. The goat track over stony ground. The prickly pear bushes growing rampant. The artichoke grounds where we used to picnic round a wood fire. Collecting firewood, from trees shattered by strong winds off the sea. Quite exposed. The last time I saw him live, he put his face close to mine and warned: "Don't go playing on those hills, son. Full of rubbish they are. Those soldiers play their dance of death as if it was a wedding feast and leave their rotten litter when they go."

"Not all of them are bad," I argued. "We do well out of them for sugar."

"Bah! Sugar we can live without. It's women want the sugar."

"Then there's the cinema. Rani gets me tickets."

"Oh yes, they give us films all right," he had said. "His royal mightiness Il Duce strutting over boundaries. Makes sure he bamboozles us. While grabbing all he can. All that Fourth Shore business. Arrogance I call it."

I remember my father's face, his mouth twisted in disgust. His expression bullish with injured pride. He had pounded the table with his fist and his next remark was without words. Just a look. Straight into my eyes. A look of sadness, really. The skin around them creased like worn leather, weathered tough by the Qibli off the desert.

"Don't go playing there, that's all," he said.

Round the curve of land is the old harbour, now disused. Left to rack and ruin. Crumbling walls, waters choked with sunken ships. No one ever bothered to clear it. The place where big games were played between the nations. We played games too. Oh, blundering games of tug and push, Italy seizes the town. Graziani rules the roost.

Talk of blunders – I did my share, though yet a lad. Me and Rani thought we had it made. Bits of Italian, useful when you needed to placate the soldiers, to get some contraband like cigarettes or sugar. Laugh we did with them. Thought ourselves so grand. The real masters while our fathers kept their distance if they could. Fools we were, thinking we could roam the place like they did, smashing it to bits it was a playground in their own land.

Broke his own rule, didn't he. On that fateful day. Oh, I'm familiar with blunder. It's been a lifelong friend.

"Need you today, son. Need you big time. Lots of produce for market. Takes two donkeys, four basket loads. Takes two to handle two donkeys, you know."

Yes, I am familiar with blunder. Familiar indeed. Complained, didn't I? Rani had two tickets for the cinema, a film 'Four Steps in the Clouds.' Didn't say, 'No'. But slipped away on his own. That day of all days to disobey him.

The cinema was closed, it turns out. Night before, the Italians had up and left, moving west. Early morning there was rumbling in the east, dust rising way far back as far as the eye could see. Rani had a friend who was imprisoned on suspicion of peddling ammunition. He hadn't quite be let free but escaped and came to tell him the prison guard had told them all to scarper. Couldn't keep them any longer in the name of Mussolini. Had to run himself. The streets were empty. Then as sudden as a clap of thunder, the road from Tobruk was filled with all the faces of the world, turbanned brown faces, sunburnt white faces, bearded faces, men walking, men on tanks, men on bikes, engines roaring. Rani and I watched all day.

On returning home, we found father not returned home and were sent to look for him along the goat track, and found him still alive but badly injured, thrown against the earth, leg blown off. Great gaping hole. Donkey dead. Vegetables scattered and rolled down the hillside. We dragged him on a makeshift sled all the way to the Italian hospital. One of those land mines, wasn't it? The rubbish they left behind.

"I'll be okay," he said. "Good doctors there. The nuns brought me into this world. Don't you forget that. Might have died without them." I couldn't tell him the doctors had all run off, along with the retreating Italian troops.

No doctors were there to attend to him. The nuns would never leave. They made him as comfortable as they could. And then he died. Bled to death. Not important that I never got to see the film. There on that brown-grey hill, bright with spring flowers, I let him down. I failed the father who had taken care of me. Can I be forgiven? I was just a boy. I can be wiser as a man. Better now at listening. Better at keeping my word. Worthy of a child's trust.

Hassan saw his grandson's expectations of him as a chance for atonement, a shift of loyalty to a father passed over to a grandson, a debt to repay across the generations. He must turn his face from the past and confront the future.

Part Five – A Breach

Large drops of rain spotted the women as they turned to go their separate ways; but then they dried in the desert wind in the instant of their touch.

Chapter One

Sandstorm

The light streaming into Sally's apartment through the partially opened wooden blinds had dimmed suddenly. At first she thought it must be an approaching raincloud, but this was not the rainy season. She tugged at the cord to raise the heavy blinds as fully as she could and saw the sky was turning rusty brown. A curtain of dust was making its way across tops of buildings in the distance, heading for the wasteland. It dropped its belly and scoured the ground, dragging debris into its mass. It was fast approaching the honeysuckle trails and binds along the garden walls. Soon the view all around would be completely blotted out. She had to rescue the washing hanging out on the washing line.

She rushed down the stone-clad stairwell, catching her breath as the clear air was invaded by the dust. The red cloud had passed over the villa and was sagging into the canopies of the orchard. Soon it would cover the orchard and reach the beach and drop its suffocating talcum out at sea. Hoping to beat the red fog in its approach, she ran to the line and reached up to pull at the pegs.

Something moved beneath her fingers and slid away – it was smoother than the feel of wood, more like plastic, cool and brittle like the back of a beetle. Squinting through the gritty haze she saw it was a locust, pale yellow-green, its hard casing patterned like a moth's wing. Preparing to fly, its body lifted up and filled her view entirely as it launched itself into the drizzle of dust and was gone. Sally shuddered.

As she plucked away at the pegs, the line bounced free each time, hurtling other creatures and sand into the dense cloud. The still damp sheets were fast turning rust in the swirling descent of under-clouds triggered by the swinging arc of blue plastic washing line. In minutes, everything in the garden would be thickly layered with terracotta talc. Green leaves and tiled paths were smothered. Everything was coloured a pale russet brown. Drafts of air corralled the heavier grit and litter into little drifts, filling crevasses and corners.

The bundle of stained washing in Sally's arms trailed behind her sweeping through the sand. The marble staircase was now awash with it. Once inside, she readied the rooms for the storm. Doors onto balconies were firmly shut and sealed with damp cloths. The wooden blinds were shuttered down, as closed as she could make them. The children rolled wet towels and laid them along the window sills and at the foot of the front door. Even so, in the space of an hour the air inside was fuzzy with a rosy mist. The dust seeped in, finger-creeping under doors, through broken blinds and places they had not thought of.

The darkness and uncertainty excited the children. They hid beneath dusty blankets and rugs, playing hide and seek. Excused from school which had closed for the duration and the burdensome task of learning texts by rote, they made their own entertainment, drawing patterns in the dust, smearing mirrors with their sweaty red-stained fingers, beating upholstery to reveal the patterns underneath, watching ants as they struggled over banks of sand in single file, weaving in and round the legs of chairs. In the dusky half-light, they scooped up floating particles from the air, and jumped over alternating lines of shade and light cast by a pink-tinged twilight that poured in through the blinds and shutters.

But as their eyes and nostrils filled with dust, as the floors and walls of their living space became smeared with trails where feet had traced their meandering through the rooms, the delight of strangeness began to pall. Their hair, their faces, their clothes all turned sandy red; and there was no chance of washing clean, no point in changing clothes.

Tap water came only as a dribble and then with a hollow rumble not at all. For some reason the tank on the roof had emptied and would not fill again. Sally was ready for this problem since the supply of water had been intermittent for weeks; she had filled the bath and stored water bottles in the fridge. Now the water in the bath lay still and turgid under a skin of dust. Fathia had called up once or twice to check that they were fine. But on the third morning of the storm, they felt they had been cut off completely from the world outside.

There was a single knock at the door and Sally opened it to find no one there. The soft sand covering the steps in drifts bore the imprints of shoes. Someone had placed a tray to one side of the door – most probably it was Hassan since Fathia could not climb stairs without suffering pain in her chest. There was a dish of stew, covered with a cloth and some little fish-shaped shortbread cakes in a tin. Sally ventured down a short way and called out but her voice would have been muffled by the constant booming of the wind.

She paused at the staircase window halfway down. It had been without its glass for some time, hence the heavy deposit inside. Plants in the garden just below were bowed under the weight of dust. Acacia branches and tumbleweed had accumulated in untidy piles outside the garden walls, stopping where the wind had blown them. Broken twigs of honeysuckle and hibiscus flowers, dry thistle heads with their fluffy seeds long since dispersed, and the empty seed cases of eucalyptus revealed themselves in strangely shaped lumps and knots round the house and filled the grids under drainpipes.

It was as if the desert had come to stay. How would they brush it all away? It must have come first to the outskirts of the town where the flimsy shacks of shanty town offered precious little shelter. The dust and grit had penetrated everywhere from the suburbs to the town centre, into the residential areas and right up to the harbour, obliterating all distinction between the different areas, rich and poor; everything under a single blanket cover, and everything separately confined.

The big front door downstairs slammed. Though it shook the walls, it sounded a long way off. The drop of the metal handle of a bucket set down somewhere in the garden rang like a distant bell. Water gushing from the garden tap hissed like the wind itself, out there in a wasteland of sameness. There were no sounds of birds or wild dogs. If the garden cat had still been there, they would have given it shelter.

Carrying an empty bucket, Sally trod carefully down the slithery steps, feeling with her bare feet for the hard marble beneath the soft talc. She rinsed the bucket at the garden tap and filled it almost full, finding even then that the polluted air had turned it murky. She made several journeys, leaving a wet muddy trail up the staircase. No one it seemed had heard her, nothing stirred in the villa below. Not even Mohamed the gardener was about. A strange sense of being adrift overwhelmed her. She closed the door behind her and leaned against it, exhausted. She would need to dispel the gloominess – time for the box she kept for just such occasions.

Sally's box was full of little things salvaged from the detritus of broken toys and worn clothes, walks on the beach or in the orchard. She was a hoarder of trinkets that for some small reason had a significance that elevated them above the merely mundane or useless. They were the sort of items fortune tellers might keep to throw and read as omens in the way they fall. For Sally they were merely memories, stories to be told.

The children were becoming fractious. So Sally found the box in the bookcase, wrapped in a silken cloth, a gift from Mecca. She turned off the ceiling light with its yellowish glow, and lit instead a candle. Then she placed it on the rug that Saad had bought from Misrata long ago, a stretched-out panoramic margin round an oasis, with palm trees, camels, gazelles and even planes flying across the geometric grid of its pattern. She tipped the box and spread the contents. Then with slow precision lined them up to catch the children's attention; and they nestled up for a session of storytelling.

"Do you remember," Sally began, "we were walking in the forest and you found this cone, Neda?" Sally looked into a distant space where pine trees stood sentinel like arrows to the sky.

"In the forest," Neda echoed; she did not think of trees. "We went with Daddy a long time ago and these? Long time ago too." She took hold of a pebble and hid it in her palm, then let it fall with a heavy drop, "and this?" Neda took a shell, "That's from the beach, isn't it, Jeddi found it by his boat, lots of them, shells, and the feather over there." She reached across the rug.

Nizar took it first, placed it sticking up in his hair at the same time wondering why he did this; a memory of another place perhaps, one he had visited in storybooks. "And this one, too. Daddy made a pen," he said.

Neda shuffled the shell from hand to hand, palms open, and let it rock from side to side. Then she traced its whorled lines in the little pile of sand it had dispensed onto the cloth.

Nizar seized on the broken nautilus shell, its interlinking caverns just showing through the break where it had smashed, a fragment of another world, its occupant was gone. "An animal lived in here. Once. Who broke it?" he protested, looking at his sister.

"Oh, no. It shattered by itself, in the suitcase," said Sally as she fingered a ladybird button salvaged from an outgrown child's dress. Saad had been with them then.

Neda pulled the knitted baby bonnet onto her head, its spindly strap hanging loosely like her curls where it rested on her cheek. Sally watched her and for the moment Neda was once more the new-born infant safely delivered by Saad who had just in time removed the umbilical cord wrapped around her neck. There were other items lingered over, stories told: a metal-coloured aeroplane tumbled from a pulled cracker; some polished pebbles and resin stones, one with a fern-like fossil and another with the body of a wasp-like insect trapped inside, souvenirs from a museum; eucalyptus seed cases from the trees that lined the road up to the villa, collected from the gutters after heavy rain; the pressed petals of hibiscus flowers from the garden; a piece of antique masonry found on the path to the Greek amphitheatre that nestled in the shelter of a mountain slope some miles away. Sally told them how she and Saad had heard a camel moaning there and found it rolling in the shade of a tree within a low stone wall built round it for protection. She told them about the silver leaves of *silphium*.

Beside the antique fragment, a small medallion owl glazed with green enamel, a favourite thing, fell into view. It lacked its silver chain but Sally would find one somewhere. Neda saw her mother slip it into her apron pocket. A drawing of a bean flower, folded now and placed in a small envelope, was passed over. Saad had planted beans in the kitchen garden years before. They grew each year without fail, a memorial to Saad. And there was the hand-made casket constructed from a cigarette packet – inside it lay the butterfly with its wings spread as symbol of freedom to its creator.

"What happened to the camel?" Neda asked. "Did it get better? And what's the story for the owl?"

"Oh, we never found out. I expect she lived, if she was lucky. The owl is just that I love them. Once I saw a picture of a famous artist with his pet owl. It was black and after that I always wanted one just the same. But perhaps it's cruel to keep an owl. It is a free thing after all."

"Is it cruel to put pins in the butterfly's wings?" asked Nizar. "Did Daddy hurt it when he did that?"

"No, your daddy wouldn't hurt it. It was probably dead already and he found it lying somewhere. Most butterflies don't live long, you know. Beautiful for a gift, don't you agree?"

"S'long as it didn't hurt. But it's sad butterflies don't live for ever."

"Nothing lives for ever, Nizar."

"Do we die for ever then?" he asked.

"For ever?" echoed Neda.

"We live for a long time really. There's always lots to do and lots of time to do it in, if you're lucky."

Sally removed the butterfly in its case from the collection and tidied things away. She found a book on butterflies and decided she would make notes. She recorded in detail the markings on the wings. Later that evening, she made a brief note in her diary:

I lifted up one wing very carefully so as not to break it. The under-wing is much paler than the surface pattern. It has soft brown irregular lozenge shapes on a white ground. The tips are shaded dark gradually giving way to pale and deep oranges with warm brown camouflaging spots, and all along the edges there are scalloped white ovals making the wing look fragile, perhaps to waft the air. The eye-spots are dark with amazing turquoise centres, perhaps fading a little now. Do butterfly colours fade?

Next she found a silver chain and threaded the enamel owl onto it.

Chapter 2

The owl

The period after the dust storm was a frenetic time of sweeping, swilling steps, endless dusting, watching dust fly from the duster, wiping walls and beating carpets. Sally learned that soon after leaving the tray of food at her front door, the family had left to stay with Hassan's brother until the storm was over, mainly for company but also because his brother's apartment in a block of flats was more sheltered from the dust and near the shops for ready meals and bottles of water. The chauffeur had driven them there and stayed with friends as did the gardener. Fathia had explained this casually but with a trace of guilt. Sally said nothing to add to her discomfort, even though she knew that leaving a woman on her own was not considered proper. She helped with the clearing and cleaning up in a subdued mood, the initial pleasure of being in company scarred now by the shock of their secret absence. She understood the meal had been an apology, and that there would not have been sufficient room for herself and the children in the car or at Sidi Ahmed's apartment.

After days of tiring physical work, Sally found that her taps, previously run dry inexplicably, were now gushing with water just as inexplicably. She wondered if there was a valve that someone had closed and opened without her knowing, but put the idea away as too disturbing and wildly paranoid. She showered herself with new-found pleasure and oiled her skin. She drank the water from the tap not minding its salty taste, something she had adjusted to, though this had taken time. She put on a long white Egyptian shirt, baggy and airy for extra comfort and hung the little owl pendant round her neck.

The children played in the garden that was losing its spring greenness. She could hear their laughter. Standing on the balcony from her bedroom she called down and attracted their attention.

"Come down," they called.

Fathia stared at her daughter-in-law, standing in the shade of the veranda, her expression a picture of disbelief, her voice low and intense with straining indignation.

"You wear a white dress, Sally. It's the colour of a shroud, a widow's mourning. Are you in mourning for Saad then? And then as if that isn't enough, you wear an owl round your neck. Don't you know about the owl? It makes a call like the sound of women wailing. Think what you are doing! You will bring us all bad luck! Are you trying to tell us Saad is dead?"

Fathia fled into the villa, leaving Sally shamed by the shock of her cultural ignorance.

Chapter 3

The photograph

Fathia decided she had waited long enough for action. She could no longer abandon her son's fate to the capricious whims of destiny. Someone had to find him before it was too late. It really needed a man, operating in a man's world, to do it; but, if no man would, then she would have to use what access she might gain for herself to the offices of power, as a woman in a woman's world.

Throughout the waiting for others to act, she had nursed her memories of Saad, fondled photos, kissed his image, as though through memory she might restore his life to natural justice. But the photos were fading fast, fixed in the slots between the frame and glass of the mirror on her dressing table. The edges of them had curled and split with too much handling, too much touching every prayer time. Sometimes she showed them to her grandchildren, letting them touch the contours of his face.

But the drama of the stories they gave up had faded too with the passing of the waiting years. His absence had become the only story and a grandmother's longing must keep him alive for them. Her tears, his children's imperfect memory and the presence of his strange wife were all that remained of him for her.

After Sally had arrived with the children, it had seemed that things must improve. At first they had. But then, there were no more prison visits, only a long period of anticipation, cruelly stoked with rumour or even lies. Right up to the last promised visit when the families had been turned away, they had dared to hope. Now she began to think that Sally was the problem. It was then that the going got harder. A long winter had taken its toll on her health and she was tormented by the thought that she may never see her son again.

Fathia did not know that the regime in the prison had been a harsh one, all winter long. Salem had asked Fathia to pack a small holdall of winter clothes for Saad – he knew someone who would make sure they reached him. He would not reveal a name or a place and Hassan had again been skeptical. All winter through she had been consoled by the belief that Saad at least had been warm, that he would have recognised her hand in the selection or the shirts and woollens, the hope that prison routines were not entirely heartless. But the bundle of his winter clothing had been dropped anonymously at the garden gate, the same clothes, untidily pressed into a plastic bag, the holdall not returned with it.

It was Salem on a visit who had found the bundle at the garden gate. He shrugged off the implications, distancing himself when Fathia questioned him about its provenance.

"How can it be they are so mean? What trouble is a woollen sweater?" she asked. "You must try again, Salem. It can't be right."

Salem left the bundle on the table with nothing more helpful to say than, "It's the rules. You can't expect them to make Saad a special case. That's life."

"I'm not asking for a special case, brother. It's only something due to any man no matter what his mistake, no mistake at all. The sin of asking questions, is it? The sin of wanting answers? Are they sins to be punished in this way so wickedly?" Fathia could never find the words to say what she really meant.

Her brother, it seemed, no longer cared to take the risks. There were limits to what he would do, even for her. So she must now be prepared to stand alone, without husband or brother to support her. She would pay any price, take any risk, compromise her dignity even by appealing to the vanity of the most untrustworthy of men, reaching them through their indulged and spoiled wives. She was prepared to make her moves without confiding in Hassan. For now his approval or disapproval no longer counted.

What would you say of me then? That I was prepared to humble myself by waiting in the street outside the residences of mayors and army officers? Or that I humbled myself by visiting the sitting rooms of their wives, eating their dainty cakes? Or that I sat on Persian carpets smiling sweetly? Oh yes, their wives lived in splendour. Their husbands were well rewarded – they were you see the kind of men who were prepared to persecute their fellow men, to take part in the torture and interrogation of prisoners, prisoners like my son. I wonder now if they were even present at my son's interrogation. Who can tell? Was I a fool to beg of them a favour, to make a special pleading? Did I demean myself?

You must remember that at that time I didn't dare to think that maybe my own son was among the tortured. It's impossible to imagine the pain of your own child, so far removed from you, crying out and you the mother unable to respond and do what mothers do – wipe away the tears, and declare that no one will ever hurt them again.

No one will ever hurt them again? Could you imagine that? A foolish thought. It's a promise a mother cannot make. The son grows up and grows away from her. He chides her for her too much caring. Tells her not to cry, to be brave. But what is bravery to me? Is keeping quiet brave when wicked things are done? Or is waiting at the gate of the leader's fortress brave, pleading with the soldier who stands immobile with his finger on the trigger of his gun? Is it honourable to accept praise for showing patience from the one who turns the key, when your heart is fit to burst inside your ribcage?

You could call me sycophant, or fool, or opportunist, but there was nothing that I would not have done to secure a meeting with someone, anyone, who had some kind of influence. In the end, I chose the quieter way. You could call it self-demeaning but I feel no shame for that. It was not a conscious decision. It was just the one that presented itself to me. I could show a pious humility that might induce pity in the hearts of those whose clutches my son had fallen into. I had to be a model of virtue, conforming to what is generally thought

to be virtue in these terrifying times. I made use of contacts.
You can be the judge if you will of the compromise I made.

It took some time for the way forward to present itself to Fathia. When the moment came, its path unrolled like a thrown carpet for a guest of honour. She knew that she must tread its length with no idea of where it unravelled to. The route was forged this way and that by the ambition of her daughter, Halaa. She was the closest friend of the mayor's daughter, a surprise connection Fathia had never before considered. She would exploit it now.

The mayor of course was influential, notorious too; mostly known for the irritating smile on his large round face. More a fixed grin, it stretched his fleshy lips tight across his jawbones to reveal large white teeth. His grinning image appeared everywhere, on posters, on television, always next to the Leader, so that he was immediately recognisable in a crowd, partly for his stature but mainly for the smile. It was said that he attended interrogations and tortures, sometimes getting so involved that he would add the weight of his own large physique to the pressures applied. Sweat would shine on the soft features of his face, so great was the effort he would stoop to. It was said the smile never faded during these exertions. But surely this was merely the fancy of gossip.

The mayor's daughter was said to have the ear of her father, she could persuade him to satisfy her every whim. He had indulged her desires from infancy so that now as a young woman she understood his weakness, as only a spoilt child might. She had her own reasons for promising Halaa that she would bring the plight of Saad to her father's attention. She would happily arrange an audience for Fathia.

Halaa too had reasons for doing what she did, but the plan was vague as yet in her own mind, too risky to define in its full portentous burgeoning. She let it be, unformed, let it incubate, let it grow into a monster acting of its own volition. It hatched itself like a cuckoo in a sparrow's nest and she watched it, still feeling herself to be a neutral observer of its unfolding, merely assisting what was meant to be. She said nothing about it to her mother, yet involved her crucially in it.

The involvement was no more than a simple handing over of an item which seemed innocuous in and of itself but which from the outset bore the mark of a scheme. It was dishonest in that she used her unsuspecting mother as the facilitator. Fathia could not have imagined the way in which a simple act would reach far into the political arena and rebound.

Halaa was on her way to a wedding, when she paid her mother a flying visit. Her mother would not go to weddings, this she knew, but she wanted her to admire the dress she was wearing in any case. More importantly, she needed something from her in order to initiate her plan. Halaa talked briefly about her contact with the mayor's daughter who wished to meet the family. She would see her at the wedding and would be bringing her the next day to see Fathia; and so Fathia was to make sure the villa would be looking its tidy best. Then quite abruptly, making no effort to disguise the incongruity of her request, she told her mother the mayor's daughter had asked for a photograph of Sally. Would she please have one ready?

A strange request it might seem to you, but not to me. The mayor's daughter surely only wanted to check Sally out and this would be the best for Saad, I thought. She would be impressed by the efforts she has made to be like us, to adopt our customs and speak our language. Sally herself will dispel all suspicion that she has turned my son into a traitor.

Fathia asked, "Why not let them meet in person? It might help if she sees the kind of person Sally is. She is quite harmless. She might like her as many do."

"She could meet her, at some point of course." Hala threw in some helpful procrastination. "But Sally might prefer not to. So just in case, I need the photo first. It's very important. I really need it. Have it ready but don't let Sally know. Oh, and one of Saad, too," she added casually.

Halaa left as swiftly as she had arrived, leaving her requests behind to trouble Fathia. Firstly, she did not have a photo of Sally and would have to ask Neda to fetch her one, concocting a reason good enough for her to do this without her mother knowing. It was not Fathia's nature to be devious. But when she weighed up the balance of possibilities, of pleasing and of not pleasing her daughter's friend, she knew that contact with the mayor's family loomed large as the only chance there was for Saad. She persuaded herself that a photo was a mere trifle, quite incapable of doing harm.

It was, however, a moral shift that set new priorities in train and subtly changed the feelings that she had for her daughter-in-law. Sally was no longer a close ally she could discuss things with. She was even someone who would not understand, who might muddy the waters and be the obstacle in her way.

Fathia persuaded herself that her daughter needed the photo because she was helping in the only way she could, through her unique contacts. It was a simple matter, a praiseworthy thing. She had no choice in the matter and would only be helping things along. More to the point, she secretly cherished the hope of an audience with the mayor, and even with the leader himself. It would be foolish not to cooperate.

At the first opportune moment Fathia asked her granddaughter to find a photo of her mother, to find it without telling her, in secret, because it was to be a surprise. Neda liked surprises and wanted to prove that she was grown up enough to keep a secret. Choosing a moment when her mother was busy, she searched in the family album for the best photo she could find. Her hand hovered between two taken at a time when her mother seemed less troubled and smiled more easily. Should she give the very best or the one that was almost as good but without the smile? She decided that the photo with the smile was the right one for a surprise. She lifted it out carefully, held it close to her person, and rushed to give it straightaway to her grandmother.

"Here it is, Jdaidi." Her breathless voice was lowered to a whisper though they were well out of Sally's earshot.

"Well, done, my little girl. You have been very smart." Fathia slipped the photo into an envelope which she popped into a drawer.

In that moment of handing it over, Neda felt a tingle in her stomach. Her grandmother had not bothered to examine the photo as she had expected, or to pass a compliment as she might have. This would have been the natural thing to do, especially as her mother looked so beautiful. Something was amiss. Should she take it back? But Neda could not put her doubts in words or tell another lie. The awkward moment passed and she mistook the uncertain feeling in her stomach for the excitement of the surprise that was now to be waited for. Despite all this self-delusion, the deception they had shared was a sign that all was not right between her mother and her grandmother.

Chapter 4

A betrayal

The next day, Neda watched her grandmother dress grandly for the special occasion of the mayor's daughter's visit. She noticed the various objects on her grandmother's dressing table, and there amongst the old-fashioned perfume bottles was a crumpled photo, its edges peeling slightly. She watched her tuck this photo, along with the one of her mother, into the folds of the broad sash that she wrapped around her hips to hold the skirt arranged in pleats around her body. Her grandmother did not pause to share this second photo with her, to explain its purpose. She had not explained a second one was part of the surprise.

So if adults did not explain everything to children, there must be a reason. In the bigger adult world, a child would lose track of the deceit that was now unfolding in a hidden way. She was distracted by her grandmother's appearance, the flowing pleats of her skirt that swung round in a single wave as she turned away. She studied the bright colours in her headscarf as she tied it in a knot under her plaits. How wonderful she looked, like a statue. And yet, without knowing why, Neda was worried.

In the mirror, Fathia saw Neda studying her as she hid the photos. She registered the quizzical expression on her face and the smooth skin of her child's brow knitted now in vague consternation. Her heart missed a beat for the dishonest way she had taken advantage of a child's innocence.

"Now, shush. Remember it's a secret." Fathia surprised herself with the force of her whisper. Somehow the moral ground had shifted to the child.

I follow on the tails of her big skirt. Jdaidi going into the special lounge. The shiny folds sway from side to side. Her

scarf is slipping off her head. I like to copy the way she walks,
but it isn't easy. She has trouble with her knees and it's
difficult getting up from sitting. Sometimes she puts her hand
on her heart.

The guest is sitting on the big sofa. She looks small though
not as small as me. She isn't very pretty and her clothes are
quite ordinary, not as grand as Jdaidi's. No one says who I
am. She doesn't speak to me at all, but I watch and see Jdaidi
pull the photos from her sash. She holds them for a minute.
Then she gives the woman my mother's photo, the woman who
says nothing to me.

What does she want with my mother's photo? I wait for her
to say something but she says nothing. Then I wish my mother
was not smiling in this woman's hands. But it is too late. The
photo has gone. I cannot put it back in the album. There is just
an empty space where she should been. And she will find it
gone. And it was me. I took it. Only because Jdaidi asked me.

Should I tell my mother? Should I break a secret? But I am
frightened. I don't know what is right or wrong. I feel sick in
my stomach. That is not excitement but a worry. I have to keep
it to myself and hope that nothing has happened.

Soon after this, came news of an invitation for Fathia to
meet the mayor's wife. Fathia's heart rate quickened as she
heard the news from her daughter. She felt pain stab
intermittently at the side of her ribs. She generally ignored it
but this one was more severe. The thrilled expression that had
lit her face before she grimaced returned, a little jaded. But
there was still that gleam in her weary eyes which said that she
was pleased.

The gleam dimmed the effect of the small tattoos on her
forehead between the eyebrows and on her chin. It sealed the
beauty of her face and gave vitality to her clear brown skin.
Neda often wondered about the tattoos and hoped no one
would tattoo her. Otherwise she bore the same features as her
grandmother and her hair was curly to the same degree. When
she looked up at her, the likeness reflected back was uncanny.

"Neda," her grandmother whispered. "You like surprises, don't you? Especially exciting ones. Can you imagine what surprise I have for you? You remember my promise? Oh, you do. Because this is the surprise I promised you, remember. I always keep a promise, don't I? You must know that very well by now. You are a big girl, not a baby any more. Would you like me to let you into a secret? It will be our secret. No one else must know about it. Can you make a promise? Remember a promise must be kept. Always keep a promise and a secret. You think you can? Then, I'll tell you if you're sure you want to know. Well, I'm going to meet someone, someone very important, someone who can help us find your daddy. Isn't that a nice surprise?"

Neda looked up startled, wanting a surprise but feeling confused. Her grandmother had not mentioned the photo again but somehow there was a link. A link between a stolen photo and a special meeting made no sense at all. Besides, the bond between them was marred by a shared deception. The fact of this registered fleetingly on both their faces. Something unnatural had happened, an incursion into the closest bond there is, between child and her mother. Can a person hold together a promise kept and a deception, both at once? The possibility could hardly be supported longer than the time it took to nod her head.

"Remember now – you mustn't tell anyone, Neda. Especially not your mother." And a warning finger traced the air between them, up and down, then side to side.

Chapter 5

Perfumes

Electronic sensors operated the gates as Halaa's black saloon car drove slowly through into an outer courtyard. Guards watched from a compound enclosed by chain-linked fences from behind which dogs were barking and rattling their chains as they threw themselves bodily full against the wire.

Halaa and her mother walked through a second set of gates, the tread of their shoes on gravel muffled by the rhythmic pulse of water cascading in a moving arc across an emerald-green lawn. The mayor's wife was waiting at the top of marble steps. She looked crisp and fashionable in Western dress. The greetings were formal and a little brief on both sides. She was younger than Fathia and moved with energy. She wore no make-up but her hair was colour of the sophisticated dark red of Egyptian henna infused with the residue of a red herb, favoured by the wealthy. Fathia tucked in the orange-hennaed strands of her own hair that had escaped the scarf she had tied like a bandana over the crown of her head.

Fathia slipped off her sandals at the edge of the Persian carpet that spread before her the gloriously intricate design of the tree of life. Each branch of it was teeming with jewel-coloured birds, and the base of the broad trunk was surrounded by the fauna and flora of a mythical time when lions and wild boar roamed where now the desert is. Here tamed beasts assembled on a lawn decorated with wild flowers and cultivated roses, itself a carpet. The weft of the silken threads gleamed in dense pile and gave a little to the tread of feet the way a well-kept lawn does. Beyond the tree of life sat a swathe of women dressed impeccably in silken robes, silver and pink, silver and green, striped brocades and floral chiffon. Fathia was surprised by the number of them, all relatives. This was a family more powerful in number than her own.

The room was perfumed with the scent of orange blossom, sprayed from golden phials bought in Mecca on a pilgrimage. The phials were displayed on a silver tray. The women seated round the room, however, wore Western perfumes from the salons of Paris, Rome and New York and somewhere in the air above the carpet their aromas mingled in a heady cocktail.

Fathia could no longer detect the eau de cologne that she had sprinkled on her wrists and behind her ears. She greeted each woman one by one, all of whom she had never met before, not at births nor weddings, nor at funerals. Then she eased herself down onto a fan of sumptuous cushions plumped up with the softest duck-down. They were covered with Syrian brocade or German tapestry, and tassels hung from all their corners. The tea tray in the corner was bedecked with a hand-embroidered cotton cloth from China and there the silver teapot with all its silver accessories for making tea stood neatly arranged. The tea tray, however, was never touched. It was a decorative item. There was no charcoal burner beside it. It had become an emblem, a piece of tradition no longer of practical use since tea was brewed in the kitchen by a maid.

Conversation began slowly. There was no coherent theme other than the customary honorifics and blessings that tripped easily off the tongue. The expressed purpose of the gathering was sheer conviviality. Decorum was studiously cultivated in every line of enquiry, and conversation could not be expected to go beyond this level of social chit-chat. Chit-chat was the background musak for the display of wealth. It impressed Fathia but it did not overwhelm her. Opulence had no special value for her; there was no visual gain in layered jewellery, heavy neck chain over heavy neck chain down to waist and lower still.

Purpose in this social milieu was a complicated construct. It was hidden behind smokescreens of other more apparent design, like a masque in which the players find advantage in disguise. As in the masque, the real intention was always understood. Fathia must join in the pretence. Her sweet voice gently intoned her pleasure at being in their illustrious company. She answered their profuse blessings on her person with studied grace, straining all the while to listen to a different conversation, high pitched and spiked with laughter. Halaa was in the adjoining room with the mayor's daughter, discussing photographs.

Chapter 6

The silver tray

Fathia's hands were filled with sweets. A glass of sherbet was placed before her and she was invited to drink by the hostess who invoked blessings on her health. She drank alone, a meagre sip, as the gathering waited for the questions to begin:

"Your son studied abroad, ya Haja Fathia? We hear he is a doctor, a surgeon even. You must be very proud of him."

"We've seen his photo. It's very interesting but it doesn't show his face, does it? He's turning away from the camera looking out to sea somewhere."

"It looks cold wherever he is."

"Perhaps you have another photo, a more recent one. Well it can't be much more than two years since you saw him last."

"One where we can see his face."

Fathia could not credit the directness of their comments, so brazen and casual in the way they spoke of her son; it was much longer and more devastating than they had supposed, the time of waiting for him. She was glad the photo had not revealed him well.

"I'm sorry but that's the only one, I have. Except perhaps... but it's very precious, you understand." In an instant, she knew her mistake if not the reason why it troubled her.

"Then kindly let us have it, the better to know him. Your daughter can arrange it for you."

Two trays arrived, a silver one of sweet red tea in tulip-shaped glasses with gold rims, and another filled with small Lebanese pastries, Swiss petit fours, and Danish butter biscuits.

"Your son's wife is foreign, we hear. And lives with you."

"You have two grandchildren. They are well we hope. May Allah bless them."

"And is she a dutiful daughter, this foreign woman?"

"She has important contacts, no doubt. For it is most unwelcome otherwise to have a stranger in your midst, married to your eldest son and he so gifted too."

"We do feel pity for you."

"We hear she teaches at the college. My youngest son is one of her students, so he tells me."

"Does she have to work, then, or does she work because she chooses to?"

"And do you approve?"

"It seems so unworthy of our men to let their women toil in common places, don't you think?"

"And does she make time to help you in the home?"

Fathia answered vaguely "Yes" or "No", to each enquiry as seemed best, simple answers signifying very little when repeated quite so often. She remembered Sally's fragile face looking out from her photo. They hadn't commented on her. Did that signify anything? Worse still, had she by a foolish whim made her more vulnerable than she already was? But too late. All she could rely on now was its power to engender pity. In any case; it was a mere picture after all, nothing more.

Then she recalled the chain and pendant, briefly glimpsed. Sally had been wearing the owl in the photo. At the centre of the portrait, its definition so clear, not made of gold or silver but probably of some cheap sort of metal, the chain so short the owl rested at the base of her throat. An owl she thought. An owl, a symbol of mourning for the dead. It was a desperately unfortunate choice which she had left to a child – who could not have known its meaning.

Chapter 7

Tea ceremony

Fathia's plate was filled again, over-generously. Each woman in turn invited her to eat and gave blessings for her health. The tray with glasses was offered by the mayor's youngest daughter. She was pretty but, to Fathia, her round and large face was disturbingly reminiscent of her father.

Now the questioning strayed upon another theme, connected in a nuanced way to the first line of enquiry. She had not expected talk about her brother Salem and 'his very charming wife, Salha'. They told her surprising things and Fathia tactfully disguised the fact she did not know already. They told her about his promotion in the mayor's council; about Salha's plans for arranging the marriage of their daughter, still very young, to the mayor's son, the same who attended Sally's lectures. Their remarks were meant in praise but they hinted at the way men's careers progressed via influential marriages. It left Fathia feeling her aspirations for her son had been blocked by his foreign marriage to a woman who had no influential connections, his imprisonment seemingly contingent upon it.

There could be only one intention underlining all their comments. They were offering her an escape, dangling before her the promise of the marriage of Saad to one of their own daughters, one of the mayor's daughters. And yes, this must be the reason for Saad's photo. It was the opening shot in the wooing of the potential groom for the hopeful bride. Fathia had been tricked into collusion by her own daughter. In this shocking revelation, she understood for the first time the significance of her own part in the threatened undoing of Sally. Where was she to go from here? Should she reciprocate, make an overture, offer possibilities if Allah so willed it? She had the choice, or rather a dilemma, to proceed or to retreat. There was so much at stake either way.

A tray of little china cups filled with hot cacao was brought in, with chocolates and nuts, sugared almonds and gum arabic and toothpicks. A dainty serviette with lacy edges was placed in Fathia's lap and a little cup and saucer with golden rims was positioned at her feet. At this point the mayor's daughter, the intended bride, came in the room and noisily drew attention to herself. Her dress was immodest and she wore showy jewellery, every possible kind adorning every possible part of her anatomy. She was not as pretty as her younger sister and failed to show the guest an appropriate level of respect as if she felt the balance of esteem was so stacked in her favour that she needed to do nothing to win over her intended future mother-in-law. Fathia felt the affront as something deliberate, not simply uncouth. The idea of negotiating a marriage contract for Saad had never ever been in her mind and so the girl's behaviour could achieve absolutely nothing.

"I can't think why our men marry foreign women," the mayor's daughter complained, addressing everyone in the room but no one in particular. "When there are such beauties amongst us. I think there should be a law against it. After all, who will marry us when all our men have married out? Oh, I forgot. There is a law against it, don't you know?"

Fathia made no reply but the other women in the room agreed in principle that foreign marriages were wrong in the main. They knew nothing of the law but the leader would be right to ban them if that was what he had done. There was a lengthy silence until again someone asked about Sally and how she fitted in.

It was Fathia's chance to put the matter straight and she said that she was blessed with a daughter-in-law who had adapted to their ways, had learnt the language and agreed not to live like a European woman, and who respected the reputation of the good family she had entered through marriage. She sealed her position with a firm declaration that she and her husband had always felt that the birth of their grandson had been a blessing on Saad's marriage to Sally and this had reconciled herself and her family to the situation.

She had spoken softly as was her way. But her words struck home. The mayor's wife left the room. No more was said on the matter and it was some moments before her audience regained its equilibrium and found vacuous things to say. They asked her if she had seen the garden and would she like a stroll in it before leaving? It was a convenient way of bringing the visit to an end. A sister of the mayor's wife accompanied Fathia round the garden, and showed her its man-made oasis, its oleander trees surrounded by orange marigolds planted in the earth at the base of their trunks, the lemon and orange trees in the orchard, the hibiscus and honeysuckle bower; while all the time the dogs were barking and pawing at the metal fence.

Fathia returned to the lounge and meticulously took her leave of each and every one of the ladies, bending down to kiss the forehead of the elderly great-grandmother, even though it hurt her heart to do so and her knees were too painful to crouch. The mayor's wife popped in to say goodbye and led her guest to the hall dressing table laden with bottles of perfumes where her hand traced over Chanel, Dior and little phials of Arabian perfumes before selecting one of sweet jasmine with an old-fashioned silken spray pump and tassel. She sprayed it on Fathia's wrist as a leaving gesture. She gently grasped her wrist as she did so, turning her hand palm upwards to gaze briefly at the signs of Fathia's fortune registered there. She let her hand fall away and kissed her twice on each cheek. Everything was immaculately done.

Halaa was not coming home with her mother who would be driven home by a chauffeur. Waiting on the drive in a black Mercedes car was the chauffeur.

Chapter 8

The chauffeur

Fathia knew the chauffeur. He was much older than she remembered him. Fawzi was a visitation from the past, a little troubling in the way his unexpected rebound into her life at this juncture added new uncertainties to her quest. He stood politely holding the car door open for her. She greeted him quite formally, disguising her surprise, unsure how best to behave. He was not surprised to see her.

Her memory of Fawzi's connection with Hassan's family was a little hazy. He had been an orphan, adopted at some point by Hassan's father. He had grown up with Hassan and worked for the family. But Hassan married, and Fawzi was no longer on the scene. Later, but only for a short while, he worked for Hassan in his shop and sometimes drove the car. Hassan never explained his sudden departure the second time and she had never brought the subject up, despite wondering about the bitter exchange of words she had overheard.

Obviously things had worked out well for him. Fawzi smiled at her in the rear mirror as he drove. He looked elegant in his three-piece suit adorned with a little pocket handkerchief, but no tie as was the favoured style. His white collar was starched and stood out sharply against his dark hair. His wavy hair was greying a little at the temples but did not seem to age him.

Their conversation was restrained, befitting the distance in their relationship, but clearly he harboured no ill will. He took great pains to put her at her ease.

"I am so pleased to see you again, my dear friend," he said. "I have always had your family in my thoughts. I owe you all so much. You know, I always liked your husband but he never was a businessman, if you don't mind me saying so. He hated commerce and took no notice of all the changes that came with the oil boom. I warned him many times."

"He is a good man. I have no complaints," Fathia countered, quick to dispel any suggestion of agreement.

"Oh yes, he was a good man. A gentleman. Sometimes he'd find a way of helping me when times were really hard. But he didn't like the cut and thrust of things."

"I never understood why you left us, Fawzi. Hassan needed all your help. You would have been an asset to us."

"Oh, that's what I thought at the time. Believe me, it wasn't my choice, *Ya Hajja*. I would have stayed but as I say, Hassan was not a businessman."

"I'm sure he wanted you to stay but I never understood what went on between you."

"Water under the bridge now, I say. It turned out fine in the end."

"For you it turned out fine, thanks be to Allah. I'm glad of that."

If Fawzi detected irony in Fathia's words he didn't let it show. He did not enquire after Hassan. Perhaps he knew already what had happened and kept a tactful silence. In any case, Fathia, content not to discuss personal matters, was disturbed that he carried on with critical comments, that did not sound as grateful as he said he was:

"No, it's as I say, Hassan was not the businessman. More a recluse I would say. It always fascinated me how, in the face of falling profits, he would choose to go fishing rather than make a big push to sell his dated merchandise. He was either too much in love with solitude or his shop was not really what he did for a living. More a front. You know, to look conventional."

This last disturbed her. It was unwarranted. A little interlude of silence passed between them, while Fathia mused on his words and what they could possibly mean: his shop / not really what he did / a front. Fawzi cleared his throat and checked on Fathia's face in the mirror. He knew he had overstepped the mark, speaking out of turn. Fathia was aware she could be seen in the mirror and if she was shocked or offended she did not care if she let it show. But she smiled just the same for the mirror.

"Yes, I suppose you're right," he continued. "It turned out fine after all. Who would have guessed?"

"You have deserved your fortune, I am sure, Fawzi. May Allah continue to look kindly on you. I expected you to do well. You always worked so hard."

"Well, I didn't expect it, I can tell you that."

"Why not? Life is hard for all of us but it deals a little bad, a little good here and there. Who can tell whose face will find its fortune in this world of ours?"

"But I had a very unpromising beginning," he reminded her. "Perhaps you never knew but my father was executed by the Italian troops in the War. My mother was left to cope on her own, pregnant with me. She died giving birth to me and all our tribe was scattered in the mountains, some in concentration camps. You remember them of course. The Jews, the Bedouin. Anyone who stood in their way, on the land. Oh yes, they wanted all the land. A neighbour looked after me until she died of old age and then I wandered from place to place until your father-in-law took me in. A saintly man he was, I always say, who prayed regularly at the mosque and knew the holy laws. He took me with him and showed me how to pray, and then he let me help him in the orchard. He was a father to me until his terrible accident, with the land mine. Then of course, Hassan, his son, took over. I stayed until his first child and I was on the move again. The rest is history, as they say."

"I didn't know you'd been through all that, Fawzi. Allah has certainly rewarded you for all your patience. And do you have a family, now?"

"I have a wife and one small son, even a house of my own. What more could I want? I have moved from one benefactor to another and Allah has always provided for me. Allah has been good, it's true. I am blessed to meet you again and have the chance of repaying in any way I can. That's sincerely meant; please don't forget it. Anything at all for all your past kindnesses."

Fathia was quiet for a long time and he sensed that she was too full of emotion to speak. Fauzi watched her in the mirror.

"Hush, dear woman. I know your troubles and I would like to be of use to you. There now, don't be upsetting yourself with thoughts of hopelessness. What is it that you want from me?"

Struggling to speak calmly, Fathia said there was only one thing – her wish to know where her son was being held. And then, she added, she wanted to meet someone who could help her find him and bring him home.

"Now, as for finding his whereabouts, that I can surely do for you. No doubt about it. Be patient. I'll arrange a meeting with someone who can help. It won't be just for you, since several others have asked me for the same thing. Be patient, it might take a little while. But if I can, then why not? We can but try. To bring him home? That's another matter. But finding him should not be so hard."

This was the first time anyone had said something so definite to her. The visit had been worth it if not in the way she had expected. Perhaps she would tell Hassan without explaining everything. But as yet there was no need; she would keep her counsel until the time was right.

Chapter 9

The death's head moth

The grey sky promised unseasonal rain. A group of women were standing in the wasteland opposite the army barracks. It was a piece of land reserved for army trucks turning round, now empty. Prickly pear bush grew untidily round the perimeter of the site sprouting from the rubble of collapsed walls. A donkey was tethered to the chassis of an abandoned car. A few stray hens from a nearby housing complex scratched and pecked the dry and dusty ground.

The women kept a safe distance from the road to avoid the gaze of passers-by. Fathia was there with them, introducing Sally and the children. Sally felt the warmth of their acceptance of her. She felt a part of them, of part of their sisterhood, their shared grievance and anticipation that this day they would make some progress in their search for their missing sons and husbands.

It was early afternoon, a full hour before shops opened for business following the afternoon siesta. The air felt damp enough for rain but gusts of warm wind suggested it would evaporate before touching the ground. It scattered the dust and loosened the folds of the women's *gerids,* their long outer robes that covered them from head to ankle. The purpose of their congregation in this public space lay in the army barracks opposite, a sprawling complex of single-storey buildings. Somewhere inside was their hoped-for contact.

The women were nervous. Their families had needed much persuasion to support their mission, something Fathia had arranged. She had told Hassan nothing about this daring initiative. She might have told him as she made him tea after the midday meal; but they had shared the time as usual in their familiar silence. She felt sickly with the secret, with the deceit, uncertain of her wisdom and audacity. She had left him sleeping, wholly unaware. The other women had won their husbands over with the suggestion that a meeting with an influential army officer held promise of a further audience, with someone closer to the Leader. It was important that the agreed time was appropriate and low key, during afternoon siesta when the roads would be mostly empty. This gave their mission the necessary social decorum and cover.

But now their expected contact was late and already the roads were beginning to fill with cars. The women turned their backs and edged closer to the far boundary. Anxiety replaced anticipation.

Some time after the agreed hour, Fawzi arrived on the scene. He had parked his car a discreet distance from where they were waiting. Greeting them en masse in a breezy manner, with no apologies for his lateness, he led them across the road, halting the traffic as he did so. Sally felt herself, not for the first time, undesirably exposed and obvious by her dress, though the women kept close to her. Leaving his following on the pavement, Fawzi went alone to the barracks entrance where a guard was on duty. He made a phone call in the duty office.

Minutes later, a tall man in a flowing Bedouin toga appeared on the concourse. His long robes flapped in the wind. Then he bounced onto the pavement before them. He darted back and forth with a jerky gait and began speaking in a poetic voice, its cadence raucous and wide-ranging in pitch. The rhythm was urgent and ungainly, inelegantly odd.

The women arranged themselves in a line with Fathia at their head as their spokeswoman. The Bedouin poet, who could only talk in rhyme it seemed, spoke to each in turn, asking who she was, her family and her place of birth. To each he answered with effusive praise commenting on the purity and authenticity of her ethnic or tribal origins or on the wisdom of her age or the energy of her youth as appropriate. He was bombastic in his speech, and his compliments were overly profuse to the point of seeming improper as well as insincere. When he reached the children, he adopted a more fatherly tone, shifting from the role of pompous sage to that of gentle grandfather. The shift of attitude and bearing was patently contrived.

First, he placed a hand on Nizar's head to wish him good fortune and noble manhood, a future of great achievement and pride for his family and country. The archaic stanzas flowed and rolled and repeated their structure in a persistent beat replete with words Nizar did not understand. Next, the poet placed his hand on Neda's head and briefly wished that her beauty would find her a trusty husband who would achieve great honour, or fortune or both.

Then he confronted Sally, and paused with high melodrama. His mastery of the poetic style seemed to fail him as he withdrew in disdainful horror from her foreign appearance, her pale uncovered skin, though she dressed modestly. He threw his hands upwards to the sky, and spoke at screaming pitch, asking Allah to save them all from the evil intentions of foreigners in their midst, from the malignant glances of Western women who came from foreign lands to lure their men away from their true destiny. The poet pirouetted many times on the spot, his robes twirling, wrapping around him and unwrapping in a tangle of folds. He skipped some distance from them and as he did so the wind gathered pace around him. It caught the voluminous expanse of his toga, causing it to billow up like a sail. He spun around ever faster, his arms raised slightly from his side with the force of his spin. In a lusty voice he hurled curses at the party of stunned women.

Finally he glided away as if with some hidden mechanical device attached to his feet, and rolled through the barracks gates and into the greyness of the military compound beyond. With arms flung wide at shoulder height and legs taking great strides under his robes, the dark cloth of his long shirt was briefly revealed. He had the appearance of a death's head moth its bright upper wings lifting into flight and the fold of his turban at the back of his head assuming the iconic image of a skull. His voice whistled shrilly as he ordered the guard to close the gates against the women, leaving them bereft without.

Sally felt all eyes upon herself, wide with horror and glowing with anger. Worst of all was her mother-in-law's dismay, her understandable embarrassment that it was she, Sally, her own daughter-in-law, who had shattered the dreams of so many inconsolable mothers. But they said nothing, made no complaint.

The children clung to their mother. They held her hands tightly, sensing a harm had been visited on her – the poet's words so like a curse. As the other women seemed to move away, Sally could only guess at the full extent of their confusion at wanting to flee this derelict site yet hardly knowing how to face their families. But she knew enough to sense that, by association with her, they must have thought they had placed their sons in greater jeopardy.

Large drops of rain fell and spotted the women as they turned to go their separate ways. Heavy drops that stained them but dried in the desert wind in the instant of their touch.

For this inauspicious day, Sally's diary entry simply stated the following: 'A very awful day with an overcast sky.'

Part Six – Turn, turn

He is a poet. He does not write – he says it. If he wrote it, he would be in prison too.

Chapter 1

Aftermath

In late autumn looking up from the garden below, Sally could be seen on the balcony off Nizar's bedroom. From within the villa it was at the furthest distance from the family living area on the ground floor, and so her retreat was an easily forgotten space. Over the summer months, she had become more alert to judgements of herself, difficult to pinpoint or locate exactly, but potentially hostile. They had the power to unravel her, to question her sense of who she was and her integrity.

She imagined the family might remark on her self-exclusion with disapproval but also with some shared relief. Living more apart made it easier for both sides. However, she could withdraw from their company only on condition she continued sweeping floors and restoring order to her mother-in-law's kitchen. So she ventured into the space she felt excluded from when the family were sleeping the afternoon siesta. These unseen chores won no accolades. They defined her place. It was a reality she came to understand quite slowly, seeing how they symbolised her status – marginal and dependent. More and more the balcony came to represent a space where she could reclaim her sense of who she was, a place of solitude and repair.

Since the failed attempt to make contact with someone in authority at the military base, afternoon tea with her mother-in-law had become a difficult affair. Fathia still made tea for both of them, the sweeter version, but now she prepared a separate tray for Sally, and left it on the kitchen table. There was still the plate of cheese, butter and jam to accompany the fresh bread baked in the morning. But the rug was not spread on the veranda for them both. Nothing could be more evocative of Sally's isolation than that single glass of tea standing alone on its zinc tray. It was impossible to know whether most of the meaning was created solely by her own anxiety or whether it was assisted by her mother-in-law's growing misgivings.

One ordinary afternoon, Sally was on the balcony listening to a little wind that idled round the villa, gently rattling shutters. She rocked back and forth on the battered wicker rocking-chair, the one she had reclaimed the previous winter from the garden.

If she stood, she had an unimpeded view of the sweeping panorama of the sea and sky, both continuously blue with scarcely a wave or cloud to mark their separation. Swathes of esparto grass between the sea and the orchard were interrupted here and there with prickly pear to the west and pomegranate trees to the east. Hassan's boat was resting on the beach.

Below the balcony in the garden, she could see Fathia treading carefully along the rows of beans and courgettes. She loved its overgrown elegance, each herb and vegetable plant throwing tendrils over borders. It contrasted with the tidy husbandry of the orchard shaped by annual pruning under Hassan's careful husbandry. The branches of the fig trees with their broad sun-soaking leaves had dropped low, heavy with the weight of its swelling fruit, promising the luscious sweetness of its pink and white flesh very soon.

Impossible to garner in were the hard olives that were too many and too high to reach – some had fallen and stained the pathways with their bitter-sour dark juice. The aroma of lemon-scented leaves infused the canopies of surrounding bushes and, mingling with the pungent smells of mint, basil, coriander and rosemary in the garden borders, floated upwards in a feint mist to the balcony. In the dark shade of all this vegetation, hiding under the darker leaves of the vine, were the small white petals of broad bean flowers, their centres marked by the tiny stigma-like marks of violet-black. Moving slowly in the spreading branches of the vines, a mostly hidden green chameleon, guardian of the fruit, flicked its long tongue gathering up the aphids that thrived on the sticky undersides of leaves. She could not tell from the balcony if little movements in the canopy were evidence of the chameleon's slow progress, or just a breeze wafting through.

To Fathia, the day seemed to drag on. Everything was muted and slow. The accumulating heat sapped her energy. Fathia was waiting for the harvest in which she vested all her mother's love. She moved painfully, stretching to feel for the ripeness of the bean inside its pod. She waited for the next prayer and intercession for some release from waiting. She waited for the evening and the chance of respite in her kitchen chores, the longed-for but not-expected conversation with Hassan who felt so distant from her and was so needed.

Sally realized that she too was waiting. Not for the end of autumn, not for winter, but waiting for a sign. An intuition born of desire insisted there would be one and she would know the moment when the time was near. Now was not the time. But she waited for it just the same. She reclined back into the awkward cradle of the chair and fell into a heavy exhausted sort of sleep.

It was the voice of Neda that woke her. She was standing at the balcony door and pulling on her arm, alive with news that they had at last been promised a visit. Her little face was all lit up. "We're going to see him. Jdaidi says so, Mama. We're going to see him soon." She was so sure that this was true. The message gave the impression that more than a visit was promised, that he was coming home perhaps, and this time it was for real.

Neda said a man had rung the bell at the gate and given the news to her grandmother. She was calling Sally down to join her for tea. Sally wrenched herself out of the chair, more excited than she could remember. Could she believe it? Did she dare to? They ran together down the staircase to find Fathia, her face shining like the sun. She was almost breathless with the news and spoke in stops and starts. She dithered at the kitchen table confused about the items needed for making tea, returning several times to the cupboards and talking in a high-pitched emotional voice.

"Sally, he said that we will see Saad. And see him soon. 'You won't have to wait long, not even a visit, but something more,' he said. So that means he's coming home. Doesn't it? They've decided to release him at last, haven't they? Perhaps the barracks visit was not a waste after all. But I've been trying other things too. On my own. I've made some contacts. I don't know which it is that did the trick. It doesn't matter. We'll see him soon. He's coming home. Home at last. He said we'll see him soon. Not at the prison. So where? It could only be at home. Here. He's coming home, I'm sure of it."

Fathia was elated, but Sally could not match her faith. "You won't have to wait for a prison visit," was spoken by stranger. How much trust could be placed in a stranger? It was possible that she was wrong. Fathia did not notice the flat tone in Sally's voice.

"How did you find out? Did a man call by and simply tell you? Who is he? How does he know? How can you be so sure?"

Fathia did not care to answer but ushered Sally into the family room, where she closed the windows as if the news must be kept from the world outside. She calmed herself by neatening the folds of her skirt across her lap and over her knees, stroking them into place as she settled in her usual position on the floor cushion. Then she started to prepare the teapot, one handful of red tea and three palms of sugar. They fell like little avalanches down the chute formed by her funnelled hand. She placed the little pot on the red embers of the charcoal fire whose flames she had already fanned until they livened with a glow from the dying embers. Her face was warm from their radiating heat. She was in control now. Her eyes sparkled in a composed face as she smoothed the sprigs of mint in her hands, bruising them slightly to encourage their juices, pinched their stems between her fingers and laid them purposefully to one side on the tea tray. She spoke seriously.

"I can't tell you how I know this, Sally. You have to trust me. You do not need to know. Leave such things to me. Suffice it to say I've met some important people. Halaa has helped me there. She has a good friend, a contact. And that is all I wish to say."

She cast a warning glance at Neda who understood in her own way why the whole truth was too dangerous and fidgeted in her place on a tired old cushion.

"Perhaps one day, you will find out. But not just yet. Now we have lots of work to do. There'll be a lot of guests wishing us well, wanting to celebrate with us. And I'll need your help. We'll begin today by making *basbusa* and fig cakes, some shortbread biscuits, small custards with a dusting of freshly ground cinnamon and pomegranate salads with freshly shelled walnuts all steeped in pomegranate juice. I will show you how and Neda can learn too."

With this daunting task ahead of them, Fathia sought Sally's assistance, hoping that their combined enthusiasm would more surely guarantee the desired outcome. Searching the kitchen cupboards for what was needed, a new distraction absorbed them as they rearranged their untidy contents into a new regime of purpose. It was a welcome activity. Sally enjoyed the sense of communal endeavour, grandmother, mother and grandchild brought closer together than they had ever been. It seemed she was forgiven.

Fathia's store was short of most of what was needed. The missing ingredients were all a luxury they could ill afford, as Hassan had warned; but he was already under orders to fetch them from the market and her certainty spurred him into action. She would be ready for all those who wished her well for the expected homecoming of her son. Helped by Sally, with Neda helping where she could, she fashioned shortbreads, round and plain, dredged with icing sugar, or diamond-shaped and filled with dates, all pinched along the top with pastry pinchers and soaked in lemon-scented syrup. Then there was *kneifa* also soaked in syrup and rolled out flat, filled with chopped pistachio nuts and rolled up to be sliced in chunks. The *basbusa*, semolina sweetened and baked with eggs, cut into squares each one with an almond, was fragranced with the essence of roses

They completed tray after tray of these delicacies until they were so dexterous that there was time enough to add more nuts, to roast them and salt some, to break open the pomegranates from the orchard, beating the outer skins of the halves with a rolling pin to empty all the seeds and add the pomegranate syrup. Time enough to crack open walnuts on an upturned mortar and add them to the pomegranate salad. Time enough to collect the lemons from the lemon trees and make a lemonade. Time enough to harvest mint and dry it in sprigs hanging on the garden wall, ready for sweet mint teas and the inevitable tea ceremonies where woman chatted endlessly, and encouraged one another with recollections of life's little quirks of fate.

Chapter 2

Networks

Fathia had been drawn into the reach of a powerful family. She was sure she understood the dangers. She had learned to cultivate a dignified and prudent remoteness without seeming impolite. She knew for sure, but could not tell, that it was Halaa's contact with her friend, the mayor's daughter, that had made the difference. She was surprised at how quickly her cooperation had effected a result. It served no purpose to reveal her sources so when Hassan had assumed Salem had the credit, she let the matter rest. She knew the gossip, the mayor's reputation for cruelty. She was, she knew, crossing a certain line, a line with social and moral significance; but there was not the remotest advantage in scorning the influence of a powerful man.

Rumours of Saad's imminent release spread in the community like wildfire. Old friendships fallen away in recent years were eagerly renewed. Elaborated by gossip, the possibility became a certainty. But gossip harboured intelligence, and intelligence rippled through the conversations of women like a stream to the hidden world of secret agencies, nurturing it, sweeping it, nudging it along until it caught the attention of those who loved to analyse the routes and byways of information flow.

Fathia did not think of her neighbours or visitors as a network. They were relatives and friends whose interest was a natural expression of human sympathy. But rumour spread from friend to friend, from household to household, from gardener to gardener, maid to maid, even from chauffeur to trusted chauffeur. Fathia had no idea of the complex networks of the working lives of chauffeurs. Chauffeurs were of course discrete, an essential quality in the profession. Moreover, there was a constant supply of chauffeurs, migrants from surrounding countries. A significant few belonged to indigenous tribes whose nationality was compromised by the ambiguity of belonging to land cut in half by disputed borders.

As far as chauffeurs were concerned, the system imposed its own methods of control. Car parts could only be bought on the black market, and supply was manipulated by the state. Anything and everything to do with cars was controlled by secret agencies, each specialising in its own particular offshoot of the car industry. Then there were links between the sale of cars and the immigration service which provided work permits. Thus, a chauffeur was controlled in a kind of semi-bondage. He would be loyal to his employer only to the extent that he owed a greater debt to the exigencies of the marketplace for parts and permits and those authorities who manipulated commerce. They trod a tightrope, balanced between loyalty and personal survival.

Chauffeurs were relied on for their loyalty, called upon to drive their employers' womenfolk to the lonely villa on the coastal road, with its orchard and beach hidden from the road by fields of esparto grass. The women passengers talked as they rode home, and arriving home, slipping off their street shoes, they talked to their servants and later servants talked to chauffeurs running errands for the chocolate boxes, the visitor's gift and essential contract, that made their way to the villa. But rumour was neutral, without the bother of allegiance. It merely carried every indiscretion and exaggeration along its many pathways, without judgement, finding convenient destinations for the unfortunate chance remark.

Chapter 3

The hedgehog

The villa was an old-fashioned building, built post-war but not one of the more recent residences acquired by the new class of successful merchants and government personnel. It was set on a fertile piece of land, land that was inherited, not newly bought or awarded for services to the state. New builds stopped short a good distance away. Distance made it seem like an idyll. It was perhaps a hectare or more in size but wild acacia bushes and non-fruit-bearing olive trees had colonised much of it, reducing its productivity while adding further to the impression it gave of splendid isolation. The villa was vulnerably secluded.

Its seclusion, however, was not so complete as this might sound, since it lay adjacent and undesirably close to an annex of the military base. Within it was the Leader's new compound used by members of his family and of the regime when they visited Benghazi. There was at all times the rumble of trucks on the tarmac road to contend with, and sporadic rifle volleys in the parade ground. Military music was a strident part of this all-pervasive noise. Hassan's family had accommodated it and had learned to shut it out. It was hardly more remarkable than a plane flying overhead, unless it struck up the strains of a march and then persisted with it all day. But the same disturbances could be found on the television, daily. The accoutrements of bellicose posturing had invaded everywhere. A tarmac road separated the western side of the villa from the barracks; only a narrow strip of tarmac.

It was the villa's northern aspect that was truly idyllic, or had been. The sea was an outlet, inviting escape. You could breathe more freely there. With its constant roll, and mirage of sky unending, it outdid the barracks for engaging attention. It was Hassan's refuge.

The villa itself was small enough and modest, standing back a little distance at the front from the pink-beige walls of the perimeter. Being the colour of baked earth, it was almost camouflaged. The casual observer might wonder at its separateness, at its standing apart for all its lack of grandeur. It was kind of defiance in itself. Perhaps this was reason enough to be thought suspicious, harbouring a mystery or something that stood aloof. Perhaps this was a provocation, for good land was hard to come by. Anyone might have designs on it, inheritance no longer guaranteeing ownership.

So, when a green car delivered three mysterious women at the end of the tarmac road, where the avenue of eucalyptus trees began, its presence in the landscape might be presumed to be something other than random or accidental. The driver opened the doors for his passengers and pointed out the government store just where the road forked. There, the women asked for directions, drawing deliberate attention to their mission. Then they made their way towards the villa, along the tarmac road, leaving the green car waiting at the dropping-off and collection point.

Neda was on the front balcony, standing on the ledge of the balustrade trying to catch a waving branch of honeysuckle. It was just out of reach. She saw figures emerge in a small movement in the distance where the eucalyptus avenue reached the triangular junction with the corner shop – a place she loved for its sweets and trinkets, plastic toys and ice cream; but a place she could never go alone. Sometimes she was allowed to go with Nizar for extra provisions, with a little shopping list they rehearsed in their heads along the way.

The French windows behind her opened into the lounge, and Neda was aware of the relaxed mood inside, the friendly company of her grandmother's guests. The formal salutations had been repeated over and over and were almost done with, but not quite. They went on and on. Greetings were a familiar backdrop, lyrical like a spoken song. *How is your brother? How is his wife? Inshallah he will bring your son home. Inshallah Allah will look kindly on him. It is all in the gift of Allah. How is Haj Salem? How is Haj Hassan? Allah will bless*

you for your patience, Hajja Fathia. It is all in the gift of Allah.
Neda liked it. It made her feel safe.

The three figures were approaching the villa, almost the same in height, almost in step. More guests perhaps. They were between the lines of trees. Neda had a clearer view once they passed the copse of olive trees where the trenches had filled with water in the rainy season – still not cordoned off with a fence. Then the figures dropped out of sight. They had left the tarmac road which continued past the main formal entrance and chosen instead to use the pebbled edge between the villa's longest wall and the wilderness.

In the lounge the fragrance of tea and mint told Neda it was time for tea and she might be allowed a little sip of its froth. She heard the long gurgle as Fathia poured the sweet syrup into the tea glasses. She had helped her grandmother to choose the ones etched with vine leaves and rimmed with gold. The women's chatter bubbled up, light-hearted with talk of recent births and future weddings. Then the doorbell rang.

It was not the quiet ring of guests embarrassed by their lateness, but a series of assertive hits on the bell, each one impatiently rushing fast on the other. Neda looked through into the lounge to see her grandmother's consternation, mirrored all around in the faces of her guests. Halaa was the only one who knew what to do. She got up to answer the bell.

The tea already poured was put back in the pot. The pot was returned to the small electric plate to keep it warm, and the roasted hazelnuts were set to one side. Everyone strained to hear the voices at the door. Then three women, as similar as sisters could ever be, appeared before them. No one knew who they were and they needed an introduction. Halaa did the honours.

The strangers' names gave no clue to family or tribe. Their accents switched between different varieties, all from further afield. The oldest had the bearing and volubility of a woman used to being listened to. She was in charge of her sisters.

"We have come to help you celebrate," she said, as if there was nothing unusual about knowing there was something to celebrate, as if it was customary to join the private celebrations of strangers, uninvited. As if they needed help.

"We are storytellers," she declared, storytelling obviously being a good enough reason to invade another's privacy. She took command of the circle of women she would convert into willing listeners and beckoned her sisters to join her. All three neatly removed their strap sandals without bending down and placed their folded *gerids* to one side. "So, we've come to entertain you."

No one seemed unduly alarmed, Neda thought. Her grandmother fell in with her guests, making the surprise seem expected. Perhaps it was the way Halaa had welcomed them . Perhaps it had been planned. The guests slowly warmed to the promise of a story. And so the stories began.

They were disappointing tales, with no obvious plot. The characters were the same as you would find in old fables that even Neda recognised. The sisters took turns to stop the story-telling from flagging, bolstering up the threadbare action. The guests were getting restless and chatting amongst themselves.

"I have one more," the lead sister declared. "I insist you listen because it is an important riddle. About a hedgehog. Yes, a hedgehog. A hedgehog that lives on a balcony." She had known this would get their attention, since balconies had become the latest territory ripe for government appropriation and control.

She continued, "I only bring it to your attention because I heard it first in the company of our esteemed Leader. He gave it his approval. So I know you will be very interested."

She delayed the start, allowing the incongruous ideas of hedgehogs, balconies and the Leader's approval to sink in, all the while feigning perfect disinterest. The guests reminded themselves of the leader's latest decree, an order about which they all had something to say. Sally, being unaware of this latest dictat, remained detached, merely observant. She noticed that the dominant sister made great play at adjusting the folds of her dress for something hidden at her waist. When ready, she nodded to her sisters and launched into the riddle.

"So, as I said, it's a riddle about a hedgehog. That lived on a balcony." It sounded harmless like a folktale. "You will have heard of our Leader's decision for every household to be self-sufficient in food. Well, having hens is part of that drive. It must be done. If you have no land, a balcony will have to do. There can be no excuse. Well, not everyone has done what they were told. One foolish man bought a hedgehog instead. What do you think of that?"

"Surely that's a nonsense. He was making a mockery of our Esteemed Leader."

"At least a hen gives you eggs."

"No animal is right on a balcony," protested a third guest, unaware she was treading on risky ground. She was hushed by the others who were more circumspect, more keen to please the trio of sisters who had so bizarrely ensconced themselves in their midst. If the regime wanted hens on balconies, there would be hens on balconies – everyone knew that.

The storyteller felt the need to remonstrate with the guest who had protested and resumed with: "That's just the way it is, sister. Get used to it!" A ripple of shock passed around the guests. But she continued unabashed.

"This was no ordinary hedgehog, you must know, because it talked. And what is more, it said it could see into the future. It made just three predictions. Three disastrous predictions they were, as you will hear. And when you have heard and had some time to think, then you must decide which of the three is worst. Here are your choices. The first was a tenth year of drought. The second an epidemic and many children die. And the third is that our truly glorious Leader..." she waited for a reaction amongst her listeners and they nodded in agreement with the praise. Their heads were still nodding as she went on to say, "Our truly glorious leader will be assassinated."

Her listeners were quick to express their sudden alarm.

"Now choose carefully, my sisterhood. Delve deep into your souls and seek out the one and only loyal answer worthy of a true patriot."

Each guest kept the lowest possible profile. The eldest sister eyed them each in turn, spending more than a few seconds on Sally. Fathia called Sally to help her in the kitchen, leaving the sisters to make their inquisition without her. Then the lead sister selected one of her guests to provide the answer.

"Clearly the most terrible thing...," came the tentative answer, "...the worst thing imaginable, to my mind, don't you think, would be the assassination of our truly glorious Leader. The other disasters we would just have to bear. But the death of our Brother-Leader would be unthinkable!"

All the women agreed with exaggerated vehemence, sure that the balance of national security versus social ill had been fairly struck.

"You are all wrong, and gravely mistaken," came the sharp admonition. "Not one amongst you is a true patriot. Not one. The true patriot, my dear erring sisters, would demand the head of the hedgehog. The hedgehog must die. Because, you see, it has incited chaos and rebellion."

Finding the answer unreasonable and themselves collectively condemned, the women were speechless. Fortunately, in that briefest of silences, they heard a tape whir. and a button click to 'end'. They seized on the offending sister and pulled at her skirt. A tape fell to the floor. The women gasped. The three sisters seeking a quick exit, flung their *gerids over their shoulders,* and stumbled to slide their feet into their tricky strappy sandals. Then they fled.

From the balcony, Neda saw the three sisters rush through the gates and make their way in the direction of the green car waiting in the green distance. They cut across the wasteland, not bothering with the tarmac road as they had done before. A little dust cloud followed at their heels. They were in a terrible hurry. She lost sight of them beyond the olive trees, so to all intents and purposes they were gone, their nasty presence gone with them. She leaned further over the balustrade and reached for the curling stem of honeysuckle that was floating almost out of reach. She plucked a flower.

Chapter Four

Watched

Sally called on Neda to help her in the kitchen. They left Halaa sitting with Fathia in the visitor's lounge. Neither looked happy. They closed the door behind them, but Fathia's voice was raised and audible if incomprehensible. Sally felt she could script the conversation, Fathia questioning and indignant and Halaa hardly speaking at all. It was better that she could not hear them. She pulled Neda away from listening at the door and busied her with returning cutlery to their drawers.

"Jdaidi wants privacy, my little one. We must respect that."

"But she's angry. I know she is. And Jdaidi's never angry, is she?"

"That's true. But there must be a reason, a very good one. It's not for us to know."

"Perhaps Auntie Halaa knew them, those three funny women. Perhaps, Jdaidi did not like them. They didn't look nicely at you. Why did they run away?"

"Oh, they didn't run, I think. They just left in a hurry. No reason. Nothing to worry your pretty little head about?"

"They were in a hurry. Did they get a lift from the green car?"

"Which green car? I didn't see."

"The one that waits by the Cooperative. It's always there."

Sally did not answer. She looked into Neda's eyes to check she was speaking the truth. She had spoken with a child's directness. No guile, no pretence.

"Did you see them get into the car? No, you didn't. So you do not know. Do you?"

"I saw them get out, though."

"How could you from the balcony. It's too far away, that is certain."

"They came from there. Where it waits."

"No, they most likely walked here, in their worn-out sandals. Did you see the state of them, hardly holding together. They must have walked."

"Is it right for ladies to walk a long way? Would no one give them a lift?"

"Call them ladies if you like. They looked strong enough. Strong legs. They walked smart, didn't they?"

"Yes, they did."

"So there you are. They didn't need a chauffeur."

"They did almost run though, Mummy."

They heard the front door close. Fathia joined them in the kitchen. She thanked Sally and Neda and made them a warming pot of tea. She did not talk about the afternoon. She spread the rug on the veranda and spread the tea things before the floor cushions. She shared broken pieces of *tanour* bread she had made the day before dipped in melted butter ghee, and found a chocolate for Neda in her apron pocket. It was possible to imagine everything was the way it was before, that nothing had changed.

But looking into Neda's eyes, Sally knew otherwise. her little daughter seemed older, wiser. She had not missed the moment when Fathia had intervened to protect her. She knew about the green car always being there at the end of the long avenue of trees, with its perfect line of sight for watching the comings and goings at the villa.

Fathia needed onions for Hassan's supper, and tomatoes. Sally said she would take a walk to the Cooperative and fetch them. Neda could go with her, and they could explore. Fathia told them to be quick, it would be dark soon. Best to be back before Hassan.

The green car was not there. The roads forked in two directions but it wasn't parked anywhere. They bought the tomatoes and onions as well as some very cheap flip-flops, in children's sizes. Then as they left the shop, a green car drew up alongside. The windows were dark, impossible to see inside. The car followed them. Sally drew Neda close to her, and guided her away from the avenue as soon as she could, so that if the car continued following across the wilderness it would be obvious. The car did not follow, but stopped in the shadows of the eucalyptus trees.

Neda kicked the dry earth creating puffs of dust, enjoying the sound of her flip-flops clapping on the soles of her feet. She looked over her shoulder to spy the car, but it was gone.

Chapter 5

Surveillance

Hassan had abided the comings and goings of Fathia's visitors with growing impatience. He was irritable and difficult to approach. Fathia in turn kept her distance and told him nothing of their nature, apart from mentioning names she thought would impress him. There was little to report since the afternoons had given up nothing significant to the world outside, not until the riddle of the hedgehog.

Now she was worried and decided to share it with Hassan. Her account was a weird mix of fact and fairy tale, a shortened highly abridged version meant to test his reaction. Only when she had to explain the riddle's solution, did she realise her mistake. Hassan knew at once the riddle was a mischief, not to be taken lightly. He chided her for entertaining such idle wastrels in the privacy of their home. He felt they had been polluted. There would be gossip, and gossip was a social scourge, and dangerous, best left out there, beyond the wilderness, beyond the garden walls.

He left Fathia smarting from his harsh words. He had made a child of her. He had made her feel small. She was hurt but never show it, stowing the anger somewhere deep inside her where he could not reach her free spirit. She never let the hurt show. Hassan depended on that. He took advantage of her gentle nature letting grievance run deep. Even so, she knew she had been foolish, that the blame rested with her alone.

She had been careful not to mention Halaa's involvement and she revealed nothing of her own entanglement. Hassan must never know that, But then neither would he know that she had kept her integrity and protected Sally, as soon as she realised her mistake.

Hassan felt the rift between them widen. He needed objective advice from friends in the community. He would talk to fellow merchants who were friends of long standing, the ones he knew he could trust. Putting aside the thought of having to reveal his lack of authority in the home, he would break the habit of a lifetime, and find help.

In the event, it turned out his old friends had already heard of the numerous visits to the villa. They were pleased to see him and told him how the news had reached them through their wives. Their interest was intense because his was not the only family to await the return of a son. Husbands and wives, mothers and children believed that Saad's release heralded the return of all the other men who were imprisoned or disappeared. The whole community of his friends had been uplifted by the speculation.

This only alarmed Hassan, for public interest attracted unwanted attention to the links between them all, links that had before been hidden as a wise precaution. Intelligence would be garnered in as result of the social activity rumour generated. And something else worried him. Hassan was tormented by it; or was he imagining things, becoming paranoid. There was always the question never quite put to him, but which seemed to lodge behind the querulous looks on his friends' faces: Why Saad? Why is he the first?

Was there some undesirable infamy attached to being the first? Had Saad colluded perhaps, under pressure, and then cooperated? Would other things be expected of him? Was it prudent then for others to court his family for the advantage of association, or would it be to the contrary, an ignominy? Perhaps the family of the first would only achieve pariah status, caused by the merest suggestion of having been compromised somewhere along the way.

Nothing was clear in Hassan's mind. He did not find comfort the way others did. His friends had been unable to help. He did not air his doubts, preferring to leave them lodged at the back of his mind and their minds, unactivated.

So, the visits continued. The following weeks saw the hopes of a community revived, evidenced in the trail of boxes that were carried into the guest room. They were received in humble silence, never remarked upon, but removed politely to the darkest coolest room where Fathia kept a store. The gift bearers wished Fathia good fortune and Allah's blessing for her saintly patience. They refrained from uttering their own sorrows for fear of cloying their good will with an all too natural envy.

The growing collection was culturally strange in the way it represented a way of life somewhere far away – idyllic and romantic scenes of a world long gone. There were scenes of cottages and haywains, flowers and carthorses, horse-drawn carriages transporting women wearing bonnets, scenes of Victorian childhood games, alpine glaciers and brooding pine forests, lapdogs sitting in crinoline laps, rabbits and hunting scenes, the Eiffel Tower and the cobbled streets of London.

The boxes came in different formats, some wrapped in cellophane, some tied with ribbon or edged with lace and plaited gold cord, decked with silver borders or draped with tassels. Foreign languages described the contents milk or dark with soft centres or hard, praline, flavoured truffle, roasted nuts and brittle nougat, or Turkish delight and ginger, orange cream and butterscotch, rum and other forbidden liqueurs, their presence concealed in the foreign scripts not understood and so not offending. There were lists of ingredients of substitute cacao and butter fats with additives, preservatives and flavourings, overlaid with stickers showing expiry dates and e-numbers and guarantees of quality printed in diminutive undecipherable text.

Fathia stored them all through the hot summer. They were piled high against the wall. She measured the rising tide of sympathy by the heights they reached. They would not be eaten. They were symbols only, until Saad came home. Constantly heated and cooled in the alternating temperatures of day and night, they were most likely inedible, at the least unappetising. They sweated and crystallised, desiccated and shrivelled, oozed and dried. A white sheen settled on their misshapen forms. The cellophane wrinkled. The cardboard sagged with the strain of days, weeks and months. How long would they remain, acquiring their shroud of dust, the kind that collects even in a closed room?

Chapter 6

Like toys

Hassan hung around in the marketplace one morning, not feeling ready to return home, with still with some time before lunch to kill. He wandered about in and out of his old haunts with no proper purpose, only wishing that he still belonged there, feeling some regret. He missed mingling with his generation of self-made merchants, modest entrepreneurs like himself who had done the hard graft and progressed from being pavement vendors, most with other work on the side to keep the family provided for. All those years ago, they had steered their way through the capricious waves of fortune that came with the exigencies of war and invading armies. They had made friends with soldiers, their special customers, learning their languages. Each of his fellow merchants had a story to tell. He had loved their stories.

He walked in a circuitous route to avoid the premises that had once been his shop. He hated seeing the place all shuttered down and padlocked; either it depressed him or stirred his pent-up anger. So, his meandering led him into the old quarter of the dark covered market where the shops were cabins in the walls and the makeshift stalls were made from boxes, with goods laid out still in their cardboard boxes, stacked up under faded awnings.

He found the usual selection of spices his wife needed for grinding in the stone mill she kept in her kitchen. In addition, he had found the extra items, which she had added to his errand, in niches he had not explored before: fine caster sugar, honeycomb, baking powder, cinnamon sticks and whole nutmeg, cardamom, root ginger, ginger in a syrup and ginger ground, fine sifted flour, *sahleb* and star anise. He felt the weight of the bags cut a furrow in his palms, stemming the blood flow to his fingers.

He made his way towards the coffee shop, the one where he had been arrested. It was a bit too audacious. But he stood back away from the entrance to check that there were no indolent youths leaning at the counter. The doorway was open and uncluttered. The tables inside were empty, but in the yard at the back there was movement and voices were raised in a heated discussion. He could not be sure of the cafe as neutral ground and so carried on to the rougher old-style drinking places deeper still in the old market.

There in the oldest premises, unchanged for centuries, old men older than himself, squatted on low stools or sat cross-legged on cushions, for the ceilings of the cabins were low. They were tidy places, diligently swept but so far from the market courtyard they did not attract much light. He did not have the courage to wander in and search for familiar faces in the dark.

He preferred unkempt places, with decor unchanged since before the last War. He chose one and as it happened the tiled walls and floors were being washed down with a mop and dirty pail. But he had no need of going in since a group of men he knew were sitting outside on folding chairs that spilled across the uneven apron of tiles, a space in the sun. Some of them were smoking water pipes, a habit that did not suit him particularly. There was, he felt, too much relaxation and too much risky storytelling, encouraged by the soothing bubble of the apple-scented water of the *narghil*. He would guard against any risks. Even stopping by was a risk too far, he thought ruefully.

Burdened by his shopping bags, Hassan hailed them like the long lost friend that he was. His arrival caused a commotion prompting the cafe assistants to peer out from the doorway to investigate. Against the background smell of pungent detergent still swilling around them, the aroma of confectionary and spices in his bags invited teasing comment about celebrations and festivals, rare and curiously remarked upon in present times. For gone were the days when celebrations were made for the new car, a daughter's graduation, a return from America, Russia or Europe.

"What do you have there, old man?" one enquired jokingly. "It looks like the making of a wedding feast. What's going on at home? You must tell us all about it."

Hassan hesitated, but looking round the friendly circle, he risked confiding his concern. There had been a rumour, which troubled him. His wife was so convinced that their son was coming home. But he was not so sure. He said no more than the most unadorned detail. He had not expected them to be delighted so hurried on to explain that the inevitable disappointment must surely await them and this he feared would throw his wife into a deep depression, so great was her belief. What should he do – deflate her optimism now or wait for Time to do that for him?

"Ahhh," one old man groaned. "That old trick again. So now it's your turn, is it? We've heard it all before. They try it on each and every one of us, the waiting families. For prisoners' families are the perfect prey for the traps they lay. Take care, old man. I warn you now, like a true friend. You and I are the channels for their secret investigations. We wag our tongues too readily and reveal all they wish to know."

"That is so true, old man," another added for emphasis. "A rumour is a source for gathering information, you must know that. Who knows who, who visits which family, who is still an ally with which one, who rejoices the most and who declares their celebration most openly, attracting and alas revealing their network of allegiances."

"And then the women buy chocolates," the first man elaborated. "Hordes of them. Boxes and boxes of them. Tell me about it. I've seen it all before."

Another pipes in, "Cars transport the women from house to house. Don't they now? Well, that's a perfect conduit, isn't it? Think about it. Chauffeurs carry news. Of course they do. Then they pass it on. More chauffeurs. More news, embellished and distorted as it goes, that's for sure."

"And if they choose to walk to their neighbours' houses," the first man intoned a comment with a bitter edge to it, "the green Volkswagen is always waiting there, following slowly behind, crawling, stopping just beyond the gate in that clumsy deliberate way they have of showing that they do not even need to be discreet."

"I've even heard of old hags posing as beggars, visiting the homes of our lost sons, just to gather intelligence. They wear bugs or tape recorders hidden in their clothes. Then they go running back to their various antennae, and tell all. Oh yes, our Leader is no fool. He understands that half the population is at home, where it feels inviolate, and it talks. While those of us at work are reminded at every corner of the dangers. So beware of strangers visiting your home. You must vet them all."

The wise grizzled heads nodded in agreement. Their faces were solemn. And yet their eyebrows were raised in consternation, even as their gazes were dropped to the floor, deliberately avoiding Hassan's wide-eyed stare.

"Take care, old man, oh devoted pilgrim," the first continues. "A rumour is a falsehood, to be sure. Have you thought why indeed they would release only your son? How could it be that they would hand him over, only him, and no one else is worthy? Surely, wherever they are, they are altogether, and together they will remain. But doggedly they will always try to separate us, picking us off one by one. They use us as their playthings. It seems they do it if there's not enough mischief about to keep their networks buzzing. Information false or true is their life blood. They thrive on it. They need it, to justify their parasitic existence. Take care. Don't fall foul of their evil scheming. You have suffered enough, dear man. Tell your wife it is a mischief."

All heads nodded. It was of course a mischief.

"That's the way I see it too. You've said it all. I could not say it better." Hassan answered. "But how can I look my wife in the eye, see the hope shining there and tell her she's mistaken? I hear what you say but in the end I fear we'll just have to discover for ourselves how disappointment kills us, slowly. But maybe, just maybe, she is right. How can I be sure? How can you be sure?"

There was a collective sigh and nod in recognition of the intolerable uncertainty of it all. They suspected they would all become involved at some juncture, simply because one rumour has a tendency to herald another, one person's trap becomes the collective trap. They can think of no way of stopping the contagion.

No more was said on the matter. Already too much had been said. Hassan left them nodding at their folded hands resting helplessly in their laps. A few waved an unspoken goodbye without looking up. From a little distance he turned round and still they sat, heads down, contemplating rumour and its effects. He had not dared to put to them the riddle of the hedgehog.

So it is true. This is how the terror seizes us. It cows us first and then we are transfixed. We take some time to find an inner strength only to be enfeebled by hope. They play with us to amuse themselves, they laugh to see how many individual tragedies it takes to destroy the social fabric that once held us together as one and made us proud, held us all together in a nurturing brotherhood, how now we uselessly seek new contacts to break free from the oppression they impose. They delight in our frantic searching and in our subsequent obedient subjugation. The fear of death freezes us. And they achieve this in just one fierce stroke. It takes just one threat and we are all transformed, immobilised in cement. Then they raise us up with false rumour and fling us down again and again until we weaken and accept the way things are. How easily they do it, lying in wait in the central reservation on the highway, sitting out there on household chairs with pencil and notepad, in full public view, making sure we know they are watching us. How stupid we are that they must only follow us in their cars, and do no more than follow, knowing that their blatant observation is sufficient to restrain us, that they do not have to be more crafty than this to repress us. A simple open act of surveillance is all it takes.

And I too have succumbed. I cannot prove my own authority as father, not even to my grandson, for I have none to declare. Fathers have been deprived of paternal duty, mothers of their maternal protectiveness, families of their proper functioning and children of their fathers. We mill around in endless confusion and ill-humour, jostling with each other for basic needs under the aegis of one all-consuming leadership that amuses itself like a spiteful child, egocentric and wilful. We are like toys to be broken and put away.

Chapter 8

Striking a chord

Hassan was desperate to confide in someone he could trust with his deepest fears. If only he could disclose his worries to someone who would not be judgmental, for he feared seeming paranoid, he could satisfy himself that he was right. It would give him the wherewithal to reason with his long suffering and now impatient wife, for it seemed to him that she had disturbed the order of things in the privacy of his own home and in external matters too.

He was a man of reason, who relied only on real world proof and tangible stuff. He scorned the kind of belief that thrived on what he saw as childish hope and vague or lazy thinking. He wanted proof for everything. For the return of his son, he expected a formal visit, an official letter, the weighty presence of some dignitary or other to lend the message the substance it deserved. Rumour was a rogue means of trafficking in news, ill-mannered and untaught, a knave amongst all the possible vehicles of conveying fact.

He worried about the part his wife might have played unwittingly. Had she really kept her counsel as he had advised? Had she avoided the self-serving interests of the many hangers-on who might seek to take advantage, relaying innocent sighs and frustrations back to the fourteen or so different secret police organisations, so rumour had it, that spread their tentacles wide across the community?

For two years now, she had voluntarily curtailed her social life, attending only funerals and births, avoiding weddings, not inviting guests for tea in the afternoon. Their home had become a place of solitude for him. It was a welcome retreat. No one he could not trust had in that time entered the sanctuary of his home, at least not as far as he knew. The only visitors he had been wary of were Salem and his wife, and even they had not visited recently; a significant fact, he had noted without much regret. Isolation had allowed him to be prudent and in control. He had learned self-imposed censorship since his arrest. The lesson had been hard learned. He trusted that his grandchildren did not discuss their father outside the home. No doubt his wife had applied her own restraints. But now that she had become rebellious towards him, might she fall prey to rogue outsiders who sought influence inside his own home?

He chided himself, for these thoughts were unworthy. He felt bad about not trusting his wife, a woman with a good heart who had never failed him. He had proof enough that she was no stranger to the maliciousness of gossip and idle conversation and had always been averse to it; she was after all the family peace-maker who had nurtured her family by example and taught all her children the same. This was why he loved her and why he had often felt unworthy of her. But his new suspicion lodged like a wedge between them.

At the heart of the matter was a dilemma: while his wife had shunned social contact, he had felt safe. But he could not in all fairness expect her to keep this up for much longer. He decided he must let the rumour run its course. The chances were that he was, in the final analysis, over-cautious, paranoid even. That thought continued to disturb him. Only his brother, Ahmed, would understand. Only he would answer candidly.

He could ask Mohamed his driver to drop him somewhere near the marketplace and then he could walk from there to his brother's place, no need for Mohamed to know where he was going. Chauffeurs carry news. It was a pity, he thought. A pity that he had never learned to drive as a younger man, when he could not afford a car. A pity to be so dependent now for transport. Everything was a pity. A pity not to be able to trust a patently good man. And he knew Mohammed was a good man who was always discrete. His aims in life were harmless enough. He longed to buy a Land Rover. That was all. And beyond this or perhaps even before this, he thought only of his family, providing for his beautiful wife, Sudanese like himself, and his three small children. There was no malice or envy in Mohammed. And yet, the old man's words had chastened him:

"Cars transport the women from house to house, don't they?" he had heard them say. "That's a perfect conduit, now isn't it? Think about it. Chauffeurs carry news. Then they pass it on. More chauffeurs. More news, embellished and distorted as it goes."

Hassan hated the way mistrust could extend its reach, like a poison, deep and wide, and he was loth to include Mohamed in the class of informer, unwitting or otherwise. He did not want to forfeit Mohamed's company for there was something refined about him, something reassuring in his tall figure striding up in long white robes, always ready to help load the car with provisions. There was something safe about his easy relaxed pose as he sat waiting at the wheel, always patient, always courteous; something reassuring in the gracious way he listened to indiscreet complaints, offering words of sympathy in return. Nevertheless, he would go alone on this mission, even though Mohamed would have wondered why he had chosen to make a long walk alone in the hot midday.

There was nothing sinister about visiting a brother, nothing he needed to hide, only a possible surprise that after so many months of not visiting him he should choose to do so now. Perhaps it was this conflation of two different kinds of guilt that was so disquieting, his unnatural neglect of a loyal brother which he could not explain away, and the social stigmatising of himself as persona non grata following his arrest, perhaps even as a man who had lost control of his wife. It was his habit to harbour guilt, he thought.

Some way along the pavement, Mohamed, his chauffeur, showed him the café patronised by fellow Sudanese, where Hassan would find him waiting. They agreed on an approximate time when Hassan would return to find him there. He watched Mohamed join his friends at coffee, and, before turning to make his own way to his brother's home, he mused with a tinge of envy on the apparent ease of living that Sudanese workers achieved despite their lack of wealth. But that was just an impression, Hassan knew. Life could not be easy for migrant workers. They must long for home.

Hassan found that his legs would not carry him as fast as he had hoped. There was at first an urgency in his hurried steps, but then he felt the sweat trickle down his brow and an unwillingness in his muscles slowed his pace. He would have preferred now for the car to sweep him quickly on his way along these streets; and yet, now that he was here, he felt a vibrant pleasure in being part of the place instead of being cloistered behind glass and metal.

He admired the antique wooden doors along the walkways, set in ochre-coloured walls. They were reminders of a long-gone past, the comparatively easy years of his teenage years when he had visited relatives who lived in such a street. He caught the smells of cooking that wafted down the stone steps to greet him where street doors had been left open. He heard the calls of women as they urged their children in. As he passed, doors closed behind him with a sharp scrape, their ill-fitting hinges worn and misshapen with age making the frames drag over the thresholds, leaving narrow gaps below the lintels. And then a bolt would rattle into place. The faces of children peered at him from grilled windows. Cats darted from his path mewling their complaints. A vendor in a lock-up shop was packing away his half empty boxes of over-ripe fruit before closing up for lunch.

He paused to watch a frustrated cart-owner down a side street pathetically whip his donkey while it brayed plaintively, feet full square and stubborn on the road. He felt sorry for the donkey, mainly because it represented himself in a peculiar way; but he did not intervene. This was the donkey's lot; he was familiar with the scene and had long ago convinced himself of this. The cart was overloaded with bricks far beyond the beast's pulling capacity. A child in plastic sandals and with arms akimbo stared dumbfounded at the show. "Hey, ya Sidi, stop that!" she called. "Stop hitting him and take away some bricks." But her child's voice was too shrill to travel above the cart-owner's raucous cries and the donkey's loud complaint. Wooden shutters around him were pulled shut with clacking thuds.

By the time Hassan had reached the block of flats, he felt energised by the walk. His cheeks were flushed and burning hot. Some of his anxiety had been dissipated by the effort. The apartment block was on the main coastal road and its front faced the sea. This was where Ahmed and his small family lived. Since he had not visited them for some time, it seemed unfamiliar. But then it always did, its dilapidation striking him anew as unworthy of his brother. His home was a modest apartment in a hastily constructed and unfinished four-storey building. The owner had made a fortune from the build, and profit being his motive he had kept his future options open by having the steel rods that reinforced the concrete extend upwards in anticipation of a fifth storey. In the meantime, the exposed vertical rods served well as supports for washing lines that criss-crossed the flat rooftop.

In the winter season of forty nights of rain, the flat roof was a problem. Washing refused to dry and hung motionless, heavy with water, dipping into pools of rainwater that had saturated the surface and leaked through into Ahmed's bathroom. There was no waterproofing on the roof and each block of concrete that made up its structure had a hollow centre in which the rain collected. The dampness had caused his brother's wife and children to suffer from chest complaints. Today dry sheets were billowing up erratically in a gusty sort of wind much stronger than the gentle breeze that blew at street level.

He felt sorry that his brother had not been able to build a villa; they could have been near each other sharing their lives as brothers should. He found the apartment building dreary and depressing. Its concrete walls were stained and marked by a creeping dampness. Paint that was meant to brighten up the cement grey was flaking off. His spirits sank as he mounted the stone steps and entered the dark hallway with corners where natural daylight never reached. The entrance extended so deeply into the structure of the building that the one light that was set into the ceiling did not reach the cavernous extremities of the communal space from which each apartment radiated off. The lift was not working and he thought how difficult a dysfunctional lift must be for Ahmed with his heart condition. The lights were not working either, none up the staircase and none in the hall.

How apart their two lives had become, he thought. Their different homes, or maybe aspirations, seemed to have created a gulf between them; and yet he felt closer to Ahmed at this moment than to any one else he knew. Their occasional disagreements had always been short-lived. The vicissitudes of recent years should have brought them close together for each was struggling in his different way. But this had not happened. They had not come together.

Apart from their different fortunes, Ahmed and Hassan were different in personality. Ahmed avoided controversial matters in public or private discussion. He remained studiously silent while heated debate raged all around him. Hassan admired him for this restraint. Set beside his own irascible nature, Ahmed was a saint. In the present circumstances, he realised that in reality he could not expect an honest answer from his brother. He would as always prefer to take the neutral ground and not offend.

Chapter 9

Upbraided

Hassan did not find what he expected at his brother's home. He was greeted at the door by Ahmed's wife, Nur. Her head was partially covered by a hastily tied scarf. There was anxiety in her eyes. She ushered him in with the briefest of greetings and led him to his brother. Ahmed was critically ill. He knew at once this was not the time to air his own problems. He was of course an unexpected visitor and as soon as he stepped through the door he sensed he had invaded an intimate space.

Ahmed was at the kitchen table, leaning back in his chair, too weak to sit upright and unable to feed himself. He had appeared to faint, alarming his wife who was urging him to rest in bed, when the doorbell had rung. Formalities were dispensed with as Hassan helped his brother to his room and they left him there to sleep.

He learned that Ahmed's son, his nephew Nuri, had for the last two months managed the role of father to his family without support from anyone. Hassan was ashamed that as the elder brother he had neglected his brother's family, ashamed that they had not found it possible to call on him for help. He could have helped. But he would have known, if he had simply enquired for himself. Thought of yet another error of omission subdued him.

But Nuri was welcoming and polite. There was no hint of disapproval in his manner, or in the natural ease with which he kept him company, though they were in the visitor's salon where a stranger would normally be entertained. Hassan would have preferred the family room but there was a natural sense of decorum in the way the quiet, rarely used salon added solemnity to the moment. It was a large room, with sofas formally lined against the walls, their dark red mock velvet strident and masculine against the shiny pale green walls. A large photo of their father, his and Ahmed's, dressed in a fez and wearing a toga over his western suit was hanging on the wall opposite the door. It was imposing and patrician in its self-conscious stern pose.

Nuri was young for his new responsibilities, only sixteen, but his bearing made him seem older. His manner was gentle, like his father's. Hassan felt himself to be unsophisticated and indelicate in comparison and so the older man deferred to the gentle dignity of the youth. For his part, Nuri found he liked his uncle's direct if slightly uncouth manner and warmed to him immediately. This was the man about whom he had heard so many unflattering things, mainly referring to his legendary stubbornness, exaggerated he was sure. He was intrigued and wished to get closer to his uncle to make his own mind up. He guessed it would be easy to discuss politics with him. Perhaps he would dare to voice his own partially formed opinions, without fear of rebuttal; not so with his father whose disinterest and fear of politics made him cautious, and wary for his son's safety. He surmised he would in any case need to seek guidance on many things in the very likely circumstance of his father being unable to care for his family.

At first, their conversation was practical in nature. It took some unexpected turns and caught Hassan off guard. They talked about the substantial sums of money needed for medical treatment if they could only get his father to Europe and the necessary travel documents that would be difficult to procure. It was possible to persuade a local doctor to recommend treatment abroad in places where medical practice was thought to be more advanced. But travel documents required influence in circles which neither Hassan nor his father had access to.

Nuri suggested approaching Salem because he knew he had good contacts but he found his uncle reluctant. And here their conversation floundered. Nuri sensed an obstacle stood in the way and so he changed the topic and complained instead about a health service which served only people of influence and with the correct political allegiance. Hassan did not disagree but Nuri had strayed into illicit territory and must have known because he whispered he had heard that even private homes were bugged and walls had ears everywhere.

They had established in this brief encounter a mutual understanding that bound them in a way that needed no explaining. It surprised them both that they should feel so close. Nuri felt emboldened and dared to comment on broader themes. He spoke with anger about new forms of privilege by which only favoured people with a party loyalty card could obtain certain scarce items in the marketplace. Hassan nodded knowingly, surprised by the fervour that resonated in his nephew's voice, in one so young. This was a matter which for reasons of caution, was never brought up in ordinary conversation, but Nuri spoke easily about it, without fear.

He went on to describe how he had recently asked for a tin of black olives. They were the best, preserved in virgin olive oil. But they were perversely made to look as inaccessible physically as they were politically by being placed on the highest shelf. He was asked for his party card and, not having one, was refused. The olives were meant to be seen and the lesson to be drawn could not be clearer. The lure was a kind of lynchpin in the psychology of oppression. It worked best that way, since knowledge of what could be denied acted as an antidote to dissent, a lever to compliance. The example seemed a trivial one. Olives were merely olives. And being deprived of the best was but a small detail in the grand scheme of things. Nuri said as much; but they both understood the symbolic nature of the example.

Nuri had spoken quite openly. He had so little to hide. Hassan could not speak so easily of his own journey into this same sense of exclusion. He did not like to reveal his sense of powerlessness just as his nephew was turning to him for help. The fact of needing help himself paled into insignificance at the thought of finding himself wanting when help was so urgently expected of him. From now on, he would have to take responsibility for the wider family. How was he to manage this when he was already failing his own immediate family?

Chapter 10

A change of heart

Hassan left after noon, and went in search of Mohamed. The sky had clouded over in the time he had spent at his brother's home. Another sandstorm was on its way. There had been a record number of storms in recent weeks, and a filmy covering stretched everywhere even on the surface of the sea. Hassan had noticed that there were fewer fish to be caught following sandstorms; perhaps it was true as fishermen had complained – sand destroyed the plankton the fish fed on.

Sandy dust choked everything. It filled the drains in the garden and choked the leaves in the orchard. Now, out in the street, gusts of wind left sand heaps piled up in corners and lifted litter high into the thermals. It scattered birds off the telegraph wires. Plastic bags ballooned and sailed over the shanty town that leant up against the desert-facing edges of the town. Plastic bags and acrylic threads from shredded ropes were entangled with trees, electric wires and street lights, weaving in and out the left-over traces of illuminations for the last public celebration. Unexpectedly, as he turned a corner, grit blew into his face stinging his eyes. He put his head down into the heft of the wind.

The donkey cart was still there, but without the donkey. The bricks were stacked in unstable columns on the pavement. All the doors along the street were shut and windows shuttered, while families slept through the afternoon heat. His journey back to the marketplace seemed longer than before. He was unpleasantly tired, and preoccupied with the thought of a new worry compounding old ones.

He was brusquer than he had meant to be when he summoned Mohamed, speaking as if he were an erring child. As always Mohamed responded graciously and walked alongside in respectful silence. He must have noticed the awkwardness of Hassan's gait. He would have known the cause. That was his caring way. He drove the usual route without further comment.

At the garden gate, they smelt the aroma of freshly baked cakes. Hassan pull himself up as tall as he could, all fired up with new determination. Mohamed was not surprised when Hassan forwent his usual habit of spending time with him drinking tea in his garden room.

The hot kitchen was more busy than usual at this time of the day; it was chaotic and not the place to be. Hassan was angry; he felt himself to be unreasonably angry. Fathia was so engrossed in her project that she did not see him standing at the doorway, reluctant to come in. She was holding a hot baking tin in a damp towel, switching one tray of baked biscuits for an oven-ready one of flat biscuit dough. She was harassed, juggling for space on the cluttered worktop. Her hands were swollen and red with the heat, and recent burns marked the smooth skin on her wrists and arms.

His first impulse was to speak his mind. He was minded to tell her that her efforts were a total waste of time. Forgetting his earlier resolve to let matters be, he wanted her to listen to the wise words of the old men who had shared their thoughts with him that morning, and to know that what inspired her was nothing other than malicious mischief-making. There were other matters more pressing. Instead, seeing how she glowed with hope, he checked himself. He knew in that instant that he loved her still, just as when he had seen her for the first time as his bride.

He was moved by the ageing beauty of her, revealed by the silken scarf that had slipped off her head, showing her sometime hennaed hair with its greying roots at the parting, and the slim woollen plaits she had interwoven with her own short tresses and tied with red ribbons to make up for the abundance of tresses she had lost. He loved her smooth forehead where beads of sweat glistened and trickled down her crimson cheeks.

He knew that she would do anything for their son. She would go to the ends of the earth against his better judgment, always disregarding her own well-being. For this he could only admire her. But his love was mixed with irritation. Love for him was an emotion he had put away long ago, unfamiliar now with all that love had meant to him as a young man. Love was choked by bitterness.

Knowing in the instant, that his rehearsed words would sound uncharitable, he parted his lips to utter them just the same. He saw the pleading in her eyes. He understood that deep down she too knew it was a folly. He said nothing.

He knew it was all a front, this bustle of activity. Like him, she knew the promise of their son's return was possibly a sham, a cruel trick; but it seemed her knowing this made no difference. He watched her as she bent down to place a tray on the floor, and saw her face darken with the sudden rush of blood. He muttered something like a curse but his words were inaudible, softened by his loving of her. She stood upright, straightened herself and was pushing her fists into the small of her back. He knew that ache of hers. She wasted no energy on answering him but he knew she must have guessed just what it was he had not quite said.

"It's much too hot for all this." Now his voice was raised. "You don't need to do it. It's a waste of time, and money too." He thought his complaint was mildly spoken; but even so he had been rough. She wrinkled her nose in disdain at his uncharitable disregard for her labour of love.

Did he not feel, she thought, the same fierce longing that drove her all the while? Longing went further than logic, deeper into the soul, and certainly illuminated wisdom more than men ever could. Could he not see that she was pining? But she knew he did, always in his clumsy ungracious way. She knew that he pined too.

"It's too hot to eat in here," he moaned. "I'll eat on the veranda." Without a murmur, Fathia arranged his meal in a tray while he disappeared to the bathroom, more to put a stop to his heartless needling of her than to wash his hands.

Hassan ate alone. He missed their casual chat over the meal and the chance to talk about his brother's health. But no matter, there would be time enough later in the day to worry her with more problems. For the moment, he was focussed on his wife and her obsession with the hope of Saad's release. She did the preparations like a penance, suffering so much discomfort, even pain. He reflected on his conversation with friends in the coffee shop. He went over their words in his head: *Why would they release only one? Surely they are all together somewhere. It seems they do it just to test us – that's what they do whenever they are short of information ... Information false or true, that's their lifeblood.*

Hassan was irritated by a sense of guilt. Where did it come from? How had it taken up so much space in his thinking. He knew there never was in his mind a treacherous plot in the making, and yet he felt as if there must be. Treachery had never been his way, and yet he felt accused of treachery. If seditious thought had ever sparked in the deep recesses of his mind, he had never contemplated action. And yet he was tormented by the need to suppress his thoughts. If he was not guilty, why the need to smother thought? He felt sick with an emotion for which he could not find a word. He pushed his plate away, the food untouched. He walked through the kitchen where Fathia laboured on. As an afterthought when he was almost through the door, he threw one last remark over his shoulder and was gone:

"And by the way, don't have anything to do with these female beggars. Old hags they are, bent on mischief. You can be sure of it. And don't say I didn't tell you!"

Fathia felt the heat of guilty conscience rise up to her face and prick her eyes. She saw Sally glance at her and she managed to secure a confidence between them with a bite of the lips and an almost imperceptible shake of the head.

Hassan did not see the shock register on his wife's face but moved his weary physical self to his private room, the penitent's cell where neither silence nor the crackling wireless could console him. His inner self lingered at the table on the veranda, looking out to sea.

Chapter 11

The wire

Just when all hope seemed pointless, when even Fathia had given up and her guests had dwindled to her nearest relatives, a new promise came to lift them once again.

She and Sally had returned to the kitchen and the food store to impose a semblance of order where haste and lack of time had created chaos. Baking tins were oiled and returned to their shelves. Ingredients were audited. A mental note was made of what was running low, what was over-bought. *Ka'ak* and fig-stuffed shortbread biscuits were carefully re-arranged in tins to find the staler ones to be set aside for themselves to while away the afternoons. Whisks, wooden spoons and shapers for pinching the edges of pastries were carefully arranged in a wooden box. Sally was standing on a chair to reach the highest shelf where Fathia liked to keep things she would not need every day, when the doorbell rang.

Fathia stopped and wiped her hands on her apron. She fiddled with her slippery headscarf and pulled it over her brow, her fingers all trembling so that her appearance was less tidy than she might have wished. No matter, the doorbell rang again and she rushed to answer it.

It was Salem's chauffeur. This time he brought a brief and curious message from Salem, "Be ready this afternoon at two. I will take you."

The kitchen was now a frantic scene of packing whatever cakes and sweets could be found to take to the prison or wherever it was they were going to meet Saad, if that was indeed the purpose. Hassan urged her not to worry about food. It would not be expected at such short notice, it only mattered that they saw their son.

But would they see him? Two o'clock after midday was the most unearthly time of day, the time of the afternoon siesta, the time when the ground has absorbed the heat of noon and begins to return it to the air. The streets would be empty and eerie. Even the prison should be sleeping at this hour, Fathia thought. Now it was she who doubted Salem's word, while Hassan was perversely upbeat about the prospect.

"No this is just the best time," he had said. "Discrete and very wise. We won't be seen. So as not to cause a commotion. To make the visit as inconspicuous as possible." Fathia shook her head.

There was only one basket to take, and that was only partly filled. They were a little group, extremely exercised by hope mixed with doubt, who waited at the side of the villa, inside the garden with the gates open and ready for Salem's car. Neda was drawing faces in the sand that had collected in drifts along the hollows of the marble steps. Nizar stood still, like a child old beyond his years, beside his grandfather who had brought a chair for Fathia and now stood behind her with his hands resting on her shoulders. It was an unexpected kindness that smoothed the frown on her face into surprise. She sat with her feet astride the basket, covered with her long *gerid* from head to toe. Sally walked about trying to dissipate the tension that bound them all.

Salem arrived. His face was cheery and absurdly triumphant. He ushered them into his large saloon and drove them off. There was no chauffeur this time. Salem had little conversation to help break the monotony of the route which Hassan recognised as the same as last time. His spirits sank a little but lifted at the thought that at least the place of Saad's disappearance was becoming a fixed point, an almost reality. This was the holding for his son and he could begin to locate him somewhere in the universe. Saad was no longer haunting a parallel world of oblivion but was attached to a retraceable location. This bleak road through an almost featureless landscape was becoming a permanent feature in Hassan's mental store of all the roads he had ever travelled on. For its emotion and pain, it trammelled deeper than any other.

Sally chatted to distract the children. She wondered if taking the children with them was the right thing to do. She was apprehensive. She could not protect them from whatever might transpire. And yet to deny them the visit, when they longed so much for their father, was too unkind.

This time, the eyes at the grill in the prison entrance door met Salem's with a steady stare. The door was opened without fuss. The little group trooped in, stepping high over the threshold. They were directed to the first visitors' waiting room to the right and sat there along a wooden bench, beneath a long window high above them, with no view out. Before them was a low wall and set within the wall was a tall mesh that reached to the ceiling and from one side to the other, to meet a gate of made of similar meshing.

A guard with a friendly face stood there, holding the keys to the gate in his hand. He greeted Hassan warmly as if he did not wish to be associated with the role he played as gatekeeper, prison guard. He shuffled on his feet, and teased Nizar by pulling funny faces.

Beyond this first mesh, there was another of the same proportions and construction, and another gate to one side. Between the two meshes lay a no man's land, a gap, a forbidden place of separation. It's function vague and merely suggestive at first.

Sally imagined Saad hugging the children, how they would feel his hair and search for the mole on his neck. He would pick them up and swing them round. He would not be able to touch her, but he would be near enough to see the desire in her eyes. She must not cry. Fathia was trembling. This was her first time and Hassan was sensitive to the fact. He stood behind her and held her by the shoulders.

Then an inner door opened and let in some light and Saad's silhouette appeared in the doorway. He moved to the meshing barrier, and stopped there as he must, startled like a worried horse, shocked at the fact of his family too far away to touch. He forced a smile. He was very thin. His hair was flat as if it had lost its bouncy curl. He was not wearing his glasses. His false tooth was missing and when he grinned there was a gap. He rubbed his cheeks nervously and said, "I'm okay. Don't worry, Mother."

But Fathia was too distraught. She wept inconsolably, so that Hassan felt he had to take her back to the car to stay with Salem.

Nizar pushed his little hand through the mesh and tried to reach his father. "Daddy, I want you. Please come home and never go away again." Now with both hands pushing through and with Neda trying to reach as well, he shouted at the friendly guard, "Let me have my Daddy back."

It was enough to affect the guard and he hastily fumbled with the lock and let Nizar pass through so his father could hug him.

"You see, he is a good man," Saad said to reassure his family. "He at least does not hate us." And then he whispered something for only Nizar to hear. As he did so, an alarm sounded in the prison. The guard quickly rushed Nizar to the outer mesh, and Saad was hauled back to his prison cell.

Fathia had not been mistaken with her forebodings. Now she had seen what they had done to her son, how they had weakened him, the child that she had nourished to robust health. Now she knew how they wished to reduce him even in the eyes of his own children.

"You were lucky, Nizar," Neda said. "I didn't get a hug. The nice man didn't let me in."

"Yes. I'm sorry about that. But it was all too quick, wasn't it?"

"What did Daddy whisper so I could not hear?"

"Not so that you could not hear," consoled Nizar. "It was to keep the nice man safe. Don't tell anyone, will you. Don't tell them that I told you. He is a poet, you see. But he doesn't write his poems down – he says them. If he wrote them down, he'd be in prison too."

Part Seven – Headlong

This poem, in its fragmented and ambiguous form, was dangerously obscure, impossible to be kept at home. Its passionate words must be restrained like outcast felons. Nuri would bide his time like a temperate man for the opportune moment when he could scatter them into the public arena, like bread to hungry birds.

Chapter 1

Turning

So Salem had been able to organise a prison visit after all, such as it turned to be. It would be churlish to allege some kind of insider knowledge, for he had at least done what Hassan could not do for himself. Neither could Salem be blamed for the way the visit had been so suddenly curtained. Unpredictability was an integral part of the inventory of oppression.

Seeing Saad had been a tremendous relief, but with mixed blessings. He was alive, but his poor appearance left them worried about prison conditions. How much longer could he survive them? They guessed there was little scope for exercise. Long hours of sitting in sunless rooms, and long nights of unlit darkness sere debilitating. He was wasted. The prison diet would be meagre lacking all the good nutrition he badly. They had not been allowed to give him the basket they had prepared. So, new worries replaced the old ones.

They had been quiet on the journey home. Arriving home, there had been hardly any time to talk over what had happened, when the doorbell sounded. It was his nephew Nuri. He had tried phoning Hassan earlier. He had rung several times but thought he was simply ignoring the phone believing as he did that it was tapped. Now almost an hour later, he had come to waken his uncle from his presumed siesta and was standing at the gate in a long Egyptian nightshirt.

Hassan knew that something very pressing must have upset him for he was out of breath. He had come by taxi which had left him at the end of the road and from there he had come running. It was Ahmed. Ahmed had suffered a heart attack.

Mohamed drove them to Ahmed's house. They took him to the local hospital, supporting him on either side. This was how the two brothers had come together, each finding solace in the other. Nuri sat apart in deference, watching how his father leaned into his uncle's embrace. A bed was found for Ahmed, and Hassan and Nuri had a chance to talk while they waited to hear from the doctors..

Nuri was worried. Very soon he was likely to be called up as a reservist in the army. Every few months there was a new draft. It could happen any time. He did not feel ready. He felt he was too young for dying, too young for killing. Could he withstand the harsh routines and punishments army training was notorious for. The stories were rife. A cousin had not fared well, being an academic sort of person. He had arrived late for a morning drill on more than one occasion. Eventually, he was punished by an over-zealous officer who beat him mercilessly and then had him plunged into a cesspit and left unclean in a solitary confinement cell. His wounds were infected. The beatings had permanently damaged his nervous system causing a debilitating tremor in his legs and arms. Now he stayed indoors at home, unable to apply himself to his studies. The army was a hateful career to Nuri, and now he had the added worry that if his father died, and he was called, there would be no one to take care of his family.

"Uncle, I need your help, now more than ever. It's obvious my father can't work any more. We've no income and we'll starve. What if I'm called up and have to do my army training? I won't be able to avoid it. Who'll take care of my mother, my brother and sisters? I know life is hard for you. I don't expect you to provide for a second family. But is there any way we can work together? Is there anything I can do for you, now while we still have time to plan?"

The two men, almost father and son by default, put their arms around each other in their grief. Hassan struggled not to weep. Nuri too wanted to cry but felt he needed to demonstrate his strength and usefulness to his uncle as a man. They needed to talk but there was too much traffic in the corridor for confidences to be shared.

Police patrolled the corridors, striding up and down in their heavy boots, with their holstered guns moving rhythmically on their hips. In the café, there were youths, dressed in plain clothes but dominant in the way they swaggered and occupied the public space, their reason for being there obscure. They were the age for military service but serving in some other way was known to be a privileged exemption from the battlefield; hence the attractiveness of surveillance on their peers. They were sprawled across the visitors' armchairs, their legs stretched out and arms dangling over the sides in lazy fashion, threatening in a casual way. They talked loudly and passed loud comments on civilians who chose not to sit near them. The café had emptied, out of fear of them. So, uncle and nephew left the hospital building to find somewhere suitable in the hospital grounds.

The weather had worsened. The sky glowered red. They paused for a moment at the exit door, where dry air met humidity and took their breath away. They stepped from heat into greater heat, forced to shield their eyes as the wind sucked the dust into a swirling cloud and blew it into their faces. It was the *qibli*. The southern desert wind was blowing strongly in sudden intermittent gusts. It spiralled round their feet.

They found shelter in a vacant gatehouse, no bigger than a sentry's shelter. They hunkered down close. They would have looked conspiratorial. They made a plan to sell off the remainder of Hassan's merchandise, a portion of it being locked up in his Ahmed's souvenir shop; but the remainder, most of it, in Hassan's old one. As the only source of income at their disposal it might just about support both their families on the black market. The only problem was access.

Hassan passed something to Nuri who placed it in the breast pocket of his shirt. His uncle gestured meaning 'slow down, take care,' and he embraced him long and hard to seal the pact between them.

Hassan urged Nuri to wait awhile, but Nuri was all fired up by the chance to do something useful at last. He could not wait. he would leave Hassan to check in on his father. There was no time to waste. He held his uncle's hand in both of his, then touched his own breast in the customary sign of sincerity. His uncle watched him walk away at a brisk determined pace, while he searched the vicinity for someone who might be watching. He worried that the plan had placed too much responsibility on his young nephew. Would Ahmed have approved? He was sure Fathia wouldn't have.

Chapter 2

Tumbleweed

Nuri was nervous and kept looking over his shoulder until he was out of the hospital grounds. Once on the main road, he relaxed a little. There were no more guards standing at each turn of the path. He persuaded himself that his uncle's warnings were irrational, understandable in his terms, given all that had happened to him, but probably unfounded. Nevertheless, he was unnerved a little, even by his own reflection in shop windows, his long shirt twisting in the wind, winding round his body and billowing between his legs. He was gliding in the glass like a mirage. He looked deeper and longer into the windows for other reflected images besides his own. He stopped at intervals to scan behind him and beyond. He touched the object in his pocket, to check the way it lay there.

Bundles of tumbleweed were rolling and bouncing along the empty road. They swiftly gathered momentum on their course towards the warehouses on the harbour front that lay at the junction at the end of the road. Some broken scraps were wedged in corners where they rocked to and fro, easing themselves free to continue their bouncing progress onwards. Others became tangled with each other and continued on, bumpily entwined, until a sudden blast blew them apart.

Nuri felt himself to be a loosened tumbleweed. His feet seemed to lift too easily off the ground and his legs made long effortless strides, gathering so much momentum that it made him fear he might fall headlong.

He strained to slow his pace, leaning into the pressure of the wind behind him, realising that speed itself would single him out, a strange figure dressed in a long jellaba. He stopped for breath in a sheltered doorway. Perhaps he should return home instead, and wait until nightfall. At the very least, he could change his clothes. But he was too driven by curiosity to turn back now. He needed to be there in the half-hour still left before the shops opened for the commercial hours of the late afternoon and evening. He disguised his hesitation by studying his watch and a show of checking that it ticked. He considered his direction. The road was long and straight, and perhaps not the best route since cars passed by, slowly, and the drivers turned their heads to gaze at him. One was stationary now a little way ahead. Perhaps it had been following him.

He turned into an older street taking a less direct route, more shaded and too narrow for cars. He paused to check behind him. Finding himself alongside a stall of vegetables spread out in cardboard boxes, dehydrating in the heat, he touched them to check for a plumpness they obviously did not have, unaware that someone had stepped out from the neighbouring shop.

"You're too early," the stranger mumbled. "The old man is asleep."

Nuri peered through the open doorway and found an old man sitting cross-legged on the floor, his head dropped forward resting on his raised knees. Not wanting to disturb him, he turned to go expecting to find the stranger whose voice had surprised him but he was nowhere in sight. He looked at the adjacent porch but it was empty.

Detecting a movement across the road, he wondered if another shadow had shifted into the darkness of the entrance to a block of flats. There were children there, some sitting on the steps, others playing in the dirt, ducking down from gusts of sandy wind whose dusty path they had seen coming and shielding their eyes with their hands. They were jumping down the flight of steps two by two and challenging each other to prove who had the longest leap. The wind excited them and their excited movement convinced him that it was their actions that had made him imagine a voice. Meantime, the vendor of the shop had appeared at his side. He was clearly disgruntled at being wakened from his sleep. His expression prompted Nuri to justify his intrusion by declaring an interest in some of the dried dates that were drying even more under the glare of the sun. When the vendor produced a bag and invited him to help himself, Nuri backed away realising that he had no money on him. The man screwed up his face in puzzlement. Embarrassed, Nuri apologised for the disturbance. "Here. Try one!" the man offered. But Nuri hurried on, feigning disappointment. "Another time! I'm sorry."

It seemed necessary to complete the pretence of being out to buy groceries by leaving in the direction he had come. He did so, then slipped away down a narrow passage way that would with a few more turns return him to the main road but further along it. So much for his idea of making the journey at this time of day when there would be no one about. Observers were everywhere. He hoped that each had seen only a part of his route and none would follow him to his destination.

There was no reason why Nuri should be watched, no reason why he should have to justify himself. But paranoia was contagious it seemed. He felt his shirt pocket for the object Hassan had given him. It was still there but he worried that it could easily slip out if he forgot about it, whilst running. He decided he would not run and, should he be stopped at any point, he would say he was looking for employment at the international hotel. It wasn't far away.

Once there, he felt he had to act out his fabricated reasons but standing at the foot of the steps, he baulked at his next move. The marble stairway led invitingly into a deep recess of cool shade behind dark glass. The dark green leaves of ornate palms stood upright in shining containers screening the entrance that was open and unguarded. He started up the steps but stalled again. One leg already lifted to the first step, the other on the pavement, he knew he was being stalked from a distance, some few metres away. He had no choice but to climb the steps and present himself to whomsoever might emerge there. But there was no one. Looking behind him, he saw that there was no one in the street either.

Inside the lounge there was a long reception desk, opulent with flowers. The guest area was filled with dark leather sofas. Electric lights from the glass chandelier softly fractured the gloom. There was no one at reception, but he thought he could see a man sitting in a far sofa, only his head. It turned round and was facing him now. A voice called out but it was not his voice. Someone else was in an adjoining room. Again he hesitated between two options, to run or stay. Foolishly, he ran and was sure he looked like someone caught in the act or intention of theft. His progress was hindered by the volume of his long shirt that wrapped itself around his legs. He ran throwing all caution to the wind, holding his hand firmly against his shirt pocket.

In the marketplace something else was blowing in the wind beside the dust and tumbleweed. Leaflets. They turned in every direction flashing their slogans as they spun at the centre of the squall, moving faster than the debris on the periphery, spiralling in ever decreasing circles and rising up in the thermals, scattering dust everywhere. Nuri caught one, scrunched it up in a ball and stuffed it in his breast pocket where it now secured the key.

The hotel diversion had stolen precious time, time he had needed for reaching where he wanted to be before the shops began to open. He had taken a right-hand turning now and could see the corner where two streets met and where Hassan's old shop was. He was moving directly to his goal but still had some distance to go. The streets began to be busy. He needed to move fast if he was to reach his destination before the inevitable crowds did. He could hear the sounds of padlock chains being shaken and metal shutters being lifted from the fronts of shops, all down the side streets, creating a clanking percussion as he passed them striding out so urgently that his sandals made a loud slapping sound on his heels as they rebounded off the ground. He had not been aware of his own noise until now, until the new percussion of chains and falling metal accompanied it. He felt again the incongruousness of his own presence.

Another detour and, this time, he passed a man meticulously placing his modest goods on a small rug on the pavement. The man greeted him without looking up and Nuri responded, feeling that the voice was friendly. It calmed him, giving the false reassurance that, along with the usual opening of business for the late afternoon, he, like the world around him had returned to normal and was no longer odd in the setting.

No need to run now. It was already too late. A slower pace would suffice and he was comfortable again. The usual clatter of commerce offered him the opportunity of entering the square undetected to arrive directly opposite the shop. It was locked up still, the metal shutters were fastened with a chain to a metal ring embedded in the pavement. There was no time left to test the key.

He waited a while longer until all the shops had opened up and only Hassan's remained closed. It made an obvious statement, he thought, about the kind of retribution that would bear down upon a man who failed to demonstrate allegiance to the state. He waited longer still until the shopkeepers retreated into their shops and the crowds that thronged the street were sufficient to render him unremarkable. He left his observation post and moved towards the shop, just to practice passing by it until he felt at ease in its vicinity.

But as he stepped onto the road, his stomach churned over with sudden shock. A figure, possibly an older man, moved swiftly towards the shop, did not pass it by but stopped before it as if with purpose. The figure looked around him hurriedly glancing over his shoulder, and, after satisfying himself that all was as it should be, began unlocking the padlock on the metal shutters.

Nuri felt a sickness churn in the pit of his stomach. Clearly someone else had a key. Someone else had taken possession of the shop or had business there. Why had no one told his uncle that his shop had been repossessed, or taken over? He had thought it merely closed. He watched the intruder lift the shutters as he rose unsteadily from his bent position to up-stretched arms and then lunge forwards quickly to unlock the door. The figure disappeared behind the shutters as they were slowly guided to the ground almost without sound. Perhaps no one but Nuri had seen the intruder. The shop was now unlocked but unobtrusively so and seemingly inaccessible from the outside. The stranger clearly had business in the rooms behind the shutters, business that was not open to public scrutiny.

Nuri did not speculate on the hazards of finding out about something that was forbidden knowledge. He was driven only by the economic need to obtain access to the stocks of merchandise that he and Hassan needed. He knew now that his mission was not as simple as he had supposed. He needed to consult Hassan but now was not the time. He must watch the premises over a period of days in order to find out if they were used at set times. It he could detect a pattern, he could perhaps determine when it was safe to use the key. He resolved not to tell Hassan about this problem. It would be easier to devise his own independent plan, and act soon.

Chapter 3

Drias

It was time to leave. There was nothing more he could do just now. There had to be a change of plan. It had allow him time to watch the shop without being watched himself. For this, he needed a legitimate reason for being there, and the solution came to him. He would be a street vendor and set out his own counter on a small rug on the pavement using items from his father's souvenir shop.

He quite relished the idea of taking on the guise of a street vendor. The place he chose to lay his rug would have to be a vantage point. Perhaps the answer was the very place where he had waited opposite the shop, the corner where he had stood that afternoon, if it was not yet claimed. It seemed unclaimed as yet but he wondered if first he needed a licence. Did he need to have influential contacts? Could he just set himself up without attracting the attention of police? Is that what street vendors did? Having decided that he would not tell Hassan about the status of his premises and the possible loss of his merchandise, he realised he was making these decisions entirely on his own.

For the moment other matters were more pressing. His mother would think he was still at the hospital. She would be waiting for news of his father. He needed to reassure her. She would want to visit him herself as soon as possible and he would need to accompany her. He could not delay.

Nuri did not go home directly, however. He needed time to absorb the new realities that had begun to take shape in his innocent life. He remembered seeing the small public garden off the main highway. It had looked appealing, and he could engineer some time to sit there and think. He found it easily. It was a few steps below street level and therefore cooler. He was relieved to find such a retreat from the unexpected heat of this autumn afternoon. He welcomed the shade of the succulent leaves of desert plants that caught his shirt with their thorns as he stepped down onto the garden's sunken path. He walked slowly on the track that formed a square trench around the fountain centrepiece. There was a seat at the far end; seclusion despite the rush of traffic that was growing noisier and denser, level with his head, as businesses prepared for early evening commerce.

He felt inviolate, until a mild shock startled him. He fumbled for the key in his pocket and found it there, still secured in its place under the screwed-up paper. He was relieved. He pulled the paper out and smoothed it over on his lap. It was a disturbing document; its message strident and clumsily expressed. Its rhetoric was bold and daring, almost violent. He had never before read such audacious ideas expressed so clearly and with such certainty. At the bottom of the sheet in very small print was the name of a group who must be the authors, a resistance movement calling itself 'The Voice that will not be Silenced.' It spoke of a generation of young men, sons and brothers, boys who were not yet fathers, lost in the desert, in a pointless war, irresponsibly prosecuted by unfortunate followers of a power-crazed leader. It urged the next cohort of innocent youths to rebel, to turn against their officers, to desert the army, or to seek exile, to hide away rather than be used for unworthy causes, rather than die for no good reason.

Nuri was shocked to find his own thoughts given voice, speaking back to him with such vehemence and resonance. Was the tone of its call to rise up against authority a genuine call to rebellion? Who were the real authors behind it? Were they genuine dissenters prepared themselves to risk all or were they merely playing at heroics, ensnaring others into their trap? Was the leaflet just a decoy, a trick to see who might read it and then act upon its call? He held it at arms length as if it might have teeth to bite him with. And yet the leaflet intrigued him, drew him in to its scent of danger. He wanted to show it to his uncle, to consider it some more and discover his uncle's point of view. He was not ready to let it go, not yet, even though his conscience told him it was wise to.

For certain he would not act upon its instruction. He was not free in any case to take such action. He was not so bold, nor so sure. He could not risk his life since his family needed him too badly now. He would throw the leaflet away but not before he had learned some more. It was useful for the moment in any case, to write some random words on.

This was the way it always happened with Nuri, poetry impulsive and involuntary, insistent, coming as a whole piece, almost complete in form, always coherent to him even before the words had clothed the meaning. Words came to him uninvited. He could not remember a time when they did not do so; at critical moments they had always slipped into his conscious mind with uncanny ease, conveyed on familiar rhythms and in repetition, cyclical and spiral in form, pounding and relentless in their search for resolution, resting at a stop only when they had reached a quiet resolution:

Fear the street with its panes of glass
Reflecting the ghosts of my imagination
So wild

See figures where there are none
Watching my every move when I am still
Making me feel what I am not
So guilty

In this garden Italianate and cool
Find shelter from the glare of staring eyes
That dare to probe my empty mind
So penetrating

For me far better the ancient thirst for knowledge
Locked in the chiselled marble of this sturdy plinth
Rising up before me like an exclamation mark
So superior, so rampant

At its apex the bulbous shoot of a desert plant
Its stem sprouting flowers in a spiral round its girth
Seeking light above the barren earth
So brave, so diligent

Around me the wind quietens
The trickle of water I hear seeping down into the ground
Soothing, soothing my panic, my stricken nightmares
So secretive, so silent now.

To hold the poem in his head, Nuri needed only to record the last line of each stanza. They were all he needed to recall it, which he would do at the first opportunity:

So wild
So guilty
So penetrating
So superior, so rampant
So brave, so diligent
So secretive, so silent now.

The note he added for further research was 'to make alien.'

On his way home, Nuri passed by his father's shop, single fronted and tucked away in a side street not very far from Hassan's. It was a small business in a poor location, away from the main thoroughfare and much neglected in recent months. It too was unlikely to do much trade in the immediate future, in the present climate, since it sold souvenirs and other inconsequential or intriguing trinkets for tourists. The tourist industry was almost non-existent, the main clients being the foreign workers who worked in the service industries. The shop was safely locked up as it had been since his father's collapse, but Nuri planned to manage it himself some time soon. He would come back to see what remained of his uncle's merchandise stored there. He needed to calculate the space available for the additional stocks he hoped to retrieve from

Hassan's requisitioned shop. For this was the high risk plan he and Hassan had agreed upon.

Some days later, Nuri would hide all his poems there along with Hassan's key. The key would be wrapped in the inflammatory leaflet with his own obscure notations scrawled on the reverse. No one would find it thrown to the back of the deepest, highest dusty shelf in the poorly lit cabin that was his father's decaying premises.

This latest poem, in its fragmented and ambiguous form, was dangerously obscure, impossible to keep at home. Its passionate words must be restrained like outcast felons. Nuri would bide his time like a temperate man for the opportune moment when he could scatter them into the public arena like bread to hungry birds.

Part Eight – Where power resides

The spiral fall from the sky was dizzying. The absence of a voice-over or running commentary made it otherworldly. The image gained and lost, gained and lost, seen and not seen, was haunting; to be found again only in its cruel aftermath.

Chapter 1

On the outside

New boundary walls had been added to the Leader-Brother's fortress base in the capital city of Tripoli, the Katiba as it was called. New boundaries were usually added after a threat of insurrection. The resulting construction was a series of nested chambers, each enclosing an earlier design and each new perimeter higher and more cunningly defended. It was expected that the site would eventually encroach the ancient ramparts of the city, encompassing a tract of land large enough to be emblematic of an autocracy.

A cautious man would not dare describe it as a maze of accretions born of the fear of assassination; but even a bold and well-informed visitor would find its eccentric construction remarkable, be surprised to see how doggedly it contrived to keep the inquisitive stranger at a hundred arms' length.

The entrance was a metal door set deep into the cement-rendered wall. A grill at shoulder height was designed to limit communication with the outside world to the briefest message. It had received the knock of the new finance minister. He announced his arrival as one who had been summoned. The door did not open and no one answered him. But the grill was rattled firmly shut. He had no idea if his announcement would be acted on and was left to wait for an indefinite period of time.

He studied the door, which was not in itself remarkable. He had seen the same forbidding iron reinforcement on forts and prisons. Its setting was devoid of any architectural inspiration. The door itself was quaintly old-fashioned, perhaps a relic of a previous century, now burdened with its bracing of iron bars welded into a lattice of eight-pointed stars. He lifted his gaze upwards to take in the impression of a rough cliff face that soared into the sky. There was no shade from an overhang to shelter under. He needed sunglasses but had none.

Precious time passed. His feet were swelling in his shoes. His knees were locked into a rigid stance. He moved his weight from one foot to the other, his back to the wall, his face towards it alternately. As the sun moved across the sky, he searched for the merest suggestion of a shadow. He gained small relief as he leaned his sweat-soaked back on the wall to take the weight off his feet. With no sign of a response at the grill, he began to consider his position, the possibility that he might be turned away, despite having been summoned, that he was already turned away. The prospect of going home without having delivered his budget findings began to feel like a welcome reprieve.

Still he must wait. Always attentive to detail, his imagination conjured up a circuit of passages where he would be delayed at all the doors. He estimated just how many doors, multiplied by how many waiting hours to be endured, a final product impossible to calculate.

He knocked again at the door, continuously this time, until a pair of eyes appeared at the grill. But still there was no answer. The eyes merely surveyed the outer world. He considered the possibility that even sentries at their posts were not cognisant of the exact number of doors beyond their own, that they too were merely cogs in a wheel. Their duty was inevitably to stall proceedings, and their greatest weakness would be to facilitate progress to the leader at the hidden centre. But then again, their greatest error would be not to report a visitor at the gate. Their Brother-Leader had in the end to be all-knowing.

Eventually, in the late afternoon, the door was opened to him with a grating of metal bolts and swinging chains. He was frisked and his bag removed, along with his glasses and his watch. Stripped of all accessories that gave him a sense of human substance and control, he was led to the next door, and another grill. He knew better than to expect a chair but hoped the guard at least would help to while away the time. But there was nothing on the white-washed walls to distract him and the guard's conversation amounted to studied avoidance.

Chapter 2

The chair

Arrival at the inner sanctum was accompanied by a percussion of padlocks and chains until the final most inaccessible door was reached. The sound of an interruption came to the Brother-Leader like a warning. The door was reinforced with a mock portcullis, and made of the hardest snakewood. It opened pulling on its hinges, gouging an arced groove in the marble floor as it did so. It was said that, if his enemies ever did break in, they would not find him there for their labouring at the door would give him ample time to escape through the trapdoor under his desk.

Escape, however, was unthinkable. The Leader was there for eternity, and present in this moment to solve a crisis. This, his inner chamber was dimly lit with velvet curtains parted just a chink, like the flap of a tent. A triangle of light illuminated the almost empty room, which was dominated by a reproduction desk of dark mahogany. He sat at his desk on a low chair, too low for its purpose, his stooped shoulders just level with the writing surface. A mirror on the wall had been angled to reflect the door behind him onto the second mirror of the desk's highly polished surface so that he could see the smallest movement at his back. It was not elegant to face the door. There was dignity in turning his back to any visitor.

Sitting at his desk, on a swivel chair, he was aware that he was defying revolutionary protocol, for he had made chairs the subject and means for national censure. Chairs were banned. Chairs encouraged sloth and impeded the progress of revolutionary action. There was no function for a chair other than its inherent treachery.

Although the law must for coherence's sake apply to himself, this chair in and of itself was a useless contraption because its moving parts were corroded and its swivel seat was rusted into its lowest swivel setting. Sitting in a swivel chair that would not swivel, the Brother-Leader felt agitated unaware of the cause, and his eyes darted round the empty room looking for a conspiracy.

The greatest irritation and reason for his confusion was the need for constant vigilance, the impossibility of playing absent, of indulging the desires of his frenzied mind. There was a risk in answering his inner voices and, until now, it had been a nagging doubt that had restrained him, nothing more. But now, vigilance had become an intolerable burden and his anxiety must either let him rip or allow his exhausted body to settle into stasis like a limp doll. Which was it to be? Now was not the time to decide. This was an interlude. He slumped forwards and surrendered to the call of longed-for escape.

His head came to rest on the sharp edge of the desk. He felt its impression like the cut of a blade. He wanted to feel that pain. But again he was disturbed, this time to find his own face peering back at him from the polished surface of the desk. It was an ageing face, all puffed up and battered with the exigencies of usurped power and medications. The plaster cast on his nose disturbed him most; it was impossible to forget the nose still swollen from its recent trauma; the splintered nose that was the reason for the trilby hat which he had pulled down over his forehead. He tilted its brim further until it came to rest closer to the desk.

An inkling of some future action must have agitated him, because he jerked upright, posturing as if to address a crowd. His arms lifted in prescient salutation. But the moment left him. He fell back into the ribcage of the chair and, cradled like a helpless child, he fell into the trance that had been beckoning. There was no quiet lull to be found there, no infant's joy of innocence. His inward eyes were startled by the tricks his mind played upon him. He heard his own voice shouting accusations, and for every charge he hurled against his enemies, a contagion of conspiracies rose up against him. Glimmers of revenge shook their fists whilst ranging wide in constant motion like a hailstorm through the whirls and whorls of repeated pattern. Then they slipped away into the mosaic tiled walls of his private chamber.

Feeling the need for chemical support, he fished around inside his desk and found a small phial. He shook some of its contents down his throat and swallowed hard; he was practiced at easing stuff down his gullet. Then, he found the image of himself staring back again. He held it in his gaze for a good full minute, willing the storm hurtling round him to cease. Pushing the chair back so that it clattered to the ground, he stood up to address his imagined audience.

Chapter Three

Rapture

He waited for the audience to settle down, an unruly mob at the best of times. Now they elbowed him, jostling in their place around his desk, like leaves shaken on the branch but would not fall. His trusty cadres were rustling in amongst them. He could wait. There was time. The moment of his inspiration had not yet come.

The minutes limped along. The maelstrom resumed its play, this time with a slow floating fall of dust emanating from the curtains. He knew that given time its even spread would smother his polished desk, blanking out his reflection in it. The fall would have done its falling. It would all be still, and, in the lull, he would find himself released from the restraining screen of the concrete world, its imaging disintegrated. All visioning would be restored to him. His mind would take control and the mob would be pacified.

As he waited to be gathered up into a reverie, he was unaware of a knocking at the door, the arrival of a message from the minister waiting at the perimeter door. Nothing from the outside world came in without his say-so. Even the light from the window had become an afterimage of the blizzard. Now the dust had dulled its shine and it was dissolving into the distance.

But the voices penetrated, making their intention clear. They would be heard, they would raise their doubts and rattle his conscience. They would force him to engage with their interrogation. He stood rigidly still, raised his chin in defiance, and threw his chest out like a pigeon's, while he steadied himself with one hand on the desk. Trying one last time to resist the onslaught, he kicked the fallen chair at his feet and if it bruised his shin, he showed no sense of pain.

"Useless thing. I've no need of you. What I need is action! I'll show this mob who I really am. It seems they do not know me yet."

This was it – the beginning of a plan. They must see him as he really is. He must tell his story. He strode over to the mirror, swiping swathes through the dust as he did so and confronted the personage he found there.

"So you desire a total revelation of your inner self?" The voice was deep and uncouth. It used a sneering tone.

"Well, maybe not total? Partial? Perhaps." Was this a retraction, a retreat so soon from his plan?

"A partial revelation? Would that do it for you, then? A humiliation." It came at him in bursts like rapid gunfire, threatening to beat him back him in a rout.

"It would have to be a mild humbling. That's all."

"Like a public confession?"

"Yes. The people would understand me then, they'd see I'm only human."

"Only human? Isn't that a bit humiliating? You like humiliation, don't you?

"Not a full confession. More a declaration of my mission. The reason I suffer for them."

"A partial confession, then. Still makes you human. Does it have the necessary authority?"

"Human and a prophet, a seer. That's authority. That's real power now. Someone who begins with the rabble but rises above the commonplace. Someone who can steer his people through a troubled wilderness. They will know a prophet when they see one, when they see me standing before them, pointing the way. They will see how the storm tosses us about in a wild sea. How they need a steady pilot. I will let them see how my talks with God help me find the way through."

"You believe in that, do you? You are sure of the calling? Is that not a blasphemy? Wouldn't you be in a state of apostasy? They will tear you apart."

The leader is quiet. He frowns at himself but the frown flickers across his face and passes so quickly that he does not notice it. He turns round to peer into the crowd with his head pushed forwards and his eyes narrowed.

"The wolves may prowl and the jackals might hunt in the valleys. But I stand high on the precipice, above you all and light emanates from my soul showing me the way, leaving you in the darkness below. Let the wolves prowl the valleys, they cannot climb the slopes. I am beyond their reach."

This seems to silence the opposition, but not for long.

"Are you sure you are so far from their reach? Don't they see the signs of your weaker self? Can't you see the scars in their eyes, their hate of all you stand for?"

"So? I will destroy them, the dogs. I will have more reason to. And I will."

"That would amount to stripping away your superior aura. Would that endear you to your people, retribution, I mean? Would that endear you, d'you think? For if you strip away the aura of unassailable authority only to clothe your nakedness with the aura of no culpability, they won't see any difference, will they?"

"They will if I explain myself. Let them see my suffering."

"Don't you think that would be revealing too much? Too much humanity, too much weakness? Wouldn't you lose the essential mystery of power if you show too much of who you really are?"

"Well, now you have touched on the crux of the matter. Would it take away from my charisma? That's the question. Because I know I have charisma. I see the way they part like waves when I walk amongst them, because I am a god in their presence. They smile and make way for me, asking for favours and interventions."

"Do you want them see you as a god, then, not a suffering hero?"

"Yes, a god, and a suffering hero. It's been done before. They must see my suffering in my halting walk, in my stumbling speech, my split face. These are all the signs of suffering. They fail to see because we have pushed the idea of an all powerful despot too far and I cannot be both the perpetrator of tyranny and its victim at the same time, can I?

But if we push another idea. If we promote the idea of a destiny and a guide to show the way?"

"Perhaps you can, if you so ordain it. Perhaps you must. But do you want your people to love you still?"

"I want them to love me and admire me. Both."

"But what if you can't have both?"

"But I can. It has been done before, I've told you that already, haven't I? You're not listening?"

Here the leader turns on his audience, his eyes shining with fury. His interlocutors step back to miss the darts. They feel safer when he doesn't look at them. They fall silent and wait until he signals them to speak:

"We are sure the people can love and admire you at the same time, and fear you as well."

"But they fear me already. What is missing is love. You forget that. You have said nothing about my need to be loved. You have neglected love. That is what I said. You're not listening to me."

"But it doesn't matter if they don't love you, does it?"

"Yes, it does, That's what I said. It does. Don't you hear me? They won't see the world as I do if they don't love me?'

"Maybe not. But what if you can't have both? Which would you choose, love or fear?"

"I must have both. Why contradict me? There you go again."

"You can't have both."

"Must I choose between sympathy and fear?"

"You have already chosen."

"When did I choose?"

Here the Leader's voice breaks. Tears roll down his face. His listeners hold their forked tongues. They do not dare to contradict him.

"I asked you, when did I choose?"

"You chose the execution."

"But I was forced to. I had to show authority."

"But you wanted them to love you."

"They were defilers, they were traitors. I don't need that kind of love."

"But the people. Didn't you hear their cries, the screaming that rose up at the execution? The cheers at your command only. They cheered at your command. Isn't that the kind of love you crave?"

"I didn't hear their love."

"No? Not even as the bodies swung from the gallows? Not even as the soldiers exhorted them to cheer, when they raised their voices and cheered loud and clear? You didn't hear their love then?"

The questions were impossible. They could not be answered. Other questions jostled for attention. Which of all the deeds he had perpetrated should he take for the central event on which to elaborate his themes? Which attack on his authority should he exploit for the greatest sympathy? Which had the greatest pull? Should it be the latest, for which the punishment had just been meted out? It was gross enough to make a salutary example. The noise of the crowd was still ringing in his ears. He was still elated with the excitement of it. The story was even beginning to tell itself.

He must get it down. Words were bouncing off him round the room. He had only to capture them. A diagram would pin them down. He searched for a pen. With the devil on his left dispensing doubt in chilling terms and his prophetic self on the right imploring him to act for all his worth, he could not afford delay.

His arms swung in semaphore as he mouthed the argument, switching from protagonist to antagonist to protagonist, showing the crowd where to look for the moral ground. There were the scaffolds on either side of the curtain, the uncontested ruling of a final judgment. Grand gestures here, large sweeps of open palms there as if the hands held nothing back. An imaginary line from the door marked the path the three brothers had trod, heads bowed and wrapped in sacks, to the steps. He played their parts, skulking, each brother walking to the waiting noose accepting his fate, filling the room with the stench of their treachery, his treachery. Turning to his desk where the captive crowd shuffled their feet, he raised his fists and goaded them again to cheering. He did not see the hate that inflicted its wound in every face.

He must make them understand the burdens of state. He covered his eyes pushing his eyeballs into their sockets. He heard the cries of "Long live!" Striding over to the mirror he faced himself, hat cocked at an angle to reveal the nose.

Chapter 4

The door

As he stood there posturing, the door behind him opened just a crack. He turned with a start to watch it open further. The door remained slightly ajar and moved no further.

Paranoia was a familiar companion. It was what restrained and provoked him by turns. Paranoia confirmed his distrust. Paranoia enfeebled his vision and then it made it feral. The door still stood ajar, the reason for its opening hanging like a question mark. Who was there? Why did they wait? How long would it take for them to turn against him? Could he really trust his hangers-on? For when that point of doubt was reached, the game was surely up, for them.

He had reflected on this kind of betrayal the day before, as they had stood before him waiting for his pronouncement on the fate of the three brothers. At his suggestion of an execution, they had shuffled about with their feet. The shuffling of feet was not a good sign in the Leader's inventory of semiotics. He detected ambivalence in the shuffling of feet. They had either looked at him too directly when a downward glance would have been appropriate, or they had looked away when he expected a direct gaze. They had offered nothing but watched him without uttering a word themselves, waiting only for his decision like frightened sheep in fear of slaughter. He had detected a grudging acquiescence.

Clearly, they were not convinced of the brothers' guilt, and it occurred to him that perhaps they had always watched him with this keenness, a keenness he had unwisely read as hero worship, the admiration he had always craved. He wondered if he was mistaken.

The door slowly closed, involuntarily maybe, setting its metal tooth in the holding casement with a little click. But his watchers were still with him, just as they had been in his memory, standing uneasily before him. Only now he feared them, as he had never feared before. They were at the door, the only door. They were on the other side wanting to come in. He watched the door tremble under his gaze as he waited for someone on the other side to open it again. He shouted at the door, demanding it reveal the listener but it folded out into a contorted form, a wooden tree not growing but carved into a human shape and speaking from its trunk emitting no sound that he could hear, though he knew it spoke. The tree morphed back into the door. He found the key and struggled to turn it in the lock.

Chapter 5

A persistent knocking

Lunch came carried by his food taster, with the finance minister in tow. He was a cowed sort of man, an accountant who understood numbers better than he understood people. There was something inherently hazardous about his role and the thankless task he was about to perform.

The Leader addressed him roughly causing him to retreat further into his shell. The Leader had little respect for accountants, pedantic perfectionists, much consumed by detail and so tending to miss the grand vision.

"Your point for being here is...?" he growled, still watching his food, and deeming him unworthy of both a direct gaze and an honourable title.

The Leader watched his taster with a keen eye, lest he forget the agreed procedure. It was unusual to have these two events together, his food and a visitor. Perhaps one was meant to distract him from the other. A tin of tuna fish, unopened, was left for inspection on his desk, after first being wiped with a cloth. Next to it a warm parcel was placed; it was a round of *tanour* bread, cooked by his wife and marked in a way that proved it was the genuine article. The coffee was prepared and brewed in front of him on a small portable gas canister which the food taster carried with him. A tin of pears and a tin opener was placed carefully beside the parcel.

They retreated, the Leader and his food taster, to a dark corner of the room to sit on the floor, leaving the finance minister in the doorway, not yet having been invited in. He waited for the eye contact that would let him in. In the circumstances, his hesitation was understandable but his dithering only irritated the Leader more.

"Leave now if you have nothing to say for yourself," the Leader snapped, but the minister stood his ground. From where the Leader sat, he was hidden by the desk. His voice would have to float disembodied over or around it. He cleared his throat and coughed a number of times. This was not a propitious start.

Eventually, he said, "I have the unpleasant duty, my esteemed guide, to deliver some unpleasing news. Er, I have to inform you that our revolutionary coffers are... almost empty. We have been a mite too generous with expenditure, I fear. Or else there has been some..."

"Empty? How, empty? You have let them get empty?" Here the tremor in the minister's voice fairly warbled and he cleared his throat again. "Not me personally, sir... Well perhaps not quite empty. That might be a trifle exaggerated. Just not full enough. I have been keeping records fastidiously. And I have always kept you informed, unless for some reason my last memo did not reach you, oh esteemed and just one?"

"This is the first I hear of it. Is there someone playing games with me?" And the Leader shot an evil look in the direction of his minister. "It must be you. You have let them get empty, haven't you? I repeat, you have let them get empty and failed to tell me. Until now that is."

Silence.

"Why would there not be enough? Not enough for what? Step into the room, you wretched man and look at me full square before you say that again."

Even from his seated position on the floor, the Leader's gaze was direct and goading, daring the minister, a mere accountant, to be honest at great personal risk to himself. A terrified silence.

"I'll have you arrested if you don't answer me. Perhaps an interrogation will help your tongue. Where has the money gone?"

Impossible to say the money was spent on wars, in disastrous adventures, in endless bribes and financial arrangements for propping up illegal governments around the world in the vain hope of winning allies, in intelligence projects that tracked his enemies far and wide across the globe, in global publishing adventures, on any number of failed schemes. About this, a deathly hush.

"The people do not pay sufficient taxes, oh esteemed Leader," he tamely offered.

"Is this so? And who let them get away with this folly?" The Leader allowed him no escape.

"No one, sir," slipping out the noose, he hoped, the noose he felt was closing round his neck, tearing at his skin. "They prefer their ready cash so that there can be no accounting of it."

"And how long have you known this?" This last was uttered as a challenge and, without waiting for an answer, the Leader charged towards the door and called his guard. "Have this man locked up until he comes to his senses and offers a solution. Or until I ask for him again. He is easily replaced."

There followed an unseemly struggle, as the guard, unused to the role of arresting officer, half-heartedly pulled the finance minister who in turn pulled away. Other guards on the outer doors were called and rushed in to seize at first mistakenly the guard and then incredulously the minister whose impunity they dare not question, especially because of his impeccable reputation for honesty and diligence.

The finance minister remained incarcerated for a long time. His whereabouts were known only to the Leader and a chosen few. His disappearance was the topic of rumour, and a tool for coercion amongst those closest to the Leader. There was nothing to be gained out of delivering bad news.

Eventually, the leader's very able finance minister was forgotten. The Leader chose a replacement, someone who would be given less scope for delving too deeply into the unconventional dealings that would explain the crisis. No one would be allowed to come too close. A small coterie of acolytes were paid handsome sums for their silence and collusion. Besides this, the demise of the finance minister was sufficient reminder of his power. If the rest of the nation forgot about him, they would not. The rest of the nation kept its lips sealed, not knowing one way or another if his alleged embezzling of funds was true. What else could be surmised from the charge that he was responsible?

Examination of the balance sheets revealed there was indeed a financial crisis. The size of the problem took time to reveal itself because it extended in a multitude of directions. But when its enormity was fully exposed, as fully as the leader had allowed, there was need for a campaign of attack.

Chapter 6

The frontline

The Leader, Brother-Leader, Guide – for he was collecting many titles – had a problem. The plundered treasury. It was essential that he turn the crisis of dwindling funds into a strategy, that he turn the tables on some unsuspecting others and shore up his own line of defence. He would turn the dissent inwards, make his opposition a things bent upon destroying itself. There would be a battle of sorts, a silent onslaught, with ambushes, cornering and reversals, rather like a game of chess.

He believed he knew his people well. He knew their weaknesses, foibles which he despised them for, flaws he could manipulate and for which he could perversely adore them, since the ordinary frailties of human beings could be exploited so easily to his advantage. He remembered hearing that Mussolini before him had chosen to surround himself with corrupt men because they could be more easily controlled through blackmail. Or was it Machiavelli earlier still who had arrived at such a delicate truth, the corruptibility of ambition. It struck him that he already had the embryonic structure for such a ruse. And he had the external threat to back up the ploy.

But where was he, this rat of a minister who'd had the temerity to bring him bad news? He must be fetched out of cold storage – for further questioning.

It took a few exasperating days to discover where the ex-finance minister has been sequestered. A location in the desert was hard to identify. There was no record of his place of incarceration. Only one man could recall the requisitioning of a jeep to carry some anonymous cargo to an obscure oasis. How easy it was to lose a man, the leader mused.

The driver of the original jeep was nowhere to be found. But the Leader insisted. Strenuous efforts delivered the necessary details within the day and one early evening some few days later another jeep reached the said oasis and drew up at a white stone building. The local sheikh had the keys to a cellar, and asking no questions handed it over to the officer.

The finance minister, known as Adel to his gaoler, was at evening prayer. He turned in surprise at the unseemly interruption. The officer stepped into his cell, seeming to fill it. Adel's eyes were red and sore, his lips cracked, and cheeks hollow like those of a man starved of nourishment. He stood with difficulty, using a stick. Apart from his open mouth and the drop of his gaze, he showed no emotion. He stood as upright as he could, pulling his robe around him. The officer noticed the mark on his forehead denoting devotion to prayer. He was unsure how to greet him and waited until the gaoler had walked away before he embraced him, kissing him twice on each cheek and touching his heart with his hand. This was the gesture required to convey moral support and sympathy, a gesture he would not dare repeat again. Adel understood.

The Leader did not present Adel with a chair. According to his own dictat, they must either stand or squat. They squatted. It was very clear that all postures were painful for his prisoner, Adel, as prisoner he still was, uncertain of what was planned for him, and quite attuned by now to incarceration, feeling safer in his own thoughts, much safer in a desert hideaway. The Leader mused on how quickly a man might deteriorate, once excluded from urban comfort. But that was not his concern.

"You know Maths. You have a Maths degree. Is that correct?"
Loathe to disagree, Adel, kept silent. Silence was provocative.

"Don't antagonise me, you fool. I asked you a question. Is that correct? Are you a Mathematician? I'm waiting for an answer."

"Statistics, esteemed Leader. I studied Statistics," was all Adel would say. He had more than a first degree. He had been the best of his year. He could have carried on with his studies, for there was nothing he loved more that the beauty of numbers; but the chance never came. He had to work. Studying further would have meant travel abroad and that was out of the question, not for money reasons, but for the care he was taking of his elderly father and mother, as their only son.

"Statistics, then. Statistics, statistics. They prove nothing. Perhaps you twisted the figures. Made them up."

'No, my Esteemed Leader. Certainly not. I did no analysis. Just the accounting. The balances had to agree."

"And they did, didn't they?"

Again silence, for fear of seeming to contradict, for fear of looking less than contrite for what he was not guilty of.

"Well, you won't say, so I'll answer for you." Coward, he thought. He lacks the backbone even of a rat. "Of course they didn't! I know that. But you do not know the reason why, do you?"

"I only saw sums leaving the accounts for undeclared destinations. That was not my business."

"You didn't tell me that, man, at the time. You stupid donkey! You didn't explain the balance."

"No, I only drew your attention to the bottom line. There was almost nothing left." Adel felt he needed to change the topic. He had to avoid disagreement. He had to avoid revealing that he knew something of what he was not meant to know. So he added, "I mentioned taxes, at the time, as I remember. Then you dismissed me."

Something must have illuminated the leader's inner eye, for he lifted his chin, slowly as if it was pulled gently by a string. He looked up at the ceiling where he found what he was looking for.

"Yes, you did. You did mention taxes. And how do you suggest I deal with that – the people's unwillingness to pay them. For taxes would keep the coffers afloat, wouldn't they? Taxes would sustain expenditure. Oil revenues are simply not enough." *Certainly*, he thought, *they were not sufficient to*

307

sustain his grand vision of extending his influence all over Africa, across the swathe of Arab lands, all of which could so temptingly be his.

Adel did not need to read his Leader's thoughts. They were manifest in all the disasters he had seen his beloved countrymen endure. Like his leader, he did not reveal his thoughts, but perhaps both of them knew the potent significance of their mutual silence. *How could it be that oil revenues were insufficient to sustain such a small population.*

Perhaps Adel was after all essential to the Leader's plan. He could not be sure of the reach of his scrutiny, but he certainly knew about balancing the books, how it was to be done. He knew other things too, though he might try to hide the details. He could have him tortured, and then he would talk. Perhaps. But that risked too much disclosure. Best to buy Adel's silence. Much easier. And then have him disposed of when he was no longer useful.

"Now, Adel. I have it in my gift to reward you with a plot of land. A farm. Good land. You can work it and become self-sufficient. That is always an honourable sort of existence, living within your means. It would suit you. You like things to marry up, no more and no less. And you would be free. And always available. to me."

The Leader's voice lacked the warmth of charity. Adel knew that. The award was a device. Perhaps it was a threat. But he saw had no choice in the matter. The consultation, if that was what it was, had reached its conclusion. With embarrassing difficulty he struggled to his feet from the squatting position that had pained his joints. The Leader had turned his back already, having made no move to assist him. Farming, Adel thought. All that ploughing, planting and gathering in. Perhaps goats.

"I'll see that it is done, Adel."

Chapter 7

Repercussions

So this was the front – taxes, the people not paying them. But how to set about drawing the line in the sand? He would consult his coterie, and form a special council to advise him. Certain fringe activities they would have oversight of. But he must fortify his hold over them. Action followed fast on the heels of his meeting with Adel. He needed momentum, since that would keep them guessing. Such poor swine his people were who let their hearts rule their heads, and could not see the train coming for its speed.

His technicians set up a series of satellite transmissions, linking various key towns and cities, via television screens, controlled by a console in the Leader's own secret bunker. The technicians were held incommunicado for the duration, next to be exiled to inaccessible places in the great sand sea when the job was done. They could be fetched back whenever he required them, just like Adel. Every special council needed its pawns in waiting for back-up.

A multiple-venue interactive summit was called, to be entertained by eighteen different locations. The interaction would be all one way, with the Leader listening and butting in. All the elders of tribes would be summoned as well as key post-holders. Each of these in turn was expected to make their own selection of significant others to join them. They were to be encouraged to speak their minds on the topic of taxes. It would be an open and free debate based on the need for the Leader to know. On the day of the live-streaming, the Leader would be seen and heard making his own interjections from his own undisclosed location. He would be everywhere and nowhere specified, rather like a divine all-knowing entity.

In Sabratha came a phalanx of local officials, the Imam and members of the Leader's local cadre cell. Each was allowed a maximum of five supporters. Women might be included. Stationed round the meeting hall were those who were eager to contribute their vigilance and demonstrate their worth. All participants welcomed this unexpectedly refreshing opportunity to air their views in a democratic process, as it seemed. The chairman opened proceedings and invited contributions from the floor.

The first to speak was a local businessman whose bid for new shop premises had been thwarted by a more successful claim. "Well it's the merchants I blame. It's the merchants who could pay more if only they revealed their takings in full. For who knows what their takings are? It would help, as well, as I know from my own experience, if more of us prospered enough to earn such an honour as paying taxes."

He was challenged by a farmer who understood the contingencies of good times mixed with bad and understood the need a man had to put money aside. "Ah, you might be right, brother, but we all need to put away something for emergencies, don't we?" The camera swung around to rest awhile on his face, long enough for someone to make a note of the man who had spoken so rashly. Long enough to make him feel uncomfortable.

"And your name, ya Sidi," someone challenged. "Is that what you advise?" The voice hailed from nowhere discernible. Perhaps someone had been too slow with the microphone; heads turned in all directions looking for the speaker, until it dawned on the congregation that the Leader had interacted, as he called it. What was the rash man's name, they wondered. Some of them knew who he was, but did not wish to answer.

"He's right," came a supporter's voice. "We have no way of saving for the bad times. And there's dowries to think of, the years of drought and loss of harvest. This year the desert storm destroyed all my dates."

There ensued a battle of words. The arguments ranged over questions of what government did with their funds, the absence of insurance against disaster, the traditional function of gold as just that – insurance, a little set aside for the unpredictable future. The people, it was argued, needed to know that all the accounting for taxes would be fair and open, that their livelihoods would be safeguarded. There was unanimous support for a reasonable solution that would involve a fair system of contribution, with the addition of some sort of security when hard times came.

The Leader took no account of theses reasonable solutions. "Find that man, the first to speak, from Sabratha," he ordered. "Find out what his grievance is, and sort it. Then make him an adviser. He knows a thing or two. Then find me the other, the farmer who lost his dates. who didn't want to give his name."

It turned out that Adel and the farmer swapped places. Adel had the land. The farmer had the prison cell.. Each of the eighteen venues yielded up gainers and losers. Notes were made of all the grievances, and they were added to. Penalties and rewards were shuffled between the players. And so it was that the seeds of dissension were scattered even wider. The tax front would keep the people occupied. Suitably distracted, the leader thought.

Chapter 8

Demise

Hassan had been waiting for news of his brother who was still confined to his hospital bed but now in a bigger ward, his life out of immediate danger for the moment. He was alone in the villa, since his wife was out visiting. He had languished all afternoon in his room and given up on the radio and its poor reception. He had settled himself in a large armchair, to watch television, half-heartedly dismissing it as a fickle device for distracting people from what was going on in the real world.

Suddenly, he found he was watching a newsreel being repeatedly relayed with military marches themed as background. This was no propaganda. This was real news. He was watching a plane falling from the sky. At first it plummeted slowly, reeling in circles like a predatory eagle soaring over its prey. But then it was the wounded thing itself falling like an inanimate stone, repeatedly dropping below the camera sights so that the final landing was seen only as a backwash of dust cloud and debris. He listened for information of its whereabouts, the site of the crash. There was none. There was no voice-over to explain the incident. It was played again and again, hauntingly surreal and hypnotic.

Later, a brief newsflash presented the stark facts of a crash in the desert. Foreign visitors were being shown a rice paddy in the desert, one of the Leader's latest projects. At the last minute, the Leader was unable to accompany them but regrettably had sent his finance minister to take his place.

For days afterwards, the film was replayed, in silence. The spiral fall from the sky was dizzying. The absence of a text made it otherworldly. The image gained and lost, gained and lost, seen and not seen was haunting. To be lost and then found again only in the aftermath of the crash was cruel.

There was always this sense of an absence of an explanation. *The sequence tells us all we need to understand,* Hassan thought. *How lucky the Leader changed his mind at the last minute.*

Part Nine – War footing

They understood and ran away, haunted by new understandings, haunted by the silver screen which was no longer a plaything for their entertainment.

Chapter 1

The night closes in

It was nearing the end of summer. The nights would soon be closing in. It meant the children would spend less time in the garden. The best of the grapes had been harvested and the remaining vine leaves were too tough for making parcels of leaves stuffed with lamb and rice. That summer, they had made them in abundance for Saad and the others, but they had never made it to the prison. The season for this domestic devotion had passed with no further news of him.

There would be fewer mosquitoes. Fewer mosquitoes meant fewer sightings of the resident chameleon. His long flicking tongue and his slow revolving cone-like eyes amused the children. If they were lucky, they might they find him sitting high up in the canopy. It was this slim chance of finding him that kept them in the garden well after dusk one evening, despite the chill. After an afternoon picnic on the veranda, the light was too dim to gauge the sugar in the palm of her hand, Fathia began to sort the items on her tray, tidying the sprigs of mint leaves into a bundle. She left the children to search a little longer.

Sally noticed that Fathia was moving with more difficulty of late. The last few years had taken their toll on her health. She moved slowly, since exertion caused pain in her heart. She would bear up, tightening the muscles around her mouth and squeeze her eyes closed. Sally watched with sympathy, offering her a hand as she struggled to her feet from a sitting position. Fathia would lean heavily on her spread fingers to push herself up from the ground and before righting herself fully, she would fold the mat she had been sitting on, to avoid a second bending down.

Sally had cleared the tray of tea and bread from a picnic on the veranda with the children. It was getting dark. It was the stage of dusk, which always surprised Sally, when the house interior would look darker than outside. With just a switch the contrast would be reversed. That moment seemed to mark the definitive end of a day. House geckos would scurry to their hiding places.

The children were in the kitchen listening to the cricket that for the last few evenings had kept itself warm under the fridge, chirping away all night long. Their mother's sweeping broom had failed to reach it, luckily, and it was still croaking away. They crouched down to see where it might be, but it went silent on them. Bedtime was some way off, and this interval of time before pyjamas was precious. The adults were too busy clearing away the remains of the day to notice them.

"Let's go on the veranda and watch the dark," said Nizar. "We could have our supper there. No one would mind. You might see your cat and I could hunt the chameleon."

"My cat would chase the chameleon," said Neda. "Would that be a good thing or is it bad? Some people say the chameleon is a bad animal. Is that true?"

"No, they are wrong. People sometimes say silly things, Neda. Don't believe everything people say. Chameleons are good for the garden and especially the grapes since they eat the bugs. Daddy told me that, the first time I saw a chameleon. He said his grandfather told him. And he should know. He was a farmer."

"Is it a bad idea then to let the cat chase the chameleon?"

"I've never seen a cat do that. I don't think we need to worry about it."

"Let's find out, then."

And they both went hunting, through the kitchen garden where the herbs gave off a pungent smell, into the orchard which smelt of over-ripened fruit. On the way they discovered the bean patch. It was looking rather wilted now, so they got the hose and sprinkled the amount left inside it. Neda decided she would give them more water first thing in the morning. She plucked some leaves to keep as a reminder, and left them on the veranda wall.

Whilst the children played in the orchard, the adults sat in the television lounge and watched the news. Sally sensed her father-in-law was tense, and Fathia too fussed around him, offering tea and savouries which he refused. Fathia returned to the kitchen where she could keep an eye on the children as she prepared supper. She switched on the veranda light in the hope it would spread its beam into the orchard. But she was sure they were safe since she could hear their voices ringing out under the dark blue sky.

Chapter 2

Before the storm

"He's back," Hassan said, rather meaninglessly, out of the blue.

"Who is? Who is back?" asked Sally.

Hassan was mildly surprised that Sally did not know who might be back. Then he thought there was much in general she did not understand or know.

"Himself, our great Guide and Leader," his meaning was sarcastic. "Back after another of his disappearing tricks, only this time, it seems, is different. They got him this time."

"It's between you and me, mind you. Don't go talking outside this house?" Sally could not imagine telling anyone. "It's said that some weeks ago, a truck drove into his car, only he wasn't in it, as they had expected. He was in the one behind, which got shunted in the pile-up. The car in front was a decoy, a security he always takes. The driver of the first car was killed outright. As for the Leader, he escaped unharmed, or so they said. It's my guess he was hurt. But today being the anniversary of the glorious revolution, or coup, call it what you like, had to come out of hiding today. Perhaps he'll make an surprise announcement. Free the prisoners, say. That would pacify us, wouldn't it?"

Sally only nodded, for words failed her. It had been some time since anyone had referred even this vaguely to Saad. There had been no visits for more than a year. Not even promises. Had he died without them being told. Thoughts impossible to put into words. Had they submitted to the cold reality of helplessness, of life submerged beneath the struggle to survive. She felt sick at the thought. It was a slow dying of feeling. But now something new was crystallising. It had been time enough. For the first time, she was overcome with anger.

Hassan looked at Sally, half expecting her to answer. But seeing her face drawn and tired he realised an answer was not needed. Waiting for Saad was everything to her – the reason she was here.

Feeling his gaze on her, Sally spoke in local dialect: "Ya, Rub. Oh God!" Tears welled up in her eyes, tears of frustration, the impossibility of ineffective anger disturbing her state of sadness, for what could anger achieve but bitterness. She dipped into the bowl of roasted seeds Fathia had left for them in an attempt to quell the feeling.

They said no more, but watched and waited for the spectacle to begin. The screen showed an empty rostrum above a cement wall, below it chanting crowds no longer milling as it accumulated to fill the square. Hands waved and voices called for the beloved Leader. The strain of waiting was too much.

The screen was blurred, the reception poor. Sally thought to check upstairs to see if her set had better reception. As she climbed the staircase, she reached for the wall and touched the wings of a dullish moth that fluttered away, displaying as it did so the bright green and yellow of its underwings and emitting a disgusting smell. Many moths covered the wall all the way to her door. In her flat, in front of the television, lay a much larger dead moth, its furry body listing to one side. An army of ants trailed in and out of a hole in its abdomen. Sally suppressed a scream, scooped up the remains and threw it through a window.

She didn't stay to test the reception on the television, but slammed the door behind her, rushing down avoiding the moth-infested walls.

The Leader had just stepped up to the rostrum.

Chapter 3

Fight back

The Brother-Leader spoke with deliberation, and at times the flow of inspiration stalled. Something was amiss. He didn't have his usual poise. Perhaps he was overwhelmed by the occasion, having been in retreat so long. There had been rumours of an attempted coup, but nothing certain. Perhaps he wasn't ready for this outing; an urgency had propelled him to this place on this day, a need to show himself. Or perhaps he was moved by a curious humility.

The crowd was unaware of his difficulty finding the eloquence he so desired. The people were exuberant and relieved. They wanted him to be the Guide he had claimed he was. The hiatus in his leadership had unnerved them. It had given rise to rumour and conspiracy. The way ahead had seemed too hazardous to travel without him. Perhaps the nation would fall apart. So, he needed only to stand on the rostrum, towering above them, on the walls of the Katiba, and that simple act alone of coming to their rescue explained the magnetism, the wild jubilation. Rhythmic chants swelled to a crescendo, drowning out his incoherent message.

Sally remembered that first time when, as an ill-prepared newcomer, she had observed his adoring crowd. They had heard only fragments of what he came to say. He had supplanted a weak government, and tipped a monarchy into a republic. The moment then was scary too, and the ground beneath their feet unstable; but he had given them a vision that was sufficient to woo their allegiance. But this time, absence replenished with a longed-for reappearance, like a second coming, had recharged the waning fervour of his languishing revolution. It needed this new injection of vitality – the sacrifice of the people's freedom to his dominion, their will to his.

Sally was drawn to the screen. She strained her eyes to see his face more clearly but the image was blurry He was but a small figure, hidden by the concrete wall, above a churning sea of waving hands. The cameras did not zoom in to dispel the impression of a puppet, its shoulders swamped by a heavy toga, a trilby hat tipped to hide his eyes. His guards shuffled their positions round him, sometimes standing close and leaning as if to steady him.

From time to time, the Leader left the rostrum to return for an encore He would resume with hesitation. At times, he shook his fist and re-arranged his toga before assuming the posture of defiance. Beating hard on the rostrum, he lost his footing and someone placed a baton in his hand. Now he conducted his speech with greater force, calling his orchestra to order. It gave his speech a certain bite. But between the imperceptibly hush and the voice, there had been a shift from certainty to doubt.

"He's not himself," Hassan suggested "I told you he's been injured. They couldn't tell us, could they? No without risking a crisis. Let's see if he surprises us with a gift."

Sally wondered if tyrants under threat could ever be so magnanimous as to set their dissenters free. Had it ever happened in history? And yet against all odds, she willed it so. She could not detect a softening in his manner, no more than in her own. Despite the pathos of being so elevated yet damaged and mortal, he was still defiant, probably even more so. What hope he would shift to find a middle ground and announce an amnesty. And if he didn't, couldn't, she wanted him to go so that into the space he left behind something more compassionate and human could come.

Hassan confirmed the few details she had gleaned from the speech.: *There is only one book that carries the truth. That is his book, the Green Book. It prescribes the law. There is no need of professors. His followers are students of life. They will pass the necessary judgements. His intelligence will tell him who is guilty. Each one of us is a keeper of his faith. From tomorrow we will all have guns.'*

The Brother-Leader had left the rostrum. They stared sat the empty screen. Hassan had sat throughout with his eyes glued to this vision of what he saw as tyranny. Now he covered his face in despair. The hate that welled up was unbearable. "The man is monstrous," he declared.

This was not the right time for testing his endurance further, but Sally did just that. "*Ya Haj*," she said. "Do you know that next they'll change the currency. I've heard about it at college. You'll have to buy some gold before they do it, or it will be..."

He fumed and interrupted. "Oh, yes, and you think I can buy oranges with gold, do you? Buy gas to cook with, a sheep for Eid – all with a golden bangle. Don't pretend to know men's business. Go find your children in the garden. It's getting late. It's a woman's duty to put her children to bed at bedtime. Be a woman and know a woman's place."

Hassan regretted his words as soon as he had spoken them; but he could not explain that he virtually had no funds at all; buying gold was out of the question. Sally found his words unfairly hard, his counsel lacking sense. She had no option but to fetch her children. It was necessary anyway and she was glad to leave his company.

As she left, she heard him tell Fathia that the world had now gone mad, that men would have guns and could arrest or shoot anyone they had a grievance with. It was the new law.

Fathia did not believe him. "You are a misery," she said as she set his supper on the table in the dining room.

Sally found the children. Their faces were glowing. They had found the chameleon sitting on a vine. It had not minded them talking to it and had lazily rotated its eyes to study them. They came in with the cat following to wait nervously at the door. Fathia threw it a scrap and whispered, "Bismillah."

Hassan popped his head round the door, "So it must have hit him in the face then, the bullet. Broke his jaw. He wore a hat to shade it. I could see that plain as day."

Chapter 4

Threat

In the morning, Neda remembered to water the beans before the sun was too warm. She part-filled a watering can, not too heavy to lift and dragged it to the shady spot where the plant was struggling in the hard soil and watered it. Then she remembered another spot where she and her grandmother had planted more beans, this time at the front of the villa. Travelling round the side of the villa, the sound of a bulldozer could be heard, coming nearer. It was working on a building site at a spot just beyond the garden wall. The sound grew louder but Neda was familiar with it, working on a construction that was never-ending out there in the wilderness, so she did not worry.

She slowly poured the water from the can letting it trickle through the rose and fall in droplets over the drooping leaves. Then she sat there, waiting, hoping to see the plant lift up, though she guessed she would have to wait longer than she had patience for.

Suddenly, the great yellow metal blade of the bulldozer appeared over the garden wall and bridled up like a live animal, spilling some of its contents onto the path beside her. She ran, and as she did so, the bulldozer rammed against the wall a second time, this time shattering some of the render. The noise brought Hassan to the door. He wondered what had happened and looked at her for explanation until he saw the bulldozer rise up once more. He ran to the gate and opened it wide to shake his fist as the driver jumped down and ran away, leaving the engine roaring.

For several days after, the feeling of being under siege faded. But there were a number of incidents in the city centre following the Brother-Leader's speech. Demonstrations of support for the regime with no apparent provocation. Youths fired guns in the air. A child who happened to be deaf was run down in the High Street. Shops were commandeered and changed hands, their new owners triumphal standing in the doorways It was said that in every town and city armed youths were arresting draft avoiders A new generation of older men was called to enlist.

Even the air above was busier than usual, with fly-pasts and aerobatic displays performed by the air force. It seemed that some pilots were branching out on their own. Time and again planes passed lower than was safe. One kept recycling his swoop over Hassan's villa, the roar of the engines frightening Neda and Nizar.

After several days of becoming acquainted with the roar of planes, the children had gone to the roof to watch. One plane was so close they could see the pilot in the cockpit. They were excited now by the deafening sound of engines at full throttle, coming so near that they imagined they could almost touch the wings. Sally pulled them both inside.

Later that evening, it was announced on the news that a young pilot had crashed having flown his craft too close to land. But other reports said the plane had nosedived in a perpendicular trajectory and burrowed its way into the ground to some depth with its tail engulfed in flames. The pilot had died outright.

The hysteria had seemed to come to a violent end.

Chapter 5

Scarcity

Hassan had stayed in his room for much of the next day. Towards the evening he emerged, briefly staying in the family room where he quietly observed his grandchildren and the way they were so engaged by the ridiculous antics of cartoon mice on the television. Later they found him in the garden chair on the veranda, and bombarded him with descriptions of their escapades with chameleons and geckos, drawing him into explanations of the diving planes and daring even to talk shyly about their father.

Hassan appreciated the warmth of their confidence. Their attention kept him welded to the chair when otherwise he might have retreated to his room. He felt blessed to be playing the role of surrogate father. He enjoyed the reviving sweetness of the tea that Fathia had brewed especially to his liking, minty, strong and pungent, syrupy and far too bitter-tasting. She left him with the pot still warm for a second glass. Then to his surprise, she returned to keep him company.

The time was opportune. They seemed to be edging closer to each other and Fathia asked him to recall the Brother-Leader's speech, to tell her what he had culled from it. He was pleased she had at last reconsidered her dismissive response.

There was no doubt the speech had had its impact. There was no doubting the serious nature of it. The proliferation of guns was an alarming possibility. It was an unnecessary ploy to terrorise. Were they not frightened and cowed enough?

Their conversation skirted round the new and alarming scarcity of bread, the tiresome effort of seeking out bakeries or public ovens further afield. Daily life had become a constant search for the basic necessities. The juxtaposition of contrived scarcity for the majority with the ostentatious show of plenty by the few was divisive. But the idea of armed civilians was the truly nightmarish scenario.

"Take guns for example," Hassan complained. "Every petty-minded go-getter must have got one by now. They wear them slung ostentatiously across their chests easily discharged by accident except for the fact that most lack the necessary ammunition. I have a mind to acquire one myself. It would keep the wolves at bay," he added, taking note of Fathia's shocked glance. "I would never use it, don't you worry."

"You will never have one, Hassan. Just spend your time looking for bread and such, and don't you worry about anything else," she stated emphatically. "Let them do their worst. It's just a phase they're going through and when they think of something else to do it'll all go back to normal, mark my words it will."

Hassan was not so sure. But he appreciated her sentiment and chose to nod in agreement, to reassure her. He sensed, however, that they were about to be tested by a period of unprecedented deprivation. They would manage it somehow, since managing scarcity had already become a way of life. But he was feeling too old to master its quirks. He saw the havoc it had wreaked in the shopping precincts.

So many premises had been forcibly occupied by armed men not wearing uniform. Merchandise had been confiscated and most shops were closed and padlocked. Meanwhile a few fashion shops and furniture stores, well refurbished in the recent spate of commercial enterprise, were acquired by the state and converted into new state cooperatives. There they sold off the confiscated goods at rock bottom prices to an eager public. As stocks reduced, even these stores emptied. Food shops ran out of basics. Ice-cream melted in turned-off fridges, meat rotted and vegetables shrivelled. Survival from now on depended on who you knew.

There were mass indiscriminate arrests. Wholesale round-ups of men for the draft left families bereft of their menfolk. Grandfathers were pre-occupied with the search for food. Mothers, sisters and wives were engaged in endless rounds of social visits in the hope of finding influence to keep their sons and even their daughters safe from the draft. When this failed they sought guarantees of a comfortable posting or at least a safe training in some useful skill. Their anxieties were fed by stories of young cadets being sent to the front unprepared and poorly equipped, or of being punished for mild misdemeanours with 'drownings' in cesspits, confinement in metal containers and excessive beatings. Those who were better placed to make strategic contacts contrived marriages which gave advantage to their sons in their army careers. The contrivances and deals were endless, exhausting and time-consuming.

Everyone had to engage in the frenzied bazaar of items deliberately made scarce. What was scarce and what was plentiful were under constant revision, the market in a constant state of flux. One day it might be bread, the next tomatoes, and then meat. Or the object of desire could be more abstract like a deferment, a deceit, an absolution. The need to seek out contacts and sources was the driving force behind every social interaction reducing acts of friendship to the imperative of self-preservation. The accumulative effect was the enhancement of the Brother-Leader's hold on power.

Meanwhile production was undermined by endemic corruption and incompetence. Fear of admitting failure and thereby risking dismissal was followed inevitably by poor quality control which resulted in infected produce in the dairy industry and the spread of diseases such as brucellosis. The shortage of medical staff at most hospitals resulted in the exponential rise in the death rate.

Hassan kept his counsel and did not tell Fathia everything he knew. Of course the people grumbled, yet he knew they would never take action. You would have thought that they had suffered enough to rebel. But he knew they were exhausted, and long-suffering, and had adopted a kind of fatalism which meant they could continue in this despairing manner indefinitely, always waiting for better times that might never ever come.

That evening, when everyone had gone to bed. Hassan discovered the stem of drying bean leaf that Neda had picked from the garden the evening before. He did not know who had planted the beans in the first place; he guessed it was his wife. He found a glass, filled it with water and carefully placed the wilting stem against the rim for support.

Chapter 6

A matching pair

Hassan had never bothered with a bank account. Banking was an unnecessary hassle. So his name did not appear on the lists under scrutiny. He had, however, acquired a safe, that new symbol of treason and treachery. So now he spent the morning counting through the notes and coins he had stashed there. It had been his security against hardship, a natural worry in the circumstances. Now it was made a crime, and a new source of fear. There was no point ridding himself of the safe; that would risk being discovered. He needed to hide it but the enormity of the risk overwhelmed him and he had no idea how he might bury such an awkward cumbersome item. Neither could he risk buying gold for fear of his meagre fast-depleting savings coming to light. He was frozen between acting and not acting.

Fathia came to his aid, 'tsking' all the while, having pleaded many times with him to convert what little cash they did have to gold. Hassan neither defended himself nor admitted his error. She helped him push the safe further behind a pile of clothes that were draped in multiple layers over a free-standing clothes rack. Fathia promised him she would cultivate an impression of untidiness to shore up the hiding place and it would never be discovered. He trusted her, and left the practicalities to her.

But now action was needed to raise more cash. He was impatient for his scheme with Nuri to be up and running. He trusted Nuri was working on it but he was taking his time and so he needed a distraction in the meantime. He had heard there was a disturbance in the market place. Those whose shops had been confiscated and had their merchandise seized were gathering there in the hope of buying back their own goods which were now being sold off at ridiculous prices. And now there was a fracas in the market square, as armed police tried to identify them as traitors in amongst the unruly crowd.

Hassan felt there was no harm in being part of the action. He might even buy something himself if the prices were as low as had been rumoured. Mohamed took him there. He had his own stories to tell on the way, tales of immigrant workers who had been prised out of their shacks in the shanty town declaring their innocence while soldiers rifled through their collections of goods wrapped in layers of plastic bags against the encroaching smothering dust. They were things impossible for them to find back home, items such as feather pillows, leather sandals, and cut-glass vases, all made ready and good for a future journey which they would be making at the end of their seasonal employment. It would not be possible to declare them at customs on the border since most of the men were illegally here and would have to make secret journeys overnight through the mountain passes and attempt the hazardous climb down and up gullies that were hidden in deep vegetation where electric wire fences did not extend. The soldiers at customs would in any case take whatever they fancied for themselves.

Mohamed himself had an official work permit. He was perfectly legal. He also had a bank account and everything he did was according to the law. His family were with him and he spent everything he earned on them. He had no accumulated funds and was not at risk. But he understood why others less fortunate than himself might have to live by their wits and duck and dive between the rules. Hassan felt pleased that he had made Mohamed's life as safe as possible, a fact which Mohamed had appreciated.

They were aware of a commotion long before they approached the market square. All manner of vehicles were haphazardly parked and double parked on both sides all along the route making the road passable in one direction only. Mohamed thought it best to abandon their car some distance away to ease their exit if things turned nasty. At this point Hassan began to doubt the wisdom of his going any further and thought he would prefer to sit it out in the car while Mohamed went on ahead to investigate. Looking deeper into the tangled log-jam, Hassan could see youths scrambling over cars to get closer to the epicentre of the chaos. He really did not have the stomach for this ungainly scramble.

Mohamed agreed. He strode out towards the crowds, unafraid of the various soldiers who stood on guard with their Kalashnikovs poised to shoot, a finger on the trigger. He was a tall man, taller than most and soon acquired a vantage point by dint of the crowd giving way in deference as if he was an official dignitary. He was amazed to see a man standing on a mountain of shoes all piled up on the back of a lorry.

With great enthusiasm the man threw the shoes one by one into the air just high enough to be caught by the most agile of customers. They leapt into the air to snatch the shoe tucking it away in their clothing ready for the next catch. They elbowed and kicked each other in the groin, the stomach, the face, committing the foulest of deeds, happy to pay a nominal sum for the single shoe. Cadres milled through the crowd collecting payment even from those who had acquired nothing.

Mohamed found the whole event incredible. Grown men scavenging in the dusty ground for a lost shoe was a humiliating sight; it would have been too boisterous for Hassan. The older men there stood aghast, hardly able to believe their eyes, disdaining to take part and fearing for their safety as fights broke out around them. The man on the truck looked down in scorn, enjoying the mayhem he was creating.

Quite by accident, Mohamed acquired a shoe. It had come hurtling in his direction like a flying shuttle and would have hit him in the face had he not just picked it from the air. It was a trainer; and then he saw the irony and insult of this crazy event because of course now he needed a matching shoe where before he had needed nothing. He would have left, but he was intrigued to see if the matching shoe would follow after. He tied the one shoe to his belt and waited. Many missiles were near misses landing in the open hands of someone just behind him. He did not want to try too hard but it was tempting to stay just in case. He reached out with one hand and caught another shoe but this time it was a high-heeled boot in bright pink leather. He knew no one who would wear such an impossible thing even with its sister match. He kept this one under his arm, waiting not for its match but thinking he might exchange it for the missing trainer if he could find it. Losing interest, Mohamed collected several shoes none of which matched, all in different sizes and colours, male and female, adult and child. He kept them tight under one arm and close to his side, tied to each other if possible in a linked chain. Then he gave up as did many others, shaking their heads in disbelief and frustration.

On the way back to where he had left Hassan, he noticed groups of men gathered in huddles on the pavements. They were exchanging matching shoes. Sometimes simply exchanging shoes that were not pairs yet but which might be useful if they became pairs. Mohamed got rid of the pink boot and found a match for a child's sandal, perhaps for Neda. This was a promising start. He guessed the matching would go on for days and it would give him something to do instead of drinking coffee. He had paid very little for his seven shoes and felt in the end that the effort had been worth it.

He went back to the car where Hassan was asleep. Hassan woke up with a start as Mohamed dropped down into the driver's seat and threw the shoes on the back seat.

"It's crazy out there," was all he said. Hassan was too drowsy to ask what was crazy and told Mohamed to keep the useless shoes. Later, when they arrived home, he thought to ask what had transpired.

"Shoes. Lots of them." This was all the sense that Mohamed could muster. "And none of them matching. It's crazy."

Later that day in the evening, Mohamed knocked on the kitchen door and Fathia answered it. He insisted that she take the sandal that might do for Neda if he could find the match and three female shoes which he thought he would have no chance of finding a match for. He explained how he had come by them and she was tempted not to believe his account – for who would think of such a thing! But for the next few days, various neighbours whom she had not seen for some time, came ringing at her gate with shoes to exchange. None could be matched so Fathia placed them all outside her gate in the hope that passers-by would discover them. The next morning all but one were gone.

Hassan picked up this last remaining shoe arriving home at lunchtime, thinking one of his grandchildren had thrown it there. He started to chide them for their carelessness. Only then did he discover where the shoe had come from. Examining it closely he saw the name of the firm of a distant relative stamped on the sole. He had once been envied for his fortune but must now be in serious trouble. He wanted to investigate but was troubled by the burdensome fact that he had little to offer another family in distress.

Fathia too was concerned about the shoe. Perhaps there was a match but she would have to pay for it, and people were ratcheting up the prices for matching shoes, so Hassan wanted to abandon any search as too undignified. In the end, Fathia believed she could find its match and against his better judgement kept it. Hassan left her to her own devices knowing he had to find Nuri.

The following day, he visited Nuri immediately after siesta. He left his grandchildren watching television, and his wife hanging washing on the line. He closed the door quietly, not wanting to be seen as he left. And he was gone by the time a newsflash interrupted the cartoon show with a new decree. The Leader had cancelled the old currency and replaced it with a new one, of which no one yet had even a single note or coin. It might be some time before the new notes were printed. In the meantime, the people would have to barter with goods in kind.

Tom and Jerry continued with their absurd antics across the screen, indulging in savage acts of revenge. And the children thought it was all in jest.

Chapter 7

Souvenirs

On the way, Hassan chatted with Mohamed about the state of things. Mohamed explained he had bought his wife some gold some weeks ago and was now very pleased he had done so. He had just heard the news on his car radio, a change in currency. Hassan admired Mohamed's astuteness in buying gold but questioned his last comment about new currency.

"I would have thought you would have heard about it before me, sir." Mohamed was surprised. Hassan, too proud to answer, was struck with a sense of doom, too shocked to even think what it would mean. His startled expression was sufficient for an answer. Nothing more was said until passing Ahmed's shop they noticed the door open. Hassan prepared himself for yet another shock. Perhaps this too had been commandeered, the premises and all his precious stock.

Inside Hassan found Nuri busy in the dark recesses at the back of the shop, moving boxes and emptying their contents. Nuri turned, his body flipped with shock. He had thought the door was locked behind him.

"You should keep the door locked, my son, and the shutters down to avoid attention."

"You're right. I thought they were. It's lucky this business has been such a failure. So far, they've left us alone." They were silent for the next few minutes because the world had shifted a few degrees since last they met. Nuri had heard about the change of currency. It meant their resources were severely under threat and what had been urgent before was critical now. It was no longer possible to keep his anxious uncle in the dark about his pavement enterprise. He would have to tell him everything.

"I'm afraid," Nuri began slowly, "things are not quite as we thought. Your shop has been occupied. By soldiers, I think. They're armed anyway. They're using the place, using it for something else. Not a shop anyway. It's far too dangerous to attempt a forced entry. But don't worry. I have a plan. I'm going to watch them. I can set up a stall, on the pavement opposite. I'm setting it up using some of the things from here." Seeing Hassan's crestfallen face, he added, "Don't worry. It'll be fine. And we have all this stuff here to keep us going in the meantime. There's quite a lot of it."

This last note of optimism focused their attention on the boxes and together they selected batches of different items that each could take and try to sell on the black market. Some items were quite special being of a good quality that was no longer available. Hassan left to fetch Mohamed and the car to load it once the street was clear of passers-by. There were faces lurking at windows, which they could do nothing about, and so, they carried on regardless. Hassan left for home at dusk, his family car full of merchandise, wondering where to start selling in the ubiquitous but invisible market that was called 'black'.

Nuri stayed on at his father's shop for a little while longer. He had not yet decided which pieces he would take to sell on the street. Anything would be a wrench because he treasured every item. He would like to keep it all intact, at least until he could establish his father's shop anew. His attention was drawn to the various items on the counter that were arranged in serried rows as if being prepared for some kind of classification regarding their quality and value. There were some Roman and Greek coins, of Libyan origin, still unsorted in a small basket beside the till; fairly recent acquisitions he assumed. Alongside them, there were some marble pieces he had not seen before. Possibly, they had come from antique columns and friezes that had collapsed and been left untended in the various ancient sites along the coast; he hoped they had not been chipped away deliberately for the tourist trade. That was something his father would have worried about. Perhaps they had been set aside for that very reason. He would have wanted to check their origins and satisfy himself that they were legally acquired. They were beautifully carved shapes of leaves and fruits, or the torsos of slain horses and men, beautiful in the pathos they exuded and satisfyingly heavy when held in the hand. He understood their attraction.

Beneath the counter other precious items were displayed in a glass case. He had spent long hours helping his father to itemise each one of its contents noting the details of their provenance and dates – items such as mosaic pieces from Byzantine churches, coins his father had found in an official archaeological dig and which he was subsequently allowed to keep, pieces of amber found on desert trips they had enjoyed together, some with prehistoric flora and fauna trapped inside, and stones which when tapped had fallen apart to reveal fossils. And other stones whose polished surface showed the amazing patterns of crystals, formed slowly over geological time. There was even the little copper lantern with a globular base for holding oil. He remembered polishing it for the first time and it had been his job to maintain its shiny surface. Neglected now for some time, its patina was dulled over. He had never understood why it did not sell, but he did not want it to.

Behind the counter there were stacks of cushion covers and table runners made from damask and embroidered silks decorated with silken cords and tassels. Beside them was a shelf of braids and straps, some long enough to wrap around an animal's head as reins or to wear as an adornment over long flowing manes. They were the celebratory bridles worn by camels, horses and donkeys, all woven in wools dipped in bright dyes, and decorated with beads or buttons, some made of mother of pearl. They were Bedouin bridal items, of late considered too crude by the more affluent citizens of the town but very popular with tourists.

From the ceiling hung many metal lampshades and lamps with arabesque and geometric shapes cut out to let the light fall through in cascades. More bridles hung from lantern brackets, camel reins and mother-of-pearl shells threaded on thick cords dangled like stars in the Milky Way. Some swept his head as he passed beneath them, reminding him that they were there and causing a feint jangle of varied sounds as they swung to stillness.

Nuri sighed as he drew his eyes from feasting on all this precious stuff. He was sure he could revive the shop and make it pay again. It was a dream he had to make real. There was little chance if he was fated for soldiering.

Against this backdrop of confused emotions of hope and dread, Nuri selected his first lot of items for sale: a rose of the desert gypsum crystal, small enough to part with easily; a weighty piece of petrified forest, dark and smooth with brittle ends; a little glass bottle skilfully filled with different coloured sand to form friezes of camels and desert plants; a Bedouin flute, and Bedouin bracelets strung with silver hands and fish; a string of glass beads rippled with a rainbow collection of colours; a velvet fish with a cord for hanging as a protective charm on a child's cot, embroidered in bright silks and strung with lucky charms and tassels; silver bangles, beaten into fine decorative relief with birds and flowers. Perhaps this last item was too precious he thought as he traced the flowing procession of flora and fauna around the soft curve of metal, along the ridge and furrows of the edges. He returned it to the glass case and wrapped the rest in a cloth. This he rolled in a little rug that he would use to sit on.

There was one last thing to do. He remembered the key to his uncle's shop. He would have to hide it here for now. He took it from his trouser pocket still wrapped in the pamphlet that he had plucked from the sandstorm. He looked around for a safe inaccessible place to leave and spied a shelf behind the till, high up on the wall. It would be difficult to reach without a ladder. He tossed it up into the niche and heard its dull clink as it fell into the recess. He meant to hide an anthology of poems there with it but there was time enough for that. There the key would stay until he needed it.

He left the shop, bolting the door behind him, and securing the locks on the metal shopfront shutters. He looked around him quickly, then walked briskly home.

Chapter 8

A deception uncovered

The Brother-Leader was now monitoring everything for himself. He decided he could not trust his minions, marionettes, as he perceived them to be, for he would pull the strings. He sat alone at his console, now in his private media suite, the existence of which was known to very few. It was an antechamber constituting the innermost sanctum of his fortress residence in the capital. Anyone invited in would presume they had reached the highest echelons of favour and patronage,

Equipped with the latest in satellite technology, he had been the first to use one-way video conference event as a means for seeing for himself what his people thought. He could summon a conference at any venue of his choosing, and on any topic. Those who operated the cameras at a local level had no inkling of the network they were linked into. They were unaware that they too were under surveillance, the cameras also shone a light on them. Interesting intelligence had come his way in just this manner.

He was ready the arrival of his summoned minister, who arrived in a noticeable state of fear. His escorts left him at the door of the video suite. They spent no more time at this threshold of suspicion than was absolutely necessary, for fear of guilt by association.

"Ah, there you are, Hamad," the Leader exclaimed without taking his eyes off one of the screens. He was staring at an empty seat, empty by betrayal, a noxious something he sensed all around him all the time. A smell that unnerved him. It saddened him to think he had been deceived by one he thought so loyal, but nevertheless flexed his muscles to a steely resolve.

"I expect you'd like to tell me everything you know, Hamad," he said, not turning.

Hamad had no idea what urgent issue had brought him here at such a time, but a summons in the middle of the next meant he must be guilty of something.

"What is it that I know and you do not, esteemed Comrade?"

The Leader and Guide, his back still turned could not read his face, but heard the tremor in his voice.

"Where have you been these last few days, not to know my meaning, Adel?"

"Oh, you mean the confiscations, the arrests, Comrade. Not much to tell. It all goes well."

"You must be mad to think I don't know that is a lie. You've been away haven't you, Comrade? I call you Comrade. You call me Leader, Hamad. Don't forget your place in the scheme of things. You are nothing more to me than a slave."

"Leader..." Hamad stuttered and could not continue. The demotion chilled him. He had until now been treated almost as an equal, at least elevated above the rest, so he had thought. And where had he been? He could not say, impossible to reveal.

"There was chaos in the marketplace, I hear. What say you about it?" The Leader's probing would be relentless, he knew.

"Chaos? No I wouldn't go that far. We had it under control."

"Chaos, Hamad. Chaos is just what I ordered. There was chaos in the marketplace."

"Oh well, if you put like that. Yes, it was a bit messy at the time. But nothing we couldn't handle. We knew what was going on. And it's all sorted now."

"Is it now? You are sure of that?"

"Yes, Leader. I am sure."

"How would you know – what was going on? You were not here."

"I had my minions, my men, taking care of things." Hamad did not hesitate to defend himself. It seemed pointless to deny the charge that he had been away at some point during the recent disturbances. "They reported directly to me. I did not miss a trick, not a single deviation." The Leader found him amusingly arrogant – what does he mean by 'his minions!'

"So you had your minions. You have minions? Taking care of things? You have minions, do you? So where were you through it all? Where were you, Hamad? Tell me that."

"A family wedding, my Esteemed Leader. You were invited, you remember? My youngest sister married now to an enthusiastic revolutionary cadre. One of your best. You arranged the match yourself."

A little displeased by the touché, the Leader chose a different tack. "They reported what to you exactly?"

"Everything, Leader. They told me everything. Kept me informed with a daily log."

"A daily log?"

"Hourly, especially at the height of things."

"What kind of things, Hamad? What kind of things needed an hourly log?"

"The arrests, my Leader. The arrests you charged me with."

"List them for me. I need you to tell me all their names."

"Well they're recorded, Leader. I don't remember them all – there were so many."

"Tell me one, just one." And the Leader adopted a casual understated tone, as he swaggered round the room.

"Faiz, the butcher, sir. He was one. He deserves to rot in jail if you ask me."

"I didn't ask you if he deserved it, Hamad. And I don't need your advice. I have my own minions you see. They do my bidding. And you are one of them. And where were you when they arrested Faiz the butcher? I'll take care of him, don't you worry."

"And so they should, my esteemed Leader. So they should. He had millions stashed away, planned to take it all abroad."

"And where were you, Hamad, when they arrested Faiz?"

"At the wedding, sir. I told you, at the wedding."

"You were not, Hamad. You were not at the wedding at ten o'clock on Friday night. Nor should you have been. You should have been at your office."

"I visited my office briefly, sir. There was no business there."

"There should have been business there, Hamad. Your business. It was your business to extricate Faiz the butcher from this mess because he is my trusted mole. He's allowed whatever perks find their way to him because he is my very trusted mole. I instructed you to be there making sure the special ones were not caught and you failed, you dog, you failed. Do you see that?"

"I'm very sorry, sir. I received no such instruction."

"Of course you didn't, you were not there to receive it. You were not there, Hamad. Where were you when you were not there?"

Hamad had reached the end of his feeble prevaricating. He knew the Leader knew where he had been. He had not been at the wedding even for a short while. He did not make a brief visit to his office. He had made an urgent trip abroad, using a forged passport. He knew he could be asked about the trip but had not expected in these circumstances. He thought he would be forgiven, given the chance to explain.

"Don't bother lying to me, Hamad. You will be the first to be tried at the new revolutionary court. There is neither judge nor jury to save you there. You will have no lawyer for defence. My most devoted followers will prosecute and pass sentence on you. I leave it all to them."

Hamad attempted pleading but the Leader was circling his desk in a rage, finally stopping by the mirror to adjust his hair. He tossed his last remarks over his shoulder.

"I've finished with you, you cur. I'll call a guard when I'm ready to let you go, but before you do, I must explore your mind for any other matters you have kept from me. Tell me, do the people love me more since I have demanded taxes of them? Do they understand me? Do they know why I have taken their businesses away?"

Hamad spoke quietly, his voice trembling. One last hope of salvation gave him energy for the answer: "The people do not associate you with taxes, my Leader. They blame the cadres."

"How do they feel about the new currency?"

"They admire your profile, sir, on the notes and coins. They say there should be higher denominations and your profile on the highest only."

"Do they like my plans for a new university dedicated to me and my philosophy?"

"They think this is the best plan of all. Your name is most appropriate on such a noble institution."

"And do they like my book? Do they read avidly?"

"They love it sir, they learn it off by heart like the holy Koran. It is a guide for living life in all its parts."

"You are out of date, Hamad. I have written a collection of poems. Do they like my poems?"

"They love everything you do, oh Esteemed Leader. Have I not always told you so?"

"You lie to me, Hamad. The people do not love me and for this I will make them suffer. You try to protect them by flattering me. You try to have me think there is nothing to worry about when I need to upbraid them, when they need re-educating. All the time, they try to escape me and you try to delude me."

"I have done my best, sir, to advise you. I am sorry if my best has not been good enough."

"It isn't. You are correct. Remember I will not gloss over your misdemeanours like you have glossed over the people's."

"I have never glossed over things, sir, Leader, please believe me. I have always told the truth."

"But you did Hamad. You did gloss over things. And shall I tell you when you did that? You had a certain wily sheikh visit all the prisoners, to teach them and then to pronounce them true believers every one."

"That's true, Esteemed Leader. He was very careful and found them all loyal in their hearts."

"That was a lie, Hamad. The sheikh himself has been arrested. He finally admitted it was a lie told to protect the miserable curs. Who is betrayed when traitors are protected, tell me that? Who did the sheikh deceive?"

"He must have deceived me, sir, if what you say is true. Leader."

"No, not true. It was when he vouched for your loyalty that I knew he was a lost soul. You were his accomplice. You helped write the reports. You colluded, you dog. And you tried to fool me. That is the greatest offence you could ever perpetrate against me. I placed my trust in you. You were meant to protect me, not my enemies."

"Not true, my Esteemed Leader. Please hear me out. I beg you."

The Leader did not answer his plea. He turned his back and relayed the videoed interrogation of the sheikh. It rolled on for several minutes, the demeaning of him, his proud lifting of the chin in defiance, his silent non-compliance. The Leader laughed, then swore at him.

"By the way," he was sitting at the console now and, turned suddenly in his swivel chair. "I have just ordered the arrest of your sister's husband. An audacious display of gold he gave her, contrary to orders I am about to pronounce. The banning of gold is my next decree. Backdated a year or more, as required on a case-by-case basis. I leave it all to the discretion of my legal team, loyal youths who do my bidding effortlessly."

The Leader tapped with a stick on the floor. He watched the door, believing the doorman would be listening at the crack and open it right away.

"I'll give you one last chance to save yourself, you donkey. I am very interested in a youth who seems not to have understood his lowly status as 'miserable citizen'. He has a pavement business, but no licence. We will not bother about that. No need to blow our cover, or his yet. He has placed himself right opposite a site we have commandeered for street surveillance. The fool has no idea he is directly in our sights. Look I'll show you what I mean. There he is. Not a roaring trade is it? And yet he persists. You must follow him and report directly back to me. Your assistance will be your reprieve, and your brother-in-law's too."

The Leader slapped the door with his stick, and the doorman's face appeared round it, apprehensive and ready to do his Leader's bidding.

Chapter 9

Contagious poets

The family were watching television. Hassan disapproved more and more of their fascination for the trivia that counted for entertainment, for its distortion of the truth. He took himself off to the orchard to tend to the new shoots of vegetables that had appeared unexpectedly around its edges; they were the forgotten plantings of a previous season.

Meanwhile the family, immune to his scorn, continued watching the screen for the escape it offered them. It was safe unreality, a place where pending disaster was converted into visual illusion. It was childish innocence free in spirit yet surrounded and hedged in by adult menace. They watched it in defiance of everything, lulled into a kind of unthinking stupor, hardly blinking when the images switched unannounced and the screen moved seamlessly from the jerky cartoon movements of wheeling legs and eyes on stalks to a live human performance of different but equal unreality.

At opposite sides of a stage, two poets were poised like feral cats on their haunches, as if about to spring. Their mouths were stretched to exaggerated proportions like market hawkers bawling out their wares, ready to holler their raucous alarms. Their language was the lexicon of abuse, it was full of obscenities and primitive in essence. Their antics were random and absurd, too erratic, too full of melodramatic lunges and crazy somersaults for the camera lens to keep track. At times they stood back poised in the wings, hidden. At times, a defiant fist arced its trajectory rising from the floor, from corner to corner of the screen, or an eye glared into the camera and poked a tunnel of focussed hate straight into the viewer's brain.

Often the screen was empty, a misty grey pause drawn out for long stretches of silence. Into this vacuous space first one and then the other would leap, each a fleeting image of a screech wide across the stage, their bodies a blur of cartwheels. They hurled fantastic menaces at protagonists who were to all intents and purposes absent, or so it seemed, unless the audience was indicated. The intention was unclear until the exchanges settled into a regular rhythm and made it obvious that this was a dedication to enmity, a tit for tat exchange from one to the other. It was the 'other' that was hated. Their venom was sheer undiluted fury.

The children stared at the screen. Nizar, his sister and their little cousins had barely noticed the programme change. They wondered at the juxtaposition between the antics of Tom and Jerry and the circus antics of what seemed to them to be clowns. Perhaps the themes were recognisable but just maybe there was a nuanced difference.

Tyranny itself had arraigned the poets. Their orders were to perform poetic stunts that asserted their patron's sovereign power. Their innovations had to express the most intense expressive power. The aim was to engender awe, to gouge into the public mind a lasting impression of the insuperable force at the disposal of the Leader. He needed the skills of poets to broadcast the propaganda of war.

So then, poetry must serve the objectives of war. It must be powerful enough to silence opposition. It must imply a foe, conjured up if not real. The Leader needed poets to foment the unifying theme of hate, those within challenging those without who stood between his goal and failure. It was a way of strutting on the world stage. It was a way of parodying a larger polemic. The poets' debacle was to be a haunting of the nation.

Part Ten – Contingencies

She did not linger to hear the owl hooting in the trees but ushered in the children before its wail could dash her hopes completely. There was still Saad to pray for.

Chapter 1

The trap

So how was it that events moved so swiftly and unimpeded from a live performance of poetry to a series of gallows on a church wall? The route they took was subterranean, veiled and impossible to track. Who could say with any certainty when the plan was made, the place of execution decided on? At the shallow surface there were some seemingly unconnected assignations that marked their progress.

Imagine an earnest man, a pillar of society whose position ipse facto made him prominent. Who better to carry the project forward than the chief librarian, retainer in the Leader's personal entourage, his tutor in literary matters, and guardian of all key knowledge. As keeper of books for the nation, he symbolised the nation's fund of wisdom.

Fathi's Benghazi office was located in an imposing building, legacy of the Italian colonisation of Libya decades past with its Roman style. He was small in stature, given the enormity of the room, but nevertheless he was imposing, elegantly dressed, to the point of wearing the disfavoured tie. There were three large windows above his head so high they cast little light at the level of his desk.

Sally had an appointment with Fathi, her first ever invitation to his office. She had known where it was because it was opposite the sunken garden where she often sat, in the shadow of a plinth supporting a sculpture of the *sylphium* plant. She had wondered about the function of the building with its row of august windows. She understood Fathi to be a man of integrity, knowing he sat on the board of trustees for the Association for the Blind. He had arranged several dates before, each one cancelled at the last minute, his message reaching her at the college.

Fathi met her at the door. His smile, with hindsight, was not the friendliest, more a mask. He was uneasy, his voice terse. He explained that the original purpose of the meeting, a planning session with a fellow language teacher for a course for librarians, had fallen through, but there was still something she could do for him.

The large back of a winged easy chair dominated the entrance to the room. It blocked her view of who sat there. There were children sitting on the lap of a man who eased himself to peer around the wings of the chair. Two small boys smiled shyly, and stopped their endless wriggling. If only their father's eyes had not met hers so knowingly.

Sally did not understand the import of the breaking of recognition. Fathi ensconced himself in his leather chair behind his desk. He did not bother with introductions.

"You know this man?" he asked. "You remember him? He remembers you."

She did not know him. She could not remember ever meeting him, and said so. The father smiled and the children resumed their rough and tumble play, one slipping to the ground so that he must reach down to catch him. That was almost the end of it. She was confused.

Then the father turned again and said, "I remember you. You came to see us that night before you left. You had to leave, you remember? You came at night. It was safer that way in the dark. There had been a power cut and we had candles lit. You sat with my wife and watched television. She was pregnant then, with this our eldest child. Don't you remember?"

Sally did remember and said as much with pleasure. She was still standing behind the armchair unsure of what to do for proper etiquette. There was no extra seat. The father was rising to free his as she recalled the night before she and Saad had left Libya for exile. "You were very kind to us," she said. "It was during Ramadan and we broke the fast together."

The father looked pleased she had remembered. An expression of concern for her spread across his eyes. His smile was warm; he was pleased to have the chance to express his friendship and solidarity with her; pleased to show her his sons.

Fathi stood up, suddenly. He spoke sharply, "Well, that will be all. There is no further point in this meeting. I understand everything I need to understand." He stared at something invisible in the space behind her, the door. He swiftly made his way to it and ushered her out of the room. She found herself running down the steps into the street. With laboured breath, panicking, she fled into the street.

The sun was blinding. She halted just in time at the kerb as a large car sped at speed past her. A man, not Libyan, wearing a small-brimmed straw hat was standing on the opposite side of the road. He was very tall with fair skin that was burnt pink by the sun or glowing with the heat. He watched her cross over to his side of the road. He followed her at a steady pace until he caught up with her. He said there was a meeting planned but he had been late. He apologised but kept her there on the corner chatting about his considerable experience in setting up language courses. Sally made an excuse about a coach waiting for her. She ran, confused by the feeling that something awful and incomprehensible had happened. Looking back, she saw the stranger was still there, watching her.

Chapter 2

The gallows

Later that day, police burst into the home of the father who had been Saad's friend, a man whose name Sally did not remember. There was no warrant for his arrest, no charges pressed but they had come to take him away all the same. They had an authority that transcended law of rights and due process. His association with Saad, proven unwittingly by Sally herself, was the evidence against him. He was the required scapegoat, a local notable, lecturer in Sociology at the university, to be outcast as a warning. His exclusion to outsider status was confirmed by his execution alongside four illegal immigrants. Of what he was guilty was never disclosed or proven, but the public statement carried the legend that he had plotted against the Brother-Leader along with four illegal migrants. Together, it was alleged, they had caused an explosion at a warehouse on the harbour.

They came for him minutes following the explosion, unconcerned with the need for plausibility. They took him in a Mercedes along the coastal road to the capital. It took a day's drive with a stopover in a camp, where he was kept bound and blindfolded in a dug-out hole in the sand. They interrogated him for five days and then returned him to a military base in Benghazi, hooded with a sack. Before the day was done, in the darkened early evening they had hung him from a gallows erected on the wall of a disused church alongside the four other victims.

That night, the Brother-Leader visited the vicinity of the gallows to observe the men left hanging there. He arrived on a donkey-drawn open carriage, more a cart than carriage, with a platform laden with drums that were decorously strewn with garlands. Drummers beat a chaotic rhythm, furiously pounding the taut skins. The leader sat amongst them, drugged and entertained. At intervals the carriage stopped and various officers dismounted slipping into the night to perform their duties. They charged their way into the various halls of residence for female students. They dragged them from their beds.

Press-ganged to join the toxic melodrama unfolding at the rear of a donkey cart, their ears assaulted with the ugly words of righteous revenge and hate, they were goaded to swell the unholy chanting. A stream of gown-clad women sleepwalked, the donkey's braying adding to the cacophony. Not in their wildest dreams had they imagined such celebration, such decadent disregard for the dignity of bodies still hanging fresh and warm, names withheld as victims unworthy of remembrance.

Salha and Salem came knocking at Hassan's door the night of the executions. Salha was hysterical. They had just arrived home when they became aware of a commotion in the street below their apartment. Large stadium lanterns had been erected and carpenters were hastily constructing gallows on the wall of the Roman Catholic church which had not been used for two or more decades. The church had become a meeting place for a cell of faithful followers of the leader. Until now, Salem had thought its location had made them safe and on occasions he had been summoned there for reasons he had never divulged to his wife.

At first Salem had watched the action with indifferent curiosity. But then he began to recognise the shapes that were emerging, the furniture of execution. He called his wife to watch with him and had not reckoned with her squeamishness. Suddenly he realised it was not wise to be associated with the gruesome scene that was about to be enacted.

Unusually, the men and women did not separate but sat together round the family room at Hassan's villa. The children sensed the tension – a speechless Salha was an unfamiliar sight. Neda wanted her to entertain them as she usually did. Salem lacked the reassurance that usually made them feel safe. If anything, he seemed chastened, and even deferential to his brother-in-law. Hassan sat brooding in his dark leather chair, waiting for Salem to speak.

"There's something going on," was all that Salem could say. "Put the television on, There might be some news."

The screen sprang to life but without warning went blank again. Seconds later, it resurged with triumphal military music set to a scene which materialised from the darkness. The hanging was being filmed live and relayed to a national audience. Fathia, who had been seated to oversee the making of the tea, struggled to her feet. Nauseous, she rushed to the bathroom. Salha hid her face.

Sally was a novice, an untutored innocent who could not predict what kinds of terrifying things might happen next. She made sense of what she saw from the responses of those around her, until she saw five men walking in a file their heads covered with sacks. One by one they took their place beneath each scaffold. One of them stumbled on the poorly assembled wooden blocks that served as steps. He was pushed as he tried to regain his balance and fell headlong to the jeering cheers of the soldiers and police gathered round them. Amongst the cheers, the braying of a donkey could be heard and a drum roll announced the kicking away of the platforms on which they stood. There was no blessing, no chanting of the creed of faith, and if the condemned men uttered their prayers they could not be heard by their executioners.

"Long live the revolution! Long live the Guide!" the Brother-Leader's cadres shouted.

Chapter 3

Lanterns

The day had begun like any other with absurd normality. It was the first day without rain after many days and nights of stormy weather. It had been so bad in recent days that torrential rain had flooded every ditch and gully and some children had paddled their way to school on rafts of corrugated iron or any flat piece of jetsam, anything big enough that floated. School buses had been impossible to dislodge from ruts in muddy side-roads that were nothing more than tracks. Otherwise, the threat of entrapment in the flood had kept most people at home. Perhaps now the flood would subside and life would revert to normal, as normal as life could ever be. Sally had lost all measure of what 'normal' was.

Before breakfast the children had been in the garden talking first to the gardener and then to Mohamed the driver. Sally had watched them from her upstairs window, the formal dining room window that was large but seemed small and crowded out by the scale of the reproduction furniture. The sun never found its way far into this long room and when the sky was overcast, as it had been throughout the rainy season, it was like a cave, and damp. The olive velvet curtains absorbed the dust. No matter how often she had vacuumed them, at the lightest touch they belched out clouds of terracotta talc.

She had seen the children enter Mohamed's garden room, shaking off their sandals as they entered it out of respect for his modest living quarters. She knew they were safe. She knew he would be talking about his family, the names of his children and his wife. His room was sparsely furnished with a small rug that filled the floor space. The homely touch of delicate sprigs of embroidery on the Chinese cotton pillowcases that Fathia had given him, neatly spread on his bed contrasted with the plastic bags that held his shaving gear and washing. She had given him a small electric fire that hardly kept him warm but slowly dried his clothes, and a stool for his alarm clock. She reflected on Mohamed's gentleness and wished that the children could have known the gentleness of their own father. She was brooding, feeling her spirit plummet, unable to draw herself away from the gloom she had become so wedded to.

Looking beyond the garden gates, she saw the migrant workers digging trenches, deep and gaping foundations for new villas. She worried that they might fall into the trenches as they worked so precariously on the unguarded edges of soft soil turned to mud. The trenches were filled almost to the brim with rainwater. She had worried that the children might fall in them too on their way to school but she knew that for now Mohamed would keep them safe from wandering outside.

Reassured, she turned away from the scene and scanned the room, the heavy furniture so depressing. The bookcase stored all Saad's medical journals, her paints which she rarely used and some secret letters that had been smuggled out of prison some time ago. The letters had stopped coming. She had no idea why. She had never questioned their provenance, and could not now seek out the intrepid soul who had been the intermediary. Had she or he been discovered? Had the chink in the oppressive system of censored communication been divulged to some interloper? She wished that she could answer them but there was no chance of that.

For now, the forbidden past was safely stored in the bookcase in its separate compartments, in boxes with taped lids, in bundles tied with string, in piles neatly organised by date. The past was so safely tucked away that it seemed to have slid away even from the key that locked it up. She wasn't sure where she had hidden it. It was probably in the sideboard opposite and so she turned to stare at it to secure its location in her mind so that she would know where to look when she needed it.

As she faced its hiding place, the sight of three large black seeds from a castor oil plant caught her attention. She had not known that they were highly toxic, the source of ricin famously used by terrorists since even the smallest amount is fatal to human beings. They had been left some weeks ago on the top of the sideboard and since forgotten. She remembered being given them by the wife of a doctor acquaintance of Saad's, herself a doctor. "Eva," she had said, almost whispering under her breath, and she had thought nothing of it at the time. Eva had simply placed the seeds in her hands, as she left, saying everyone was growing them for their shiny decorative leaves.

But Sally had never felt tempted to plant them. She had been unsuccessful even with the sweet potato, the easiest plant to grow in pots indoors. She turned again to examine the seeds more closely. "Eva," she said the name again. She wondered at their purpose sitting now on her sideboard, and decided to throw them away.

Nizar and Neda had gone for a ride in their grandfather's car with Mohamed the driver. They had been gone now for an hour or more. Sally called out for them but no one answered. She thought immediately of the trenches filled with rain. There was no safety fence around them. She panicked. She rushed downstairs and outside to search for them in the streets and returned an hour later distraught, only to find them waiting in the entrance for her. Mohamed understood her distress and apologised profusely as she hugged them long and hard.

Later the same day, she sat on the balcony outside Nizar's bedroom watching her children play with their cousins. It was the Eid Milad for the prophet's birth, Allah's peace be upon him. She remembered when Saad had been with them, they had turned off the lights and lit a candle, placing it in the centre of the room. There was no carpet to worry about should the candle fall, only a marble-tiled floor that warmly reflected the candle's flame in an encircling glow, the tiles shining from being polished smooth by the daily swilling of water. The children were much smaller then and they had squatted on the floor easily, sinking into a lotus position with their feet tucked in and their little hands cupping their faces shining with delight. Saad had taught them the chorus from the chant that held in memory the Prophet's line of descent: *This is the birth of Al-Nabi, Fatma begat Ali*, it began. This remembered lineage made everything seem properly ordered. There was a certainty about it that engendered an unquestioning faith. They had danced, Neda with a toddler's gait, around the candle, chanting over and over until they knew the words by heart.

This year was different, however. It did not include Sally, or any of the adults. Instead the oldest cousins had taken over and claimed the celebration rites for themselves. Or perhaps the adults had out of weariness relinquished their control. In any case the older cousins had determined to make their own impression on the ceremony and commemorated it quite differently. They had held aloft the usual paper lanterns that had seemed too impossibly flimsy to dare to place a burning candle in.

Sally listened to their excited cries nervously, as the evening chill ushered in a cold wind. She strained to see them from the balcony as they played beneath the vines, and then proceed in a file beyond the fig tree, chasing down the path through the orchard all the way to the wooden pier and back. In the shelter of the bay on the sandy beach below the esparto grass there was usually hardly any wind coming from the land and if they held their lanterns steady, there should be no danger.

Then she heard their voices move towards the villa, and saw the lanterns in a stream of little bobbing lights following one after the other up the veranda steps and disappearing into the kitchen. They had called out her name, to tell her they were coming to wish her all the blessings of the day. She was pleasantly surprised to be remembered. Greeting them at the door, one of the children, cousin Intissar, dropped her lantern. It had caught fire and the flames had scorched her knees.

Sally attended to the child's hurt with a cold compress. She left her to rest in the apartment while she followed the others returning to the garden, concerned now by the risk of other lanterns caching fire.

There were two much older male cousins who starting behaving in a scornful way towards their younger peers. They had before been happy enough to lead them to the sea and back, chanting the children's song. Now they were intent on demonstrating their leadership in a brutal fashion – putting a sudden and violent end to the festivities. They grabbed all the lanterns and kicked them into little fires that scattered over the path and flower beds, setting alight herb bushes and flaming the base stems of honeysuckle. The children were screaming. The boys stamped out the fires, risking injury, no doubt alarmed themselves by the destruction they had caused.

Yet still asserting their burgeoning manhood, the oldest cousin boasted that next year it would not be paper lanterns that they carried but guns. They would fire them into the air and would not be children anymore. "We'll be men with guns and we'll shoot to show we're not afraid like little kids are."

The children looked forlornly at their stamped-on lanterns where they lay in the dirt, settling into ash and soil. Sally made sure her children were safe inside and went to examine the honeysuckle, while Hassan gave them all a telling off, as he shut the garden gate behind them.

Chapter 4

Omen

There was a sudden commotion at the garden gate as soon as Hassan had shut it. Someone on the other side of it was shaking it in its frame. This was followed by a ringing of the bell. No one was expected, so no one made to answer it. But perhaps it was news about Ahmed and could not be ignored.

"Be quiet," Hassan commanded quietly. "Go inside everyone and keep still."

Hassan went inside with them and shut the villa door behind him, still not realising Sally was out there examining the fire damage. She hid in the shadows, finding she was shut out. Once inside, Hassan turned off all the lights and gathered the family in the living room. He pressed his face up against the window overlooking the small veranda at the front. He could see the headlights of a car. There was shouting. Then the car drove off, its tires screeching on the stony ground. When a few minutes had passed without further incident, he ventured outside to look around for something, he knew not what.

Opening the gate, scanning the wasteland, Hassan discovered a bundle of something at his feet. He pulled the bundle into the garden and turned on the porch light. It was a blanket, loosely wrapped in plastic. Inside the blanket a shirt was untidily folded. He tugged at it, and as it unravelled, it revealed blood stains. Out fell a comb and a photograph, Sally's photograph, the one where she was wearing the owl charm.

The shirt was maybe Saad's. Hassan thought he recognised it. The comb, he could not explain. The photograph's part in this meddlesome collection he could not fathom. They were the usual tools of the trade of soothsayers. Certainly, they were evidence of malicious harm intended, or, worse still, harm perpetrated. He dared not consider which. What business had these unexplained objects keeping company with his son's shirt?

Sally approached as he stared at the bundle at his feet dumbfounded. She startling him. She was startled herself when she recognised the comb as hers, the photograph Hassan held out to her. She knew the shirt was Saad's. Neither of them spoke but each saw fear and shock in the eyes of the other. They would say nothing.

Hassan was not ready to tell family about this act of malice directed at Saad, perhaps at Sally too. He indicated this to Sally with a finger placed on his lips. He kicked the bundle along the path and asked Mohamed to get rid of it, and to say nothing.

Hassan went inside, a changed man, his head buzzing with the many possible interpretations he could make. Sally felt events bearing down on her. She alone knew the provenance of each item; she felt the message implied was meant for her alone.

Chapter 5

Suspicion

Late one afternoon, after returning from his brother's bedside, Hassan was surprised to find Salem and Salha at the villa waiting for him. Salem was in a sombre mood. His greeting was abrupt. He made it clear that he was not visiting for social reasons but had a rather more serious purpose. There was some crucial information he had to hand over to Hassan. Of course, Salem was wary of a face-to-face discussion with him, given his last ruinous exchange; he expected a rough ride from his brother-in-law. But Salem assured Hassan that this was no accusation against him. Rather it would, he hoped, for his sister's sake, be an opportunity for forging an alliance.

He wanted privacy to speak to Hassan, and the way to the formal lounge was cleared and the children ushered into the garden. Salha was particularly cold towards Sally, who immediately absented herself, self, the signs seeming ominous. Salha, alone with Fathia, talked about sally. Fathia felt this was unkind and tried to change the subject. But Salha was determined and would not be stopped.

"You know the five men who were hung the other day? At first we didn't know who they were. But since, we have discovered that one of them was a friend of Saad's. A decent man no doubt but definitely naïve. The police were not certain of this fact of his friendship and needed objective confirmation. Guess how they came by it? You should not be surprised. It was Sally. Sally spilled the beans. She it was who revealed it to a certain intelligence officer, who shall remain nameless. No not foolish. Worse than foolish. Treacherous. She provided the information that connected them. She described how after deciding to escape the country, Saad having been tipped off that he was about to be arrested, they visited this man's home and stayed with him one night for safety. They left the very next day. It was Sally who exposed him, the stupid foreigner that she is. What does she understand! She blurted it all out. And then they hung him. That was all they needed to hang him. He leaves a widow and three children. How can his poor wife support them on her own?"

Fathia took some minutes to absorb this information. It was implausible. Sally rarely spoke out of turn or to anyone outside the family. She worked long hours and tended to her family. She knew few people and had no contacts to speak of. How would she have engineered such a meeting? She attempted a defence of her, sure of her ground because in one substantial detail she knew that Salha's version of events was not correct. At no time before leaving had Saad stayed overnight in someone else's house for safety. It had been Ramadan and he had stayed with his own family right up to his departure. Fathia was astute when searching for the truth. She knew that if one small part of a story was a fabrication, the chances were that the whole story could be a lie.

Furthermore, Salha's account revealed something of Salha's and Salem's involvement. No one other than herself and Hassan had known the circumstances of Saad's flight and it was clear that Salem at least knew the said intelligence officer or else how they had come by this information. She hesitated to challenge Salha who had spoken with such forceful certainty.

"I know for sure that the story is true in every part. You need to believe me," Salha chimed again, filling the silence left by Fathia's reflection.

"No, I do not need to believe you, Salha. Your story does not ring true to me. You do not explain just how Sally had come into contact with an intelligence officer. She goes to work and comes back home by university bus. Then she never leaves the house except for basic things from the corner shop. I doubt very much she would have had the chance to meet any strange men in the circumstances."

"Well you say that. But you are too trusting by far. She goes to the Association for the Blind, doesn't she? She teaches

English there? In the evenings? There would be many opportunities which you would have no idea of. We have it in any case, from very reliable sources, that Sally provided all the evidence that was needed to hang the poor man. She really is a liability to us all – if only because she has no idea of what is going on behind the scenes. And that is Salem's opinion, too. Somehow, you need to rid yourselves of her."

"I have no intention of doing any such thing," Fathia retorted. "She is Saad's wife and the mother of his children. What meanness you seem to harbour against her."

"All right, then if you will not have it from me, ask Salem what the Leader has to say about this strange woman in our midst. He blames her for everything. According to him, it is Sally who led Saad astray in the first place. He never should have married a foreigner."

This struck Fathia like a pain in the heart. Clearly someone had had an audience with the Leader without telling her about it. Salha avoided looking at her, not wishing to acknowledge the query that would, she knew, be registered in Fathia's eyes.

"The Leader has warned us that you must be rid of her," Salha continued, careless of the impact of her words. "He will never release Saad until she has gone. That is the long-term plan and I have it on good account that Saad himself is ready to let her go, ready to divorce her."

Lies, lies, thought Fathia. Lies so impudent they could kill her. And she felt a pain stab her heart. It took her breath away. Slowly she eased herself into a chair and Salha called for help. Hassan and Salem rushed in and lifted Fathia onto the sofa while they decided how to transport her to the hospital. Fathia was too wrapped up in panic to hear the commotion around her as anything other than a muffled drumming noise, far away. Salem drove her in his car with Salha attending at her side. Fathia was placed in intensive care, the same ward that Ahmed, Hassan's brother, had only recently been transferred from.

Chapter 6

Decoy

For the next few days, Hassan spent his time at the hospital, visiting both his brother and his wife. Likewise Nuri paid regular visits. Most times he found his uncle at one or other of their bedsides, quietly scribbling in a notepad the contents of which he would disclose to no one and which he tucked away in his trouser pocket when disturbed. He noticed that Hassan was preoccupied and perhaps a little agitated but still insistent about retrieving his merchandise Nuri, He spoke earnestly on of the need for a float of cash in the new currency and Nuri could see that his evasiveness was beginning to look like lack of courage. Seeing the dismay in his uncle's face, at his prevarication Nuri tried to reassure him that the time was not yet right and insisted he had every intention of keeping his promise. Hassan let the matter rest. His wife's recovery was more urgent. He was terrified of losing her.

Fathia was making good progress and was discharged the following morning. The angina she suffered meant a change of diet and Hassan meant to monitor this himself, knowing that his wife rarely bothered to consider her own physical needs. He must concentrate on getting her back to strength and trust that Nuri would see to the financial side of thing,

Following each hospital visit, Nuri would make the journey to Hassan's shop but now with the confidence that comes from habit and a clearer resolve. On each occasion m he was bolder, paying little attention to his surroundings. Paranoia, he decided, only make him nervous and, while a certain amount of caution was necessary, it could cripple his ability to act.

In his father's shop, he had found a rug suitable to use as a mat. He had taken possession of a site near his original observation post, near enough to give an unobstructed view of

Hassan's now occupied premises, no longer a shop. Methodically, he laid his wares along the edges of the rug. There were some little antique glass vases, some Bedouin bangles, ancient earrings and hairpins, and antique coins mainly those of least value, postcards of special sites such as the ruins of Cyrene in the mountains and little plaques of Koranic verses.

At one corner of the rug he placed a fan of business cards hoping to give some much needed publicity to his father's shop. He had not given thought to curious link this display made between a pavement vendor and an established merchant. The cards threatened to blow his cover. Any thinking person would wonder why a pavement stall? Why abandon a respectable outlet for peddling wares on the street. Several enquiries were made along these lines by casual passers-by who showed no interest otherwise, certainly not in buying.

Sales were disappointing. There had been no need to replenish his stock and the failure make him feel exposed. But he was cheered by the fact that a week had passed without him being challenged about his right to be there, or asked for his license. He took this to be a good omen.

Besides, he had learned a lot just sitting there and watching. There was plenty of activity across the road. Heavy equipment had been delivered. Ladders appeared on the outside walls. Engineers in overalls quite openly installed a CCTV camera with an all-round range. Nuri worked out from the height of it that he would not be detected if he kept close to the wall, which he would have to do when it was time to break in. He did not know that more discreet devices were installed and they had an all-round range from left to right, from the sky to the ground.

The activity at Hassan's shop had stopped. Nuri decided the time had come for him to act. He could not keep Hassan waiting any longer. After another slow-trading day, as the night closed in and the market closed, he packed his merchandise carefully, slowly wrapping each item in tissue paper, hopefully for the last time. When the shop was locked and the shutters padlocked, it was safe to cross the road in the dark. Leaving his bundle on the pavement, he tended to the lock and was relieved to note they had not been changed, and the key fitted. That was the first worry sorted. He lifted the heavy metal shutters high enough to allow passage under and, after grabbing his bundle, strained to let the shutters slide down slowly, not making a sound.

Inside the shop, he quickly found what he was looking for. It was as if his uncle had been there only yesterday. He found an empty medium-sized cardboard box, hastily gathered some items from the shelves and threw them in with his own bundle, slid it through the door, under the raised shutters and onto the street. Blood rushed like a pounding torrent through the veins in his neck and his hands were trembling as he locked up. He carried all before him for the not inconsiderable distance to his father's shop, arriving still in a state of sheer terror. But terror had served him well, he thought, focussing his mind on completing the task. It had gone well, better than expected.

The next morning, a neighbour called by to enquire about his father. The neighbour was an old family friend who had taken it upon himself to keep a watch on Ahmed's souvenir shop every day it was left unattended. There had been a number of suspicious burglaries in the vicinity and neighbours had taken to watching out for each other.

Nuri peered over is mother's should and suddenly the man was alarmed. He asked if he might come inside. Once inside, he asked if Nuri was responsible for the shop while his father was ill. He spoke very quietly and commented that Nuri must be working very hard since he had noticed the shutters up and the light on since the early hours, at the time of morning prayers. He had assumed that it was Nuri but now he knew otherwise. The only explanation was an intruder.

"Well," the neighbour warned. "Don't go investigating just now. It'd be dangerous to surprise whoever's in there. There's nothing you can do. Just wait 'til this afternoon. And don't hesitate to take me with you, if you wish."

Nuri thanked the neighbour disguising his own alarm. He worried that the key to Hassan's shop might not be safe in its hiding place. He took his neighbour's advice not to risk surprising the intruders but passed by the shop with his mother on their way to the hospital. It all looked normal and the shutters were down and locked. No one else had a key so perhaps the neighbour was mistaken. This went some way to reassuring him and to allaying his mother's fears. Most burglaries, even those with a political objective, left the premises in an obviously looted state since the obviousness of each strike was part of the strategy to intimidate as wide a public as possible. It was lucky that the undisturbed appearance of the shop had been sufficient to convince her and to silence any further enquiry. Had she known the real reason for Nuri's sudden interest in his father's business she might not have approved.

That afternoon, at the hospital, Nuri was able to report to Hassan that he had collected a few items from his shop and stored them alongside the others at his father's, and he had done this without being detected. The relief that registered on his uncle's face was too heartening to spoil with the added worry of the neighbour's observation and he decided it was best to tell him only if something happened which made it necessary for him to know. In any case he would soon find out if anything had been disturbed in his father's shop. He waited until after the closing of business for the day, when he could expect the streets to be empty. His mother was sleeping and thought he was too.

It was gone ten o'clock. On arrival, he had no way of knowing if the lock had been tampered with. It all seemed undisturbed. For a split second, as he opened the door and switched on the light, the shop inside was just as he had left it. But no time to take one step further, the burning glow of a white fire lit up the space around him and burst into his face.

With a screaming thud, the blast shook the air. His body had taken the full force of it. Metal pieces flew through the air, and cut clean through his head, neck and shoulders, ripping him apart and throwing him back with the door and window onto the street. His shattered body parts were mangled with the shattered wood, glass and twisted metal of the shop front. No one came running to help. People were afraid. Explosions in the night were best not investigated.

That following morning, neighbours who had dared to venture out early found the innards of the shop spilled over the pavement and onto the road. Amber pieces and marble carvings were flung to the other side, hitting the walls opposite with a force sufficiently powerful to pock the hard cement before falling pulverised as dust to the ground. Amulets of silver hands, buttons and glass beads were small enough to remain intact, but lay strewn amongst the shreds of velvet, silk and damask. Bits of petrified forest acted like missiles and were driven into the asphalt. The fragile desert rose-like crystals were shattered into their original state of sand and gypsum, and scattered across the street. Somewhere amongst it all was Nuri.

Chapter 7

The boat

That same night, as Hassan ate his evening meal, Fathia prepared his packed lunch for the following day. In a manner meant to ward off her protest, he had announced that he was taking his boat out along the coast. It would be the last time. She complained. He remonstrated with her, and she relented. He would, he said, take a last look and satisfy himself that the fishing trade was really a thing of the past. And if that was the case, he would never venture out in his boat again. To Fathia, it was a foolish hazard, and the excuse not worth the risk. But if it really was his last...

A mild breeze was blowing in from the sea and gave welcome relief to what had been a muggy sort of day. The kitchen door was open wide so their bickering floated round the villa on the breeze. A stranger listening in might have heard an incoherent conversation and made little sense of it; but the pained voice of an exhausted woman weary of protest and the lower firm tones of an equally exhausted man, railing against each other in self-defence, was sign enough of strained relations in the household.

Fathia had saved bread from the day's baking, and was reaching for a tin of olives from a shelf, doing so against a nagging pain that she disguised, not wanting Hassan to worry. She had baked the bread in the *tanour* in the garden. It had required effort leaning over the fire, her face almost scorched by the waves of heat. It had been a foolish thing to do she knew so soon after her recent collapse. She had suffered the usual burns to the tender inside of her wrists as a result of placing the flat dough on the hot sides of the oven above the glowing ash. The burns showed pink and raw. Still smarting from the injury, she was in no mood to be placated by an implausible argument.

"It being the last time," Fathia replied, losing her patience with him, "means nothing to me. The last time has nothing to do with anything. The question is why go at all? What could be the point? No, please don't bother answering with lies. I've had enough of lies. That's all anyone ever deals in these days and it offends me that you of all people should be so devious as to even think of lying to me."

It was fair enough, this last remark, and it stung him. He had never told his wife a direct lie before. But perhaps she startled herself too, remembering the secrets she had kept from him. Yet she wondered at this sudden spike of angry defiance, nor knowing that Hassan had had his own suspicions too. Hassan of course could not countenance the thought that his wife had withheld anything from him, and to him an honest woman, who deserved to know the truth in all personal matters between them. It was inadmissible to deceive her. Yet deceive her he must. That was why he needed to rid himself of anything he had hidden from her. Anything that required a lie threatened those he loved.

Paradoxically, this final sacrifice had to be yet another deception, a story fabricated in order to protect her from all his previous deceptions. How awful that lying was self-perpetuating in this way, and there was no escape. The recent spate of raids carried out by the police in search of undeclared monies and evidence of tax evasion impressed upon him the urgency, not only for reason of his stash on money now obsolete, but also for the few remaining writing pads in which he had written his latest poems, his own private conversations with himself. He must be rid of them, precious as they were.

Hoping to curb the argument, he thought it best to admit to a minor deception rather than reveal the whole more convincing truth, he answered: "Well, perhaps it's not the last. Because if I catch a decent haul, I might yet go again. You know full well we need an income, since all our savings have gone."

It was not a wise tack, this sidetracking of the real point at issue, since it was a reminder of his most recent foolishness. The loss of their savings, or rather his failure to convert it into gold, had almost been the breaking point. It did him no credit to draw attention to the fact. As she chose the best chunks of bread and set then to one side, Fathia's face told him she was not convinced. They would never resolve their different points of view, she would never change him. She cut large slabs of cheese and stoned the olives, maintaining her silence. Hassan noticed the care his wife took of him and smiled lovingly at her as she turned to make her last plea.

"But why tomorrow? Why now? Let's wait until we hear some more from Nuri. Why not wait a day or two?"

A day or two, why not after all? Two more days was no time at all. But he was determined to act at once, since any putting off of the essential act of self-censorship could weaken his resolve. He must act while the heart was strong enough to destroy his life's work, before it ruined Nuri's success.

"There is some sense in what you say. I'll think about it before the morning," and as he watched his wife's face to measure the success of this small appeasement, he added, "I promise you, I'll give it thought."

There was a pregnant pause, as each considered the impact of his words and then a sigh as Fathia watched him put the various items of his lunch in a large bag, so unnecessarily large as far as she could tell. She knew he would not change his mind.

"I'll put some other things in there," he quickly said. "A first aid kit, and a book to read in case I get tired and need to rest a while, some extra clothing in case the weather changes."

These last details, his intention to take good care of himself, were almost enough to silence her.

"Good," she said. "You'll think better of it, I'm sure, and we'll have morning coffee together on the veranda instead."

Later that night, Hassan packed away the accusing notebooks. He fondled them as if they were a faithful animal, innocent and genuine, his constant angel. They were the secret record of his private musings, the first drafts for poems some of which might evolve into reasonably coherent verse but much of which would remain in their pristine virgin state of first jotting, too subversive ever to be made coherent. They were metaphors and only he held the key for breaking the code Sometimes the symbolism was so obscure that often he could not recall its meaning. Few of his drafts had survived his own censure to be nurtured into poems. His style he felt was amateurish, never quite becoming quite his own. It ranged from crude expression in the vernacular of non-standard language to the sophisticated forms of finely crafted classical language. For inspiration, he had drawn deeply on mystic rhythms and the sufi meditations of his favourite poet. But despite their failings, each had been a pouring out of his soul. With their destruction, he must die a little.

This, his last journey along the coast was meant to mark an end to his endless search for meaning to this life. he would no more seek a meaning that rose above the mundane and the urbane. He would submit finally to the unheroic task of earning a simple living, testing the murky waters of the black market with all his confiscated and therefore illicit merchandise. But then, every means of making a living had become a dangerous enterprise now; every option open to him involved compromise with his conscience. When he stacked the odds of one way against another, the likelihood of being branded traitor was equal,

Hassan made great show of taking his fishing tackle with him by purposely leaving it on the veranda near the kitchen door. It was the last thing he did that night before saying goodnight and she had watched him, knowing there was nothing that he did that night that was not intended to disguise a hidden motive. She knew instinctively that this was so.

Being plausible at this stage, however, was not what occupied him. It would take him time to moor his boat in the bay along the coast and climb the rocky hillside to reach the cave where he would hide the remainder of his poems. He knew exactly which niche deeply recessed into the grooved ceiling of the cavern would be large enough to accommodate them. And, if this did not take too long, there was always the outside chance of catching a respectable trawl should his spirit move him enough to test the odds against fishing in unsafe waters while enemy shipping lay in wait on the horizon.

In order that his bulky bundle of papers would not need explaining to his wife, he left early the next morning before sunrise, before even the call to prayer. He left quietly, knowing that Fathia was easily woken. He walked quietly through the orchard, treading on the balls of his feet, along the sandy path where lizards would appear later in the day to obtain some warmth from the sun. Now nothing shifted as his feet shuffled through the sand. He was lost in shadows and was as dark as they were.

When he reached the beach, a sepia light reflected off the water and he paused at the water's edge for a moment where the tide lapped gently at his feet. Then he sat for several moments on the jetty, inhaling on his cigarette, enjoying the chemical charge of the smoke, feeling the damp of the night air and waiting for the sunrise. As a faint beam of light began to spread from the horizon across the sky, he decided there was light enough to sail the boat and steer his way without a lamp, which would have attracted too much attention.

This was the right moment. He would delay no more. He was ready for the sail, eager to dispose of all the evidence against him, acquiescent now to the demise of his free spirit, beaten by economic circumstance, yet hopeful that a better day would come when he might retrieve his poems, mediocre as they may be. He was ready now.

So he boarded his boat with an agility that took him unawares as a vivid memory might. He felt pleasure at the feel of surging water under him, the steady swaying motion of his body as it responded to the movement of the craft when it tipped slightly to his stepping in.

As he reached out to untie its moorings, a flash of light shattered upwards from the hull of the boat or from beneath the wooden seat. The blaze was shot through with wooden splinters flying. It lit up his startled face. The sound of it was a deep roar, muffled by the backwash of water that rushed in to fill the hollow its explosion had gouged in the water right down to the seabed below. The weight of water falling back again downed him, face to the sea bed, and pulled him into a death roll.

A rush of sea water filled his lungs.

If anyone had been awake to hear, the sound would have registered as a distant firing way out seawards – nothing untoward or even vaguely sinister.

Chapter 8

Sally steps out

The same morning that Hassan had left the villa to make his last journey down the coast, Sally was awake thinking about the day ahead. Sitting on the balcony, she heard a subdued click that triggered her awareness of movement on the veranda below. It brought to mind the snatches of conversation she had overheard the night before – Fathia alarmed about another fishing trip. Hassan adamant. Sally had seen the sense in what Fathia said, but Hassan had clearly made his mind up. She guessed it must be the door closing behind him. It was such an ordinary small sound in the early hours of an ordinary day.

She leaned over the balcony wall to see him pass into the orchard on the path that led down to the jetty. Sometime later, she heard a crack followed by a dull thud. Far away.

Sally understood that something had compelled Hassan to go – an independent spirit. She too had reached the point where being only half alive was becoming intolerable. A life of submission and fear was like playing dead. And 'playing dead' was not a long-term strategy. There would come a point beyond which only spontaneous action was feasible, even if freedom was only a figment of desire and reaching out for it was suicidal.

Sally could not have guessed at Hassan's motivation, the stress of isolation and of not-conforming, only partly explained by his financial worries. She did know that he wrote poetry, in secret. She would not have understood that he was not, as she supposed, in a rebellious mood, but about to do something essential to survival, about to comply, when he left that morning. She would have been surprised to learn that he was ready to put an end to his defiance, in return for whatever limited existence compliance would bring him. She could not have known the enormity of the risk he was taking as he disappeared into the pre-dawn landscape.

The crack she heard in the distance was a brief piercing of the air, soon closed over by the rising calls of sea birds.

Unsuspecting, trusting in the monotonous sameness of the day, she sat with a notebook in her lap, mulling over things, before the routines would begin in earnest. Writing was essential to maintain sanity, and not something she could share. She had come to this understanding only recently and had since taking to writing in the very early morning hours when the children were still sleeping. It was a conscious decision triggered by something her sister-in-law, Halaa, had said.

As she prepared for the action she herself would take later that morning – a little skirmish not without its own dangers – she recalled Halaa's words. They were as fresh as if spoken only yesterday.

Sally had been painting. She had surprised herself with the image that had formed almost voluntarily on the canvass; it must have come from her inner turmoil. The sleeping body of a woman was floating above a dense forest. In her tangled hair was the face of a child, screaming. Perhaps it was her face, her scream, the scream she suppressed. Suddenly, she became unaware of someone standing behind her, perhaps had done so for some time. It was Halaa who spoke, questioning Sally aggressively, demanding an explanation of the image.

When Sally could not, or would not, provide one, Halaa had said, "Oh, in that case, I must warn you – there's a well-known Egyptian artist who painted pictures like that, pictures no-one understood. Turns out it had a subversive message. He's been in jail for years now. It's not a good idea to paint this kind of thing." After that, Sally had been unable to return to the canvas. All the spark had gone. But she had kept on writing.

In the night prior to this not so ordinary day of her planned 'skirmish', a poem had come to her. She had written in the dark, so her jottings were almost illegible in the light of day and she needed to make them clear in a second draft.

For you the sky is square
For me shapeless
And as senseless
As an upturned bowl
Birds fly round a domed sky
Like bikes in a velodrome
Tight and confined
Never losing momentum

But the sky is square in a prison yard
Yesterday, today and tomorrow
Without depth of field
Yet deeper than forever
For you birds fly corner to corner
Starting nowhere in sight
Leaving thoughts trapped at the edge
Where you cannot imagine

She would change it around, change the length of lines or make stanzas, perhaps find a way of making it a sonnet, if that was at all possible or appropriate. She would fix it another day. For now, she needed the nerve for something else daunting in a different way. It involved, a package in her briefcase, cards to post abroad.

Sally had prepared the day's lecture for a second year Biology class in advance. She would be screening a Libyan-directed wildlife film about a species of gazelle known as *dama* gazelle, an endangered species of the sahel. She liked the idea of using a film instead of written text to spark off an informal discussion amongst her students. She had judged the film to be neutral, given its Libyan provenance. It dealt with the issue of the *gama* gazelle being an endangered species, due to over-hunting. On the surface of it, there was nothing contentious about the film.

Sally, however, was unaware that one of her students was the mayor's son, and even had she known, that fact alone would not have held much significance for her. He was an amiable student with an easy manner that attracted admirers.

He had never been anything but courteous to Sally. Anyway, her mind was focussed on an entirely different matter.

Some weeks previously, the social worker Selma at the Association for the Blind had given her a plastic bag full of mail addressed to Saad and the prisoners with him, care of the prison governor. Selma did not divulge how she had come by this mail, and Sally did not ask. The bag contained literally hundreds of greeting cards from members of an international human rights organisation. Sally had kept them hidden at home, not knowing what to do with them. In the end, she had decided to reply to as many as she could who had provided a return address. She designed a card for the purpose.

The first batch of replies was ready for posting today. After the first lecture, she would have an hour before the next, time enough to slip away and return without being missed. She had a plan in case she was followed to visit the French bookshop, the Chinese linen shop, and the Swiss jeweller's. Expecting surveillance as always, she would have to shake off anyone shadowing her.

But Sally had not reckoned with the fact that today was not an ordinary day after all. There was a tense atmosphere in the college, caused but something additional to the usual student informers posted at strategic positions. Perhaps she should have been more alert to the little changes such as more watchers than usual. But student informers never normally bothered her. Even so, when one took exception to a fellow lecturer giving her assistance, she should have drawn some conclusions.

The lecturer in question had offered to help her lift the heavy projector onto a trolley and push it down the corridor to the lecture theatre. They chatted briefly. A student informer beckoned to him and whispered something in his ear. The lecturer took fright and left without looking back at Sally. The sign was obvious enough but not sufficient to make her rethink her plan for the morning.

The film opened with an expanse of desert in all its photogenic beauty. The cameraman had taken the long panoramic view, panning over the dunes. Then it slowly zoomed in on a lone gazelle grazing on an acacia bush in the far safe distance. Its silhouette was memorable for the curved and ringed horns that swept back from its narrow head, its large black-rimmed eyes appealing to the treacherous void. Then, the view switched to a rally of jeeps giving chase to the lone gazelle. It started to flee, the distance between hunters and quarry narrowing rapidly. The lens held still on the creature collapsing with exhaustion. It was easily staked to the ground held by its horns and waiting for the slaughter.

The commentary switched to comment on the risk of losing the *dama* gazelle this way, and spoke of herds of hundreds as recently as ten years ago, now reduced to tens and often less. The jeeps that replaced hunters on camel-back had radically shifted the odds.

Operating the projector from the back of the hall, Sally was aware of the anonymous informer standing behind her. She was also aware of her students growing restless. Passionate exchanges between them were drowning out the sound track. Some voices were louder and more sustained than others. She had not expected the film to create so much division and had certainly not expected anger.

Before the end of the film, the informer slipped away. It was the mayor's son now who challenged her. "You have no authority to make this accusation," he shouted. "Who are you, a *frangi*, to criticise us? Our desert and our wildlife are not your concern. You'd do well to keep out of it."

No one came to her defense, though most seemed distressed for one reason or another. She had drawn attention to herself as the vulnerable outsider and had to feel her way back somehow to more neutral ground, which was her role as teacher. The teaching objective had been to explain the functions of the passive and active voices in describing cause and effect – grammar pure and simple.

"The point is," she pleaded, "we are just looking at how cause and effect is expressed, that is all. The *dama* gazelle lives in a fragile ecosystem," she continued, sounding like a textbook, she thought. "The switch of verb from active to passive voice can be used to remove the focus from the actor, as the subject becomes the agent..."

She hesitated. There was an uncomprehending silence. "Now I want you to do some transformations using statements of scientific fact. I will show you how." She stressed 'scientific fact', attempting to turn what might have sounded like opinion into a universal statement, to make safe what had clearly become unsafe.

As she turned to write some examples on the board, the class was disturbed by a commotion in the street outside. The students rushed to the windows to see a roaring motorcade pass by. The mayor's son seemed well-informed. He explained there was a visit to the college that day by a foreign dignitary; possibly two or three motorcades would do some practice runs. Furthermore, since the Brother-Leader was expected to accompany his guest, there would be an increased level of security.

The mood of the students went from mild interest to excitement. At any minute, their Brother-Leader would be in their midst at finger-touching nearness. Sally thought of abandoning her plan. The place would be swarming with agents, or 'antennae' as they were commonly referred to. Then it occurred to her that the whole college would be too distracted to notice her. This was just the opportunity she was waiting for.

The lecture over, she hurried to the college entrance, passed quickly over the threshold with its bright mosaic of the *sylphium* plant. The public square lay in front of her, empty, bleak and concrete grey in the glaring light of midday. Just a single palm tree gave it definition. She looked down to check her bag. The postcards were there, tucked in an inside pocket for ease of retrieval, all with stamps and ready to go. She was at the curb hesitating for a second before stepping out. Barely had her stride reached the inside lane than she was struck by a motorcade, appearing, it seemed, from nowhere.

Her bag was torn from her. The postcards were scattered across the road, exposed for all to see. Some of them bore the face of a child drawn inside the spread petals of a bean flower, the central petal reaching out like a prayer. Others carried the legend: "Your kind support gives us hope." They lay in the melee around Sally's body, crushed, their message struck through by the weals of tyre treads, almost obliterated.

Chapter 9

The prisoner

There was a long and dusty track that ran due south from the capital city of Tripoli to an obscure unnamed location, in the desert region. The road, a track across sand, was rarely travelled except by army trucks. It was a secret place, its ancient site fading on old hand-drawn diagrams and not marked anywhere on official maps. Desert dunes erased it in places. First trailed into the desert by the slave trade, it was now the route on which a truck was travelling, its cargo concealed by green canvas awnings.

No doubt the path was a little deviated from its original trajectory with the shifting of dunes but most likely it still meandered in the same south-easterly direction until it lost itself in the shifting mass of sand where only sand lizards, gazelle, Tuareg, Amazigh and Bedouin knew the way onwards. The truck moved slowly, mindful of the damage that steep inclines and slopes would cause its cargo. Reaching the track's end, the driver's eyes were dazzled by a pool of intense light in the distance, no mirage this as well he knew.

The track, known only to the expert guide, petered out and its faint margins dissolved in endless ripples of dunes. So it was surprising that here Modernist erection appeared in view, poking its blunted apex above the dunes. With its foundations burrowed deep in the desert floor, it supported a glass dome within a steel frame set on its upper rim. Seeming to flash light like the flame of a torch, the desert heat was mitigated by a screen and rotating overhangs. The structure of the cone was bold but otherwise uncompromisingly bleak. Its surface was polished smooth so that sand did not erode it. Sandstorms threw their pitting debris but barely etched a mark. This brave new architecture was a place of abominable human incarceration.

At its gates, the truck deposited its cargo, a human frame, onto a stretcher. A troop of soldiers quickly dispatched this burden to the officers within, and the doors were closed.

Some metres below the surface of the desert, at infrequent intervals, prisoners languished in grave-like cells. At intervals they were corralled and circled in the sun's glare underneath the dome, goaded on to walk for hours, fatigued by thirst and the heat that was magnified a hundredfold by the glass. No doubt its imaginative inventor-architect had envisaged air conditioning and perhaps there were structural details intended to accommodate such a convenience. If so, there had been no intention to install such, or perhaps they had simply not been maintained. Denied sufficient water for the duration of their exercise, the inmates collapsed, dizzy and nauseous. They longed then for the tunnels that burrowed at cool depths, but their cells were nothing more than fox-holes.

It was at the end of one such tunnel that Saad could be found, in a solitary confinement, a cell set aside for non-compliant prisoners. The one week assigned to him had been extended to a month, and the month to yet another ad infinitum, so that he knew he had been forgotten by the governor.

Before being isolated, he had managed to hide on his person a small box of chocolates, his clothes being loose on his skeletal body. The chocolates had been given to him by his last visitor, a sympathetic sheikh; he kept them now as a reminder of the world he had left behind. They had never been good enough to eat, having been heated and cooled so many times that they had lost their original shapes and were covered with a grey bloom. He had not expected how much of his time would be filled by this decaying confectionary. The protection and survival of it became his own undiminished will to live.

Despair was a constant haunting. It reached an unbearable low at times. When he sank into that hell, feeling he had been reduced to mere animal, he reached for his secret cache of chocolates hidden in his lumpy mattress. It was a way of reminding himself of his humanity. He lifted up the corner of his mattress and pulled the thread that secured the thin pouch of cloth he had sewn with the aid of a chicken bone for a needle.

Saad had been deprived of human contact for weeks the number of which he could no longer count. He suffered pain in all his limbs, an ache in his kidneys, his hair was thinning and he felt himself old before his years. He longed for a cleansing shower; he wanted to clean his teeth and wear a clean vest. He wanted to stretch his full body length and smell fresh air, to touch his children and console his wife. He wanted human kindness.

One morning, a morning indistinguishable from any other, he decided that he had reached the limits of his endurance and needed protection from his own tormenting imagination. His spirit had been dragged so low that the taste of even stale chocolate, no matter how unappetising, might seem to serve as something welcome for the simple fact of being different from his daily gruel, the unseasoned watery soup that a disembodied hand placed daily on the dirt floor of his cell.

He needed something to restore his will to live just a little longer. It seemed a paltry craving in the circumstances, insufficient match for his indescribable suffering, but there was nothing else to lift him from the sinking to which he was slowly and inevitably succumbing. He was, he thought, becoming part of the desert itself, soon to be absorbed into its obscurity. Chocolate itself fell short of representing the fullness of his longing, but a small morsel might signify a faint remembrance of a trivial but gratifying pleasure. It was now a simple matter of having to accept the smallest action, with aspiration reduced right down to the most minimal possible. It was at least a reachable goal.

Some weeks before, afraid that its hiding place might be discovered or the mattress removed, he had dug a shallow hole in the dirt floor under it and there in the hole he kept the box. Its list of ingredients was blurred now by green dampness. Had he been able to read it he would have seen that the so-named cocoa used was a low-grade substitute and the ingredients further degraded by the addition of flour and potato starch. In fact, these ingredients from the start had been so old and badly stored that insects had laid their eggs in it and grubs had eaten of it and passed their faeces grovelling in it. The chocolate was now worm-ridden, infested by a cocoa grub.

As Saad lifted the disintegrating lid of the box, a stream of brown moths with thin yellow lines across their upper wings flew out. They had hatched from the chocolate. The dirt floor beneath his mattress was a perfect breeding ground for insects that loved the dark, especially for a species of moth which in its grub stage forms a chrysalis shaped like a ball as small as a sugar granule. The original moth was most probably hatched from an egg laid by a moth in the cocoa pod itself. The moths had a distinct odour, which now assaulted his nose, only with its unfamiliarity, not with any sense of being unpleasant. The chocolate chunks had deteriorated into crumbling pieces and were wholly inedible.

The prisoner was not too dismayed. Chocolate was a dubious source of nutrition and likely to upset his inflamed digestive system. More importantly, he had developed a coping strategy which taught him how to refashion all the negatives that life apportioned him so that they might serve his own advantage. In fact, he was in awe of this unexpected form of life surviving in such a miserable place. Despite their mainly dull appearance, fine yellow lines provided colour as if it was a feature designed for him, colour serving no obvious other purpose in this godforsaken place than his delight. He was fascinated by the moths. They were after all a sign of life continuing despite incarceration.

Since he could not be sure how they had come to be in the chocolate, he was intrigued. How, he wondered, had life burgeoned in that fragile box? Dissecting one piece of chocolate, to test its texture, he found some tiny balls embedded in the greying mass and assumed they were the moths' eggs. But to be sure, like any scientist, he must design an experiment that would fairly test his hypothesis. From the box he fashioned several smaller boxes, and in each placed one small piece of chocolate containing one small egg. Some eggs he held in reserve.

Days later, time which he must now record, he explored the boxes and, as he had predicted, one moth flew out of each. Next he salvaged some prison meal combined with flour, a mixture which he called *zumeeta* out of remembrance of the real thing. He rolled it into shapes into which he placed more eggs and stored them in the box. In this way, the prisoner went on creating moths ad infinitum.

Incarcerated in this dark place with the moths, the prisoner never saw the sky not even as the reduced rectangle Sally had imagined for him. His place of disappearance was more a grave than a dungeon. Here, there were no reverberations of traffic overhead, no voices in dispute or harmony, no rumbling of wheeled trolleys down a corridor, no sound of doors opening and closing, or keys turning in lock, no illicit communication by means of tapping on conjoining pipes. And so he assumed he was trapped in an unreachable place, far away from the city that was his home, locked in an earth burrow, awaiting the time when his biological self would become one with the earth.

Lying prone, which was the only position allowed by the coffin-like chamber, he felt the monstrous structure of which he had become an organic part bore down on him. The prisoner could not have conceived of such an enclosure of space that harboured the conditions essential for a living death. It was evil in its perfect geometric symmetry, its towering walls sloping inwards and upwards to a glass ceiling, sprawling outwards at its base and trammelling the depths beneath the shifting dunes like the roots of trees. Nor could he have guessed at the existence of its sister structure, the new university in the city which promoted and propagated the Leader's philosophy, the new proselytising brand of learning in which the brutal voice of authority was the only voice. Of course, it was always a straight choice between indoctrination and banishment.

The symbolic butterfly of his freedom had long since flown its short-lived life. But more unlikely still was thought of the possibility, the audacious thought even, that the emblematic butterfly would be returned to him, even in its damaged state, and was this same day being transported in a truck from the city to this desert prison stronghold.

Sally had been severely injured in the so-termed traffic accident. There was no evidence that it was not an accident. Still in an unconscious state, far too fragile for the long journey along the coastal road, transferred from van to truck to van at the army's convenience. None of her broken bones had been attended too, internal bleeding had not been checked although a glucose drip had been connected to make sure she would last the journey and serve the purpose that her condition now made feasible.

The prison governor was the only man privy to the plan. He gave the orders and was never countermanded by his guards. They dragged Saad from his solitary cell. They were ordered to hose him down for no other reason than his presence in their midst should be made less offensive, and he was given fresh clothes. He leaned against the wall, his legs giving way beneath him. He was a crumpled figure and wanted so much to stand tall and be defiant. But he was cowed, knowing that at any minute a kindness could be converted to a cruelty, suspecting all the time that a kindness was a cruelty in disguise. Someone gave him a chair.

"Prisoner. We have your wife in the room adjoining this one." The governor's voice was piercing to his ear.

"Did you hear me, pig? I said we have your wife." It seemed improbable. "You have one last chance to redeem yourself. You may see her only after denying her, only after signing this form declaring your intention to divorce her. You know that marriage to a foreigner has been made illegal. But in his inestimable mercy, the Leader, Our Guide, has relented just a little, given the fact that your marriage took place before the law was made. He has agreed that you may be forgiven your misdemeanour, on condition that your wife is sent away. She will be safe. We will not harm her. But only on condition that you rid yourself of all association with her. Divorce her. You must divorce her. You must see the sense of that. Be wise now and have done with her. Do yourself a favour. She's finished anyway."

Some partially comprehended bits of meaning began to dawn on him. He sensed the way each hint of leniency was cancelled out by threat. He sensed the capriciousness of the reasoning intended to confuse him. He knew their foibles, knew he could never trust them. They would not keep her safe no matter what. In any case, it was unlikely, he thought, that she was in this wretched place with him. He must remain unmoved.

The governor sighed with extreme impatience and took himself off to a corner where he lit a cigarette, taking time to summon up a fiercer disposition. Throwing the match to the floor, he turned with a bullish aggression.

"You fail to understand me, prisoner, you wretched dog. You really have no choice. I can see you don't believe we have your wife here. So if I tell you she is unconscious following an accident you probably will not believe that either. And if I tell you more and explain she has not been operated on but needs an amputation which if not done will cause her imminent death, will you still not believe?"

The governor's voice had almost reached hysterical pitch, his words spoken in a screaming monotone without inflection. He could see from Saad's dull eyes that he had made no impression at all. This quiet rebuff quietened him, perhaps partly out of admiration for the prisoner's self-control and partly out of puzzlement. He ordered two guards to carry in the stretcher on which Sally lay unmoving. They placed her on the floor before Saad. She had not been washed. Blood had dried on her skin and clothes.

A groan escaped from Saad's dry throat. He heard it as an alien animal noise, not like any human sound he had heard before. He threw himself on the stretcher to lie alongside her and howled. Now he had reached this place in his soul where there was no way forward, no escape, the sheer dead end.

He felt for her pulse in desperation. It was very weak, almost gone. She was dying. His butterfly of freedom was almost gone. There was only one way out now and that was up, up to the highest plane of human dignity and love.

"I will never divorce my wife. What have you done to her? Do with me what you will. I will not divorce her."

No more words passed between this defiance and the blow which the governor himself delivered to his head. Saad fell to the floor gripped in the paroxysm of a seizure. His body convulsed with violent tremors for more than twenty minutes, after which he lay unconscious, drifting in and out of consciousness for two whole days. In the hospital wing of the prison, medical staff kept vigil by his bedside, with the sights of guns trained on them.

When he recovered, he was returned to the company of the other prisoners. He heard no more of Sally.

Chapter Ten

Missing

sand-blasted palms
wail on the coast;
clashing fronds
release their shrill tale;
flocked crows
scatter though the air

the wind roughs up the sea
and tears across the shore
wearying itself and bedding down
in a deep scythe-cut
through esparto grass;
buffeted and plummeting
a fist of black birds falls
colliding with the stone wall
of a prison yard

feathers splatter the concrete
in a melee of dark confetti
the dried bloodstains
of many-coloured black birds
while at metal grills
prisoners' eyes watch
stock still

Epilogue

Fathia had been collecting coriander and parsley to hang to dry for her winter store. Bending down to kneel on the pebble path was not easy for her, but this cultivated plot had become her refuge, and she did not complain. It was a modest acreage, enough for her to manage, less demanding now that the fruit harvest had been picked, mainly with the children's help. For herself and the remains of her family it was an inviolate place, the garden, a place of welcome distraction. It consoled her. And though it sapped her energy, it gave back in abundance in a good season.

The children were busy stripping desiccated leaves from the spent stalks of herbs, casting the brittle debris onto the fire that she had lit in the bread *tanour*. When its crackling embers spat out glowing sparks, the children ran off to the orchard to search for the chameleon's hiding place. It would be in a lemon or an almond tree, holding on with its tail coiled around a swaying branch. As they rushed along the earth track, they brushed against a host of moths. A fawn cloud flurried at their heels and sprinkled into the dusty air.

Fathia's body ached. She stretched her back and wiped her soiled hands on her pleated skirt. Then she pressed a hand against her heart, that old angina pain. She looked up to the fig tree, her only lasting memorial to Hassan, a faithful man of good heart who had taken far too many risks. The fig was his favourite tree, his favourite fruit. It was a mature tree whose canopy of broad leaves was spread in dark silhouette against a fluorescent pink sky. At its furthest reach was the balcony, the one that had been Sally's retreat. She remembered her standing there that day some time ago, dressed in the offending white shirt, wearing the owl charm, and innocently waving. Every day she felt the pull of her absence, a mother's absence she could not explain to her children who were now her own.

Fathia wiped away her tears, smearing her cheeks with red earth as she did so, unaware that her youth's beauty was still etched in her ageing face. Traces of the past were enlivened by physical exertion and the gleam of the sky.

Fathia felt a chill touch her skin. The warmth of a late autumn afternoon was dwindling, undercut by riffs of a cool sea breeze. The contours of foliage were lifted in a slow curvet around their scalloped edges. Between the fading light and the coming darkness, she found a momentary release and wondered in that lull how things might have been different.

Not lingering to hear the owl hoot in the trees, she ushered in the children before its wail could breach the silence. There was still Saad to pray for.

END